TANGLES

KAY SMITH-BLUM

Black Rose Writing | Texas

ISBN: 978-1-68513-506-5
PUBLISHED BY BLACK ROSE WRITING
www.blackrosewriting.com

Printed in the United States of America
Suggested Retail Price (SRP) $21.95

Tangles is printed in Baskerville Old Face

*As a planet-friendly publisher, Black Rose Writing does its best to eliminate unnecessary waste to reduce paper usage and energy costs, while never compromising the reading experience. As a result, the final word count vs. page count may not meet common expectations.

Dedicated to the thousands of men and women
on the home front of WWII and the Cold War

We will remember the sacrifices made, and be forever grateful.

Praise for *TANGLES*

"In her knockout debut novel, *Tangles*, Kay Smith-Blum sheds new light on the Hanford Nuclear Plant - the largest environmental disaster site in the United States. Skillfully blending historical details and nail-biting suspense, Smith-Blum weaves a harrowing story over two decades and delivers two complex protagonists you can really root for...a fast-paced, and unputdownable tale."
-Kevin O'Brien, *New York Times* bestselling author of *The Enemy at Home*

"In a well-crafted debut, Smith-Blum provides the reader a ringside seat to the birth of the nuclear age. *Tangles*, a tale of tragedy and loss, but also hope, is beautifully written. An important story, much like *A Civil Action,* it packs a punch and hits close to home."
-Robert Dugoni, *New York Times* bestselling author of *The Tracy Crosswhite Series*

"*Tangles* is a brilliant, captivating ride through a very dark period in America's nuclear history. Although fiction, Smith-Blum reveals many truths about our radioactive legacy."
-Joshua Frank, award-winning investigative journalist and author of *Atomic Waste*

'Based on real events, *Tangles* is an ambitious debut novel that is at once labyrinthine and simply and deeply human. At its heart are generations of secrets and horrific sacrifices played out in the twisted shadows of personal, corporate and government corruption during the advent of the Atomic Age and Cold War. In stunning and engrossing multiple narratives, Smith-Blum reminds us about the devastating and lasting costs of love, loyalty and freedom and, above all, the enduring solace of nature and family."
-James Anderson, award-winning author of *The Never-Open Desert Diner*

"The world of *Tangles* is brought to life with Smith-Blum's vivid, rich language...an epic historical tale."
-Samantha Dunn, author of *Not by Accident: Reconstructing, a Careless Life,* and *Failing Paris*

"Kay Smith-Blum's voice radiates, delivering an Annie Proulx-like exploration of America's Northwest at the dawn of the nuclear age!"
-Cam Torrens, award-winning author of *Stable, False Summit,* and *Scorched*

"*Tangles* is a fascinating read, and a convergence of clues that keep the reader guessing. Set against an important time and little-known place in American history, Smith-Blum has given us a unique tale. I couldn't put it down."
-Michele Gerber, Ph.D., author of *On The Home Front: The Cold War Legacy of the Hanford Nuclear Site*

"Kay Smith-Blum's debut novel *Tangles* is a gritty and compelling environmental thriller set in Eastern Washington during the Cold War...that exposes the government coverup of the devastating effects of nuclear weapons production...a tangled tale dedicated to the people who unknowingly paid the ultimate price."
-Clare Hodgson Meeker, 2020 Washington State Book Award Winner for Young Readers

"*Tangles* is as gut-wrenching as it is heartwarming. A cast of characters as memorable as the setting...a backdrop of nuclear warheads, and life-altering consequences that are mind-blowing. Smith-Blum is a master storyteller, now on my "go to" list of authors...she should be for you, too! A 5 Star, Must Read!"
-Joseph Lewis, Author of *Blaze In, Blaze Out, Fan Mail,* and other tales of the Evans Family

"[In]Smith-Blum's excellent debut novel...both the history and the science are meticulously done, but with a light hand. The story takes the lead...a powerful inter-generational story of environmental crime, state secrecy, and the redeeming power of science."
-Ronald Niezen, anthropologist, author of *The Memory Seeker*

"If I hadn't known going in this was a debut novel, I never would have believed it. Well written, smart, and deeply engaging, Smith-Blum's uncanny ability to make her characters come alive on the page [made me feel] as though I knew each of them personally. *Tangles* is a book I know I'll come back to again and again."
–Brooke L. French, author of *Inhuman Acts, The Carolina Variant,* and *Unnatural Intent*

"*Tangles* intertwines a poignant love story with a gripping narrative about a government conspiracy linked to an environmental catastrophe...the novel vividly recounts...the government's mishandling of radioactive waste. Smith-Blum deftly raises critical questions regarding and...prompts reflection on the true cost of technological advancement and the ethical responsibilities of those in power. Skillfully balanced threads of conspiracy, romance, and environmental accountability, ensure each theme maintains its significance and emotional resonance."
–5 Stars, *Literary Titan Reviews*

"*Tangles* is an ode to the human condition, to the irrepressibility of caring in the face of uncaring dangers. It is also first-rate literature."
–Morris Hoffman, author of *Pinch Hitting*

"A beautifully written historical novel with tragedy and heartbreak delicately woven in, but it is the characters' persistence and love—the will to have a better future that will leave each reader with a book hangover."
–Meghan Redmile, author of *Hold On*

"Kay Smith-Blum delivers a powerful novel about a time in history we should never forget. Set in the beautiful Pacific Northwest against the backdrop of unchecked industry, *Tangles* is a story layered with complexities and mystery. A story of loss, regret, hope and love...keep the tissues handy, as it comes with an ending that will shed the tears."
–Chris Riley, author of *Went Missing*

"Kay Smith-Blum's debut novel *Tangles* is a love story folded inside a mystery, told with precision through two distinct timelines...harrowing and heartbreaking, with chilling ties to recent headlines. Get ready to be disturbed...and enthralled."
–Brian Kaufman, author of *A Persistent Echo*

"*A* dazzling combination of love story and edge-of-your-seat suspense...told through the eyes of two star-crossed heroes, Smith-Blum deftly transforms the complicated history of the Hanford Nuclear Plant into a heartfelt, moving story."
–Brian Christopher Giddens, Writer, Poet, Contributor Evening St Press

"Based on actual events, *Tangles* shines a light on the darker episodes of the nuclear arms race. Separated by a decade, Mary and Luke struggle to make public the horrors of nuclear contamination and personalize the Hanford disaster for the reader in the same way that Rose and Jack did the Titanic tragedy. You won't want to put it down."
–Gary Gerlacher, M.D., author of *Last Patient of the Night, Faulty Bloodline* and *Sin City*

"Smith-Blum's debut novel, blends a riveting plot with hard-to-forget characters, and shines a spotlight on a period we don't often read about in fiction."
–Sheila Myers, author of *The Truth of Who We Are*

"Smith-Blum's expertly weaves alternating perspectives of a Hanford secretary with her one-time neighbor who [through] scientific study [is determined] to prove the harmful effects of nuclear production. Filled with memorable characters and unexpected twists...put *Tangles* at the top of your reading list!"
-Travis Tougaw, author of the *Marcotte and Collins Investigative Thriller* series

"This beautifully written story hit close to home for this PNW reader. Hope for the indomitable characters [offset my] anger at the injustices suffered [because of] of government subterfuge...[but this is] a touching and tender story. I left my heart on the last page. A timely reminder that the human spirit can endure, heal—and begin again. You won't be able to put *Tangles* down!"
-Catherine Shea Matthews, author of *Releasing the Reins*

"Through dual perspectives, Kay Smith-Blum weaves a compelling historical tale...revealing the tragic consequences of the creation of the atomic bomb...kept secret from American citizens. *Tangles* will keep you turning the page and questioning where our government's allegiances lie."
-Jaime Grookett, author, *The Invisible Ones*

"After Oscar-winning *Oppenheimer*, [I could] not put this book down. *Tangles* shows the other side of the creation of the atomic bomb which affected innocents...on the U.S. home front. Think *"Summer of '42"* and *"Erin Brockovich,"* Smith-Blum's writing style [is] fast-paced...but, pulled on my heartstrings."
-P L Jonas, award-winning multi-genre author of historical fiction, romantic suspense and more

"Smith-Blum has gorgeously re-created an obscure time and place that were critical to the future of the planet. Her story speaks to us all."
-Steve Olson, Award-winning author of *The Apocalypse Factory*

TANGLES

"It is hardly enough to retell accepted history with dramatic embellishments; there should be a ghost clamouring for justice to be done him."
–**Captain Robert von Ranke Graves,**
British Poet, Writer, and Historian

Prologue/Mary

Late Summer 1947

Scientists and supervisors, workers and wives, shopkeepers and servicemen packed the still-new town auditorium. Toe-taps of teenagers and tots echoed off the pine rafters. Puffs of Lucky Strikes and Camels trailed out the double doors thrown open to capture any breeze. The Richland Singing Cops entertained during band breaks, the four-part harmonies threading the night in a prelude to the final set.

Amid the not-so-lonely Saturday night my next-door neighbors the Hinsons glided across the crowded dance floor—slow slow, quick quick—foxtrotting to Benny Goodman's solo. Well, not that Benny. Our Mr. Goodman supervised a production line at Hanford Engineer Works, aka The Area. On the weekends, he played clarinet to Mr. Clark's sax and Mr. Joseph's horn. Mr. Joseph was no Bix Beiderbecke, but he had a feel for the shifts, jazz in his soul, beer and only God knew what else in his belly. Mr. Drummond—and I'm not making this up—was the drummer.

Mr. Clark winked my cue, and I angled my shoulders to the spotlight with hands hidden in the folds of my swing skirt. My gaze floating above the crowd, I aimed for a cross between Billie Holiday and Rosemary Clooney, and to—just for a moment—forget where I was. My home-permed waves fell across my cheek, concealing the fresh bruise. The crowd wanted an encore, so we gave them Carmichael and Parish's tune to dream on.

Folks spilled out of the hall, inhaling the sage-soaked night air. Mr. Clark's teenage daughter, Janet, dawdled behind her family, her blonde ponytail swinging and petticoat rustling. She kept turning back to look at her fella, a prolonged goodbye—the kind where feelings are bigger than words.

Calculated releases rode the breeze south from The Area, across the expansive desert that bound Eastern Washington. The mix of gas and particles lit up the moss along the banks of the Columbia where salmon fed on their way to Baker Bay. The breeze torqued and stole its way northeast to Spokane and Idaho, where dairy cows and wool-laden sheep grazed, and human young slept, eiderdown quilts tucked tight.

The wind whipped up at ground level, taking the loose dirt with it, shooing folks inside their government-built houses. A star shot across the sky, doling out wishes, but mine wouldn't be granted. Because I just wanted to go back. Undo that moment when I said yes to the man who brought me here where the stardust was lethal, and so was he.

Chapter One/Luke

September 13, 1963

Industrial chains stretched off the rusted metal winch to eight points of the whale. The torso overwhelmed the flatbed trailer parked alongside the waterway, the back and belly ripped where the harpoon's barb had struck, not once, but three times. According to the boat crew, the fin whale had been slow in the sea compared to the rest of the pod, but not an easy mark. A bomb-lance had torn her open, and the inner flesh glistened in an otherworldly sheen.

Ready to serve up blessings, a dozen members of the Tututni Tribe dotted the narrow bank bordering the strip of the Skipanon River that fed into the coastal Oregon marina. The hive of activity on the dock area invited curious seagulls, their fly-bys skirting our heads as we unloaded.

An onsite test of the whale's blood had triggered my summons. Teddy—as in Theodore Roosevelt—Walker, a state-employed biologist and an informal partner in my doctoral research, had called me saying I should see the catch before BioHarvest took over. The tribes were the real stewards in the region, and Walker, a mix of Yakima and Wanapum, was pulled into environmental tussles more often than not.

"Luke," Walker said, extending his hand.

"Walker." The nickname Teddy had never seemed to fit the man. "Could someone jar up water samples from the mouth of the bay for us?"

Walker side-eyed the scene. "Among other things?"

"Much appreciated." I turned to the whale, the stench permeating my protective gear.

My lab mate, Roy, his freckled face obscured behind his mask, scooped out part of the stomach contents, mostly krill. We bagged and bucketed everything into a series of coolers. The product of our work lined the dock like a clam dig haul.

Tribal chants started up, a steady low-pitched cadence. I swished the whale's blood in a test tube with a solution from our portable kit to check for zinc. Zinc was prevalent in the production process near my hometown, among other elements strong enough to kill a whale and sure to kill a human, which was the point. The sole reason Richland, Washington had been built, and why I left when my father died. Bombs never kill just the enemy.

Across the inlet, the lumber yard spit up sawdust like wedding rice. Wishing away the sore throat I had coming on, I raised the vial to the midday sun. "A potpourri of problematic activity."

"If the whole pod fed on this plankton, we could use the hot zinc to trace their route," Roy said this with a grin, not having lived where I had.

Walker had mentioned that the whale was pregnant when he called. "Where's the calf?" I asked.

Walker giant-stepped over a cache of buoys and drew back the flap of a smaller tarp. "The cow damaged the whaler's boat pretty good."

The sun's glare obscured my vision, but the fierceness of expectant mothers made me smile. I blinked into focus, and a sick sensation invaded my belly.

Roy peered over my shoulder. "About halfway through gestation, maybe six months?"

"This far along it should have fins." And it didn't. Just two stubs and eyeless sockets flanked both sides of the snout, black vacuous tunnels that bored into my memory banks. The chanting rose in volume, drowning out my moan.

I'd returned home for the holidays after vagabonding around Europe a couple of years ago, needing a job before starting my doctoral program. My mother had suggested the Johnsons might want help at their ranch outside Eltopia during the lambing season. A shotgun blast woke me from my bunk in the dark morning hours. I'd found Mr. Johnson in the barn, kneeling in blood-soaked hay next to a dead ewe. Said her insides were completely broken after birthing.

As he spoke, he held a lamb underwater in one of those large tin tubs. The legs of the newborn were fused like someone had bound them with an invisible ribbon for Christmas. Mr. Johnson had already dealt with the other. Belly up at the far end of the tub, it had four stubs for legs and black holes on either side of its cherubic snout. The Johnsons lost forty ewes and seventy-three lambs that season. I had helped deliver them all—to the tub.

• • •

A semi-truck towed the whale into Warrenton, Oregon. BioHarvest, Inc. allowed graduate students the occasional use of their lab with its razzle-dazzle equipment, which was nonexistent at the college level. BioHarvest's chief chemist analyzed everything aquatic, hoping to find the magic ingredient for the next miracle pill. Word was the new line of plant-based immune supplements would heal all that ailed you.

The containment area accommodated the fifty-five feet of blubber, most of which would be sold. The idea of a gamma ray-emitting whale's innards being consumed, even if the majority went to the mink farmers, bothered me. But with the environmental movement gaining momentum, the whaling biz was waning.

Roy supervised the unloading of the carcass, and I signed in at the front desk ledger. We hauled the coolers into the cool white lab.

A jumpsuit-clad tech separated the krill samples. Plankton typically occupy water bodies, but airborne versions can live part of their lives floating in the atmosphere. If subject to a downwind current, they could sometimes travel hundreds of miles and evidently, these had blown a ways before resettling. Baker Bay, Washington, where I had a cabin, was inside the mouth of the Columbia River.

The tech removed more tissue and organs under my direction. "Freeze those. The stomach contents, liver, eye-ball, and intestine, fix in formalin."

Roy fired up a Bunsen burner to start on the oily tissue. "Luke, how much ash do you want?"

"Enough for a five by five inch." The fancy scintillator counted two hundred gamma rays per minute, and the analyzer with a magnetic core memory spit out results fast. The Buck Rogers aspect of my work always entertained, but it was no substitute for real passion. In that arena, I was sorely lacking, never quite getting past the first date.

My attention shifted to the eyeball. I measured it lens-down on top of the crystal, checking for any irregularity in growth. After most of the samples had been analyzed, I said, "Let's chart it."

The BioHarvest tech flipped a few switches, his confident motions reflecting a superiority over us lowly students. The machine spit out a chart, and Roy pinned it on the wall. The most prominent peak in the spectra was zinc-65. Potassium-40, the naturally radioactive isotope found in the ocean, was next, followed by niobium-95 and cesium-137.

Isotopes are one big happy family of the same element. As with any family, some offspring can be problematic due to varying numbers of neutrons that define them as radioactive, not unlike an adolescent rebellion rooted in hormonal imbalance. The whale's organs hosted seven such wayward children. The cow's liver had traces of cesium and a distinct peak of manganese. The tongue housed niobium, which was more than just a little unusual. A harpoon had felled her, but there was no doubt what had made her vulnerable. Small amounts of radioactive elements can have large effects.

Roy tapped the chart. "Manganese was reported in seawater and marine organisms last month in Southern California." Whales get around, but they usually stay along the same route, migrating north to south and back again. The Washington and Oregon shorelines provide access to the sea for the bountiful Columbia. What that bounty included appeared to be a problem.

"Larger peaks of manganese were just found in the river," I said. "Freshwater clams."

"The level of zinc in the plankton is comparable to that in the whale." Roy scrunched his forehead in thought.

The BioHarvest tech jumped in. "We can't rule out previous exposure to fallout."

Roy smiled like a game show host handing out a consolation prize. "Manganese is present in fallout, yes, but," Roy's smile turned to a dare. "It takes niobium only thirty-five days to decay. So, you figure it out."

The event that contaminated the whale had occurred in the last two months. I sucked in air, thinking of every plant and animal that drank from the waters and of the factory, far upriver, resting on its bank, the likely source of all this trouble. My mother still lived in Richland, but the papers wouldn't have reported anything. Incidents involving the reactors, even if they were major, were classified.

The tech dug his hands into his jumpsuit pockets. "Still, I don't see any health hazards for humans here."

He and I exchanged a long cool stare.

The Atomic Energy Commission funded some of BioHarvest's research, and the tech had no way of knowing I'd lost my father to unidentified health hazards. But that conclusion, full of government gloss, pissed me off. No hazard to human health had been the AEC's party line for the last twenty years. Mary Boone, my former neighbor, had called it alternate truths, a concept that, among others, she had introduced me to.

"When five thousand-cubic-feet of radioactive blubber lands on your doorstep, don't you think it's time to acknowledge a regional health hazard?" My glare reduced him to silence.

Gamma rays, hot zinc, radionuclides in the liver, lungs, and intestines, and a deformed calf, all pointed to one thing. As my mother would say, "That damn Hanford."

·   ·   ·

A crisp breeze forced fall in hard the next weekend. Walker met me outside his cabin. We slapped away the gnats as we trudged to a small shack on the backside of his property where he smoked meat, a side gig to his work for the Washington State Department of Transportation. The samples of bay water had shown low levels of radioactivity, arguably natural or at least not deadly, but his phone call summoning me had indicated there was something else.

Along the side wall, the hand-built smoker, a metal-and-steel contraption crafted out of castoffs from the WSDOT salvage yard, offered an array of savory scents, duck most likely, making my stomach growl. In the center of the shack, an enormous buck hung head down from a two-by-four pine ceiling beam that Walker's head barely cleared.

"Where was the kill?"

"An island about a hundred miles upstream. They got him crossing the shallows." Sun permeated the cracks in the single-plank walls, shooting lines across Walker's tall frame and lighting up the deer's rack, which overwhelmed the narrow work counter.

"What's the spread on those?" Mule deer have bifurcated antlers that fork off the main beam, and as they grow, they fork again.

"Almost thirty-eight inches."

I whistled. A typical mature buck's crown is twenty-five inches. Shreds of velvet cover still clung to his rack, as if the buck had been midway into the stripping process. Maybe he'd been leaving the island to find larger trees to do the job.

A chunk of velvet was wedged between the deer's front teeth. After getting my master's at MIT, I'd done a two-year research stint at the Scottish Marine Station in the Firth of Clyde where, despite our ocean focus, two of my colleagues were obsessed with tracking and photographing deer on the moors with flasks full of Oban. I had tagged along for the scotch, watching many a buck hack away, clearing his mantle for battle, but I'd never seen this.

"He was eating his velvet?"

"Yeah, spooked the hunting party too, which is why they brought him to me." Walker laughed under his breath. "They think I can shoo away the evil spirits. They don't realize we elected them."

The shot at political powerbrokers brought up my smile. "At least President Kennedy signed the nuclear test ban treaty."

"Keeping it underground isn't stopping. He needs to do more."

Small scars pocked the buck's coat. Had irradiated releases traveled hundreds of miles, infecting cheat grass and sagebrush that the deer fed on? I ran a gloved hand down his backside, my resentment for all things nuclear mounting. "Like sparks from a campfire burned his flesh. We need to test every part of him, just like the whale."

"Could have been a brush fire, but I already told the hunters they shouldn't eat the meat. Said I'd mount the crown as a consolation prize." Walker handed me two jars. One held more velvet strips. Inside the other were deer pellets. "Harvested from the rectum."

I slid the jars into my pack, and we stepped outside. The valley spun out below, a rolling mist pocketing the forest and solidifying the chill in my chest.

Walker lifted his face to the breeze. "Not long after our tribe was forced out of The Area, my grandfather said the Air Force tried to track the releases. Figure out where they went, but they couldn't."

"Wondering what's under every step you take?" I shouldered my pack. "I'll be back."

•   •   •

The recently renamed Oregon State University sprawled across four hundred-plus acres on the south side of Corvallis. The quintessential college town hosted one of the top engineering colleges on the West Coast, thanks in no small part to federal and corporate dollars that came with the new name. Well-placed money controlled everything and everyone on campus, including me for the last two years.

The fellowship to fund my doctorate in biochemistry was solid bait, but the School of Sciences had a burgeoning activist side that had drawn me in. The nuclear debate had only gained momentum since The Bay of Pigs. The other cause du jour, a multitude of pesticide studies, occupied the Forest Research Laboratory and agricultural departments. My pitch for tying pesticides to the failing animal life around Baker Bay and upriver had been an easy sell to my dissertation advisor, Dr. Miller, but that premise needed tweaking.

I slid inside the lab at the back of the department, waved at Roy, and approached the glass-encased realm of the department head. Some Halloween jokesters had stretched a grim reaper poster across his door. Miller most likely hadn't seen it yet.

His bald pate down, Dr. Miller motioned me inside the office, the kind stereotypes are made of—dust-laden piles of folders, a half-eaten lunch, pencils hidden between text pages, and cabinet drawers half open as if a sudden thought had pre-empted the act of closing them.

"I won't take much of your time, sir, but as I said on the phone—" An involuntary cough made me pause. I couldn't shake this damn sore throat. "I have a request, a minor change to my thesis."

Miller raised his eyes to mine. "Is this request justified by new findings?"

How to explain this request was not research-driven, but rather by gut: the whale's, the deer's, and mine. I swallowed hard. "You heard about the whale, I assume?"

Miller's face remained neutral, but his eyebrow ticked up, indicating for me to continue.

"Considering Osterberg's findings regarding manganese in Columbia shellfish, I'd like to pivot from just concentrating on pesticides to all potential sources of poison."

"Careful to not sound like an activist, Mr. Hinson. You're a scientist. At least I presume you still want to be." Miller's tone held a warning.

"Yes, sir," I said, showing as much deference as I could muster. "One wanting to explore all the possible causes for the rise in cancer in our region."

"Sounds like two separate projects."

"A comparison, if you will." What I was asking—to include nuclear waste findings in my study—was tricky. No OSU department was immune to the AEC's copious amounts of money, but I forged ahead. "As scientists, we should maintain objectivity, shouldn't we, sir?"

A risky comeback, but Miller's reputation was that of a relentless pursuer of the facts. You couldn't be that and filter out the thorny ones.

Miller eyed me. "All right, send me a revision of your proposal."

"Yes, sir," I said, about to issue a thank you, but Miller cut me off.

"You know, Luke, there is no lesser. Evil is evil, but only if you can prove it."

If nothing else, my father's death had taught me that.

Chapter Two/Mary

Late September 1944

Why I ever thought I needed Matt to provide for my parents, specifically my father's medical bills, just shows how infatuation can sway a girl. Make her change her lifelong plans. The U.S. government had a plan too, but there was no changing it. And the thing was, no one in Richland knew the whole plan. If you worked in The Area, you knew what you needed to know to do your job, but your puzzle piece was not something you were allowed to fit into any board.

No one had all the pieces, except maybe the higher-ups at DuPont like Dr. Jackson and maybe Colonel Matthias. The colonel was in charge of our part of the puzzle. A puzzle not set up on anyone's dining table. Pieces were strewn across lab countertops in Chicago and Berkeley and down the dark hallways of power in Washington, DC. Even more were scattered across the hills of Tennessee and the deserts of New Mexico.

And here, beside the Hanford buses in the line of employees that bubbled with cheery morning greetings and wound through the lot across the street from Sacajawea Elementary School. Bus passes cost fifteen cents, and the buses ran on time, so you had better be.

Sally, my typing pool mate who lived in the new hastily-erected trailer park on the edge of town, linked her arm to mine, pulling her coat closer against the nip of winter. "You got the dress!"

"Anniversaries should have some reward, right?" I twirled in place, my new frock spinning. "What do you think?"

"Matt won't be able to keep his hands off you," she giggled, not knowing.

No one knew. What I endured to keep my parents afloat, much less get permission to buy a new dress, but I wasn't about to tell. Instead, I said, "What do you hear from Mick?"

Sally's husband was a pilot somewhere in the Pacific. His letters arrived after workers at three different post offices inspected them, the last being Richland's, their black markers wiping out any hints of his whereabouts. An unfamiliar woman in front of us crooked her head.

Sally mouthed, "Later."

Anyone could be a spy. When you first arrived in The Area, you signed a Declaration of Secrecy and pledged your faith and allegiance to the United States, as if we all hadn't had our hands on our hearts from first grade on. I had led my class—a privilege earned by perfect attendance—but this pledge was much more specific in its demands. Any information about your work at Hanford, classified or otherwise, was not to be discussed with anyone, including our own families. I was pretty sure my husband Matt, the Hanford spokesperson, knew what was being engineered in The Area, but, of course, he didn't talk about it.

Any violation—here's where I wondered how they'd know what I said in my kitchen—would land you in jail for ten years unless you had $10,000 to pay the fine. No one had $10,000 at the end of 1944 unless you were a Rockefeller. You signed. They gave you a badge.

We climbed aboard and flashed our passes at the driver. The ride to The Area, depending on your assignment, could be anywhere from fifteen to forty-five minutes. The serial bridge game garnered those with the longest rides and took over the back of the bus. A gaggle of nurses in front traded recipes, and a few senior managers buried their heads in newspapers. Sally and I chatted with two other typing pool pals about the upcoming town picnic until the bus came to a halt at the 300-West entrance.

"Morning Mr. Joseph." My favorite horn player was also a gate guard.

Mr. Joseph scanned my badge with what looked like a big pencil and motioned me forward. "You sounded great on Saturday, Mary."

"No glitches?" I winked. If your badge had a glitch—a glitch no one would define—you marched upstairs in the gatehouse, got a new patch that looked like a film strip, and marched back down again for work.

"Only in Mr. Clark's bridge." Mr. Joseph's poke at our bandleader's tendency to riff a bit too long on his saxophone when he got the spotlight made me laugh, but my amusement faded as Sally and I navigated the labyrinth of walkways.

Our jolly workplace occupied one of a myriad of mundane administrative buildings on the far south side of the massive Hanford Engineer Works. The network of structures sat amidst the otherwise desolate landscape, dotted with only the occasional sagebrush and withered phlox.

Sally and I made our way to our tandem desk, and I shoved my purse and lunch inside my drawer. Sally issued an "uh-oh" under her breath.

Our supervisor, a balding man with a pot belly and a penchant for leering, sidled up beside me. "Mrs. Boone?"

Certain he was trying to peek down my dress, I stepped back. "Sir?"

"Follow me to my office."

Retracing the aisle between the rows of desks, I plucked the pencil from my ear and twirled it in the air to the Merry Macs' peppy "Mairzy Doats" piping through the incessant sound system. The girls tossed grins my way. The questions would come later when we broke for lunch. My supervisor stepped inside his paneled office, wedged his belly behind his desk, and motioned for me to sit.

Another man held the chair for me. "Mrs. Boone, I'm Todd Stordahl. I have the pleasure of working closely with your husband." His smile enhanced his handsome face. "I understand today's your anniversary. Three years?" His smile deepened into best wishes, but the reminder of my third wedding anniversary was not a welcome opening.

"Yes, thank you, but we don't discuss his work." My grip tightened on the pencil.

"Precisely. We need a highly competent, but equally discreet, secretary for the lab in the 3706 Building."

That number resonated. Our former street address in Boise—that's BOY-see, not BOY-zee to you non-Idahoans—was 706. Newlyweds nestled on a maple tree-lined block in stark contrast to the 200-Area that was twenty miles away and strictly off-limits to more than half of Hanford's thousands of employees.

Rumors—most absurd—fed more rumors speculating on the product that was being produced. More than one of my pals perpetuated the toilet paper-plant theory, but even a casual observer could see that there was a lot more going on at Hanford. Matt could have told me the truth, but he hadn't. Our secretive interactions were physical, and being on the receiving side required an extra layer of pancake makeup. But why they had plucked me out of the pool, Mr. Stordahl still hadn't said.

"What exactly are you suggesting, sir?"

A handsome smile locked in, his jaw set. "Less of a suggestion and more of a reassignment. Your country needs your special set of skills in a key area for the war effort."

Declining appeared not to be an option. "What might this entail?"

"Unfortunately, our scientists are not particularly adept at recording their work legibly. We need someone to organize and type up the handwritten records." Stordahl shot me a look that said he knew things about me. "A skilled secretary who understands scientific vernacular and knows the symbols from the periodic table of elements. A familiarity with chemistry, if you will."

Majoring in science had suited me. The solitude of study and the methodical pace, balanced by madcap parts in the drama department where I played at who I wanted to be. Then, stupidly thinking Matt was offering me my dream part, I left college after my third year of study. The passion-charged gale blew me here, but not before I had banked two-thirds of the science credits needed for my major.

A caution bubbled. Labs could be dangerous places, but happy that my unfinished college degree had merit, I said, "I would be inside the laboratory as they work?"

"Inside the building, yes, but not the lab." Stordahl proffered a paper. "Your classified clearance."

From my work in the typing pool, I knew this type of clearance only came after multiple background checks: the FBI talked to your neighbors, your former teachers, your second cousins, and anyone else who knew anything about you. I tucked the document into my pocket. Secrets I could keep.

•   •   •

Early Monday morning following the celebration-packed Thanksgiving Day weekend, Mr. Parsons made his rounds like an ice cream wagon in any middle-class neighborhood in America. His bell woke the entire block of identical company-built A-houses, annoying some, but in my case, it was a welcome excuse to leave bed.

Ralph Hinson rustled around in his bathroom on the other side of the shared wall of our duplex. I applied makeup to cover the evidence of last night's scrape: a scratch by my left eye.

Matt needed to trim his fingernails. Not that anyone would say anything. No matter what a neighbor might overhear—and I was pretty sure the Hinsons heard everything—questions like that, as well as the ones about The Area, just were not voiced.

Out on the porch, I lit up my first cigarette of the day, talking myself out of leaving Matt for the hundredth time. Ralph emerged from his side of the duplex with two milk bottles, except they weren't empty, and it wasn't milk. His monthly "gift to the gods," as Helen, his wife, put it. Ralph shot me a sheepish grin, and I was struck again by the innate kindness of his face.

I grinned back, slipping into my home state's vernacular. "Prolly why the toilet paper rumor has legs." Speculation as to what might be produced in The Area fueled absurd guesses, a running joke about town. Party napkins? Toilet paper? Clothespins? Fireworks?

Ralph laughed, but it seemed like his heart wasn't in it. He placed the two bottles labeled with his name in the metal box, which also contained his work badge and boots, and scurried back inside. Workers from the 300-Area peed into bottles at the end of long weekends.

Mr. Parsons parked his truck emblazoned with the lettering "Hanford Instrument Division of Hanford Medical Department" at our front walk. He loped up onto the porch, his khaki jacket flapping in the breeze. He transferred the urine samples into a carrying case and ran his magic pencil along the bottoms of Ralph's boots and badge, taking readings off both, and grimaced.

"Something wrong, Mr. P?"

His frown reverted to neutral, but his expression was far from cheerful. "Nothing at all, Mrs. B. Just realizing my instrument might need recharging."

A beat passed as I assessed the level of truth in his reply, but I knew better than to dig. Folks who questioned procedures were almost always fired. I wrinkled my nose, blowing one perfect smoke ring into the air as if I wasn't concerned about what he may or may not have found on Ralph's boots. "What do you do with it all?"

"Safe to say, it's flushed down a toilet somewhere, eventually."

"But first, it's tested? Urine being critical to our mission here at Hanford?" I winked, but Parson's tone shifted.

"Don't have to tell you that the HMD is watching out for all of us."

Matt delivered a similar mantra at the end of every community meeting. What would be manufactured in The Area was "critical to our war efforts and absolutely not a danger to the public." Any good American supported the war effort, period.

Mr. Parsons moved onto the next block, passing the coal truck lumbering down the block. Luke, the fourteen-year-old Hinson boy, stepped out onto the porch with a glass of milk in hand, a shy grin on his face.

At least someone was happy to see me. "Interested in a rummy game later?" We had a running card game with penny bets on the nights Matt was at Jimmy's ball games. Basketball season had begun.

"That'd be...great." Luke's eyes flashed with adolescent adoration, a look so distant from the ones I experienced from Matt it made me shiver. My days of being adored had pretty much ended at the ripe old age of twenty-three.

"Luke," Ralph hollered from inside. "Come help with the coal."

Wishing that my stepson Jimmy was half as cooperative as Luke, I slid into my Idaho twang, "Careful, it's the sutt that'll kill you."

I headed down to the basement to open our hatch. Black coal pummeled down the metal chute, kicking up a thick cloud of dust. Covering my mouth and nose with my handkerchief, I noodled on what the instrument had registered on Ralph's boots and whether the HMD was watching out or just watching.

· · ·

An army private chauffeured me along a dirt road on the southern border of the Hanford site. Geese took flight off the broad blue expanse of the Columbia River, casting a chilly morning shadow across our path, pocked with the remains of last night's storm. The jeep jostled past yards of barbed wire fencing and sign after sign warning not to go any farther without authorization. The perimeter fence read aggressive, as if it might pull up stakes and redefine the wiry boundary. Take in all that was vulnerable.

The land for The Area had been taken from the Indians who had hunted and fished it for centuries, as well as newer white settlers who had lived there for at least one hundred of those years. All booted off their land for a paltry sum, because when the government wants something...well, you know.

We came to a halt in front of a large sign beside the entry that read: Technical Building 3706. Other low, flat buildings of the 300-Area flanked it. The rapid erection of a much taller building with large circular chimneys, unseeable from my vantage point, had fueled rumor upon rumor, but no one really knew.

The private pushed open the entry door, saluted a superior, and announced me. The lieutenant dismissed him and addressed me. "Your supervisor, Dr. Griffin, will be here in a moment." He motioned me to a chair by the wall. "Make yourself comfortable."

Prefab walls with loose-fitting panels did little to make me feel comfortable. Minimal protection from who knew what in the lab beyond.

A door behind the lieutenant opened, and a man of medium height, dark hair threaded with gray, stepped in. "Mrs. Boone?"

"Yes, sir," I said, taking in his boyish face and thinking the gray must be premature. Stains on the front of his lab coat and the absence of a ring on his finger indicated bachelorhood.

"Dr. Griffin, but please, call me Harry. Everyone does."

Warming to Harry, I smiled. "And I'm Mary."

Harry led me into a larger room with a glass wall along the far side. "That's the general technical lab." Through the glass, several white-coated men had their heads bent toward a counter laden with beakers and microscopes. "We monitor the jacketing process."

"I assume there's not a row of tailors manning sewing machines behind the counter."

"Those skills might be of merit, but no." Harry chuckled as if he was stalling, deciding how much to tell me.

"Right," I said, not really apologizing. "I think you're going to have to back up a bit."

Harry's smile thinned. "Sorry, I assumed they briefed you. We make sure the jacket, or 'can' if you will, won't disintegrate." He took a seat on a long wooden bench, one end filled by a tipsy-looking stack of manila folders. "As you can see, we're in dire need of your services."

"Perhaps a bit more context first?" In science, it's what you don't know that can kill, and though I danced with danger daily, Matt was familiar, navigable. This looking glass stretched into the unknown and required a language I hadn't learned yet.

"As you know, our production facility is under contract to the Army. This lab tests the integrity of the 'jacket' for the base metal before it's sent on."

"Where?" I asked, my mind spinning as to what the base metal might be.

"To where the product is purified for delivery to the Army." Harry paused, looking for evidence of my comprehension, but I was still struggling. "In the course of your work," he said, answering my unasked question, "you'll be transcribing classified technical information of the highest significance."

"So, the government isn't manufacturing clothespins or toilet paper," I murmured, puzzling out that the new building was most likely where the product went, and it had something to do with the 'gadget.' A term I'd seen used in the typing pool. "Much less campaign buttons."

A grin flickered on Harry's face. "No, but we may attach an FDR button to the next shipment off the production line." His face sobered. "Stabilizing the jacket design has been the most frequent cause of delay in the Project." Harry said the word 'project' as if it weren't entirely benign. "We have but one job here. To make sure the 'jacket' can take all we throw at it."

"And my job?" I attempted a smile, stanching the cold dread that inched up my spine.

Harry peered over his readers. "To make sure all our data is typed up accurately for the rest of the team's use. Critical to our process. Think you can do that?"

My head spun, thinking of the possible danger surrounding this process, but I wasn't about to let on, so I rescued an overstuffed folder from the top of the pile. "Where's my desk?"

Harry opened a side door I hadn't noticed. "This is you," he said, pointing to a small desk with a typewriter. "And this is me." More folders covered Harry's desk.

Another teetering tower of files occupied the hardwood desk chair. "I'll need a cushion."

"I'll call the supply officer." Harry tossed me a fatherly smile, seeming eager to please.

I smiled back, thinking this was a man I might trust. Leaving my husband would require allies.

Chapter Three/Luke

November 1963

Ocean Beach Hospital was a short drive from Baker Bay, and the storm coming off the Pacific justified taking a day off from fieldwork. My sore throat had swelled, making my voice squeak at random moments as if Mickey Mouse had invaded my being. An orderly directed me down a long corridor in my search for Dr. Tall's office. A nurse at the desk took my name.

I'd already self-diagnosed, sure that they'd want to take out my tonsils. Surgery would gum up the remaining days of fall. The time when conditions were still good for the incubation of bad stuff in both flora and fauna. The stuff that fueled my research. The whole thing was annoying. My research timeline did not include a tonsillectomy and recovery time.

"Lucas Hinson?" A nurse at the door nodded at me. "You can come in now."

She showed me to a small windowless exam room. "Remove your shirt. The doctor will be here in a moment." A child's drawing of a Thanksgiving turkey was taped to the wall. Its neck stretched across the page as if waiting for the axe.

I hung my shirt on a wall hook and sat down. Moments like these could turn into years. The cold of the metal chair sent a chill up my back, pushing me forward. The door clicked open, and a relatively short Dr. Tall entered, a clipboard in hand.

He cast an eye at my throat, scanned the record on his clipboard, and set it on the counter. "Mr. Hinson, may I call you Luke?" He grasped my shoulders before sliding his hands across my collarbones and thumbing up either side of my Adam's apple. Dr. Tall swept one hand around to the back of my neck in a quick assessment before pressing both of his thumbs down the sides. "How long has your throat been swollen like this?"

"It's been sore for a couple of weeks, maybe three." I swallowed with some effort. "The swelling, not so long."

Dr. Tall's face twisted into a grimace. "I see your family doctor was in Richland. How long since you've seen him?"

"Undergrad, I think. I'm a PhD candidate now."

Dr. Tall nodded and put his hands back on my throat, pressing gently from right to left. His frown intensified.

"Tonsillectomy, right?" I said, to get the guy to grin.

Tall picked up his clipboard. "I think we'll start with some pictures."

"X-rays?"

"The swelling makes it hard to tell, but you may have some rather prominent nodes on your thyroid glands." Tall made a couple of notes. "The only way to be sure is to take a photo."

Nodes. Thyroid. My mind leaped from annoyance to terror. Thyroid cancer was a malignancy delivered like rounds of a Gatling gun, sprayed in all directions in my hometown. Old, young, and several of my high school classmates had been diagnosed in the past few years. In willful denial, I thought I'd dodged the bullets until now. I shivered.

"You can put your shirt back on."

I studied my buttons as I asked, "Cancer?"

Tall looked at his watch. "You do the pictures, we'll meet back here in two hours."

He was out the door before I could disagree, not that I would have. My ear pain revved again, and I realized I hadn't told him about that part.

My brain pinged to my mother. She would not be pleased with my waiting so long to see a doctor. She'd begged my father to see a doctor for weeks before my father lay down on our couch for the last time. So, I wasn't trying to die on my mother, but the side effects of surgery could make it impossible to work in a lab. Not just for a few months, but for the rest of my life.

The exam room door popped open. An orderly motioned me onto a gurney as if I'd become helpless. He whooshed me down the corridor and around two bends before coming to rest outside a metal-encased door. The orderly pushed a button, and it clicked open. We rolled in. The large cylindrical bulk that housed the lens of the X-ray machine dwarfed the small room.

The radiologist stepped out from behind a small screen. "Lucas Hinson?"

I nodded, and he helped the orderly wheel the gurney under the machine. My valet took his leave, and the radiologist got to it, positioning the contraption over my throat.

X-rays have an exceedingly short wavelength that allows them to penetrate matter—me—and gives the physician—Tall—the ability to view the inner molecular spaces—my throat. Several head turns later, the radiologist rang for my valet, and we glided back to the clinic waiting area. My pictures would need washing, rinsing, and drying, and the radiologist probably wanted lunch, as did I.

The receptionist gave me directions to the cafeteria, where the soup of the day was a surprisingly good clam chowder that made me wonder if they'd stolen my pal Harry's recipe. My rumblings satisfied, I loped back into Tall's reception area in time to see the handoff of a large manila envelope marked "Rush."

In a game of hot potato, the nurse snatched up my photos and ferried them into the hallway and out of sight. A medical journal held my attention until Tall strode through the reception area toting a brown paper sack and, without so much as a glance my way, retreated behind the door to the exam rooms. Everyone has to eat.

I slumped in my chair, watching a seagull soar over the parking lot and out of sight. A dark cloud drifted across the clearing sky. The seagull circled back and dropped his white load on the window.

Tall's nurse opened the door, relieving me of the mounting metaphors. "Luke?"

Back in exam room one, Tall clipped my X-rays up to the lightbox. X-ray film is essentially a shadow photo. Dark regions represent the penetrable parts, my thyroid, and lighter regions are opaque, meaning possible trouble.

Tall tapped at a lighter area. "Here, and here. Outsized nodules we will need to investigate further." He turned to me. "Biochemistry, right?"

He'd looked at my file. "Yep," I said, not yet willing to say I didn't fully understand the implications of the pictures, even though I'd counted five troublesome spots. Bile rose in my already sore throat, and with great effort I swallowed it back down.

"Water?" Tall drew a cup off the shelf and filled it from the tap.

No filter, but in light of my possible new circumstances, why not? The irony of the situation made me laugh.

Tall turned to me, a questioning look on his face.

"Unfiltered water, my work," I realized it was too hard to explain. "Never mind. Just tell me what you think." My knees would not support standing any longer. I plopped onto the chair.

Tall's pencil tapped an X-ray. "Could be benign. Only way to tell is a biopsy."

A fierce pain brought my hand up to my ear lobe. "Ear pain. That's a symptom?"

Tall nodded, his expression turning grave. "Clear your schedule. My nurse will call with your appointment time."

I must have looked pathetic, because Tall put his hand on my shoulder, the way my dad used to. "Aspirin will help with the ear pain." And he was out the door, leaving me with the real dilemma. Should I call my mother now or later?

•   •   •

The research grant paid for the small cabin on the backside of Cape Disappointment, the perfect location, considering my new condition.

The Cape straddled the Washington-Oregon border. The point at which I separated from my old certain life to enter my new unpredictable one. After years of bumping around the Western Hemisphere, I chose to live near the last place Mary had been. Beautiful Mary, my first everything.

When my mother came to Boston in 1950 to visit me at grad school—MIT—and shared the news that Mary had been declared missing, I was too far away to help with the search. But an inane longing had lured me back to this spot. A place where she was nowhere to be found.

Harry's crab shack occupied the midpoint of the longest pier on the sandy side of Baker Bay. I set aside thoughts of a possible cancer diagnosis, as well as treatments that wouldn't lead to a cure and guaranteed unwelcome side effects in favor of cracked crab, a far safer choice than fish spawned in the Columbia. The walk along the weathered planks took me well beyond the shoreline to the depths that housed a legendary undertow.

What looked to be a mass of red hair bobbed on the far side of a dinghy floating near the pier pilings. A boy in the boat clutched at the oars receding into the brine. On the water's surface, fiery tendrils strayed in all directions, undermining any defined center. A tangled mass, dry to my eye, as if the wet of the entire ocean could not tame it.

The boat and the boy, along with the tresses of copper-red drifted under the pier. I galloped to the other side to spot them, oddly frantic. The water at the tide line had turned winter cool, fair warning to swimmers.

The dinghy poked out below me, its bow pointed toward the shore. A blanket, it must have been folded before, bundled up what seemed to be another child in the boat. The red mane obscured the face, but I guessed she was maybe seven or eight.

Harry stepped out of the shack's back door, handed me a mug of coffee, and leaned over the rail. "Ah, the boy's coming in." I raised a brow in query and Harry said, "I loan him the dinghy ever so often."

"How can anyone be out in that cold?"

Harry shrugged. "The boy stays in the boat." Harry motioned toward my Impala, parked at the edge of the pier. "Need a ride home, I reckon."

"How far?"

"Too far to walk before dark. A couple of rises over."

The hills began about a mile beyond the shore, rising above the Columbia's mouth. My cabin rested on the first one, just beyond the Washington hamlet of Naselle. Only a few tract houses and an abandoned development scattered across the bare, rolling terrain. An area I deemed suspect, and where every drink of water should be questioned, but few folks knew anything of the real havoc wrought by the Hanford nuclear plant three hundred miles away.

The scientists at the inception of nuclear production had believed that errant, airborne radioactive emissions would just float up and away, and never reach this far. The Hanford engineers had submerged the irradiated fuel slugs under water in large tanks, creating a barrier between the engineers and the slugs. A faulty uranium slug could necessitate a shutdown, and engineers would scramble to remove it before damage was done to the hardware or worse, a uranium fire erupted. They dumped any ruptured slugs into more water to cool. The effluent was flushed into the Columbia, a circuitous path, but one that led to the sea.

The boy, a redhead too, pulled the dinghy up on the sand above the tide. The girl hid behind the blanket before breaking free of it, the light turning her luminous. Her clothing puffed out in the breeze, completely dry, as if never immersed at all. I shook my head at the thought of it, figuring she must have been swimming naked, and the clothes donned after she climbed aboard. The boy shook the sand from the blanket while the girl stayed back, a step or so behind him. He folded the blanket and placed it back into the skiff.

Harry waved, and the boy lifted his hand. He climbed the ladder from sea level, the girl almost overlapping him like a shadow. As he swung a leg over the rail, I caught a glimpse of her face. The shock of their faces, side by side, rocked me. Familial look-alikes. Twins except for the age difference, the boy older, maybe by five or six years. I pegged him at thirteen or so. The girl gave up a half-smile, fading before it began, and the sun blotted her from my vision.

Harry spoke to the boy. "Luke's headed your way. Told him you might want a lift."

The boy nodded. "Shall I bring the dinghy up?"

Harry shook his head. "I'll take her out to check the pots." He handed me my crab order.

The boy turned to me. "Ready, mister?" The girl's hand disappeared inside his palm.

They followed me to the car and slid into the back seat. I tossed a conversation starter over my shoulder. "Lived here long?"

"Since my grandmother came to get us." The boy didn't offer more.

"What grade are you?"

"They've got me in seventh, but I'm older. Just taking enough math to pass the GED."

The boy shot me a fierce look through the rearview mirror. I envied this little man with a plan. My own plan, a PhD in biochemistry, a professorship, and eventually tenure, was bogged down by my pending diagnosis. My research grant, with its required reporting schedule, would keep me somewhat on track. But no denying that my focus had strayed, despite Dr. Tall's assurances that survival rates were far better for those under the age of forty-five.

The boy sat up straight near the window, peering out at the marshes that divided the shore from the rest. A divide that had proved penetrable, according to my initial testing, though the results had been more pesticide than radiation-laden. Both ignored manmade boundaries.

Pearlie's Mercantile slid past, and I made a mental note to buy more bottled water. The girl had slumped into a gray woolen blob under the boy's arm. I caught the boy's eye in the rearview. "Which turn?"

"Just pull over at the crick, I'll walk from there."

I startled. Crick was the way Mary had said it. "Clouds rolling in. I'll drive you."

"A car can't make it up the farm drive, too many ruts. I'll be home before," he paused. "Before it gets dark." The way he had hesitated gave some new agency to the dark, but I didn't pursue it. A clump of hemlocks signaled a stream ahead. Distracted by a long-bed truck loaded with timber barreling toward us, I pulled well off the road.

The boy exited as the truck blew past. He pushed his head back into the open car door. "Appreciate the ride, mister." The girl must have slipped out before him.

"Call me Luke. What's your name?"

"Ben." He tossed another thanks over his shoulder as he strode down the dirt road riddled with rain puddles and tractor tracks. The girl had moved out of sight.

Chapter Four/Mary

Spring 1945

DuPont had hired an architect who envisioned a community rooted in equality, modest but ample housing from A-H. Five exact replicas, A-model houses, duplexes really, lined our side of a treeless block. Six H-houses rested opposite, ample side yards of twenty-foot or so separating each. Several L's in the next block, the only homes with four bedrooms, were reserved for the higher-ups at the plant and were part of my husband's ever-present aspirations.

The stairs in the middle of the A's floor plan provided a separation between the two living spaces, but the living room and third bedroom walls were shared. Walls built with no insulation, so I heard pretty much everything that went on with the Hinsons. Folks must have complained, because the contractor was adding insulation in the new ones being built two streets over.

Home early on this particularly warm April day, I crammed myself into a chair on our half of the tiny front porch. Legs propped on the railing, I considered the struggling Potentilla bushes across the street. Nothing grew here without a struggle. I lit up.

Ralph Hinson stepped out his front door and tipped his hat. "Good afternoon, Mary."

Typical Ralph, always so respectful. Strong, but kind. There wasn't enough of that going around. Helen Hinson gifted me homemade jams when we first moved in, promising to teach me to can. Helen followed

Ralph out the door, her voluminous red hair cascading off her shoulders. A decade my senior, she embodied a serenity that I dreamed of.

"Off to take in a picture show?" I asked, even though I'd already heard their plans for the four o'clock matinee of *Arsenic and Old Lace*—Richland got movies late in the rotation, and Helen loved Cary Grant—and dinner at the local diner—Helen needed a break from cooking dinner.

Helen nodded. "Luke's home, doing his homework. Don't let his music get too loud."

"It can't." My smoke ring drifted toward Janet Clark and her fella strolling hand in hand down the block. "The Ink Spots are one of my favorites," I said, thinking the young in Richland had no idea what might be born of their union, much less what love could do. For me, that question had been asked and answered.

Janet's fella had his sleeves rolled up against the heat. What was it about a man in shirt sleeves? Matt's suit jacket had been flung over his shoulder, on that warm day in Moscow—"MOS-coh" not "Mos-COW"—as he supervised the hanging of a large semi-centennial banner over the entrance to the university library, workmen hanging on ladders in precarious fashion, doing his bidding. I had hesitated, viewing their progress.

Matt had tipped his hat. "Miss. Please, go ahead." And even as he said it, one of the workmen lost his hold on the cloth. In a giant whoosh, the banner swept across the steps, wrapping me up in its path. I stumbled, trapped, my balance failing. Matt caught me. "Are you okay, miss?" He kept one arm around me and wrestled the banner with the other. The banner flapped its way off me, but Matt didn't let go. The next thing I knew, he and his young son, Jimmy, were meeting my parents.

Matt and my father, home on sick leave from the Stibnite mines, had a lot to talk about, and me being a naïve almost-woman—not that much older than Luke Hinson is now—I was happy just to watch Matt's mouth move. Matt was a government liaison with the University of Idaho, something to do with mining zinc and cobalt. My father's heart and lungs were already compromised, and the mine accident had impaired his vision, making it impossible for him to work.

Pancake makeup cost one dollar and twenty-eight cents, but my father's medical bill for one month alone was one hundred and twenty-two dollars. The sum was half of the monthly salary my father used to collect and far more than the stipend Stibnite gave him now. Matt had just given me a check to cover it.

I stubbed out my cigarette and swung my feet off the rail, resigned to fixing the ridiculously early dinner Matt had demanded before Jimmy's baseball game, when Luke stepped outside. His normal spectacles had been replaced with a pair that had a solid tortoiseshell rectangular frame, giving him a scholarly look.

"Hey, new glasses," I said, smiling my approval. "Very Ivy League."

"Pays to turn fifteen." Luke grinned. "Like the scientists in the newspapers."

Our common love of science had created a bond between us. He ate up my stories about failed college lab experiments and the joy of discovery. Joy lost to me.

"Who knew Dr. Butt had style?" We both grinned. Binyon Optometry on George Washington Way was yet another government-subsidized service. The powers that be didn't want us straying. Every need—housing, businesses, schools—was backed by the Feds.

Our grins faded as Jimmy and Matt pulled up to the curb. Jimmy's mother had run off when he turned four. Matt's explanations early on garnered sympathy for my stepson, and Matt's generosity toward my parents sealed the deal. The difference in our ages had bothered my mother, not to mention the problems a mother-abandoned eleven-year-old might cause, but who listens to their mother? Mesmerized by first-time-ever sex, I said yes to Matt's proposal, with one condition. I insisted on working.

My reluctance to become a full-time stepmother had been the initial source of conflict between us. Jimmy, already a bully in fifth grade, caused disagreements and small flare-ups. I glossed over them all in lieu of the all-encompassing lovemaking and the much-needed financial support that Matt provided my parents. Jimmy's pranks escalated as he moved into his teens and high school. Quiet, studious boys like Luke suffered the consequences.

Luke moved to the far side of the porch, giving Matt and Jimmy plenty of room as they approached.

My husband put on his plant spokesman's false smile. "Afternoon Luke." Jimmy brushed past without a greeting, and Matt cast a dark look my way. "What's for dinner?"

I stiffened, realizing I'd let the time slip and knowing that cooking would take too long. No way to get it on the table by three-thirty. "Thought I'd warm up the leftover pot roast."

"Second night in a row?" Matt chuckled, but I knew he did not think that it was funny.

That chuckle was for Luke's benefit, as if he couldn't hear through the walls on his side too. The slow creep of Matt's anger was visible, an achingly, long approach to the inevitable. Luke eased back inside his half of the duplex and closed the door, but I glimpsed his silhouette through the Hinson kitchen window.

My husband's humor turned to derision. "Are you trying to make Jimmy late for his baseball game?" He crossed the threshold, one he hadn't bothered to carry me over. That was two houses and many anguished nights ago.

I used to draw hearts on the calendar, just to keep track of the good days, the ones where Matt loved me, but once those days did not outnumber the others, I stopped. Now I record it all in my diary, locked inside my dressing table. A record just for me, along with my father's treatment, a litany of medical procedures and medicines, as if they might balance out the pain.

"I'll make a stir-fry too, some spuds and carrots." Matt ignored me and stomped up to our bedroom. I popped the roast into the oven to warm and lit the burner under the skillet. At least something would be hot. I'd peeled two potatoes when a footstep startled me, and I turned.

The slap hit my cheek broadside. I fell back against the stove, my arm grazing the hot cast iron skillet. I yelped in pain. Matt smiled.

On the other side of the kitchen wall, Luke switched from the phonograph to the Richland radio station. Jimmy entered the kitchen clad in his uniform, busy scraping his pocket knife under a fingernail. I ran cold water over my forearm, a red welt rising.

"Careful you don't burn the potatoes," Matt snarled. "Dinner is already late enough."

I'd learned to decipher his tone, full of regret or threat. He wasn't done yet.

Desperate to derail Matt's trajectory, I said, "Jimmy, how about a pop?" I dug into the fridge for a Coca-Cola. "Fuel for the game?"

Jimmy grunted. "As if it'll help." The other team had beaten them every season for the last decade.

Matt extracted some ice cubes for a pre-game drink, not my arm. The bourbon bottle rested above the fridge, only a couple of shots left in it. *Damn.* That would be my fault too.

Matt emptied it into his highball glass and slammed the empty bottle on the counter. "Too busy chatting with the neighbor boy to make it to the liquor store either?"

Jimmy retreated to the unset dining table. With a load of silverware and placemats, I followed, putting some distance between Matt and me.

"I only got home a couple few minutes before you did." Out the dining room window, two boys were playing catch in the dirt between the houses. "I had to finish a report for Dr. Griffin before I could leave."

"Ah yes, the good Dr. Griffin." Matt sneered, sucking in bourbon. "I've seen the way you look at him from the dance hall stage when you sing." His voice had lowered a notch.

"I don't look at anyone, not Harry, not anyone. I look at the tops of folks' heads when I sing." I went back to the kitchen to scoop helpings of the stir-fry onto plates. The welt on my arm pulsed, needing some salve.

"Harry, is it? Mighty informal with your supervisor." Matt hovered in the doorway, blocking my ability to open the fridge. "I'm not blind you know."

"I need to get the ketchup and mayo for the fry sauce," I said, bracing myself against the sink, wondering if he would do it with Jimmy sitting right there. Matt had never been quite that brazen before. Not that Jimmy didn't know. His bedroom wall adjoined ours.

The clock ticked toward three, and the voices on Luke's radio traveled through the wall. "We interrupt this program to bring you a special announcement from CBS World News. A press Association has just announced that President Roosevelt is dead. The President has died of a cerebral hemorrhage, and all we know so far is that he died in Warm Springs, Georgia."

Matt anchored himself against the door frame, staring at the radio. I sank into my chair, sorrow swelling in my chest. Chatter fired up in the streets as folks exited their houses, the news too big to stay inside. Radios blared up and down the block, announcing Truman's presence in the White House. Jimmy scraped his plate clean, his appetite undeterred by the news.

Matt stepped outside, and a neighbor crossed the street to commiserate. Another brought a bottle out to the sidewalk, and filled several glasses, including Matt's. They toasted the presidents, dead and alive. Men asked Matt what this might mean for the plant. Would it affect the work? Every response Matt delivered was never an actual answer. Questions from the community were to be fielded and batted away, all in the name of security. But whose?

"Boys," he said, as if all those around him weren't men. "Our work is critical to the war effort, and I'm sure President Truman is aware of that."

The Hinsons scurried down the block. Helen took the porch steps in a leap, and Luke met her at the door. They fell into a hug. Neither tried to shield their eyes, wet with tears. Luke's eyes traveled my way, but I let the curtain sheer on the kitchen window drop between us, ashamed of my relief. The President's death had put Matt off his game, but there was still a night to get through. He mostly did it at night.

• • •

Victory in Europe had been ten weeks prior, but the war in the Pacific continued to rage, along with rumors that our boys in France and Germany, bedraggled and exhausted, were going to be transferred in droves to the opposite side of the globe to fight some more. The gossip swirl in town spun off whispers of our boys winning islands throughout the South Seas that summer, many more than the newspapers reported on.

My new assignment had kept me from regular lunch breaks with my typing pool pals at the 200-Area administration building for weeks. The temporary quality of the picnic area gave me hope that once the war was over, most of this would simply be packed up and carted away. But the longer I worked with Harry, the more research and data I transcribed, the harder hope was to grasp. They might call it 'base metal,' but even I had figured out it was uranium, and the 'product' was fuel for the unspeakable.

Big band tunes piped over the speaker system, a constant loop of upbeat tunes that inundated the entire Area. Artie Shaw's peppy clarinet accompanied this particular workday as if the music would keep us from concentrating too hard on what had brought us here. But on the Fourth of July, I'd only mouthed the lyrics to the national anthem. No rampart could protect anyone from the waste we were creating. Off gases I suddenly realized, that could have peppered the path I walked toward my lunch dates.

My pals from the typing pool surrounded me as I neared before settling at a table on the edge of the others. The noise level generated by workers seated at a dozen such tables created a screen for our conversation.

"So, spill." Sally, my former desk mate in the pool, was always tempting fate, or at least the powers that be. "What's up in the 300-area?"

With an eye roll, I said, loud enough so that anyone around might hear, "Now, Sally, you know I can't say a word about my new assignment, just like our boys in the Pacific."

This sent everyone into giggles. Some women seated near us edged closer to their pod, disassociating themselves from our disruptive gaggle.

Sally swept her brunette curls off her shoulders, cast a look at one of the women staring our way, and lowered her voice. "Mick's certain something big's going to happen and soon." Sally and her husband Mick, an Air Force pilot stationed somewhere in the South Pacific, had worked out a code in their letters regarding any major changes in Mick's status.

Artie Shaw ceded to Jimmy Rushing and his band, giving our conversation some cover. Nosy Nellie kept her back to us, but I suspected she was eavesdropping. Snitch-or-be-snitched-on was too often the case at Hanford, not that anyone reported abusive husbands. The hot breeze did nothing to ease the spiking late July temperatures or my annoyance. I swiped at the perspiration sliding down my neck and said in a hushed voice, "Weeks? Days?"

Sally and Mick's code included references to dates of special occasions that, in turn, relayed clues about his status or possible relocation. We all huddled closer, and Sally leaned in. "Mick said the only thing he wanted for his birthday was to come home to me."

Nosy-Nellie's head twitched, her blonde Betty-Grable waves swaying ever so slightly. Putting a finger to my lips, signaling Sally to pause, I pushed off the bench, stepped backward, and bumped Nosy Nellie just as she lifted a pitcher of iced tea off her table. Such unfortunate timing. The pitcher launched out of her hands, contents gushing and backwashing onto her lap. She jerked up, slapping at the brown liquid staining her dress.

"Oh, clumsy me," I said, sarcasm dripping along with the tea. I proffered my napkin. "Here, dear."

Miss Nosy stomped off, followed by the rest of her gang. My pals tossed more napkins onto the puddle and huddled back into our circle.

"When's Mick's birthday?"

"The first week of August."

•   •   •

What I didn't discuss with the girls was my work detailing the base metal's path. The 314 building had been completed the year before, with the installation of the one thousand-ton extrusion press completed the past spring. Supposedly, Mr. Thompson, who had lived down the block from us, had been fired for mentioning to his mother-in-law that his crew had finished it. His mother-in-law bragged about it to the gals in the beauty salon. Newly promoted Ted Jackson and his family had moved into the Thompson's C house after they were evicted.

According to Dr. Griffin's dictation, the press allowed the processing of raw uranium billets, extruded rods that were transformed into fuel cores that were then outgassed and straightened. After machining, the rods were sent to our lab to test for proper sealing and then transferred to the 313 building for insertion. As I plowed through the folders from 1944, it became apparent that the scientists had an awful time getting the jackets to fit.

Harry leaned over my shoulder. "That year was a blur of false starts."

"All those faulty jackets, all those misfits had to be disposed of somewhere," I said. "But I can't find the info on that. Don't you need it for the file?"

"We've stored them in vaults."

"Like a bank vault? But isn't some of the waste liquid?"

Harry cast an eye to the cracked door. "You've seen the trenches along the fence line?" The trenches were on the far side of the plant, acres away from the river. My turn to nod. "Most of the sludge goes there," Harry said. "The rest of the water waste is filtered and then discharged through a pipe under the plant and into the riverbed."

My eyes widened, thinking of the favorite fishing hole Luke always talked about, a warm spot in the river he occasionally waded in, even in winter. "Isn't that putting the fish at risk?"

"They're testing them—sheep, cattle, and any wildlife that drink at the river. Tracking the radiation levels against acceptable limits."

Something in Harry's face made me question his last statement. He'd said tracking, not taking action, but I asked, "And all those slugs, the ones that were not quite right?"

"Sealed away for decades."

Chapter Five/Luke

Mid-November 1963

Brenda Lee's pithy version of "Break It to Me Gently" piped through the Muzak of the Ocean Beach Hospital, making me wonder who crafted these music tapes. Dr. Tall performed his perfunctory physical exam, feeling around my throat and pecs. I straightened my back, as if my posture would somehow influence the biopsy results.

Dr. Tall made some notes on my chart, stood, and pointed with his pen at a nodule on one of the old X-rays. "We found malignant tissue in several areas." The look on Tall's face was neutral, but the X-rays posted on lightboxes across one wall of his office took on a sinister glow. "Here, and here, are the most worrisome," Tall said, tapping his pen to the backlit cavities. "But best to get them all if we can."

My hand went to my throat as if the shape of it had suddenly changed and I could massage away this evil inside. "You think you can?" My shoulders sagged out of fight stance into flee-and-hide mode.

Dr. Tall took his seat behind his desk and laced his fingers together. "The good news is, it's not very far along."

The cancer on the lightbox morphed into an animated character that the doc could surely eradicate by erasure or drawing a new page or two in the flip-book. Change my story. One that could use some changing, at least according to my mother during our last exchange, the one where I chickened out of telling her anything about this thing in my throat. I didn't know how, any more than I knew how to go about indicting the U.S. government with my thesis.

Mary and I used to discuss this kind of thing, nothing specific of course, generalities, the whys and wherefores of the hypothesis, the proof needed. In the absence of proof, there was nothing to tell. But now, the telling had to include more. Something that wouldn't send my mother off a cliff.

"You said we'd discuss options today."

"I've consulted colleagues in Eastern Washington. They've seen a lot of thyroid cancer, especially in young people in the region."

No surprise there, I thought. The only puzzle was how I had made it into my thirties without something like this presenting itself, at least according to the paltry data I'd been able to find during my research on the subject. Of course, I did my own research. Who trusts a pamphlet from the company that makes the machine or pill that will treat you?

Dr. Tall cleared his throat, glancing at his notes before continuing. "We have three ways to attack the problem. Surgery, fairly radical, where we take out as many of the cancerous nodes as possible."

"You can't get them all that way?" What about complete annihilation, like Hiroshima? Obliterate the enemy. Leave no nodule standing.

"We can get most, but maybe not all," Dr. Tall said, jolting me out of my happy-ending-laden WWII fantasy and back into my not-so-certain reality. "Along with the surgery, we would do a massive cobalt irradiation of your neck."

"And the third thing?" I prompted, knowing already. I'd devoured every article on ablation therapy and the data on survival ratios.

"We'll follow the radiation with an I-131 ablation treatment." He dropped back in his chair, as though dispensing the list of options exhausted him. But more would need saying.

Scientists are not immune to the reactive feelings of a layman patient. My mind replayed the photos of radiation machines I'd studied in journals, moving in a rapid clip like a jumpy black-and-white documentary. A hulking mechanism, the Maximar 250-III had been manufactured by GE even as they were making more and more bombs in the 50s. And how does one reconcile the fact that the machine that would deliver the death blow to my cancer was developed by a Japanese company we bombed—at least probably?

Nothing like a good conundrum to keep me from going into full panic mode. Clarifying questions first, I reminded myself. "Can you avoid taking out the parathyroid glands?"

Dr. Tall shrugged. "We'll try, but no guarantee until we get inside."

The parathyroid glands control a person's calcium levels. My mother had described in detail a neighbor's spasms after a similar surgery, a condition called tetany. A condition that would make lab work impossible, according to my research. This was the stuff they didn't put in the pamphlet.

Just thinking about a surgeon let loose in my thyroid and me knocked out helpless on the table rattled me. All the surgical residents, at least those I'd come across on the UW campus during undergrad, were narcissistic dicks. The horror of their possible lack of finesse replaced my fear of "it."

"And nerve deterioration?"

"Most likely."

I shot Tall a wry smile. "Any other benefits?"

He mustered a grin. "A remarkable scar to tell the ladies about. Ear to ear."

"The new study by Haynie and Beierwaltes." I'd done lots of reading. "Almost seventy percent of two hundred subjects treated with the radioactive cocktail tested cancer-free afterward. What say we skip the surgery and move straight onto the radiation?"

"Lowers your odds quite a bit."

The whale calf would not have survived, but the cow could have gone on for years had the whalers' harpoon not found her. The sheer mass, the amount of fight she must have had to keep going with all of that inside her, wasn't something I thought I could match.

Is it real if you can't feel it? I put my hand to my throat. Nothing. Or more to the point, was it even large enough for a dickhead surgeon to distinguish? My choice would take some serious explaining to my mother. "Yeah, well," I said. "Let's start with the cobalt anyway."

•   •   •

The sun had not even thought about fading when I cracked open a beer, chugging it for fortification. After dragging the phone cord through the window and scooting the small table closer to the rocker, I pulled on a sweater against the chill and aimed an eye at the clouds approaching from the south. I belched and dialed.

My mother picked up on the fifth ring.

"Mom? Catch you in the middle of something?"

"Just unloading groceries. How are you?"

An odd pang of homesickness shot through me at the sounds of cans being put away. Not that I missed Richland. I missed her, Helen Hinson, my mother, the neighborhood go-to. She always knew the right thing to say, the right time to say it. I didn't know how to do that. Not to mention the serious doubts I had about what I needed to say.

"About that, I'm..." I hesitated, realizing I didn't even know how I was really.

It's one thing to summon a false bravado with a doctor, or a relative stranger, and entirely another to try any of that with the woman who knew you best. I gulped in air, the cold filling my chest. "I'm okay, but something's come up."

A silence entered the line, potent in its possible assumptions. A paper sack rustled, and I pictured her running through the possible problems: a girl, school, money. She wouldn't think of this, but then, maybe she did because she said, "Should I sit down?"

"Listen, it's going to be fine."

"Maybe start over." A long slow exhale threaded the line.

"So, I've had this sore throat." I paused, hoping she'd take it from there, but she didn't. "I saw a doctor at Ocean Beach last week. He did some X-rays." Giving up that much drained me. I had to say it, but then again, if I didn't say it, then it wasn't real. She wouldn't have to go through this again. Well, not exactly this because I'd gotten X-rays, something my father never would do, no matter how many nosebleeds. But a time like this is when you learn how selfish you are. I didn't want to go through this alone.

"They identified five problem areas."

"When are you scheduled for surgery?"

"Not yet. I want to try something else first."

Her voice ratcheted up to an unfamiliar pitch. "We both know surgery first, then all the other stuff." Demands were not how my mother operated, at least not most of the time, but her tone held one.

"Look, a lot has happened since my classmates were diagnosed. I'm going to try radiation first, then, we'll see." I exhaled, knowing she'd fight.

"Luke, you can't risk—" her voice dropped off. She must have muzzled the phone, because I couldn't hear anything.

"Mom, you there?" Silence. "Look, I promise I won't die on you."

Her voice choked through. "That's what your father said."

The line went dead.

●　　●　　●

Ionization knocks electrons out of atoms. So, ionizing radiation blasts the hell out of atoms in living things, like me and the mule deer. While the latter had unknowingly ingested the strontium-90 tainted sagebrush or cheatgrass, I had made the deliberate decision to submit myself to cobalt irradiation. Whenever I was sprawled under the machine, I pondered how we used poison to kill the poison, finding no philosophical resolution.

Side effects proved less daunting than I thought they would be, though my five o'clock shadow became splotchy like the deer's hide, maybe more a reaction to knowing I would have to face my mother soon.

Harry had driven me to the hospital for my fourth round of cobalt, which toppled me, making me a prisoner in my bed. I forced myself up and out when I had to, but my vision blurred to the point that I invariably stubbed my toe. The shooting pain almost made all the other stuff bearable, but not quite.

My mother, Helen, showed up to take things in hand, her trademark serenity competing with anger at being kept out of my decision. She had stayed away as long as she could stand, she said. I was still not on her good list, and she made no mention of putting up a tree for me. But I'd spied a box of lights in the back seat of her car on my first brief foray outside. A tree would need presents underneath, and I'd given us plenty of reasons not to celebrate. Merry Christmas.

Walker, whose uncle had been the tribe's healer, dropped by with a salve for the minor burns on my neck. The salve did indeed have magical powers, but Walker confessed he'd bought it at a homeopathic store in Portland.

The sun had poked out from the thicket of early winter clouds. My mother and Walker moved out to the front porch, chatting as if they were picking up a conversation they'd left off a while back. I sank into my suffering and the front porch rocker.

My mother's volunteer work had her administering to various farm families with a variety of maladies, but cancer the most prevalent. She'd been quizzing Walker about illness among his family members. "It must be very worrisome on the reservation."

"Food is more of a problem." Walker scraped at a small piece of driftwood with a smaller version of his hunting knife, transforming it into some kind of animal. He had gone to Eastern, suffering through a slew of racist taunts to a Bachelor in Biology. "My cousins go far to the north now. Fish above the reservation. But, when you are starving, it's hard not to eat what's available."

"I shouldn't stay in Richland either, but I can't seem to pull away despite..." My mother's eyes misted, my father's death still fresh even after a decade. "There's always something, someone that needs my help." My mother reached over, grasping my hand, her eyes searching mine. "You know I'm not angry, not really. Just..." She didn't voice the rest.

If she did, how would that change things? Would it allow her to say she lived in the thick of it, every day? A fear of the thing so entrenched in Richland that most longtime residents no longer took it seriously.

Only when a cancer diagnosis landed in one's own A, B, or H house, did it become real. But they could always chalk it up to smoking or coal dust or pesticides on the vegetables they ate, not The Area. The revered Area, never the real tyrant, but I couldn't give my mother the comfort she sought.

My choice to eschew surgery was a crapshoot, and the flip side of seventy percent was thirty. A not-so-small possibility that my research career might be short shrift. Research that probably won't change anyone's mind about anything. Still, I had to try. Who would demand change if I didn't?

"You're just annoyed," I intoned, finishing my mother's sentence and attempting humor, however feeble. "That I can't come home to play Santa."

Walker grimaced at my comment. No way I would be able to drive home for the holidays, but the minute I said it, I was sorry. Sorry that she had to go through this. That she had to give up anything, any celebration that might bring at least a smile to her face. Real joy she had buried with my father. My mother was the strongest woman I knew, but my condition tested her strength at a new level. Selfish not to recognize that before now.

"Sorry," I said. "Radiation must affect comedic timing."

Walker shot me a look that said, enough.

My mother gathered herself. "In the midst of everything, I forgot to tell you something. Relevant to your research."

Her eyes held that look that could only be bad news, making me afraid to ask. All I could do was raise an eyebrow, feeling the nausea begin its stir in my belly.

"You remember Linda Wilson?"

Linda and I had gone to high school together. I nodded. "Her family lived along that stretch the locals call Death Mile, right?" A series of small communities in the farmlands near The Area had served up more than their fair share of cancer and deaths. A woman who lived on one of the farms had been mapping it for several years, different colored dots for each diagnosis along a mile or so of the farm-to-market road that threaded the region. Dozens of dots.

Walker looked up from his carving. The Yakima reservation was near that community.

"Eltopia." My mother continued. "Anyway, she just had a little girl." My mother paused, her eyes welling. "Born with no eyes, like the lambs a couple of winters back."

Mr. Johnson's lambs had been the first, but not the only. Hundreds of lambs on farms and ranches near Hanford had been born with multiple defects: missing feet, fused legs, no mouths, and eyeless sockets that provoked demonic images and newspaper headlines declaring "The Night of the Little Demons." Hanford men showed up to sample livestock. They clicked across the entire expanse with their Geiger counters, but in the end, had declared "no risk to human health" in the farmland dirt. The government had refused to take responsibility, driving multiple sheep farmers, including Mr. Johnson, into bankruptcy.

I made a mad dash for the toilet, hurled, and sank onto the cool bathroom tile floor.

My mother's words floated through the window. "That damn Hanford."

•   •   •

The fifth round of radiation went better, but the sixth almost killed me. My mother sat up all night, convinced her sheer will would disallow me from dying. I drifted in and out of consciousness, glad to dive into my dreams only to break away, sweating and terrified of what I had seen in them. A cascade of broken and bent animals barreled through long tubes, funnels immersed in water that kept rising over my head.

My fever gave way at some point, and I sat up in bed, allowing my mother to spoon-feed me some tasteless soup. Not that it didn't have taste, but my taste buds only recorded a chalky substance that remained after every hurl. When nothing was left in me to eject, my mother situated me and a jug of water on the front porch and headed to the store to pick up more food for me to regurgitate.

The bay lay flat before the sinking sun, but the winter breeze encircling me meant things wouldn't stay that way. A jackrabbit bounded across my sightline, disappearing inside a shrub and a sunbeam. I blinked the huckleberry bush into focus, seeing red strands weaving among its dark berries and copious leaves.

"Who's there?" I sputtered, knowing full well who it might be.

A rustle produced the waif of a girl, not twenty feet away, but the sun struck her from behind, making her a shimmering silhouette without distinguishable features. The breeze gave up a whisper. "Me."

"Hello," I said, stuck for what else to say. Something about this child had me in awe, as if seeing a great work of art for the first time or a hidden treasure not meant to be found.

The rabbit crept out of the bush and rested below her. A gust knocked her red locks into a frizzy curtain over her face, covering any nod she might have given, the frailty of her frame even more noticeable in silhouette. It puzzled me how she could have traipsed up the hillside. Not an easy hike.

"Where's Ben?" I asked.

"School." Her response was hushed, as if the breeze had to help deliver it.

"Why aren't you there?"

"Got sick." The silhouette shifted. "You too?"

I nodded, forcing myself out of my rocker, only to grab hold of the porch post lest I collapse. "Sort of. Cancer, but it's not catching. Treatment's worse than the illness." I pulled my baseball cap down a bit more, self-conscious about my patchy hair beneath.

"If it doesn't go on too long."

Before I could ask her how she might know, the sun vanished, leaving the ground between us dusky. The sound of tires on the dirt road stirred a flock of sparrows out from the bramble behind her. The downshift of gears signaled my mother's return. The jackrabbit loped toward the bushes.

"Gotta go." Her words bounced across the distance between us.

My mother's car inched up the drive. I raised my hand in farewell.

"Well, hello to you," my mother said, exiting the car.

"Just saying goodbye to the girl," I said, wishing I had the energy to go after her.

"What girl?" My mother extracted grocery bags from the back seat.

"Just a neighbor child," I murmured, staring at the rent between the dirt and sky, wondering if she had been there at all.

•   •   •

My radiation treatment would have been out of reach financially, had it not been for the work done at Hanford. The apparatus suspended from the ceiling bore the GE logo, creating a tug of war inside me, gratitude versus disgust.

The tech spread a lead-lined drape over me, his demeanor all business. He aimed the cylindrical protrusion at my neck, aligning the machine head. "Ready?'

Two interns peered through the viewing window. Unable to read their lips, I closed my eyes to them, grimacing. "Ready as I'll ever be for megavoltage radiation."

The tech chuckled, and laid a shield across my face. "Happy New Year."

He stepped back, his only protection a white lab coat. The lazy Susan table, on which I lay face up, rotated me while the machine pumped out gamma rays. The tech had me flip to my stomach. He recalibrated the machine and rotated the table the other way. A flip of a switch signaled that my last "cobalt bomb" was complete.

The procedure was not without its radioactive waste. The tech stripped his lab coat and tossed it into a metal can. The orderly arrived to gurney me back to a changing room, and tossed a metal-filled quilt over me, pinning me down. Two male interns stepped away from the door to allow my exit. The orderly paused to let another patient trolley pass. The interns' chatter reached my ear. "Necessary I suppose if you're going to beat it, but what a trade-off."

"Yeah," said the other. "De-spunked in your prime. Tough."

Were they talking about me or just radiation treatments in general? I cranked my head toward them, wanting to ask, but the orderly pushed off, taking me around the corner and out of shouting distance. I scrambled back into my clothes and trudged to the far lot behind the hospital. I only had a couple hours before the side effects kicked in, and the cabin and my toilet were an hour's drive away. I turned the key in the ignition, but instead of entering the highway, I detoured to the small front parking lot.

It was packed. In desperation, I pulled into a doctor's spot. Dodging outgoing visitors, I dashed up the walk and down the north corridor, bypassing the reception area. Dr. Tall's office door loomed at the end of the hall, and I burst inside.

Tall scraped back his chair in surprise. "Luke?"

"Why didn't you tell me sterility was likely?" I demanded, despite a rising sense I'd been the one to miss it.

Tall motioned for me to sit and rifled through his desk drawer. He extracted another copy of the extensive pamphlet he'd given me before. A never-unfolded copy of the same still rested on my chest of drawers at home. My research was better, I'd told myself. Judgmental about the manufacturer-generated handouts, I hadn't read them at all.

"I'll run more tests in a couple of weeks once the radiation in your system has subsided. Check on a variety of things."

I jerked to my feet. "So, I have to wait two weeks?"

"It's a possibility, not a *fait accompli.*" Tall leveled his gaze on me. "We are still studying this treatment and all the side effects. But regardless of the test results, it will be a few years before you may be able to father a child. Your sperm has to replace itself." He left out the if-it-can part.

May be able? Years? I stumbled out of Tall's office and staggered to my car. A Volkswagen sedan blocked me from behind.

The driver backed up a bit and rolled down her window. "Hey buddy, I must warn you. Taking a doctor's spot will get you fined." She flipped her long hair over her shoulder in a sign I interpreted as exasperation, stirring a memory that I ignored.

"Maybe you should put up warning signs," I growled, before screeching out of the lot.

Chapter Six/Mary

August 1945

August 14th left no doubt where the perfect jackets had landed. One week after Mick's birthday, we woke to the paper boy shouting the headline as he flung the *Richland Villager* onto front walks up and down our block. "Peace! Our Bomb Clinched It!" Overnight, Richland became the Atomic City and the pride for what we as a community had done ran rampant. Jimmy and his pals partied day and night at the local drive-in and burger joints. The flurry in Matt's office kept him in The Area for almost forty-eight hours straight.

Luke stepped out onto the porch with a bowl of Rice Krispies. He shot me a lopsided grin, eyes drifting to my legs. When had he started noticing?

My smile broadened at the unspoken compliment in his eyes. "Your mother's letting you have cereal again? And right before supper?" A posting in the weekend newspaper had warned against local milk, saying unpasteurized milk was unsafe, but it gave no specifics as to why.

"She picked up milk on her way home from her aunt's farm in The Dalles."

I grinned, masking my concern that while Helen wasn't buying milk locally, downstream wasn't necessarily safe either. "When that runs out, how about we make a batch of treats to share?"

"That'd be...great." Luke drained the rest of his cereal as Matt pulled up in front and clipped up the front steps.

Still jubilant about Hanford's key role in America's victory, Matt said, "Looks like you'll dodge the draft after all, young man." Matt pushed past him.

"Yes, sir." Luke took a backward step. "I best go. My chores need doing."

I sighed and pushed out of my chair and went inside.. Matt held up a bourbon for me as I started dinner, but his second bourbon drained away any elation.

"We're shutting down production, Truman's orders." His tone downshifted.

My eyes on the stove, I flipped the chicken-fried steaks.

"DuPont's asked to be relieved of the responsibility of operations at the plant," Matt was technically employed by DuPont, not the federal government.

"But who will run things?"

"General Electric is taking over. Nuclear-powered electricity, they say."

Armed with plates and silverware to set the table, I paused in the doorway between the kitchen and dining room. "So, the reactors will still operate?"

"Worried about your job?" Matt's face tightened. "There's talk of a new Atomic Energy Commission. I'm sure your pal Harry will bring you along."

But Matt's job might disappear along with DuPont. "Surely they'll need someone for messaging."

"They want a scientific voice now. You heard Dr. Jackson last night, assuring the good people of Richland that they were not living in the City of Pluto?"

"Jackson may have developed the safety standards, but," I took a step toward him, reaching out. "With your experience—"

His hand clenched mine in a flash, twisting my arm behind me and twirling me at the same time. The china plates flew, shattering. My good silver—I'd wanted to make our first peacetime dinner special—crashed onto the linoleum.

"What do you know?" Matt shoved me out of the kitchen. "Always Little Miss Mary Sunshine, never realizing the gravity of the matter." He spun me off with a force that slammed me face-first into the dining room wall.

I pushed off, but not in time to dodge the blow. His fist landed in my back, and pain shot up my spine. The dining room shades were drawn, making me invisible to any passersby. When had he pulled them down? Before I could puzzle it out, Matt backhanded me across the cheek, and I grabbed at the table to keep my balance.

"Do you think we can survive, much less your parents, if I don't have a job?" He sank into a dining chair, and I put my hand to one, but he glared up at me. "Were you planning on burning the steaks too?"

I dragged back into the kitchen, picking my way across the broken china and palming my cheek. After flipping the steaks, I put some ice into a cloth and held it to my face, gritting my teeth as the pain shot up my spine.

The first time, early in our marriage, I'd teased him about a bad haircut. The slap had caught us both off guard. Matt had stared at his hand as if it operated alone, said sorry over and over and brought me an ice pack for my face. He had gathered me up in his arms and carried me up the stairs to our bedroom, the one in Boise. He told me then about his father, the one he rarely spoke of. How his father had hit his mother. How he'd been powerless to help her.

He had laid me down on the handmade quilt my mother had given us as a wedding present and undressed me in slow deliberate moves, before taking me. Lovemaking I wanted as much as he, thinking it proved he loved me. But after our first anniversary, and a few more "accidents," the apologies stopped. I learned that resisting the reconciliation sex only hurt more. Even the hint of defiance would be punished, so I endured what I must. My revenge would come, but I was still working that out.

He doesn't take very long, but that night, as I lay under him, all I could think was: please, don't let him feel the diaphragm inside me. I closed my eyes and pictured the change inside my coin purse, leftover from the day's grocery shopping, and the Mason jars hidden in my sewing basket. He rolled off me and headed to the bathroom. The shower I deserved would have to wait.

Coin purse in hand, I limped into the spare bedroom. A room that I was determined not to make a nursery. Not with this man. Not another Jimmy. I sank into the chair and cradled my head against the sewing machine. Fiery little demons drove spikes up my vertebrae as I placed the silver on the sewing top. Seventy-five cents. Whores made more.

Luke's ham radio setup was in his bedroom on the opposite side of the shared wall. A blues station announced itself in Mississippi. Muddy Waters in a slow repetitive rhythm lamented the death of his girlfriend as she was lowered into the grave. Would Matt care if he killed me?

The tap, light at first, sounded again. A deliberate, yet erratic thump on the wall. Morse code. A math teacher, another ham operator, had taught my class the basics in my junior year at Moscow High School. The thumps started up again, repeating the pattern.

".... . .-. ." Just one word. "Here."

•   •   •

A human mind can work its way around just about anything, and that is what I did to survive and to keep the checks flowing for my father's treatments. But, something shifted in my head. *Odd how one person's belief in you can beget confidence,* I wrote in my diary, creating a record of everything Matt did after he did it. There's something healing about putting the abuse into written words.

Every insult, every blow, every everything that Matt levied on me, with dates and places, filled the pages: The Boise bedroom, June 1943 (I questioned our move to Hanford, the postman witnessed the blow through the window); my parents' living room in July 1943 (I still hadn't wanted to move to Washington state, my sister had arrived in the middle of it); our Richland kitchen in March 1944 (supper was late again, Helen noticed I was favoring my left hand); the Richland bathtub in September 1945 (Matt wanted to shower first, Luke was on the other side of the wall again). I found an odd solace in citing the witnesses, verification that all of this happened, not that any of them, except Luke of course, would remember.

It would be hard to go it alone. Divorced women were regarded as pariahs. Maybe that's why I hadn't discouraged Luke's adolescent adoration. I needed it. Paging through the last year, I convinced myself I could find a job in Idaho to provide for my father's needs. My little sister, Ellen, was almost old enough to get a part-time job after school. I wouldn't be alone.

I tucked the receiver between my neck and shoulder and dialed. "Mother?" My father's cough in the background threatened to put me off my mission, but I held tight to my resolve. "I'm coming home."

"Oh Mary, I was just going to call." My mother went on. My father's treatments were not having the desired effect. "They are talking about surgery."

"What kind?" I asked, but there was only one kind, the expensive kind. The Stibnite mining district in the hills beyond Moscow, where my father had worked the last fifteen years, produced most of the country's antimony, that's gold to you, and tungsten. Both are vital to manufacturing the weapons of war. Problem was, that inhaling the stuff for long enough causes damage to your eyes and skin, not to mention the effects on lungs, heart, and stomach, but it wasn't until the Meadow Valley mine collapsed, my father inside it, that Stibnite put him on permanent leave. That's when Matt came along and saved the day—or at least my parents's house—with his checkbook.

"The doctors say his lungs are filled with stuff. His cough is so much worse, constant chest pain and fatigue..." Her voice faded.

"What are they proposing?"

"Wait, I wrote it down." Coughing in the background echoed through the line, and I tightened my grip on the phone cord. My mother came back. "A lobectomy and maybe a pulmonary resection? What does that even mean?"

It meant that the poison that my father had inhaled for years on the job had permanently damaged his lungs. The mining company should have paid for the surgery, rather than just doling out a meager pension, claiming generosity, but companies don't pay for their mistakes, people do.

I didn't say any of that. I said, "I'm not sure Mother, but if the doctors think it will cure Daddy, then..." My voice trailed off into the then. Then, I couldn't leave Matt, not until the surgery was paid for.

•   •   •

Matt got a temporary job in Union negotiations with a subcontractor who was doing conversion work on multiple buildings in The Area, newly renamed the Hanford Nuclear Reservation, not that anyone called it that.

Matt's duties involved evening meetings, eliminating multiple nights of angst for me, and allowing me time to plot my escape. Jimmy marched toward graduation, talking of joining the merchant marine. Thoughts of freedom from both Boone boys preoccupied me as I entered the technical lab building. The lieutenant who manned the front counter had stepped away, but a recognizable voice on the other side of Harry's office door made me pause outside.

"The emissions from the stacks combined with the effluent." Dr. Jackson spoke in almost whispered tones. "Releases far above safe levels, almost since we began."

"What do the livestock tests show?" Harry asked.

"In their thyroids, almost 1000 times the activity of concern."

Harry pressed. "And the effluent?"

"The waste ponds in both D and F areas have leaked again. Millions of gallons." Jackson's voice trembled. "We're estimating a cumulative release of over 40,000 curies."

A shudder racked me. That meant the river. Water that Pasco and Kennewick residents drank and bathed in, water that Richland drank from the tap, was most likely higher in radioactive concentration just by proximity.

"What are you suggesting?" Harry asked. The lieutenant would probably be back any minute, but I stayed put, wanting to hear Jackson's response.

"I've recommended we shut down production until we have a filter system that works."

"The war is over. No need for more bombs when we already have a stockpile."

Out in the entry, I blanched at Harry's reply. How many bombs had the workers of Hanford made?

"But, the Russians have the higher-ups worried, and," Dr. Jackson cleared his throat. "The most we can hope for is a temporary lull in production."

The lab door creaked, and the Lieutenant returned to his station, casting a curious look at me. I smiled, popped off my hat and gloves, and pushed into the office.

The two men spun in my direction, and Dr. Jackson grasped Harry's hand in a hurried shake. "Thanks again for your support." The half-smile that normally lived on Jackson's face was missing, his face drawn tight as he exited.

"Morning, Mary," Harry managed.

"What have you gotten us supporting now?" I hung my coat and hat on the pegs and shot Harry a smile.

"Just some issues at Swedish Hospital in Seattle. That's where Jackson and I met." Harry cast a glance out the window. The sun blanked out Jackson, striding away. "Just before the war began."

"Is that how you ended up here?"

Harry nodded but appeared lost in another time. "Let's get back to it, shall we?"

My personal situation had blinded me. No one in the region was safe.

•   •   •

The fall flowed into holiday celebrations that pushed out a new year and a spring full of babies. The *Pasco Herald* reported a record 300 births in the Tri-cities, and 1946 was only half over. A new sign on the outskirts of town declared us: "Richland the Atomic Bustin' Village of the West."

Any withdrawal at the bank had to have my husband's signature. So, the spare change from the pharmacy or fished from Matt's pockets on laundry day I hid in my thread basket. The canning jars Helen had given me went from empty to full.

My getaway and hopefully my divorce would be funded a nickel here, a quarter there. I'd enlisted Luke to help me convert the change to bills, one roll at a time. No one at the bank questioned a young boy who collected coins. Luke didn't have to ask what I was saving for.

My job at the lab had shifted from typing up past notes to taking dictation from the entire team and composing daily records of the technical lab's work. Harry's manner shifted too, a growing uneasiness that infected our work. When an interoffice memo arrived, announcing that GE was inviting bids for a new waste storage farm, Harry had his back to me, buried in a file.

I touched his shoulder. "Got a moment?"

He jerked up, and a worried look encompassed his face.

"Right, didn't mean to interrupt, just..." I hesitated, not wanting to overstep, even though Harry freely shared information with me now, a trust solid between us. "The construction on the new bypass, for dumping the sludge."

Harry raised an eyebrow. "Yes?"

"Why aren't they moving the waste to the 200-Area first? To deactivate before storing it?"

"They attempted transport to the 241 storage area last week, but not successfully. The existing tanks are full." Harry paused, as if willing me to understand something I wasn't altogether sure I did, other than it sounded like a toxic mess, and maybe that was the point. "We'll need even more space when production resumes."

"They're starting up again?" I asked, thinking Jackson must not have been successful.

"Early next year, most likely." More production meant more jobs, but workers wouldn't know the dangers. Harry turned back to his file, pulling out a page and laying it on top of the filing cabinet. The headline, stamped "Classified" read: EMISSION LEVELS IN RIVER.

He turned back to me. "An old college pal teaches chem at Richland High. He asked me to speak at the high school career day next month. You know, opportunities at Hanford for the class of '47."

The change in subject threw me off. Where was Harry going with this? "Show but don't tell?" My quip didn't draw a smile.

"I was thinking we might donate some 'radioactive wear' to the school chemistry lab. We've got a surplus of goggles and protective garb. Think your stepson might like that?"

"Jimmy wouldn't be caught dead near a science class, but my neighbor's boy, Luke, he'd love that. A scientist in the making."

"I'll fill out the requisition for Supply." Harry bent back to his desk. "Oh, and Mary, make sure there is one in both our sizes. You'll accompany me, yes, in costume?"

Richland High was consistently ranked among the best in the state, but Harry had never shown interest in the high school's curriculum before or its students. A confirmed, childless bachelor was how he described himself, but I suspected a broken heart figured somewhere in his past.

"It'll be fun," I said, and moved back to my desk, certain that whatever Harry was really up to wasn't about fun.

•   •   •

The kids in Luke's chemistry class loved their getups. Harry's animation around the splitting of the atom won the students over, surprising even me. The teacher ushered us out to the car, profuse with thanks for starting the new year with such a bang. The pun made me flinch. Harry lobbed our protective gear into the trunk, held my door open and I slid into the car.

"Well, you've got a fan club." Harry raised an eyebrow at me as he settled behind the wheel, clearly amused by Luke's obvious obsession with me.

Luke had hovered, taking boxes out of my hands, as we came down the hall. He asked me questions during the presentation, rather than Harry. Luke would most likely move on at the first pretty teenage girl who paid him any mind, but I hadn't discouraged him. Was I so desperate that I needed his attention as well as his logistical support? Uncomfortable with my delight in Luke's adoration as we eased out of the parking lot, I pivoted. "You had them all so engaged."

Harry let loose a half smile but kept his eyes on the road, leaving me to bridge the silence. "And I'm sorry to give the suit back to supply. It's what I should wear when I'm canning fruit."

"Let's hold off on that." Harry stopped at the red light. "We might have another occasion." The light changed, and so did Harry's face, deepening into what appeared to be an internal argument. Whatever Harry was contemplating, he seemed reluctant to say it out loud.

We came to a turnout overlooking the river. Harry pulled in. From our vantage point, we could see the Yakima River join the Columbia and the growing spread of houses in the Richland Wye. The government had whipped up a trailer park for the latest influx of workers. Close to the bank, a few geese with goslings in their ranks poked their heads in and out of the river searching for sustenance.

"Quite a few babies are not making it to term. And others aren't making it at all." Harry paused. "Paul and Laura Fletcher just lost their son." Paul was a nuclear engineer who lived a street over from us. Their son was born over the weekend. Helen Hinson volunteered one day a week at Kadlec. She had mentioned two other stillborn babies just last week.

The horizon swallowed up Harry's words. Two large barges with old barracks buildings floated into view. Unused army buildings were being repurposed for the new influx of workers. Nothing cold about the way production had fired up again in anticipation of the next war.

"Luke's mother says it's more than a couple few," I said, my belly twisting like a vice. "Is there more than anecdotal evidence?"

"Hospital records, though I haven't seen them." Harry shifted in his seat. "Just the growing number of gravestones in the baby section of the cemetery."

"They've been monitoring releases since production began. I've transcribed plenty of data."

"Yes, they keep testing the single-pass cooling system." Harry peered at the river as if the geese cruising toward the sunset held the answer. "But it isn't the reactors that worry me the most, it's the canyons."

The canyons in the 200-Area were massive buildings, each three football fields long, capped by steel reinforced concrete roof panels and encompassed by walls sixty feet high that extended another forty feet underground. "Why exactly?"

"Gaseous iodine-131 from spent fuel assemblies. Routine, classified, late at night."

Late. When I couldn't sleep, but most did. Releases that endangered all of Richland and beyond. A town of innocent, well-meaning citizens lured here by the promise of a better life, a life with purpose. Dedicated to a common cause, the people of Richland had embraced something bigger than themselves and unknowingly risked everything. The government they trusted was testing the air and the water, but they weren't telling.

But the good folks of Richland wouldn't be the only reason I would help Harry if he asked me to. Derailing the secret practices could have many benefits, including the removal of a spokesperson who might no longer be trusted. Maybe, just maybe, Matt would agree to a divorce if he lost his job.

Harry motioned to the glove compartment.

"Open the jockey box?" I couldn't help but snicker. "I'm not going to find anything untoward in there, am I?"

A small grin pierced Harry's dour expression. "More than anyone, you should know I haven't had a date or anything else that would require—shall we call it—protection."

"That doesn't mean you might not be prepared," I teased. "Seriously Harry, Sally can help me sort who might be available and fun in the typing pool. Why don't I fix you up?"

"I'm afraid a blind date won't fix anything, just confuse an already confused old bachelor." Harry's eyes glossed over, and he gripped the steering wheel with both hands, as if grabbing onto something external would steady something on the inside, making me sure I was right about a past broken heart. "Go on."

I pulled out a barely legible list of radioactive isotopes. "Good thing you found me," I said, studying his handwriting.

He shot me a half-hearted smile. "That's all in the reactor cooling water. The effluent is cycled back into the Columbia River. The containment process isn't adequate."

"But how..." I didn't finish, not able to imagine how Harry got his hands on such a list.

"Some researchers from UW set up troughs outside the reactor basins. They've been bagging and analyzing fish, finding that list of elements in the fish. No one told them about the uptick in production." The more production, the more irradiated elements dumped in the river.

"The project team just recommended raising the acceptable levels."

"Wait. You're saying that rather than controlling the radioactive releases, they want to adjust the 'safe' level and tell people they are safe when they're not?"

Harry turned toward me. "That's what I'm saying."

We locked eyes. "How can they do that?"

"Nobody to stop them." Harry did not sound convinced.

"Unless evidence comes forth that isn't classified?" Large male geese lit next to the moms and goslings in our sightline. "Matt has a regular meeting across the river at the USO one night a week, and Jimmy almost always eats at a pal's house."

"How about we have dinner that night?" Harry said. "Take a walk along the river after."

"Shall I bring the gear and my rubber boots?"

"And some spare canning jars." Harry went silent again.

The sun dropped below the horizon. A perky poster board sign had been installed on the edge of the turnout: "Highlights of Hanford – Work for Victory!" Three male construction workers, arms laced on each other's shoulders in an all-for-one kind of way, standing in front of the five stacks of an area plant, dark smoke spilling into the sky. The thing was, no one questioned the "what" we were all working for.

"Did I tell you I joined a bowling team?" Harry shot me a wry grin.

The change in subject threw me off, but I said, "You, the consummate loner, socializing?"

Harry shot me a wink. "Turns out I'm pretty good at taking down the kingpin."

Chapter Seven/Luke

February 1964

The final round of cobalt had left me weak, rudderless. My first attempt at my thesis led the reader down a rabbit hole full of fiery declarations. My original premise was lost to my obsession: daylighting the truth of the practices at Hanford. My mother insisted I take a break. She gave me directions to a farm just beyond Ringold Springs, saying to meet her there, as if it was on the way to the grocery store, and to bring Harry.

Harry drove his jeep. I was still unsteady behind the wheel, and navigating the intermittent areas of frost in February took more traction than my tires had left. We emerged on the other side of Kennewick to a clear cold day. Police patrol boats dotted the river, part of a decades-long surveillance that culminated in armed security guards at the gates to The Area. The network of irrigation canals along the river banks had multiplied tenfold since my youth. Water, drawn downstream from the reactors, flowed up and over the layers of lava that capped the back end of the farms surrounding Mesa, Connell, and Eltopia. Basalt bluffs provided daredevil opportunities.

"Look at those crazies," I said pointing to a dozen or so bodies swimming in the frigid water.

Harry glanced over. "The Atomic Ducks Diving Club, most likely." He shook his head. "Fools know no bounds."

We turned off the county road at a mailbox marked "Wang," and eased down a dirt one with a modest farmhouse at the end. A collie trotted up to sniff us. I held out a hand for approval, noting its empathetic eyes. Dogs can sense illness, though no one gives them credit. Two cats rested on the fence by the house, assessing us with arrogant gazes.

My mother stepped out onto the porch, followed by a man, small in stature, with a face swarthy from the sun. Harry joined them and gave my mother a hug.

I followed suit, noting, "Here we are, as commanded." The sweep of the farm I estimated at a thousand acres, half of it tilled. I cast an eye at the man. "Mostly corn?" Withering stalks, soggy after the morning frost, covered the closest field.

The man scratched under his chin, a morning shadow showing. "For now."

My mother jumped into my lack of manners. "Luke, Harry, this is Joe Wang."

Harry and I extended our hands for a shake. The collie nuzzled my knee. The wind played kickball with two tumbleweeds across the space between the house and the barn.

"Come in, please." Wang led us inside. The main room hosted a small sitting area with a desk centered on a side wall. A framed diploma, a doctorate in chemistry from the University of Washington, hung above it.

"Go Dawgs," I said, and still not understanding why we were here, took a seat. The collie tucked itself under my chair, its tail flapping on my boot.

My mother shot me a look that said, behave. "Mr. Wang inherited this farm from his father, but our host works for the Pasco Water District. He's privy to papers of interest."

Wang leaned forward, resting his forearms on his knees. "This goes no further than this room?"

Harry nodded, and I noted an odd look of recognition in his eyes for something, but what I didn't know. Out the window, a tumbleweed high-jumped the low, side yard fence, threatening to wreak havoc with the vegetable garden.

Wang delivered the information in a low rhythmic pace that belied the urgency in his words. "You've seen the published study, of the

Ringold subjects? Where they credit global fallout for most of the atmospheric radioactive iodine in the region?"

Harry nodded again, and I leaned down to stroke the collie's flank, thinking my scientific reading had taken a detour that needed rerouting. All I remembered was that twelve of the twenty subjects— farm families who ate off the land—in a recent study by the HID, had submitted themselves to whole body counters by Hanford scientists. They'd been told that though their iodine count was elevated, especially the children, that it was all within the permissible limits.

Wang steepled his hands, but this was no prayer. "In April of '62, about 440 curies worth of iodine-131 was accidentally released. An intentional, smaller release occurred the following September, for a test. Found high readings as far away as Moses Lake."

"How do you know that?" I asked.

"A memo at the water department. Plus, they sent out an army of men with Geiger counters that April, scanning dirt from here up to White Bluff and over to Eltopia. Government guys are kind of hard to miss, and now, they're asking for more volunteers." Wang grimaced. "To monitor health-wise, using whole body counters."

Whole body counters measure gamma rays only, and Iodine-131 has an eight-day half-life. Exposure that occurred a few months back would be impossible to count, much less reconstruct from a whole-body spectrum.

Harry pulled up straight on the couch. "How many families?"

Wang shot him a look, making me think Wang knew who Harry was from before. "About twenty, I think, including our neighbors to the north, fruit tree farmers. Two of their children are a part of it."

"The families around here, they all eat off the land?" I asked, thinking of the deer and my tests on the roots of plants.

"Almost entirely. Folks fill out diet surveys, and the Hanford takes samples of their produce at various stages of growth." Wang frowned. "Just like they did the year my mother died."

My mother filled the quiet. "Mr. Wang's mother had a cardiac event over a decade ago. His father found her in the vegetable garden."

Ringold's water was sourced from the Columbia, a dozen or so miles from the reactors, chemical separation, and fuel fabrication plants. The small community rested on the leeward side of the bluffs. Conventional thinking is that the closer you are to the source, the higher the dose, but plumes are subject to the wind and weather. After touching down once, the wind can grab irradiated material back up, and blow it for miles before it nestles into pockets of land held captive by freezing temperatures or heavy humidity.

Hanford scientists liked to draw tidy circles to show a release's projection, but a radioactive plume is more of a bell curve, and if you are downwind from any release, accidental or not, look out. Imagine a church bell full of particles swinging in a tower above Wang's fields, and every time it rang it dispersed its load on the crops to the right and the left, depending on wind direction.

"Anyway," Wang continued. "More than one confidential memo from the AEC warns of radioactive moss along the river banks downstream from the N Reactor. Whitefish have been consuming it."

"Do you have the memos?" I asked, knowing that would be almost impossible.

Wang dashed any hopes with a shake of his head. "They number every copy. No way to remove them, much less the original, without someone knowing."

Harry didn't talk much about Hanford, but he had been right in the middle of it in the '40s, railing against the sloppiness of it all. He'd lost his job. Wang still had his to lose.

My mother and Harry exchanged a look I didn't understand before Harry asked, "The AEC keep classified documents pretty close to the chest. How'd you get access?"

"My security clearance at the water department. I see everything to do with the river."

"But they watch everything you do?" Harry's tone had a lived experience to it.

Wang cast a look out the window. His son led a cow out of the barn. "Yes."

"What are you going to do?" I asked, knowing how hard it would be to do anything. My father's death had not moved the needle, not even a decimal.

Wang looked at my mother and then back at me. "Well, I'm certainly not letting my family eat whitefish anymore, or any other fish out of the Columbia."

I gazed out the window. "Or the corn either, I suppose."

A look of alarm razed Wang's face. "They tested my neighbor's kids, their animals. Told them to drink powdered milk."

My mind twisted back to pulling a baking pan out of the oven, pretending to smell the Rice Krispie treats when I drank in Mary's scent. Baked treats hadn't required milk.

My mother uncrossed her legs and addressed Harry and me. "I thought you might have some ideas, based on current and past research projects." That same something flickered between my mother and Harry.

Wang's face softened. "You study fish in Baker Bay, right?"

"Among other things," I said. "Why?"

"Maybe a link could be found. You could warn folks." Wang glanced at Harry. "Like before."

I flashed a look at my mother, wondering if she'd told Wang about the whale. A guilty suspect if I ever saw one, but before I could ask, Harry said, "Before got me fired without a pension. All I've got is the crab shack."

Wang crumpled in his seat. "Can't risk losing my clearance. It's the only way to feed my family in the winter."

Out the window, an older boy swung up and over the fence and headed into the barn. Across the yard, a small girl entered the chicken coop with a basket. Harry and my mother seemed glued to the scene. A snowflake pasted onto the front window.

Harry eyed Wang. "Let me percolate on it, but I expect they're watching, even now."

Harry stood, shook Wang's hand, and walked out the door. Snowflakes swirled, and my mind did too, wondering what the hell happened before.

•   •   •

My mother had promised a Zip's Drive-In burger for my trip. We pulled up to a spot between carloads of teenagers, half in and half out of their cars, sharing trays of fries and exhibiting the normal adolescent mating behavior despite the snow flurry.

The girls giggled, their skirts much shorter than in my youth, and the boys leered, sweeping their long waves up from their foreheads in an attempt at Elvis-like nonchalance. After we ordered over the intercom, Harry excused himself to use the restroom. He disappeared through the doors laden with Valentine's Day hearts and names of patrons.

A brassy blonde carhop approached, intoning the joint's motto, "Thrift and swift." She clipped our tray of food to the driver's window, complete with scattered candy hearts. Each bore a Valentine's wish, wishes I'd long since given up.

My mother noshed on her crinkle-cut fries, assessing me. "How are you really feeling?"

I chomped down on my Wrangler burger, savoring the taste of red meat and knowing I would pay for it later. "Glad to be done with the cobalt."

"Follow-up test results yet?"

My mother had shown unusual restraint when it came to inquiring about my treatment. Hard for her, considering my father's sudden death had followed a series of simple nosebleeds.

"Not yet, but Doc says only one problematic node left, and it's shrunk considerably." Determined to avoid any discussion of my ability to give her grandchildren—which, oddly, I thought more about lately—I pointed to a woman exiting the interior restaurant. "Didn't I go to high school with that gal?" The woman looked twice my age, her face drawn and pale, walking with a prominent gait.

"That's Janet Clark. A couple years ahead of you in school."

"She looks terrible," I whispered.

My mother lowered her voice. "A music major at Whitman in Walla Walla. Came home for Christmas vacation in '49, looking like she'd aged thirty years. They diagnosed her with hyperthyroidism. She's lost all her hair," my mother whispered. "Had a stillborn a while back."

While I was doing the math of that, thinking it was odd my mother remembered the year an old classmate came home from college, Harry slid back in. My mother handed him his burger. Harry chomped down.

My mother waited for him to swallow before asking, "So, what do you think?"

Harry took a long, slow swig of his shake. "I think Zip's should have been open when I worked in Richland."

My mother cast him a withering glance and looked at me for reinforcement.

I set my burger aside on the seat and took them both in. "Don't you think it's about time I knew the whole story?"

"Depends." Harry countered.

"On what?"

"How deep down the well you want to go," he said.

My mother jumped in. "Remember how Mrs. Evans used to say she didn't feel well because there was something in the water?"

"I guess," I said, struggling to remember anything about Mrs. Evans other than the eggs we bought from her farm kitchen on Saturdays.

"Well, her husband used to say, 'You crazy woman, that's a 1,200-foot deep artesian well.'" My mother paused.

Harry finished for her. "But she would draw buckets of water and leave them on her screened-in porch at night so they'd be handy for the morning. Downwind from Hanford's releases."

My mother wagged her head. "That one and more, it's in Mary's notes."

I jerked up in my seat, my head swiveling between Harry and my mother. "What the—?"

Harry dipped a couple of fries into ketchup. "Your neighbor, my former secretary, Mary Boone, made carbon copies of a lot of our work and others. Kept 'em hidden for me. They disappeared along with her."

Back down the rabbit hole I went, imagining my missing Mary, somewhere out there, guarding that box with her life, living. Maybe, just maybe, she was living a life I could share.

•   •   •

Harry dropped me at my cabin well after dark, but unsettled by his less-than-satisfactory responses to my nonstop questions on the way home, I woke early to clearing skies. My pack with various sampling supplies hung on the pegs by the door, untouched for days. I pulled on my waders, layered up against the cold, snatched my scoop net off the porch, and half-stepped down the steep part of the hillside to the tail of the bayou.

The Columbia fed Baker Bay, but shifts the river had taken over time created an assortment of reed-filled swamps, slow-moving bodies of water that held onto almost everything the river delivered. I whacked off some reeds for later analysis and slogged into the center. The unexpected sunshine took some of the winter chill off the water.

Knee deep in a small circle of water, I scooped sediment off the bottom, stirring up the minnows in a cloud of silt. A blue heron lit at the rim of the swamp, side-eyeing me, stilled in place. Still was something I wasn't willing to give up, not as long as my profession required a steady hand. The heron and I stood together, the light rising, until Gene Pitney interrupted.

The boy Ben, a fishing pole over his shoulder and the slow, melodic mourn of a "Town Without Pity" flowing from the transistor radio in a pail, stepped into view. He startled as the heron took flight, soaring low over the marshes, but he didn't seem surprised to see me.

"Fishing for supper?" I asked.

He shrugged a yes. "What ya doing, mister?"

"Research." I shifted the silt into a small jar and secured it into my pack.

Ben took in my mud-filled scoop. "There's stuff worth studying in the mud?"

"Sometimes." A wicking in the water caught my eye. I eased the net out of my back holster and swiped through the water the way Walker had taught me.

"Nice work, mister." Ben beamed at the sockeye, flapping in the net.

"Best pull your radio out." I waded toward the bank.

Ben removed the transistor and scooped a bit of water into the pail before tilting it to receive my catch. "Small, but worth frying." The boy set the pail on the bank, baited his line, and waded in. His overalls were patched in two places, and his flannel shirt showed plenty of wear. Someone had given him a haircut, clipped well above his ears and shaved high up his neck.

He cast his rod, sinking his line with precision about ten yards beyond where we stood. "Your dad teach you to cast like that?"

The boy snorted. "He never taught me nothing. Gran's the angler. Taught my sister too."

Hard to miss his disgust of his father, but if I hadn't been watching, I would have missed his wince at the mention of his sister. "You like living with your grandmother?" I resisted asking about the mother, sensing she was not in the picture.

The boy slowly reeled in his line and reset, his line flying a few feet farther out. "She's okay. Better than a Dad who doesn't want you." He kept his eyes straight ahead, not inviting a response. The transistor pumped out the top one hundred from the bank.

"You keep your radio on while you fish?"

"Fish like it." Ben mustered a half-grin. "Brings them to me."

My father did that. Eased folks along to his way of thinking, advice always insinuated, never direct. A joke here, a quip there. Folks got the message without a heavy-handed delivery. A gift I didn't think I'd inherited.

The boy's line went taut, but he let the catch wander a bit before cranking the handle backward in rapid motion. The small sockeye skimmed the surface. "Hey, Mister, the net?"

Galvanized into action, I swooped the net under the salmon, and we trudged in tandem to the boy's pail.

"Should do it, I guess," Ben said, pulling a large rag from his overalls and tossing it over the bucket. "What do you think you'll find in that mud?"

"Not sure," I said in a sudden, protective tone I didn't quite understand myself. "Have to put it under a microscope and run it through a few tests to see."

"We looked at water under a microscope at school." The boy almost smiled. "Kinda weird to see all the stuff going on in there, but I liked it."

"I like it too. It's what I do, look at what a naked eye can't see."

Ben studied me a moment, raking his hand through the red prickles of his kitchen table crewcut. "I've got a project I have to do, sort of like that. Maybe you could help me?"

"What about your grandmother?"

"She's good at the writing, but it was my mother who understood science." He swiped at a bunch of reeds as if annoyed that he'd given out more information than he meant to. "She's not around anymore."

We stood in the shallows, but I suspected a drop-off waited not too far out. "How long have you got? For the project, I mean." My ablation therapy would begin in a few days, and who knew what I would be capable of afterwards? But something about the way the boy looked at me, as if I was the only one who could help, even though Harry surely would.

"Fourteen weeks."

"Okay. I've got something for the next couple, but then, how about I call you?"

The boy pulled out a scrap of paper and thrust it at me. A phone number, in a boyish scrawl, made me think he'd come looking for me. So, I asked. "What's your project about?"

"Something other folks can't see," he said, before turning on his heel and darting back up the path, the strains of "Moon River" flowing in his wake.

Chapter Eight/Mary

Summer 1947

Night fishing was my young neighbor's favorite, just the moon, the stars, and me. Only, Luke didn't know that I was here, sampling the river. Harry was upriver in a spot downstream from the F reactor, as close as he could get without being detected by Area security.

Luke followed the path down to the river's edge, and I crouched, dropping out of his sightline. Laughter sounded above. Luke shoved his bait bucket under a shrub but kept the rod. The sapling pole wasn't thick, but I expected the whip had some kick.

Luke scrambled up a scraggy cedar. A blonde head at the top of the slope reflected the moonlight: my stepson, Richland High's biggest bully. Ugh. I'd heard Helen tell Luke that the boys who follow Jimmy around don't have minds of their own and to take no mind of them. But, when you're the target, it's their fists, not their minds, that need your attention.

Jimmy loomed above the bank, two other shapes behind him. Luke shrank into a crook of the cedar. A cloud shifted over the moon, taking dark to another notch, but no mistaking the glint of Jimmy's pocket knife hanging off the belt loop of his jeans. I felt for my penknife and thought better of it, but three against one wouldn't fly. Not if I could help it.

Jimmy craned his head, searching, but the cedar's foliage wasn't giving Luke up. One of Jimmy's gang started down, but he slipped on the slick clay and skidded the rest of the way, grabbing at a shrub. "Jimmy! Over here." The boy thumped Luke's pail of snails.

"Lukie, Lukie, Lukie!" Jimmy sing-songed. "Come out, come out, wherever you are."

The three bad boys plopped down, arms on their knees, eyes combing the brush. There weren't many places that Luke could hide except the cedar. If only my knife were bigger, I would have carved off a branch for a weapon. Parrot the jungle warfare that was still playing out in the Philippines under the same moon, thick tropical forests hiding enemies unwilling to surrender. But here, cover was sparse, and my knife was no machete.

Jimmy's face broke into a grin. "Ah. There you are."

"Holy Hannah," I muttered and stiffened, trying to think of next moves. Counting on the camouflage of my gear, I moved closer. One of Jimmy's boys monkey-bar-jumped to a lower branch and then dropped with a yowl, clutching a hand to his chest. The other boy took a run at it, but, in short order rolled onto a large bough near the bottom of the tree, moaning and clutching his groin.

Luke muttered, "You're it."

The moon broke through in full force, and a flick of Jimmy's knife blade caught the light. Like father, like son. He didn't care about fair. A gurgling at the river, my *raison d'être*, distracted at just the right moment, and Luke took a swing. The bamboo whipped across Jimmy's hand with admirable precision, flinging the knife into the brush, but a bloodied fist caught Luke under the chin, knocking him cattywampus. He grabbed at his enemy's chest, and they both fell between the branches to the earth. Luke landed on top.

He rolled off just as Jimmy threw a left hook. Luke dodged, but Bloodied-fist caught him from behind, pinning Luke's arms at his back.

Luke stuck out his chin, bravado all he had left. "Go ahead, coward. Everyone knows you can't win a fair fight."

Taunting didn't bother Jimmy. He punched Luke in the belly. Luke folded. Sore-groin-boy took his revenge, and I'd had enough.

"What's going on here?" My best authoritative, masculine-sounding voice shot across the space between us like a sniper's bullet. I had played a male role in the summer musical with much success. My get-up reflected the moonlight and spiked off the metal patches on my chest. Spooked, Jimmy and his boys hustled up the path, tearing away from the scene.

Luke stayed down, holding his privates. My mud-coated boots stopped at his feet, but I kept my eyes on the ridge, making sure of Jimmy's departure before looking down.

Luke's eyes scanned up my jumpsuit to my face covered in the clear plastic screen topped by a gas mask. He knew it was me.

I extended a gloved hand. "You okay?"

"I'll live," he said, his voice thickening in embarrassment most likely.

"Pretty late to be out here." My voice softened in sympathy. The thought of the Hinson family eating one of these fish dissolved my smile. "And prolly not the best idea anyway," I said.

"Maybe not."

The sound of a fish jumping made me twist toward the river. I had another sample to take. "You should get on home." We exchanged a look. "I think it's best we not discuss this with anyone, don't you?" I sounded just like the security folks at the plant.

"But why are you—" Luke started, but I cut off his question by pointing toward his snails, escaping the bucket prison in the moonlight, inching toward the brush. He tipped the pail, scooped a few back in, and straightened.

Protective on a level that surprised even me, I thrust his bamboo pole at him. "Stick to day-fishing from now on. And farther downstream. Prolly a lot safer." My eyes darted about, knowing the night held more danger, stack releases almost always in tandem with effluent discharges. "All the way around."

Luke hesitated but trudged back up the path. A southern gust pushed the clouds back over the moon. I eased down the bank, filled my mason jars full of river water, and checked my watch. Just thirty minutes before I should have been returning from the gig Mr. Clark had booked for the band in Ringold. A spot where no one would realize it wasn't me singing that night. Mindful of my pack full of jars, I scurried up the bank to find Harry waiting, the engine idling.

•   •   •

The morning sun beamed steady and bright through the one office window. Harry entered, closed the door behind him, and perched on the bench near my desk. I cranked the return lever onto a new line space and looked up from the typewriter. Harry had that serious look about him.

"What is it?" I said, knowing I might not want to know.

"A former colleague, Lou Barnes, and his wife just moved to Pasco. She has aging parents. Farmers, not doing so well. Kind of out of the blue." Harry shot me that look. "He wants to help."

"How?"

"Access to a lab, for one thing. He's set up one in his garage."

"And the other thing?"

"He worked at the federal water division lab in Austin, Texas for the last five years. Knows his stuff. Accumulated some comparative data."

We'd couldn't do tests on our water samples in any lab in The Area. Every Hanford lab was subject to record. Failure to record any analysis could lead to immediate termination or at the very least, a thorough interrogation of any person involved in any unauthorized tasks.

"Lou found Iodine-131 in the cow's milk at his in-laws." Harry continued. "Up for a field trip a bit later today?"

"Just let me get the latest round of mishaps recorded, should someone, somewhere actually care about the amount of radioactive waste going into the Columbia." I finished typing the disturbing summary before we headed across the river to Pasco.

Harry pulled up to a nondescript ranch house, opened my car door, and raised a hand to the man who came out to the walk.

Lou shook Harry's hand. "Who's this?"

"Mary, my assistant. She's part of this."

Harry's words closed around me like a straightjacket.

Lou shook my hand and motioned us into the garage. "This way."

A low wall partitioned the back end of the garage from the car park. A small counter held some rudimentary laboratory equipment. Lou and Harry pulled on protective gear and put our jars out in a row. Finding a small stool away from the action, I suited up and pulled out a small notebook and pencil.

Harry and Lou worked in tandem, jar by jar, for hours, mixing sub-samples with various reagents to isolate the specific radioisotopes. They separated the isolates onto filter paper and counted them with a shielded Geiger counter. Their work covered the entire bench as, one by one, they confirmed the radioactive isotopes in the water: phosphorus, arsenic, zinc, chromium, and Neptunium. All radionuclides, most beta-emitters that could affect any animal's gastrointestinal tract, infiltrate bones, and generally muck with reproductive and blood-forming organs. Double-timing my shorthand to keep up with their dictation, I scratched off page after page.

Lou spoke first. "I thought the water from the reactors was diverted to an underground cooling site? These samples show hot."

Harry nodded. "It's rare, but sometimes the cladding around the fuel ruptures. When that happens, the effluent is sent directly to the retention ponds, but after a time, it too is pumped into the river."

Lou held up another beaker. "Over 50 micro-curies of radioactivity in this one. What's the cooling cycle?"

"Should be 65 days, but..." Harry shook his head. "Some inferential evidence last year indicated that fuel may have been reprocessed in less than three weeks."

"Lingering war-time mentality. Expediency over safety." Lou cast a look my way. "It's why I don't work in The Area, just in case you were wondering."

Not that you are any safer in Pasco, I thought, but I nodded, my mind chasing numbers I had typed up last month. "The T and B plants have reprocessed over 3000 metric tons of fuel since 1944." I did the calculation in my head, my hand shaking. "Eight thousand gallons of waste for each metric ton of fuel produced," I murmured, as if the FBI was outside listening and I would be arrested for treason any moment.

Quantification of fuel—exactly the kind of thing our enemies would want to know—was highly classified.

"Highly radioactive waste is piped into the cribs," Harry said, filling Lou in. "But the rest is pumped into ditches." Harry cast a glance at the row of jars. "And they're leaking, goddam it."

The rare swear on Harry's part made me snap my pencil lead.

"And this." Lou handed Harry a newspaper, folded to a page with a map of the region. The caption blared: "Designated Fishing Areas Set by County Commissioners."

Harry read out loud. "Using scientific data, the regional environmental contractor has determined that certain areas are off-limits for fishing. Fines will be levied on those violating the mandate." Harry peered over his readers. "All of the places are immediately downstream from the reactors."

Lou added. "A warning without giving up the truth. My father-in-law worked in The Area the last two winters. He said they discharged waste into a low spot in the ground. Contaminated the wetlands. So, they dug reverse wells and contaminated the aquifers, but nobody told anyone."

I gulped in air, my stomach clenching. Lou shot me a questioning look.

"My husband, he's the one who spins the tale on behalf of Hanford." I held Lou's gaze. "Not such a good guy otherwise, either."

"Rumor is, they're starting production back up. More reactors being built. A race." Lou shook his head. "As if it takes dozens of bombs to beat the Russians when one will do it."

Harry grimaced, reading the rest of the article. "Nothing about the thousands of curies released into the air and the river since they began. Just don't fish here or there."

"As if fish don't swim, and the river doesn't flow," I said with a bitter smile.

•   •   •

Matt had been in rare form on Friday night, threatening to not let me sing at the dance hall anymore. I had countered by saying that my singing had been his idea in the first place, part of his grand scheme to keep up morale. He hadn't appreciated being reminded, and I had several large bruises under my rib cage to prove it.

Helen knocked on my door early that Saturday, saying time for a canning lesson. Her friend, Mrs. Evans, who lived on a farm across the river, had dropped off a basketful of tomatoes and peppers, a seemingly innocent fall bounty.

A pot of water came to a boil as Helen wrapped me in an apron. "This was my mother's lucky apron." Most folks in Richland came from outside the region, leaving family behind. Since what we did during the day was off-limits, we shared stories of family, relishing the memories.

"My mother would approve of me finally learning how to can veggies like a real housewife." I smoothed my hand across the faded calico and tried not to wince. Lifting my left arm was not an option this morning. "You grew up east of The Dalles, right?"

"My father had a farm a mile inland. My mother worked part time in the hospital kitchen. Passed down a lot of tricks." Helen handed me the colander full of tomatoes. "Rinse those under cold water."

"My mother grew up near the ocean too," I said, as I ran the faucet. "She always said the hucka-berries grown in sea air were sweeter."

"Bet she makes an excellent huckleberry pie."

"Blue ribbon at the Idaho State Fair." The wistfulness in my voice surprised even me.

"Guess we all adjust to where we have to be." Helen smiled, pressing the juice out of a lemon. A dozen more waited on the counter. "Didn't you visit them recently?"

"My father had an operation. Recovery is taking a while."

Helen kept her eyes on the lemon press. "Why did you come back so soon?"

I spread the rinsed tomatoes out on a dishcloth. "Matt doesn't like fending for himself."

Helen cut me a sidelong glance, but only said, "Now, we boil the tomatoes."

The tomatoes roiled in the boiling water, making me wonder if the rush of hot effluent was doing the same thing to any life in the Columbia.

Helen ladled out a blanched tomato and removed the skin and core. "Some folks like to dice them for sauces, but I like them halved." She handed me an empty jar and a funnel. "The secret is to not over or under fill the jars."

I skinned. Helen cored. She spooned tomatoes and their juices off the cutting board and into jars, before adding a tablespoon of lemon juice into each. We worked side by side until the tomatoes were all in cans.

Luke came into the kitchen, rubbing his belly.

Helen pulled a warm plate of eggs and toast out of the oven and cast a smile my way. "He usually makes his own breakfast, but I didn't want him underfoot this morning."

Luke shot me a sheepish grin and raked a hand through his hair, that adoring look still in his eye, but more mature, somehow. He seemed taller, like I'd missed a growth spurt when I was in Idaho. Luke retreated to the dining room and picked up the morning paper.

Helen followed him with her eyes. "Since I could only have one, I'm glad it's him."

"Mind my asking?"

"Complications when he was born. The doctors had to perform a hysterectomy to stop the bleeding." Helen leaned against the counter, her gaze taking in the fact that I was holding my left arm like a wounded duck. "Some things you have no control over."

I dropped my arm to my side and a pain shot through my chest, making me flinch.

"Are you alright, dear?" Helen asked, but I was certain she knew I wasn't.

"Bumped into a door frame last night. Bruised my rib cage." I guess being smashed against a door frame qualified as bumping.

Helen put her hands on my side before I could stop her, applying pressure across my lower chest and up under my arm. "Nothing seems broken. Have you wrapped it?"

"Not yet." I winced. The last of the gauze had been used up on a previous injury.

"Happy to help if you like."

The tomato jars sat idle on the counter. "Shouldn't we seal these first?"

Helen held my gaze for a long minute before turning back to the stove. "Fill each with boiling water and leave about a half-inch of headspace."

I dunked her Pyrex pitcher into the boiling pot and poured a little water into each jar.

Helen wiped the rims of all drippings and twisted the lids on tight. "Now, we boil them again," she said. She arranged the jars in the boiling water canner and set a timer for forty minutes. "Okay, let's get you fixed up."

Any effort to refute her kindness would be futile, and I needed a bit of mothering. Helen followed me into the bathroom, armed with a roll of gauze. I unbuttoned my blouse, and Helen slid it down my arms.

Helen's face constricted. "Oh, Mary." The medicine cabinet mirror magnified my bruises, fresh and from previous battles, in varying shades of blue.

"Boise State fans bleed blue," I said, with a pained smile.

Helen flashed a look my way but didn't laugh. "Hold the end at your sternum while I wrap." Her touch, gentle but firm, pushed my emotions to the surface, and my eyes welled. Helen, intent on her task, seemed not to notice.

Out the window, the shared clothesline between the Hinsons and Lois, our affable neighbor, flapped in the November breeze. Another year had passed, and I still hadn't left. As if I had hung all my plans out to dry, my father's needs having wrung all the oomph out of my own.

Helen slipped the edge of the gauze into itself. She held my blouse for me to slip back on, squeezed my shoulder, and went back downstairs. I splashed some cold water on my face and stared out the window, missing the far-see from my childhood bedroom in Idaho. Here, house after house, repetitive structures gobbled up the landscape, filled with folks who pledged everything to the government's mission and spoke of none of it. Not to mention the things they didn't know, nor would they be told. Helen wouldn't tell either, or would she?

When I returned to the kitchen, Helen was mopping down the counters. I moved to the sink and added some dish soap to the pot soaking the funnel and other utensils we'd used. The timer ticked, the boiling pot steamed, and the kitchen curtains billowed, letting in the nip in the air.

"Ralph could help, you know." Helen's eyes were pleading with me, but before I could respond, Luke came into the kitchen holding up a suit pant.

"Mom, they're too short. They'll call me flood pants."

Helen let out a small laugh and kneeled to check the hem allowance at the bottom. "Plenty of material to let down."

Luke glanced my way, his eyes catching mine. I suspected he did not realize how handsome he'd become. Wondering if a girl his own age had finally caught his eye, I met his gaze, full of something, a shift I couldn't quite define as he backed out of the kitchen.

Helen murmured. "When did he get taller than his father?"

Taller than Jimmy, too, I thought. A good thing. Out loud I said, "Thanksgiving Formal?"

"Last one," Helen sighed. "Hard to believe he'll be off to college next fall." She picked up a dishcloth and began drying the utensils.

I grabbed a cloth to help her, and a shooting pain made me clutch the counter.

Helen put her hand on mine. "The offer stands."

I nodded but said nothing. The thought of bringing the Hinsons into it, the possible repercussions, I couldn't put them at risk too. I'd already risked too much with Luke.

Helen turned to the stove. "Are you spending the holidays with your family in Idaho?"

Matt would never agree to the holidays with my parents. "We'll prolly stay here. Jimmy might get leave from the merchant marines."

"You're welcome to join us for Christmas dinner if you like." The woman had a capacity for kindness I couldn't comprehend. She sent me home with six jars of tomatoes, along with instructions to make sure they were completely sealed once they'd cooled.

Matt met me at the door. "Where have you been?"

I offered up the box of jars. "Canning lesson, with Helen Hinson."

Matt grumbled something about having to cook his own breakfast and left, not saying where he was headed. Something that had happened more than once, lately.

I set my box down on the kitchen table and pressed each lid at the center. Helen had said if the dip holds, then the jar is properly sealed. The lid of the last jar popped back up at me. I tapped a spoon on top, the way Helen had shown me, and a dull sound signaled an improper seal. Maybe I'd use it for spaghetti tonight. I pulled it out of the box and opened the fridge. An empty egg carton rested on the top shelf with a note in Matt's handwriting: "Too busy again?"

Fear snaked up my back at the underlying threat, and I glanced over my shoulder, just to be sure he had left, before unearthing a half-used roll of masking tape from the tool bin. I tore off a small piece, put it in the center of the unsafe lid, added the jar to the others, and headed down to the basement to store the jars. Back upstairs, I started a grocery list. We needed a lot more than eggs.

Chapter Nine/Luke

Mid-March 1964

In the days leading up to ablation therapy, eating bored me. Pre-treatment regimen disallowed salt, dairy, eggs, chicken, or fish, not that I would have eaten the fish. I opted for liberally-peppered green beans.

Walker showed up with a vegetable stew of sorts, seasoned with unfamiliar herbs that made me hungry again. After I scarfed down the first decent meal I'd had in a week, we worked side by side at my makeshift lab counter, recording various tests on both the bay water and the marsh. Manganese was the common element in the bay, and traces of multiple irradiated elements were present in the marsh samples, but at very low levels.

Frustrated, I pushed back my stool and muttered, "It's not enough."

"Maybe we're looking in the wrong place." Walker pulled a worn map from his pack. Spreading it flat, he traced an old trade route that his family used to travel between the coast and the desert above The Area. "The wind's in our faces for half of the trip, the other half at our backs, or so the old songs say. Maybe there's an inversion zone at the halfway point. That could explain the concentration of radioactive nucleotides in certain places."

Behind Walker's back, fog infused the forest, hovering near the cabin and clouding the lower half of the window, a sign that March would push out winter. "Half," I said. With Mary, the wind was always at my back, but my life had split in two: before and after Mary.

Theoretically a stable human, I had the requisite number of fingers and toes, protons and neutrons, but when Mary came to Richland, my heart—my nuclei—had grown exponentially, along with my desire. After she went missing, I'd become unstable, like an isotope losing its positive charge. I only remained viable because of the tiny hope that Mary would come back. Recharge my heart.

Walker nodded. "The trace amounts indicate the half-life, twenty years, has passed."

I stared at the slides again, thinking that adolescent crushes, even though it was more than that, have a half-life too. When I pushed back my stool again, the fog had melted. The door must not have closed all the way, because a gust blew it wide, rattling the spoons left in our bowls on the table and jolting me back to the present. "The first reactor began production in 1944. What the hell happened then?"

Walker pulled a worn Farmer's Almanac off the shelf. "Weather patterns," he mumbled as he flipped pages.

Lost in my what-ifs, I shuffled over to close the door and checked the cloud formations before lowering my gaze, catching a narrow shoulder topped by a swath of red hair fading into the bramble.

•   •   •

The medical center in Olympia offered the region's only radiotherapy treatment for miles. Treatment that would have been out of reach financially had it not been for the work done at Hanford. The charge nurse led me to a lead-lined room that would be my home for a few days. The apparatus suspended from the ceiling bore the GE logo, creating a tug of war inside me, gratitude versus disgust, and the ablation treatment required barriers far more secure than the holding tanks at Hanford.

"I'll bring you fresh linens and a new gown each day." The nurse handed me a gown to put on, wished me good luck, and scurried off, saying a tech would be in shortly. Inside, a single bed, stripped of anything that might collect "debris" hinted at sleep, but a light switch on the far wall had a piece of tape over it.

Just in case I didn't get the message, the tech, this time in a rubberized jumpsuit, entered and told the hospital-gown-clad me not to touch the switch.

"The staff controls the lights," he said. "They'll check your vitals at regular intervals during the first forty-eight hours."

Great, no rest at all. A small intercom threaded the wall, and a lead-scored, thick glass window with a ledge on my side provided the only access to the outside world.

A doorless alcove housed a toilet. "Flush the toilet twice, to wash down your waste thoroughly." The tech continued. "And try to shift your position as often as possible after the treatment. Don't stay on one side or the other for too long when you are sleeping. Any questions before we begin?"

Amused at the thought of waking myself to turn over, I said, "April fools, right?"

The tech didn't laugh. "Today's the 2nd," he said. "Let's get you numbed up."

"Oh, boy." The most painful part of the procedure, Dr. Tall had assured me, was the injection to numb my neck. After that, just pressure. The cocktail should burn up any remaining tissue the radiation treatments hadn't. That was the theory, all theories being temporary until proven.

A couple of white-coated figures stopped at the window to observe, lips moving in profile as they chatted. When the female turned to face my window, I realized it was the Volkswagen-driving doctor who had nailed me in the parking lot at Ocean Beach. She winked, or did she? Embarrassment inundated the space between my gown and my skin like seawater filling a wetsuit.

The tech pinched a piece of my neck. I clenched the sides of the bed as he pumped in the needle full of anesthetic. He stepped away to load the cocktail, and Dr. Tall, who had made the drive as well, replaced the others at the window, holding a thumbs-up. I nodded, wincing at the after-sting of the painkiller. The tech returned, blocking the doc from my view.

He aimed the lead-encased hypodermic holding the cocktail of radionuclides at the center of my neck. Steadying my neck with his other hand, he pushed the poison in, swamping my nodes like a targeted tsunami that would hopefully take out the cancer in its wake.

I closed my eyes and smiled.

"What's funny?" The tech inquired, pulling out the needle. He dabbed at my neck with a gauze pad and placed an ice pack at the injection site.

"Floods have always been good to me." I didn't explain. I'd told no one about my night with Mary, a secret I'd kept for more than a decade.

•   •   •

My mother peered through the lead-lined window, cocking her head at my misshapen neck. I'd parked my chair on the inside ledge and wrapped a blanket around my legs against the morning chill in the room. Because I still had my thyroid glands, my neck had swollen like a balloon animal's belly.

My mother fiddled with the intercom, before realizing she had to keep her finger down for me to hear her. "How long is that swelling going to last?"

"A while. You'll have to keep your distance." No one could come within ten feet of me until the radiation in my system dissipated to a non-radioactive level.

My mother raised an eyebrow. "As if I haven't been exposed to radioactivity for the last twenty-two years."

For the first time, I noticed a bitterness in her voice. My father had been dead for almost thirteen years, and though I had railed against DuPont, the AEC, and anyone else that I could hold responsible for his death, my mother had kept most of her thoughts of who was to blame to herself. Now I wondered if she had taken on the mantle of blame, hindsight being an unparalleled driver of guilt.

She switched subjects. "Did I tell you they have almost completed the demolition of the work camp?" A trouble-dominated area in the '40s, the Hanford work camp encompassed hundreds of empty barracks rotting in the desert sun. The community of Richland had been lobbying for its removal ever since a thousand new ranch houses had been erected in the now non-company-owned town.

"What are they going to do with all that land?"

My mother rolled her eyes. "They're saying agriculture."

"That close to the reactors? Seriously?"

My mother grimaced.

Behind her, nurses and doctors strolled down the hallway, dodging orderlies pushing gurneys. A head of dark hair caught my eye. I craned my neck, peering over my mother's shoulder.

She followed my gaze. "Who's that?"

"Someone who threatened to have me fined."

My mother shot me a quizzical look, but I didn't answer her unasked question, being too busy panicking. The dark-haired doctor approached my window, her smile offering up a tease. A flush worked its way up from my toes, and I tucked my blanket up around my waist, loosening its hold on my groin. My mother, who never missed a thing, gave up a wry smile.

"Hello, I'm Doctor Jackson. I'm doing a special rotation one day a week on the ward here. And," she definitely winked at me. "I believe we've met. In the Ocean Beach parking lot."

Certain my heat flush read like a blush, I couldn't think of a comeback.

My mother jumped into the silent fray. "I'm Helen, Luke's mother."

The perfectly lovely Dr. Jackson offered her hand to my mother. "How's the patient?"

Sweat beads had formed on my forehead, and I took a swipe at them as I said, "You most likely know the drill, pass the radiation, flush, repeat."

The extremely attractive Dr. Jackson grinned and pushed the intercom. "Dr. Tall says scientists make interesting patients. He didn't mention you were a comedian too."

Maniacally happy that she'd asked about me, my flush became an official blush. "All part of the doctorate program. How to write a thesis that will keep 'em laughing."

My mother's face lit up, witnessing my attempt at flirtation.

That was what this was, right? It'd been a while, but I was in the groove when a sudden need to urinate overtook me. "Sorry, ladies, you'll have to excuse me." I padded to the toilet alcove, making a mental note to ask Dr. Tall about the amount of radiation passing out through sweat, saliva, and well, you know.

The alcove shielded me from view, and there was no way my visitors could hear, but performance anxiety set in. My neck tightened, a side-effect that the doc had predicted, but I was sure it was more about my unease at my mother hanging with Dr. Jackson, saying who knew what about me, and my having no editorial control. My pee finally initiated, but by the time I flushed twice and returned to the window, Dr. Jackson was gone.

"She got paged," my mother said in answer to my unasked question. "She reminds me of Mary Boone."

My mother was right about the resemblance, but what she did not understand was that no one could compare. Mary had taken my hand and led me to her bed, expecting nothing in return. But that night, the night of the big flood of '48, as magical as it had been, had also jump-started the most difficult days of my life. I had to pretend everything was just the same when my entire existence had been tossed into the spin cycle.

My father had kept me busy ripping out ruined flooring all over town, stacking furniture in piles for pickup, but nothing could stymie the flood of feelings that flowed through me every time I had caught a glimpse of Mary, my unbearably beautiful next-door neighbor.

•   •   •

The hospital kicked me out three days later, still radioactive. My mother insisted on following me home from the hospital in her car, "Just to be sure you make it safe and sound," she said. Per doctor's orders, she stayed at arm's length, waiting for me to go inside and return to the threshold, assuring her I had everything in hand.

But that had been everyone else's doing. Inside my now impeccably clean cabin, the pantry was stocked with soft foods: Mother. A new ream of typewriter paper stamped "Property of OSU" and two recent issues of *American Science* rested on my lab countertop: Roy. A pot sat on the burner, lid on. I lifted it. Steam escaped: Walker.

After some soup and perusal of several medical journals with unsatisfying reports on radiation treatment side-effects, I tucked into my cot, noting the clean sheets—Mother—and dozed off, musing about what Dr. Jackson might be doing.

A noose tightened around my neck, and I couldn't breathe. My fingers couldn't get under the noose, something burned, and something else crept up my chest, threatening to paint me red. I woke in a sweat, most likely radioactive, and dragged myself to the toilet. My urine didn't look any different. The Hanford Instrument Division had tested urine mostly after workers, including my father, had been home for a holiday weekend and shed most of the radiation. A full forty-eight hours of pee down home toilets before the HID collected samples.

A flush of warmth traveled up from my feet, and I plunked down on the side of the bathtub. Dreams aside, I needed to get back to my research, regardless of my spine feeling like it was about to give out. I popped an aspirin and dragged myself back to bed for what turned out to be a week. When I finally came up for air, my neck was stronger.

The pain had lessened, which meant my nerve endings were most likely dying, failing to send pain signals. Every time I looked in the mirror, I blushed like I was continually embarrassed by everything and everyone, which I was with the roster of folks monitoring my poops and pees. Dr. Tall called twice a week. Visiting nurses came to the cabin every other day, and of course, my mother drove back down on the weekend.

Dr. Tall had assured me I would be radiation-free at the ten-day mark. Desperate for company other than medical, I called Harry. He came bearing fried cod, ocean fish being less suspect than salmon that bred in the Columbia.

"Your voice is deeper," Harry said, as he put out plates and forks.

"More authoritative, right?"

"Maybe you should apply for a broadcaster position." Harry teased. "Ladies love a star."

"Like anyone would listen to me if I was on television." I slumped, eyeing my sweat with suspicion. "Plus, it'll be months before I can chance sex."

Harry guffawed, well, as much as a former scientist can guffaw. "You were planning on having some soon?"

"Maybe." I tried not to sound defensive. "A gal doctor actually, at the hospital. She seemed interested." I leaned my head, still too heavy for my body, back against the rocker.

"A doctor, huh? Sure she's interested?" Harry teased, but his face held something more. "You might just be an odd specimen for her to study."

"Hang on. Is this a clue to the dark past of Harry Griffin? Some female scientist took you for a ride?" The moment the words were out I realized I'd hit a nerve.

"Just saying, she'll know the risks." Harry ran a hand over his face as if dragging away a bad memory. "Some women just want safe."

The term 'risk' was always coupled with 'no' or 'minimal,' but stories my mother had conveyed when I was only half listening contradicted that. Plus, in my current condition, I wanted answers, and not just about Harry's love life.

"Mother said it snowed one summer, the mid-1950s I think. What was that all about?"

Harry closed his eyes, shaking his head. "Not snow, radioruthenium. I'd been fired a year or so earlier. A colleague called me. Flakes fell all over The Area, Richland proper."

My fork clattered to the plate holding my cod. "What did they do?"

"Hanford?" Harry pushed away from the table. "They put up signs. Thousands all over the desert, saying 'Don't walk on the grass.'"

Imagining mothers with baby carriages strolling downtown Richland in the supposed snow destroyed my appetite. Harry stepped outside. I followed to find him staring into the bramble as if some answer to the insanity of it rested there, but there was no answer to madness. Not really.

Harry cleared his throat. "Have you seen the boy lately?"

The science project. I'd forgotten, and at least three weeks had passed since I'd said I would help. "I owe him a call." Where had I put that scrap of paper?

"His grandmother would appreciate it." Harry's comment held something else. Had the grandmother been asking about me? Before I could find out, Harry took off, saying he had the dinner rush to deal with, and that my next crab dinner was on the house when I got my appetite back. If I ever did. I called the boy.

• • •

My mother had left me a stack of old *Look* magazines, saying I needed some pictorial relief from scientific journals. Listless, I plopped into the front porch rocker and flipped through the 1961 April issue that declared Richland an All-America City, a designation that underscored the depth of the government's deception. The logo for the award, a shield bearing the new title, had been added to the welcome sign on the outskirts of town. The moniker sent a jolt of fear through me as if all of America might become subject to the Richland formula.

"Whatcha reading, mister?" Ben surfaced at the top of the drive, several poster boards under his arm. He must have hitched a ride. A growth spurt had stretched him close to my height.

"An entirely untrue article." I motioned him to the porch, noting his red hair needed trimming, and a bit of teenage acne dotted his cheek. "Let's see what you got."

Ben spread the boards at my feet. Photos, most likely taken by a Brownie camera, covered the first board in what seemed to be a progression. Flashes of light, dramatic against a dark paneled wall, went from a vertical shape to a crouch.

Another set, blurrier than the first, shot out from a bramble in spits, going from a glow to a glare emanating from the green leaves, then narrowed into nothingness. The final series must have been taken at the pier, pilings providing a counterpoint to the gleam that played hide-and-seek with the photographer. A shimmer in one, a glitter in another, and then a sudden, joyful sparkle. Each image was spaced at precise increments to pull the viewer along in the game.

"You're it," I whispered, releasing another, harsher memory of the last time I'd tried to hide. It felt oddly like a puzzle piece to this particular moment, as if every step I had taken in my entire life had brought me to this place at this time.

Ben sat back on his heels. "Yeah. It's like a game of hide and seek we—I played."

"Light changes speed when it changes direction," I said to myself, but the boy understood.

"That's why you can see her better, here and here." Ben pointed to images at the end of each series. In both, the light had brightened from the previous image and stretched, like waking from a good night's sleep.

"Her?"

The boy shrank back, not making eye contact. "You know, like in a lighthouse or a ship. The light's a her."

The second poster held a few newspaper articles about other ghostly sightings across the globe. The most prominent, a photocopy of a *London Times* story about a family estate famous for ghosts, was at the center. The light in the *Times* images were almost exact duplicates of Ben's, but the boy's supposed evidence could be fodder for the school bullies.

The last poster board just had text, summaries of the circumstances around his photos, resembling journal entries, in various shades of ink. Most likely done over days, and he had never been able to locate the same pen. Each bore a date and time. The series of winter night and early mornings accounts painted a portrait of a lonely boy awakened in the night, alone and desperate for what he'd lost.

A small knot formed in my stomach, the same one that had lived there since my father died. This boy must be seeking answers for why his mother was gone, as if he couldn't compute being abandoned, so he presumed her dead. And this report was a study of light. Light that took the form of a spirit. A spirit that may or may not be his missing mother.

I couldn't let him turn this in, not like this. "You think the light is more than just a reflection?"

"That's what I need you to help me prove."

"Then, I would recommend a more data-driven accounting of the episodes." I motioned to the third poster. "If you want it taken seriously, you should present both sides."

"You mean, say it might not be true?"

"As scientists, our job is to provide the evidence." I shrugged, thinking of the decades of denial in my hometown. "Folks choose what they want to believe."

"I used up all my money on the posters. Can't afford another."

"Don't worry about that. First, let's make an outline, from hypothesis to discovery. Or not. We'll need to analyze the conditions."

"Like the ocean water, you mean?"

Ben's hair caught the light, and I flashed back on the tangle of red I'd first seen under the pier. I blinked the image away, rubbing at the goosebumps on my arms. "Yeah, like that. Explain the factors that might affect the light." Who was I trying to convince, Ben or me?

Ben's jaw jutted out. "Okay, but it's no mirage, mister."

"Hang on." I padded inside and returned with a stack of index cards, half white, and half yellow. "We'll put your theory on the white ones, then the counterpoints to it on the yellow."

"You gotta radio? Music helps me think."

I suppressed a grin, moved back inside, set my radio on the table by the window, and tuned it to a folk station. Mary's voice, sans Peter and Paul, threaded the air with her message-laden solo "Follow Me." I couldn't help smiling.

"What's so funny, mister?"

"Been so focused on myself, I've forgotten how fun it can be to follow the science."

Ben cocked his head like I was just another weird adult and picked up a white card. "I read that when light travels from air into water, it slows down considerable."

A plume, stagnant until the wind and weather take hold, can spread in all directions. I nodded. "Water can make it travel at a different angle or direction."

"Slower means you can see it better?"

"But there are lots of reasons folks think they see a ghost," I said, thinking of the times I'd wished my father back, pictured what he'd say about this or what I was doing, feeling his hand on my shoulder. A ray of sunshine pierced the raised windowpane, sparking light off the radio's metal trim, and a sudden static disrupted the broadcast.

The night I'd taken Mary's hand, the storm had done the same thing to my ham radio. Even now, I sometimes thought it had been a dream and might have chalked it up to that. But the void inside me meant something had been there before. An emptiness that I wouldn't let any other woman fill. One-night stands felt less disloyal. I had let my work consume me, hiding from any love that might find me, saving myself for Mary's unlikely return.

At least my thesis might provide some answers about the loss of my father. Reasons for his death which I could hopefully prove and hold someone accountable. The posters spread across my porch, I suspected, were less about a science project and more about a boy searching for answers, but loss rarely comes with those.

"Anyway," I said. "A lot of data shows that you can't always trust your eyes. Or your brain, for that matter."

Ben's eyes found mine. "But what about your heart?"

Chapter Ten/Mary

February 1948

The snow began mid-afternoon, wispy flakes that didn't stick. Flecks bounced off the office window as I incorporated the folders of notes and my latest summary into the cabinet bank, my back to the office door when Harry entered.

"Join me." Harry's tone was one I'd learned to not ignore.

I clicked the filing cabinet closed, turned the key, and took a seat by his desk.

Harry passed a folder to me. The notes, in Dr. Jackson's handwriting, told a story of various releases since the plant's inception, some smaller, others up to 7000 curies of irradiated materials.

"Not accidents?"

Harry's chest seemed to sink as he nodded. "But, Jackson just got GE to agree to a 125-day cooling period."

"Let me guess." I rolled my eyes. "The AEC is fighting it."

"Some idiot zeroed in on the fact that the cooling times for past releases varied. So, if it's already happened that way—"

"Lesser cooling periods, more plutonium?" My frown deepened as I flipped through the summaries, wincing at Jackson's notation in the margin of one page about possible public panic. "He was worried about people panicking?"

Harry gave the slightest nod, as if he was admitting to his guilt.

"But, why give this to you now?"

"Not sure." Harry shoved his hair off his forehead. "They must've stockpiled over thirty bombs already. How many do we need?"

Thick globs of snow smashed against the panes, soggy and signaling a change in the storm's intensity. "The plot thickens?"

My quip did not move the frown on Harry's face. He lowered his voice to a throaty whisper. "The Air Force is beefing up troops locally."

The proximity of the Air Force was a blessing or a curse depending on your perspective. My father had taught me five-card stud and most importantly, how to read the other player, small ticks or movements that signal your opponent's intention. Movements in military personnel were like a tell in poker. I scooted my chair closer.

"Who are we playing this time?" No one trusted the Russians, but the Chinese communists were more worrisome, according to recent editorials in the *Richland Villager,* and Korea hosted an ongoing tussle that even Matt said was a situation that Truman couldn't ignore.

"All signs point to Korea, but it's not Korea that I'm worried about today." Harry pointed out the window. A swirl of tea-rose-colored flakes blanketed the ground, burying the walkways, and depositing movie-glow canopies on every rooftop. "It's the piping in T-plant."

My little girl wonder at the pink-tinted snow turned to fear, the same panic Jackson warned of in his notes. "So, the pink is rust? The radioactive toxins are eating the pipes for lunch?"

Harry nodded. "Among other things. Jackson's crew is analyzing every square foot of ground in the Area."

"How long does the danger last?" I asked, glad I'd brought my sturdiest snow boots.

"A day." Harry closed his eyes. "Or fifty years." His shoulders sank into his frame.

"So, they're replacing the pipes?"

Harry nodded. "But they'll have to stop production to do it, and I guarantee you that the AEC won't let that last for long."

Out the window, the snow consumed everything in sight, a raging, pink wildfire.

•   •   •

Harry was right. Jackson's crew tracked the pink snow, finding milligram-sized radioactive particles, hundreds of millions of them, rolling in tumbleweeds found as far away as Spokane. Despite all that, the Hanford Medical Division bowed to the AEC. Just two weeks after T-plant was shut down for repairs, the AEC advisory committee rescinded Jackson's recommended cooling periods. T-plant resumed production in early March.

Harry and I took off early and headed to Pasco on the other side of the river. High above the Columbia, each reactor had its basins, places for the effluent to cool before it was flushed into the river. Lou had been testing fish and their spawn. He'd netted sockeye salmon fingerlings downriver from where the effluent pipes beneath each reactor entered the river bed. Fish absorbed the radioactive effluent through their gills, in addition to feeding on irradiated microscopic algae and plankton.

Lou's initial test results showed that the salmon's bodies contained almost thirty times the level of radioactive elements as the water in which they swam.

Harry centered himself on a stool. "The project lab in Seattle, Dickinson, a former colleague of mine runs it. He's doing this same study." Harry cast a glance around Lou's makeshift lab and shot me a wry grin. "Wonder what that's costing the taxpayers?"

Lou pointed to two fingerlings in a large cylinder. "Something funny about them, like their bodies are off somehow."

Fingerlings live off their yolk sacs. These sacs seemed to bulge, making the fingerlings look skinny in comparison.

"Dickinson put some fish directly into the effluent. They all died, but when he diluted the effluent with more water, the fish multiplied, outgrew the tank." Harry moved closer to the fish. "When he tested again, they contained sixty times more radioactivity than the water mix."

"So less is more?" Lou shook his head. "Lower levels of radioactivity inside a body take on a life of their own?"

"Putting every fisherman downriver at risk." Harry sagged against the garage wall.

"And their families." I shuddered, checking my watch before inserting my notes inside the shoebox. "Better get home before I'm missed."

Lou stashed the box onto a shelf in the far corner. He backfilled with some old paint cans. "As good a hiding place as I can figure for now."

Harry took the green bridge back across the river and we threaded our way through the new construction. A thousand new ranch houses were being built and those proud new homeowners didn't have a clue what was in their water.

•   •   •

Matt waited on the porch for me when I arrived home. He handed me a bourbon and clinked my glass. "To my new job at GE."

The wind was picking up, a fierce undercurrent to it. I took a tentative sip before asking. "How'd that happen?"

"They finally realized they needed a local to be the messenger. Way too many folks riled up about this and that."

"You mean about the Thompsons? The scientist and his wife that both died?" I swallowed, trying not to choke. "Not to mention their infant son last year."

Matt shot me a warning look. "You know not to perpetuate such rumors."

"It's hardly a rumor when their graves are just across town."

"Maybe it's time you started dinner." Matt stomped into the living room and flipped on the television.

I sloughed off my cardigan and placed a pot of water on the stove to boil, wondering how many radioactive elements were in it. A burst of thunder made me jump. Lightning bolts pierced the clouds, and fast rain peppered the kitchen window.

Beyond our front yard, water rose in the gutters, overwhelming the sidewalk across the street. I moved out to the front porch to assess the flow. The houses on our side of the block sat up higher on a small slope. Both side yards already hosted multiple rivulets, threatening a mini-mud slide. The Hinson's screen door creaked open, and Luke stepped out, eyeing the horizon.

"The radio says the river's just below cresting. Spring snow melt." He grinned my way, a spark in his eyes as if we shared a secret, and we did. Several.

His eyebrows had darkened, and his skin, clear of blemishes, had deepened into a rich summer tan, giving off an attractive glow. His shoulders seemed broader, a new strength to them that hadn't been there the last time I'd looked. He still didn't have a girlfriend, according to Helen, but the puppy-dog adoration for me seemed to have dissipated. My relief at that mixed with a longing for what I did not have.

"Feels like 'termination winds' in the works," I said, grinning. The Area still had problems keeping new hires, especially those who arrived in the summer. Many potential workers, some who had traveled hundreds of miles for the higher pay, would experience the dust-bowl-like winds, and the blistering heat and climb back aboard the same bus they rode in on.

Luke shook his head. "Nothing dry about this storm." He stretched a lanky muscled arm to the porch post, his palm pressing against the surface. "I'm thinking about burying a time capsule. The ground will be soft digging after a day or two of this." He raised his chin to the blowing rain, the innocence of his face a cross between boy and man. He still believed in the future, even in this place full of hidden dangers. I wasn't sure I could.

"What are you putting inside?"

Luke's face went shy. "Things." He murmured, gripping the railing with both hands that looked strong and soft at the same time.

Putting my back to the torrent, I took a seat against the railing and let the rain spatter my back, thinking how I missed soft hands. My father would stroke my cheek before bedtime when I was a girl, lulling me to sleep. A sleep so deep that my dreams, always good ones, remained vivid the next morning. Now, the only thing I remembered when I woke was the violence of the night before. Luke's presence on the other side of the wall wouldn't last much longer, not with college looming.

"How about I donate one of my jars of peaches, a sweet reward for the finders?"

Luke scrunched his nose in a little boy's way. "I'm thinking more popular things—of my time."

My laughter bubbled up, that lightness I always felt when it was just Luke and me. The light that let me imagine again. A light that led to a future without all the pain. "How about Benny Goodman? Not our Benny, the famous one," I said, hoping that if the entire world blew sky-high, Benny's music would reach the stars.

Luke's grin lit up his dimples. "Yeah, maybe the Ink Spots too?" His brows lowered into serious mode. "Would we have to bury the phonograph too? So, they could play the records?"

Luke's visible horror at having to give up his record player made my lightness soar, as if the world I stood in, just this moment, could be one where only things could be lost, not souls.

"I'm thinking research scientists, opening such a treasure, would have all the equipment archived for such finds," I said, winking.

Luke leaned into the corner of the porch railing, his cheeks catching wind-driven raindrops. "Maybe Mom's vegetable dicer." He heaved an overly dramatic sigh. "One must give up something for science."

"I doubt Helen will agree to eliminate carrots and green beans from your diet quite yet," I said, grinning.

Luke snorted and dropped into the sole chair on his side of the porch. "Maybe her Dutch skillet?"

"No way." I shook my head, giggling. "Her Mixmaster?"

"Not even in the name of science will I go without cookies." Luke's face broke into a grin, adolescent fun prevailing over his adult-serious side.

"Wait, my Mixmaster." At the thought of no more cookies for Jimmy, I wondered what I could bury that would stop Matt from—well, everything.

"Definitely," Luke said, his tone matching mine. "And of course, a newspaper."

"We should each write a letter, talking about our daily lives, normal things that will seem odd a hundred years from now."

Luke stared out into the storm. "You think a hundred years from now Richland will even be here? Or, the Area?"

His serious tone brought me back. We sat in the present, somber, silent, the rain tempering off, the wind changing course. Our side of the street, A-houses stark against the clouds, looked like building blocks that could be knocked aside at any moment. Everything about Richland felt temporary, subject to removal. The government gave and the government took oh-so-much more.

A fiery gust of wind splattered us with rain, pushing out my wish. "I hope not."

•   •   •

The seep of water began early Memorial Day weekend. Late spring snows melted in record time as the heat soared, feeding the flow. Heavy rains nudged the river across its banks, the wind herding a relentless surge that only heightened as the weekend progressed. Matt called to say they were sending folks from The Area home early and to stay put. I hung up the phone thinking he had sounded genuinely concerned, as if something happening to me worried him. The conundrum of Matt pricked at me as I moved into the bathroom, and removed and rinsed my diaphragm.

Luke had set up his ham radio on the front porch. The rain petered out for a bit, and neighbors stopped by for updates. Other ham operators confirmed flooding throughout the Richland Wye neighborhood, and that Badger Mountain looked like an ice cream scoop on top of a float. Rattlesnakes were reported floating on driftwood, escaping the flow. The river disregarded any boundaries made by man, taking over farms and towns one by one to the south.

By Monday, our neighborhood, the higher section of Richland, was completely cut off from Pasco and Kennewick, which suffered even more destruction. The Army Corps of Engineers was building a dike along George Washington Way to stave off complete disaster in the business district. Earth-moving equipment arrived from all over the Northwest. Every able-bodied man, including Ralph and Luke, took off to haul sandbags as brown silty water inundated the surrounding neighborhoods. Jimmy disappeared with pals. Helen Hinson had decamped the day before to care for elderly relatives downriver. Telephone poles fell to the Columbia's will.

My phone rang one last time before the lines went down. "Highway 410 is cut off."

"The borrow pits aren't enough?"

"Every roadside ditch is overrun, and there's flooding in the 300-Area. We're hunkering down for the night." What Matt didn't say was the reactors stopped for nothing.

"The waste ponds?" I swallowed hard. "They're flooding? Holy Hannah." Only one place for them to flow: over the bluffs and into the river.

Matt ignored me. "Boil any water before you drink it," he said and hung up.

Having stocked up on canned goods on Thursday when the first warnings were issued, I had filled the bathtub to its brim on Friday night as the river crested its banks. An ample whiskey supply rested above the fridge. I took a watch position outside, somewhat enjoying the uncertainty of being cut off from almost everything and everyone.

The heat of the day had lessened with the rain, and stars poked the fading summer light when Ralph and Luke plodded up the porch steps, covered in grime.

"I've got gallons of water in the tub, and Matt won't be home tonight. Stuck at the Area."

Ralph let loose a weary smile. "Let me get some jugs." He stepped inside, but Luke lingered, leaning against the railing.

"How was it out there?" I ask.

Luke turned toward me, a man's face replacing the boy's. "The water's waist deep in Kennewick and mud abounds." His cheeks were streaked with it.

I moved inside, filled a water glass from a large bowl I had staged on the kitchen counter, and grabbed a dishcloth from the kitchen rack. I stepped back out and handed both to Luke. He wet his face and rubbed, but the boy didn't reappear. Luke wrested off his muddy boots, keeping his eyes on the flow skimming the street.

Ralph came back out in his house slippers, carrying four large, empty jugs.

"You know the way," I said, smiling.

Luke followed Ralph up the stairs to my bathroom, and they returned two-fisted.

"I have whiskey too, if you like."

Ralph said. "Thank you, Mary, but I'm beat. Think I'll turn in."

"Goodnight then." Luke and his father went inside. A steady drizzle persisted, a harbinger of more. I counted the cigarettes left in my pack, thinking I needed to pace myself.

A storm gust lifted my hair off my shoulders, making me want to strip everything off and give my body over to the wind. Let it carry me up and over the mountains, all the way to the sea. Dip my toes in the tide, scoop foam on my palm, and watch the bubbles pop like I had as a child. The bubble of hope, too big to squash, expanded inside me, the desire to escape this place filling my chest.

Luke appeared with a fresh shirt and his ham radio. He centered it on the small table, putting the bluesy heartrending tunes between us. "I've been listening to the jazz station out of Seattle." He grasped the railing and leaned into the coming night.

I rose and placed my hands on the rail next to his, my fingers wired with new energy. "Not sure the Feds would approve."

"I'm less and less concerned about what the government thinks."

"I'll drink to that." I moved inside, lit a candle, and placed it in the kitchen window, before filling two highball glasses with Black Velvet whisky, lemon juice, sweet syrup, and the last of the melting ice from the freezer that had lost its freeze.

The night descended in earnest, but didn't eliminate the humidity. After swiping a washcloth under my arms, I pulled at the back of my dress that was stuck to my shoulder blades. Dim shouts and the occasional distant flashlight beam signaled that work continued on the dike. I pushed back out, handed Luke his whiskey sour and stepped to the railing.

"An Idahome specialty. Man's work deserves a man's drink." An inexplicable shiver overtook me despite the nearly constant spate of warm sticky air.

Luke wrapped his slender fingers around the glass and took a tentative sip. Maybe his first.

"Cheers," I said, clinking my glass to his before downing half my drink.

"Good practice for college, I guess." He sucked down a large gulp and choked. I patted his back, but he pulled away, as if shunning the motherly gesture.

"Decided yet? U-Dub or Wazzu?" Helen had told me Luke had scholarships for both.

"Seattle or bust."

His shoulder brushed mine, sparking a selfish wish that he not go, but the recklessness of making this boy my ally hit me. Luke had his whole life to live, and I needed to get on with mine. My seat on the steps next to him, the closeness of it all, urged me to tell him the plan I'd voiced to no one, not that Luke did not know already. The coins he'd converted at the bank for me were clue enough. The whiskey warmed my throat, and any concerns strayed, the urgency to tell lost in the first stars.

Luke smiled into the blue of the night. "What with the flood damage, you think they'll cancel Richland Days? Let Nancy Meyers keep her crown another year."

"She'd like that, I bet." I laughed. "Put her out in front of the hoard of girls getting their MRS degrees at Eastern this fall."

Luke smirked and dropped to the steps.

I stared at the rising moon, letting the secret fall out. "I'm leaving soon, too."

"I figured." He let loose a breath as if he'd been holding it for months, just waiting for me to say it. "Do you need help?"

I sank down beside him. Our eyes met. "I think I'll be okay." The radio sputtered, recovered, and Peggy Lee belted out her latest hit. Luke took another sip of his drink. This time it went down without a fight. He leaned back on his elbows, his torso finally in proportion with his limbs, the adolescence of him almost gone.

His eyes brimmed with a longing I'd not seen before, not just in Luke, but in any man that I had known. The naked need for a specific human, the one who saw you, all of you, and still wanted you. All of that sat next to me. Matt had never seen me. Not then, not now.

The difference was that Matt had never been mine, but I was his, a possession that once acquired held less value. His blows, the physical violence, separated us, but it was the lack of real union that left me adrift, searching. A long time had passed since I had wanted to be touched by a man, but this night, the uncertainty of it necessitated touch. Something solid to hold on to.

Along the block, most shades were drawn, the dark complete except my candle on the kitchen windowsill. A coyote scooted down the middle of the block, searching for a place to hide. The trumpet riff suddenly seemed too loud.

"Maybe turn it down," I meant more than just the radio. "Shouldn't spook the kai-ote."

Luke grinned and put a hand to the dial.

The man who had never seen me wouldn't be back tonight. Except for a dim night light here or there, the homes around us darkened. "Folks seem to think they are safe in bed now," I murmured, my needs surging, a flood of a different sort but just as unstoppable. My eyes found Luke's.

"We would be too." Luke held my gaze, all of him, waiting for me.

My mind played with how this moment might be judged. An older woman, even though I was only twenty-six, and still a girl in my father's mind. A girl taking advantage of a younger boy, even though Luke was draft age, and could shoulder a rifle in Korea if not off to college. But reality can be shoved away, risks shelved out of reach.

Squelching the greed of it, I stepped inside, leaving the door open, and gathered up the kitchen candle to light the stairwell. The front door clicked in its lock, and Luke's shoeless tread on the stairs rustled like leaves behind me.

How does one reclaim a room of violence? Keeping my back to Luke, I set the candle on the dresser top and dropped my dress to the floor. Luke trembled. I snuffed out the candle. A hot breeze blew through the open window, making the wick end glow bright. He took a step toward me. I put his hand on my waist.

His palm slid down my slip to my hip, sending a long-forgotten jolt through my belly. I unbuttoned his shirt and smoothed my hands across his chest. His lungs heaved under my palms. My hands dropped to his belt buckle, loosening it. He tugged down his trousers. I shrugged my slip off and stepped closer, wanting to see that look again.

An ache had overtaken his face, creating lines across his forehead, questions in his young brown eyes, and a pain that needed easing.

"What's your full name?"

His eyes never left mine. "Lucas Benjamin Hinson."

"Mary Margaret Peters. Nice to meet you." I murmured, before clasping his palm in mine and pulling him under the sheets.

Maybe he'd been thinking about this longer, or maybe he'd simply been paying attention to the tender affection his father showed his mother. Whichever it was, his first action was to stroke my cheek. All the rest that followed, the initial, explorative kiss that solidified a mutual consent negating my sudden hesitation, the slow caresses, and the final rocking all-consuming explosion, laid us both bare and in need of more. Sharing of individual pleasures relegated sleep to the last moments before dawn. Luke slipped out just before sunrise.

I moved into the bathroom to give myself a quick sponge bath, hoping the lightness would last. That was when I noticed my diaphragm on the back of the toilet.

Chapter Eleven/Luke

May 1964

Harry was washing barware when I entered the crab shack, the last of the lunch crowd hanging at a back corner table. I dumped the folders of research data onto the bar. The accumulated results on plants and animals living along the banks of the bay that Walker and I had compiled had to have some answers, but any real ones eluded.

"Got a minute?" I pulled up a stool.

Harry slid a club soda down to me. "How are things?"

He knew not to ask how I was feeling. That changed by the hour, a rollercoaster ride of uncertainty. Second-guessing every minor ache, feeling up my throat ten times a day, and studying my waste in the toilet bowl, my life had turned into an unending analysis of how I was with no answers in sight until the next follow-up scans. Like the irradiated material I was studying, I felt like I'd reached my half-life, my energy spent with no way to replenish what had decayed.

"Busy," I said, squeezing the lime wedge into the soda.

Harry eyed the pile of folders. "Need a second opinion?"

"Yeah. We think that most of the radioactive material reached its half-life before the effluent reached the bay, which in turn, should still mean a health risk." Reaching half-life means things are only half as dangerous. I spread the charts of summary data across the bar. "But the deer and the whale, their tissue shows damage that may be a result of exposure to larger doses of radioactivity or waste products."

Harry flipped open the folder labeled: Deer's Organs and Bones. "You found strontium-89 in the bone marrow?"

I nodded. "Along with plutonium in most of the vital organs. But based on his hooves, he couldn't be over ten years old, too young to have been around in those sloppy, early days." Hanford's approach to waste disposal in its first years had been haphazard at best. My father's death was proof of that.

"They're still sloppy." Harry picked up another folder, data on plant life and small animals: raccoons, river rats, muskrats snared near the bay. "Genetic mutations, large levels of radionuclides in their livers and kidneys." Harry tossed the folder on the bar.

"It's as if just a little radioactivity, no matter how small the amount, migrates through the entire body," I said. "And more disturbing, plant roots retain all the bad stuff when they go dormant."

"Old news."

"Are you talking about Müller's work, in the twenties?" Müller had won the Nobel for his research proving that X-rays caused damage to the chromosomes in fruit flies.

Harry shook his head. "Nope, I'm talking about government-funded research daylighting unusual levels of strontium, beryllium, and phosphorus, just to name a few."

The name phosphorus is derived from the Greek word, *phosphoros*, the bringer of light. I wagged my head. "Where, when?"

"Jacobson and Overstreet, at Berkeley, in '45. They were concerned about waste being pumped into the ground, the reverse well idea." Harry laughed. "We shipped them topsoil to California. They grew barley, I think, to test how crops might be affected. Watched the plants drink up the isotopes, the highest concentration was in the roots rather than the soil."

Reeling, I said, "The government knew? Before they started disposing of waste in the ground, they knew it would irradiate edible crops?"

"The Hanford Medical Division knew. Who the HMD told, I don't know." Harry raised his hand in a high sign to a table in the back of the cafe. He dashed off a check and ferried it over, leaving me gobsmacked. I chugged my club soda, needing more. Harry returned, refilled my glass, and took up the stool next to mine. "And they monitored soil after most accidental airborne releases. All that's still classified, in case you were wondering."

"So, my working theory—that even small amounts of radiation have a devastating effect in all life—has already been proven?"

Harry raised an eyebrow. "Harold Jackson still acts like the Berkeley research never happened. That said, no one has predicted the long-term effects of low-level radiation. Not yet."

"So, if I can get published..." My voice trailed off, thinking about *Nature* magazine, a British publication, but read worldwide, their integrity unquestioned.

Harry nodded. "Heard through the grapevine, there was a blue light accident in the 234-5 facility last year. Three workers were exposed. Jackson's crew couldn't wait to do tests on them, kind of joyful about the opportunity, or so my source says."

"Did the operators survive?"

"Miraculously, yes, but the latest tests show they don't have sperm anymore."

I grimaced at the reminder of my possible peril.

Harry circled the counter and picked up a dishcloth. "I've got chores to finish, but if I were you, I'd go back to the whale. He's new news."

•   •   •

The curves along the coastal highway I could navigate in my sleep, though I resisted trying. My car crested the bluff. Before me, the mid-morning rain pelted the hospital, giving off a relatable weariness. I threw the gear shift into park and closed my eyes for real.

If the scans still showed cancer, I'd told my mother that I would have the surgery, a late Mother's Day gift I couldn't imagine putting a bow on. The thought of allowing some knife-happy surgeon to invade my throat made me shiver, or maybe it was just the chill of the wet day.

Dr. Tall's receptionist shot me a smile. "Hi, Luke. He'll be another five minutes."

Only three had passed when Tall strode into the waiting area and motioned for me to follow. He clipped down the hallway, and we landed in the same exam room, my latest pictures already hung on the light boxes.

"The radiation appears to have done its job." His pencil eraser tapped the spots where the nodules had been. "Four of the five are completely gone, and the fifth has shrunk to about a third of its original size."

Not allowing my joy to surface quite yet, I said, "What do we do about that one?"

"I think we watch it, give it another blast if it grows."

I let the bubble out of its box and gave way to a grin. "That works."

Tall smiled back. "I want you back in here monthly for a while."

"Aye, aye, doc." I bounced out of the chair, made a quick stop at reception to set my next appointment, and skipped into the hallway. At the end of the corridor, I recognized the back of a head and loped toward it.

"Dr. Jackson, I presume," I intoned, pulling up short from behind her.

She turned, a grin flashing as if she already knew who would be there, and I reveled in what I was sure was her delight at it being me.

"You're a lot peppier than the last time I saw you."

"Tall has ousted the evil demons inside me. How about a celebratory lunch?" The unfamiliar ease with which I extended the invitation spread inside me. This was how life was supposed to be lived. Moment-by-moment happiness.

"I'm afraid all I have time for is cafeteria food."

"Lead on. Tapioca puddings on me." I couldn't stop grinning.

By the time we pushed through the double doors to the cafeteria, Ellen knew I was obsessed with fishing, and I knew she loved hiking. We settled into a table for two and the inevitable interrogation.

"I'm from Moscow, Idaho," Ellen said.

"Better Idaho's than the other." We both laughed. "How'd you end up here?"

"My mother moved to the Washington coast after my father died. The full ride that UW Med offered me sealed the deal."

"A Brainiac. Who'd have thought."

"Why are men always surprised that a woman has a mind as well."

"Not surprised, challenged. We know that beautiful and smart won't be easy."

"Should it ever be?" She winked before losing her smile. "Although, looking back, most likely my ex thought so."

I wondered what kind of fool would let her go. "College sweetheart?"

"Mid-Med-School crisis. Seemed like a good idea at the time. Lasted less than a year. Changed my last name but not much else." She ran her finger around the rim of her tapioca bowl, but whatever emotions she was feeling, she shook off. "And, you? Hometown?"

My smile dissipated. "Corvallis for now. Lived west of the Cascades for the last thirteen years. Can't see myself ever going back to Richland."

Her face deflated. "My sister lived there for a while until..." She batted the last of her peas around her plate. "Right, bad memories. She went missing a while ago."

A ping reverberated in my head, that moment when you know the universe has taken over, that nothing you can do will stop what's coming. Mary's hand in mine, her eyes penetrating my soul, and then, "Nice to meet you," she'd said before sliding under the covers. Before I stroked her cheek, like I still did in my dreams. How could I not have seen it? Ellen looked like her, and even my mother had noticed.

I pressed my fingers into the table, uncertain how to proceed. When I garnered the courage to make eye contact again, Ellen's face held a realization of her own.

"Hinson." She said, repeating the name she had surely seen on my chart. "My sister lived next door to the Hinsons. Mrs. Hinson taught Mary how to can."

"You met my mother, Helen. After my ablative treatment." I waited, fearful of what a big sister might have told a little one.

"My sister spoke of her kindness often."

A silence enveloped us, full of things to say or not say, like someone had tossed a fishing net over our table, locking us in. Fishing. The grandmother.

"Your mother, does she live outside Chinook?" I asked, knowing the answer and finally understanding why Harry had thrust me and Ben together.

Ellen nodded but said nothing. She must have had her own net full of revelations to sort.

"Ben, he's your nephew," I said, puzzled over why his sister looked so much younger. Must have been her size. Fraternal twins can be quite different, and I hadn't seen them since they were toddlers. "And, his twin, your niece."

Ellen's head jerked. "You knew Lucy?"

Confused by her use of past tense, I said, "Ran into them at the pier in Baker Bay."

"When they were little?" She toyed with her tapioca, sadness flooding her face.

"No, I..." Whatever reply I was going to give lodged in my throat, as if any answer would be the wrong one.

The shake of her head told me before she said it. "You know Lucy died, right?"

•   •   •

In science, if your baseline is assumptive, on any level, then the rest of your assumptions can shift like sand. A sandbox of assumptions buried me now.

Snippets of my mother and her early-on involvement with Mary's twins, born while I was an undergrad, ran through my mind's movie reel. I'd only seen them once, maybe twice, the last time when my father had died. My mother must have lost touch when Mary went missing, because I didn't remember her talking much about the twins after that. That made little sense to me, but not much about this did. The Lucy I thought

I'd seen was a vivid anomaly. Had I made her up because I'd wanted to see something outside myself, assumed she existed, ignoring additional data buried somewhere in my memory banks?

Harry and I fought the wind to the end of the pier, the southwest incoming storm whipping white across the ocean. Fishermen unwilling to fight the bluster had left a couple of rickety stools by the railing unoccupied. I anchored my foot on one and leaned over the rail. A seagull plummeted into the waves a few yards away, but flapped back into the sky, beak empty.

"She was eight I think." Harry began. "Her grandmother brought her in, saying she was finally hungry, and wanted crab."

"She was in between treatments," I asked, trying to imagine how an eight-year-old could live through the barbarous cancer regimens of the fifties. Had she wanted to show me? Wanted me to see if she could do it, so could I?

Harry shook his head. "The things we did to those children."

His statement was full of guilt that I was only just beginning to understand. A litany of horror that encompassed so many more victims than my father. The whitecaps danced higher, matching my froth of anger at the brutality of what Lucy had suffered in the name of science.

"Still," was all I could muster, seeing the faces of children in Tall's waiting room.

"She never held hands, except with Ben. Not since she'd been a toddler and was forced to when she crossed the street. She reminded me so much of Mary, despite the red hair. Just being in Lucy's presence made me believe." Harry choked up. "That Mary is still alive, I mean."

Harry swallowed and continued. "Anyway, we were standing here, and Lucy linked her hand to mine. There was a school of dolphins, not too far off the pier, they were jumping in pairs, like they'd been trained in a circus. You could almost see the smiles on their faces. Lucy pointed at them, saying, 'See Harry. There's no pain in the sea, only joy.'"

"And I," Harry swiped at his cheeks and coughed, covering up a sob. "I squeezed her hand and said, 'Yes, today, only joy.' Maybe if I hadn't agreed..." Harry's voice trailed off in the wind. He scanned the ocean, eyes searching. He pointed to the north. "See. Dolphins."

He said it as if they had her. Holding her close, caring for her, not letting her be afraid. Maybe they did. I hoped so. The salt-worn planks rough against my touch, I put my back to the sea, the dolphin's exuberance suddenly unbearable.

Harry sank onto the other stool as if his body weight was suddenly too much. "I said her crab would be ready and we should go in. And she said she wanted to watch for whales. I don't know why I didn't stay with her. Maybe I was afraid the pot would boil over. I can't remember why. Just that I told her to come inside in five minutes. Said she should button her coat. It was a cold June, but she didn't, too busy smiling out to sea."

I swallowed. "That's the jacket Ben carries?"

Harry didn't look at me. "Caught on a peg, otherwise it would've blown away with her."

Blown away was one way to look at it. But according to Ellen, a delivery man at the far end of the pier had glimpsed a small child perched like a seagull on the rail searching the waves for food. The man hadn't thought a thing about it. Kids climbed up on the rails all the time. Harry had checked on the crab, and he and Mrs. Peters chatted about the weather. When she came out to bring Lucy in, the child was gone.

"Mrs. Peters thought Lucy was playing hide and seek. We scouted the tool shed and looked under some tarps and behind some barrels, before realizing she had to be in the sea."

"They searched?" The undertow would have made fast work of a lithe figure.

"Never found a thing." Harry studied the planks beneath him. "Odd, don't you think? Ben brings clothes for her when he looks for her, but I think she still has every stitch on."

She does. I hugged the thought to my chest. A distant freighter blasted its horn, a long, low mournful moan signaling its departure into the open ocean. An ocean that, despite its vastness, could not swallow Lucy's heart, otherwise how could she ever have come to me?

Chapter Twelve/Mary

July 1948

The flood left thousands homeless but alive, but many not. Every day after, I woke in the rubble of my forgetfulness, only to revel in the delight that I experienced when I imagined a child born of Luke, a good soul filled with truth and honesty. But the other things that might be inside my baby lit up my fears. Every report I typed—summaries of mishaps, tallies of false starts—revved my dreams of running away to a speed that I could not maintain within the mousetrap of our A-house. A house I felt lucky to have, based on the devastation up and down the Columbia.

At the first sign of morning sickness, thankfully at the office, not at home, the escape fantasies shattered along with the coffee mug I dropped on my way to the restroom.

When I returned, Harry viewed me like a specimen, already surmising my truth. "Mary, would you be...?"

"Yes." Plain as that, but not so plain was how to finagle the rest.

I had to make sure Matt had no reason to suspect anyone else was the father other than him. His constant accusations regarding my supposed flirting had subsided a bit since the flood and I suspected that more might have happened that night besides Luke and me. Not that the carnal side of me cared, only the chemist side held a slight concern about disease. With my diaphragm in place, I invited Matt to maul me, provoking him. The only way I could protect the child I wanted. My morning sickness allowed me to purge the evil of him after the fact.

By mid-August, my condition and the secret work on river water—
not that Harry let me anywhere near the river once he realized I was
pregnant—had exhausted me to the point of breaking, which was what
Harry suggested I do.

"Take a break," Harry advised. "Don't you have parents in Idaho?"

"Matt refuses to visit them."

"Isn't that the point?" Harry turned back to his desk, and I studied
my calendar.

•   •   •

My father's condition had worsened, and Matt would rather brave the
termination winds in Richland than spend two weeks with my parents,
so off I went to Idaho alone.

The minute my mother saw me, she knew. "How far along?"

"Almost three months."

"You're sure?"

We both knew what she meant, but no one said that word out loud.
The doctor in Boise who helped with that sort of thing lived only two
blocks over, and the money Matt had given me for my parents' mortgage
would more than cover it. While sparing her the gruesome details, I'd
admitted to my mother a while back that my relationship with Matt was
not a happy one.

"It's not how you think, Mother. I want this baby."

She put her hands on my shoulders, holding me in place as the foyer
clock chimed the hour. "Maybe I should live closer."

"But not too close to The Area." The unsafe part I didn't say out
loud either.

"I miss the ocean." My mother had been raised on the Washington
coast.

"How would Dad feel about a move?"

My mother stroked my hair and kissed my cheek like she used to
when I was little. "I don't think that will be an issue." Our eyes locked.

"Your sister's applying for medical schools already, hard to believe we'll have a doctor in the family." The too-late-of-it went unspoken.

Wincing at my lost dreams, regret rising from my toes about being so far away from my father for so long, I grasped for words that eluded me. What to say in this moment I had known would come? "Where is he?"

"Out back. Can't get enough of those Blue jays and their birdfeeder antics."

The man of giant bear hugs had morphed into a slumped, shriveled torso. The man who had tossed me up in the air with joy, a joy I hoped to know soon, turned toward me, struggling to right himself in his rocker. The smile that had warmed up any room lopsided.

I would not have to stay with Matt much longer.

•   •   •

The filter system in the Sears catalog might have seemed like overkill to some, but I had a baby to protect. The carbon filter rids the water of chlorine, but it could trap other things too. Things I didn't want my baby to consume. With little hope that Matt would agree, I plunged ahead, an expectant mother full of expectations. I laid the catalog open on the kitchen table, anxious to get his approval. I'd need his signature for the money order. Matt's favorite chicken and rice dish was in the oven when he trudged up the steps.

"Drink?" I said, as perky as I could muster, wiping my hands on my apron. Matt gave me one of those looks, and I wondered what I would have to endure to get the water filter.

Extracting an ice tray from the freezer, I sidestepped him and worked the metal lever to loosen the ice. I poured us both a bourbon, handed him his drink, and held up my glass. "I have some news."

Matt raised an eyebrow and took a swig of his bourbon. "Well?"

"I'm pregnant." I exhaled, hoping he wouldn't notice I hadn't given him any ownership of my condition. Pretending the baby was his was not as difficult as saying it.

"When?" Matt's face proved unreadable as if he didn't know what he felt.

"Prolly early March." I forced a smile, trying to gauge if he was doing the math.

He moved to the table and smoothed his hand across the open catalog. "What's this?"

"With the baby, well in my condition, the doctors suggested a drinking water filter."

Matt sipped his bourbon. "Did we become royalty, and I missed it?"

Shrugging, I turned back to the salad I was prepping. "Filters have become relatively affordable." I split a tomato in half, feigning nonchalance. "It protects all of us."

"From what?" Matt's laugh consumed the entire kitchen. "Did you think we were planning to drop a bomb on Richland?"

The threat in the laugh made me tremble, but I pushed on. "I think we both know there are other threats than just the bomb itself."

He drained his bourbon and slammed the glass down on the table. "Be very careful what you say next, Mary. The windows are open."

"The windows are always open, but I can't filter the wind, only the drinking water."

"Precisely, and while your work with the inimitable Dr. Griffin may have revealed much, I remind you that all such information is classified." Matt's face had gone cold. "You're not immune to prosecution."

My chest caught, draining any resistance. He would throw me on the tracks before he would let me risk his standing, marriage be damned. No one could protect me, and worse, any objection I might make would be a trigger. I sank into a chair opposite him.

"Look, it's a small thing," I said, lowering my eyes. "The filter can protect against chlorine, iodine..." My voice trailed off, thinking of the thousands of curies of iodine that had been released since we moved here. I risked raising my eyes to meet his and when I did, there was something new in them.

"Your parents know about the baby?"

"Mother guessed. I went to the doctor in Moscow to verify."

"But it's early yet, right?"

The question sent a clear message. The baby made me more of a target. I took a step back. My mind spun, trying to work out the right defense to what he might suggest. "Almost three months, and the doctor said everything was as it should be." I pasted on a smile. "Helen Hinson guessed this afternoon, said I glowed."

Matt leaned against the sink, and I wondered if he was calculating what would seem natural and what would not. I crossed my arms over my chest, guarded, waiting.

"When's dinner going to be ready?"

"About thirty minutes."

He brushed past me. "I've got an errand to run." And off he went, making me surer than ever that he had another woman, since the night of the flood, maybe before, and whoever she was, she lived nearby.

•   •   •

Matt insisted I get a confirmation at Kadlec, the company hospital. I did not trust the doctors there, but it wasn't likely they could do anything to my baby without me knowing. The family clinic should have had a standing-room-only sign. A mother nudged a young boy in an arm cast to get up. I slid into his seat with a smile of thanks and scanned the room.

Two older men with nasty rashes on their faces had their heads down into the folds of magazines, which made their red faces even more suspicious. A boy who must have been college age, hunched in a corner looking at no one, making me suspect he had an embarrassing condition. A baby carriage at the end of the chair row held a mound of pink. I put my hand to my abdomen, hoping I'd need blue.

The nurse stuck her head through the door and called in the rash twins, but no one took their chairs. That was the thing about Richland, you said nothing, pretended you saw nothing, but nothing was everywhere. No one was going to sit in the chairs of folks that had that kind of rash. Whenever my guilt pricked, holding back the truth from

Luke, not to mention Helen, I stomped it back down, focusing instead on the chance to raise a kind man, like Ralph Hinson and my father.

The nurse popped back out. "Mary Boone?"

Everyone gaped, likely stunned that I had rocketed to the top of the list. Matt's position in the Hanford hierarchy gave me some perks, like setting appointments at the walk-in clinic. I followed her down the hallway.

The small, stark room held little in the way of creature comforts. The nurse handed me a gown and exited. I half-sat on the exam table peeling off my layers, of which there were few. Late August sun permeated the room, threatening to turn it into a sauna. I slipped into the gown and began tying the back ties.

A doctor knocked and entered without waiting for a response. "Mary Boone?"

People said my name with a question mark as if hoping for more, a chance for an autograph of a descendant of Daniel. Sorry to disappoint, I thought. "Yes."

"You are requesting confirmation of pregnancy?"

"And an estimate of how far along I am, if possible."

The doctor flipped to a second page on the chart. "When was your last cycle?"

"Early June." I kept my voice steady in the lie. Two weeks should not matter at all in the grand scheme of things and, in my case, it was an essential distinction.

"Well then, you do the math." He did not say this with a smile. Bedside manners must not have been covered at medical school. "We'll send a urine sample off for the frog test."

The thought that my urine might also be tested for radiation occurred, but I didn't ask. "Not even sure that's necessary, since I'm tossing every morning like clockwork."

The doctor managed a half-smile and motioned for me to lie back. The cold vinyl of the exam table sent a chill through me, making my nipples stiffen.

The doctor put his stethoscope to my chest, not ignoring my perky breasts, but not visibly reacting either. After a beat or two, he moved the ring of cold to my belly.

"Can you hear anything?" I said, eager to know my baby was in there.

"Not yet, but that's pretty common. Another month or so, and I'm sure we will." He pointed to a small jar on the white desk. "Take that down the hall to the lavatory. The nurse will be back to collect it."

And off he went, no congratulations in order yet, I supposed, as I trundled down the hall to do my business.

The nurse met me back in the room and helped me zip up my dress, saying, "Your diet is critical to your baby, you know."

Something in her tone made me hesitant. Trying to maintain a neutral look, I said, "Any specific recommendations?"

The nurse turned her back to me and busied herself arranging something in the shelving. "B vitamins, and citrus, from California preferably, the best Vitamin C, but I think milk is overrated." When she turned to face me, she had a smile pasted on her face. "Canned foods are so much easier to prepare. No use standing at a hot stove if you don't need to. You won't believe how your ankles will swell in your last trimester."

She ushered me out the door and down the hall. I exited, her words rolling over in my mind. A Kadlec nurse had just told me not to eat locally.

•   •   •

Harry started the day by dropping a plethora of data on my desk, an old folder with a fresh label in Harry's handwriting that read: Summaries: Bioassays. The studies on the effect of radioactive effluent on fish, flora, and other fauna, most of which had spawned near the plant, reflected Lou's findings, but these were over three years old. Research conducted in multiple venues of the Manhattan Project.

"How did you get this?" I asked.

Harry winked. "Still have a pal or two in the medical division." Which meant he had circumvented Jackson.

After a brief scan, I shook my head. "The margin notes show that Campbell, DuPont's early-on project manager, was worried about the emissions even during stable weather."

Harry's frown held more than disgust. A fierceness lit his eyes. "The higher-ups weighed battlefield casualties against possible nuclear side effects, and prioritized what they thought would save lives."

I sorted through the folder stamped "Classified," skimming the highlights. "So, as early as '44 they believed the releases were problematic?"

"In fairness, Campbell was probably so distracted by his inability to finish the build, not to mention dealing with impossible turnovers in staffing, that he simply embraced the notion that the Columbia River would just carry it all away." Harry chuckled. "He wasn't entirely wrong. We just haven't found it in the ocean yet."

"And to reroute the effluent discharge piping would mean major delays?"

"There was a war to win, remember? And it appears we are still dancing with that devil."

Harry plucked out a study by a small group of geneticists in Chicago and handed me a document entitled: Fish Studies. "Remember the Dickinson study? He and his assistant, Allen, weren't the only ones to see the effects." Harry handed me the charts. "The Chicago data tags with our lab's uptick in production in July and August of 1945."

My hand flipped through the data, my eyes darting left to right, horror filling my already crowded belly. "So when Allen used river water to dilute the effluent, he had no way of knowing the waste emissions into the river had quadrupled with the increase in production."

Harry nodded, his face sagging. "No one was focused on anything but meeting the goal and ending the war. And we did it, thank God. But now..."

I kept reading, my stomach warning of upheaval to come, but it had nothing to do with the baby. "Berkeley, Chicago, Oak Ridge, they all had a study that tagged with everyone else's, but no one person put it together."

"Damn government secrecy."

The folder had proof of the devastating effects of radiation exposure, not just if you fished the river. Downdrafts thwarted the supposed too-high-to-be-a-danger releases. Pockets in the atmosphere pulled the radiation downward, and such concentrations of emissions blanketed populated areas, farmlands, and desert plains. The night of the flood there had been sirens galore for the rising water, but in all the months of Hanford production, not one warning had been given about the releases from the stacks. Nights that I believed were full of promise had also been filled with poison. My insides felt like someone was scraping a razor through me, shaving away any joy or hope, but I had to hear Harry say it out loud.

"If it lodges in our bodies," I said. "Like the fish, there might be a lasting—"

A noise in the outer office startled us both. I pushed the papers back into the folder and smoothed my hand across it, waiting for someone to enter, but no one did. A full minute passed before I whispered, "So, it's out there now, penetrating on a mass scale, not just here?"

Harry dragged his hands down his cheeks, his voice low in its verdict. "Unstoppable evolution, in the gene pool." We both went silent wondering if someone was outside listening.

"Victory at the risk of all mankind?"

Harry grimaced. "It's a catch-all folder, they keep adding to it, but never really look at it." He shook his head. "Hard to believe that no one puts it together."

"These are originals," I whispered, knowing I couldn't do anything other than copy lab names and dates. Making photocopies of the charts was too risky. "How long do I have to type summaries?"

Harry nodded. "An hour, maybe two. I have to get it back before it's missed."

The phone shrilled like a warning siren. "Mary Boone," I said in answer.

A Kadlec staffer intoned, "Congratulations. You're pregnant."

The smile that should have come, didn't. "Yes." Harry's file had snuffed out any joy.

The staffer took no issue with my less-than-enthusiastic reaction. "The doctor will want to see you again in October."

I dropped the receiver back in the cradle and tapped the folder. "The new label, you put it on because want someone to notice the file?" Harry gave the slightest nod. My breathing spiraled, my chest tightening. "How can I bring a baby into this?"

Chapter Thirteen/Luke

May 1964

My lab mate Roy agreed to accompany me to The Area, despite my warnings. With nine reactors pumping out plutonium day and night, releases had multiplied tenfold since I'd been a teenager. Hanford scientists had been collecting dirt samples again from farms, according to Wang, as well as taking bioassays of livestock and wild game. His pal at the Pasco slaughterhouse said government inspectors were collecting necks, which meant thyroids, my newly acquired expertise.

We snaked up the long drive to Hanford, the road bordered by barbed wire and other equally prickly barriers. A large sign loomed at the gate, anchored by iron stakes, ominous in its irony: 'Welcome to Hanford, A U. S. Atomic Energy Commission Site,' as if this place or the AEC welcomed outsiders. I pulled up to the security gate, and two armed guards took positions in front of the car. Two others appeared at our doors, inviting us to step out. Roy shot me a look.

Grim-faced, I just nodded. "Morning officers," I said, with unfelt deference.

"Badges, please."

I handed over the passes and the letter Dr. Goodman, our contact, had mailed the week prior. His older brother, a lifelong Hanford man, had played the clarinet in a band that I'd danced to as a teenager. Dr. Goodman, a former colleague of Professor Miller, had worked in The Area in the early 50s, left, and boomeranged back twice. Something I couldn't understand. The guard read through both pages of the letter from Goodman and handed them back. "Pop the trunk for me."

I keyed it open while another guard rustled through the back seat and under the front ones. Satisfied, at least for now, the officer in charge held open my door. "Stick to the designated roads." The guards stepped away from the front of our car gate, the pole sprung up, and Roy let out a low whistle as we eased forward.

"Yeah," I said. "Designed to intimidate."

Puddles from last night's rainstorm—holding who knew what—dotted the land beyond the road. A few dozers and tractors lined a rectangular perimeter, generating a flurry of human activity. If more holding ponds were in the works, that did not bode well for anyone. Two patrol cars slowed, going in the opposite direction, the drivers ogling us as they passed. On the other side of the barbed wire, the plutonium finishing plant came into view, and I fought the reflex to stop inhaling. My gaze followed the clouds moving eastward over the building, and a shudder wracked me.

Roy shot me a sideways glance. "You okay?"

"Residual side effects," I said, not enumerating the other source from which they arose. My father's accident had been at the finishing plant.

We pulled into the 200-Area parking lot, situated well beyond a small building that housed Goodman's lab. Two larger ones on either side dwarfed it, giving the impression that what happened in between was inconsequential.

Roy whispered, ogling the tops of the buildings. "Is that a guy on the roof with a gun?"

"Keep your head down and stay quiet," I said, eyeing the guard at the building entrance.

Goodman met us at the edge of the parking lot and held out his hand. "Luke. How's the fishing?" Goodman had been my father's occasional fishing buddy.

"Not without its surprises," I said. The biggest surprise was that anyone at Hanford would compare notes on research. I introduced Roy, wondering what Goodman's motivation might be.

Dr. Goodman panned the landscape, his arm extended in a pointed-finger guided tour, pausing at different buildings, all built in the past five years, describing their functions to Roy. The clouds banked in the distance, shadowing a cordoned-off area filled with waste tanks. Single shell tanks that I was certain would disintegrate in my lifetime.

"Can't go there," Dr. Goodman said, as if reading my mind. He ushered us toward the metal-sided building that served as his lab.

The place was empty of workers, the morning shift having finished the hour before. Inside the lab, a large tank occupied the back wall, a slew of whitefish and sockeye salmon languid in the water. An air hose pumped in fresh oxygen, dispersing Lawrence-Welk-like bubbles on one side of the tank.

Goodman motioned to the tank. "We've been studying the release of radionuclides into the river almost since day one."

Roy rocked back, as if the shock of how completely cavalier Goodman was about disposing of waste into the river shook him. A hand on Roy's back, I guided him to a table in the center of the room, extricated a pad and pencil from my pack, and asked, "You've been here for how long?"

Goodman shrugged. "Off and on since '54." Anticipating my line of questions, he said, "Our cooling periods have increased since the late '50s, from a couple of months to over 200 days now."

According to our research, the subsequent releases peaked in 1960, but most of that radioactivity had been diluted. "The river, floods, regular dam releases, did their thing?"

Goodman shook his head, not meeting my gaze. "Not entirely. Some worrisome levels in the fish."

Some things never changed, I thought, thinking of how long ago Walker's family had stopped eating the fish. But nobody had warned the people of Richland. "Size of the doses?"

Goodman extricated a folder, sorting its pages of data across the table. "Say I started eating five six-ounce meals of catfish, bass, or salmon per week when I came in '54." He passed us a chart. "And assuming consistent consumption up to now, that could have resulted in doses greater than 100 millirem per year."

Rem stands for roentgen equivalent man, a measure used to assess the damage to human tissue from a dose of radiation. But this measurement was based explicitly on a Caucasian male, the "typical radiation worker" in weight and height. Not the lesser mass of a woman or a child, made more or less vulnerable depending on their stage of development. Millirem is 1/1000th of a rem. Enough apparently to hang on in a liver or kidney and wreak havoc, according to the fish data before me.

Imagine a one-year-old enjoying their first solid foods downwind. What fraction of the "permissible intake" would be in that first bite, and what burden would it place on their organs?

Roy grabbed at his gut, issuing a "Holy Moly." He picked up fish and chips at least four times a week at a local Mom and Pop diner near campus.

"Relax," I said, masking my concerns with a grin. "Elmer's only serves Alaskan cod."

Goodman went on. "Of course, the doses would vary depending on the consumer."

I fingered a chart with river data. "And the water?"

Goodman glanced behind him at the closed door and lowered his voice. "That's been a problem. A repeat of the early days."

Harry had confirmed basin leaks in passing when I told him of the irradiated plankton samples. Slapdash, he'd called the early processing plants, in a non-stop push to produce. Both basins of the D and F reactors had leaked significantly, but according to Harry, the 300-Area waste pond had fed millions of gallons of active waste solution directly into the Columbia, a side-effect of the great flood of '48.

With any flood, groundwater rises, and this was a hundred-year event, unstoppable, liquefying the soil and overrunning the waste pools. Not that Harry had anything to substantiate it. Any documentation had been secreted away in a classified file long ago.

Goodman lowered his head. "The river's been too warm to cool the reactors."

I leaned in. "But the Columbia averages 68 degrees in the summer."

Goodman met my gaze. "On May first, it was averaging seventy-eight. Too hot. They had to shut down three reactors."

This meant that any effluent pumped in prior was just hanging out, stymied in one spot. A lot of it causes a temperature rise.

Goodman lowered his voice. "They've been trying to flush it."

Roy raised his eyes from a chart of data. "Who?"

"The Feds," Goodman said. "Extra releases from Coulee to chill things down at night."

Always at night, I thought. Grand Coulee's releases were regulated by the Department of the Interior, which had just signed a new treaty with our neighbors to the north. It's their water too. "Do the Canadians know?"

"Probably not." Goodman plucked a paper off his desktop, recent temperature readings on the river. "But it appears to have solved the problem. They're planning on restarting the D reactor in the next few days."

"But won't it just heat up all over again?"

Goodman shrugged. "There's a bit of a double-down mentality around here."

"Do you have water quality data?" Roy asked. Higher temperatures slow a river down, more junk accumulates, creating a quagmire of problems: oxygen levels decrease, pathogens and invasive species increase, along with the concentrations of pollutants.

Goodman shook his head. "But I wouldn't recommend drinking the tap water in Pasco. Another study is underway. Out next year."

"Tell that to Wang's corn crop," I mumbled, thinking of the randomness of it all. Targets not chosen strategically, just wherever the wind blew and the river ran.

Roy separated another folder from the pile and shot me a sideways glance. "Livestock bioassays?"

I plucked the folder from Roy's hand and studied the worn label.

The ink had faded, and the handwriting was bad, but I'd paid enough tabs at the crab shack to recognize the scrawl: Harry's. Goodman's face took on a dour look. As if we had found something he hadn't meant for us to see, but something made me think he had.

Goodman cleared his throat, but the lie was in it. "Not sure I've seen that one. Must have been grouped with the files I had my assistant pull for you."

Roy paged through the folder. Research data had been collected from multiple labs across the U.S. between September 1943 and March 1950, the month before Harry had been summarily fired. Harry had run the technical lab, far away from the scientists monitoring the flora and fauna of The Area, and Harry's name was nowhere in the documentation. Why had he been the one to label it?

Roy extracted a chart and pointed to a spike in the data the second week of December 1949, a spike far higher than Goodman's 1960 reading. Roy traced his finger across the readings done for November and December 1949.

"No unusual radiation levels in any livestock or fish during November or on December first. Then, all hell breaks loose the morning of December 4th."

I scanned the chart encompassing January 1950 through March of the same year, consistent bad news, showing levels of radiation in livestock over 1000 times the norm that had been established in the Spring of 1949.

"There's a break in the chart, nothing charted from December 3rd until December 7th. Where did everybody go?" I shook my head at the chart. "Did they all take a few days off to hang the Christmas lights on Main Street?"

Goodman snatched up the document and the coffee-stained folder, stuffing the chart inside. He clamped it under his arm, revealing the stamp on the backside of the folder: Classified.

Aware that our presence there had been an informal agreement between Miller and Goodman, I searched for the right words to defuse the situation. "Let's get back to the present, shall we?"

Roy's mouth hung agape, but Goodman's glare softened. He pulled out a file with wildlife data, showing more bad news, spikes that made ours pale in comparison. "I was thinking this might help with your research. Of course, we'd like a chance to review it. Tag to our data." His smile was almost benevolent.

We spent another half hour making notes before gathering our things. Goodman ushered us to the door. "Safe drive back," he said, sounding just like my father. "Say hello to Miller for me."

"Thanks for your time sir, and we greatly appreciate the share," I said.

Roy shook Goodman's hand and stepped outside.

I extended my hand, but Goodman put his hand on my shoulder, his eyes pinning me in place. "Did you know your father and I were fishing buddies when we were a lot younger?"

"He spoke highly of your work."

Goodman's grip tightened on my shoulder. "Your dad always had the best bait. Said it was the only way to catch the bigger fish. The ones with so much history in the river, that they thought they couldn't be caught." His hand dug in deeper. "But, he caught 'em."

What was he telling me? "Yes, sir," I said, my shoulder aching under his grip.

Goodman released me. "You remind me of him." He stared off into the sunshine. Dust swirls danced across the barren terrain like miniature cyclones, the first of the summer wind storms not far behind. A hawk drifted across the horizon, catching a downdraft.

A thunk signaled Roy had gotten into the car, but I didn't walk away, waiting for what I didn't know. I just knew Goodman had something more to say.

And he did. "Your father always said accidents could be avoided." Goodman paused. The hawk circled, homing in on a target. "He was right. Nothing here was an accident, not really."

The hawk dove. A jackrabbit scampered about a hundred feet from us. The hawk swooped in, yanked it up in its talons, and sped away, up and over the reactor building. Goodman stepped back inside and closed the door between us. The hawk spiked out of sight. A lock clicked on the other side of the lab door.

Goodman had wanted us to see that folder. The question was, why?

•   •   •

Dark descended as I pulled into the cabin drive. The boy was sitting on the porch, poster boards by his side. He did not look happy. Before I could exit the car, he was on me.

"Where ya been, mister?" His voice shrill, his anger forcing a soprano that proved he wasn't a man yet. Maybe neither of us were.

"A research trip came up last minute," I said, trying to keep my tone even, knowing it wouldn't work. The boy wanted a fight, just like I had at his age. A simmering anger at the injustices of my teenage world, but mainly angry at Jimmy Boone, the high school bully. I couldn't beat him, so I kept my rage pent up. Never let it out, except to Mary. She was the only one who had heard my frustrations, made no judgments, and just listened because, in the end, that's what we all needed and why I needed her still.

"So, you just forgot we had a date to work on my project?" Ben spit through his teeth into the bramble. "I shoulda known I couldn't count on you."

The number of people counting on me put me on tilt: my mother, Harry, Roy, Miller, Goodman, and now this boy. My inability to swing up my end of the seesaw, with all of them weighing down the other side, clouded my response. I barked. "Look, if you're looking for someone to do the work for you, that's not me."

The boy delivered a swift kick to the gravel at our feet before leaping back onto the porch. "You're a jerk, just like my father." He snatched up his poster boards and darted past me, but not before his tears started.

My arm shot out to stop him, but I wasn't quick enough. My legs weakened. I dropped to the ground, following the boy's back down the drive with bleary eyes.

After Ellen's reveal, I'd convinced myself that Harry had put Ben and me together because of our similar loss. Ben's sister, my father, but now, finger-dozing the sandy soil of the drive, I thought maybe Harry had more reasons. The heavier dirt fell to the bottom, sifted by gravity. Sandy peaks can't last very long, wind and rain taking them down with a storm or two, just like the radiation spike in the livestock chart, dissipating in only three months. But elements from whatever had happened in December of 1949 would still be in their first half-life.

Roy and I would have to do some digging, literally, around The Area. The only way to have true comparisons to our bay data.

I'd fix it with the boy later, maybe even try to make sense of what I now knew to be the ghost of Lucy. His project wasn't due till mid-June, after all. A stir in the brush made me look up, hoping for red, but it was only a squirrel. The truth has a way of piling on.

• • •

Walker, who lived farther north, met us at the bend in the road near Toledo. Roy shot him a triumphant grin, having already claimed shotgun. Walker climbed into the back seat. We'd determined that reservation land would be the least disturbed since 1950, and if there was any clear evidence to be had, it would be there. Only tribal members were allowed on the Yakima Reservation, and Walker was our get-in-free card, warranting the longer route on Highway 12.

The Impala groaned at the change in altitude, and I downshifted, following the upward grade to the top of the rise before shifting into third. Halfway through the mountain pass, a smattering of buildings were tucked inside in a carve-out, including an outdoor gear shop, a gas station, and a café.

Roy pointed at the café. "That place serves a life-changing peach cobbler."

"We'll stop on the way back," I said, taking in the Packwood Pass sign. A nagging sense told me I knew something about this place, and it wasn't the pie.

Walker filled the drive with anecdotes of his boyhood summers on the reservation, a wasteland of bare plains abutting The Area, a stone's throw from Richland's riches. Yakima land flowed west, encompassing a portion of one of the largest forests in the U.S.

Walker launched into a story about his first encounter with a rattlesnake. "I was three, I think. Reached out to pet it." Walker gut-laughed. "Grandfather decapitated the snake before it could strike." Walker spread his arms across the back seat, a grin still on his face. "Anyway, the best advice for here, or anywhere, watch where you're walking."

An involuntary shiver ran through me, thinking of my father's boots and what he and others must have tracked home.

A dirt road led to the main road through the reservation. Flanking it was a small village. Beyond lay streams, rivers, foothills, and canyons. Just over a million acres, a pittance compared to the ten million the Confederated tribes used to roam.

Walker's other ancestors, The Wanapum, never signed a treaty and had lived along the Columbia near White Bluffs until 1943 when the army forced them out, driving them north to Priest Rapids. Unlike the Yakima, they never fought a battle, despite the white man's constant interference. The River People, as they were known, protected prehistoric archaeological sites and their elder's graves long before any laws did. Traveling in dugout canoes, the original river patrol intermingled with both the Yakima and the Sinkiuse-Columbia tribes. Walker's immediate family included all three: Wanapum mother, Sinkiuse father, and Yakima grandfather.

Walker directed me to park in front of a small, clapboard structure. The poles of a teepee poked out behind its shed roof. To the right of the front door, a circle of stones corralled a fire pit surrounded by assorted chairs in various states of disrepair. An erect 80-something man emerged from the house.

Walker moved to greet him. "*Áay,* Grandfather."

The older man embraced his grandson before turning toward us. "The other scientists?"

A blush rose on my cheeks at the undertone of respect the old man's voice held. Not sure we had earned it, Roy and I offered our hands, introducing ourselves.

"John Walker," he said and motioned to the ragtag group of seats.

The chair I chose had a slight tilt to it, perfect, I thought, but I said, "Sir, we're researching the disposal of waste from Hanford. The side-effects in all surrounding areas."

The old man looked across the terrain, speaking in a low voice. "Hanford does not have side effects. It has a direct effect on all life. Our lives are not," his face took on a pained look. "An aside."

Dually chastised, I grappled for the right thing to say next. "Yes, sir. We want to..." I hesitated, still uncertain of my words. "We want to prove that the government knowingly put your people in danger."

"You believe there is someone of power in your country who doesn't already know that?" The old man folded his arms across his chest. "From the very beginning, we have suffered."

Walker waited for a nod from his grandfather before speaking. "The same year Hanford began production, a young Klickitat maid swam in the *Chiwana*, the big river. When she came out of the river, she had an angry rash on her belly. By nightfall, it had spread to her back, burning her skin. Chronically ill ever since."

"We net fish with no fins, no eyes." The old man looked across the terrain as if seeing the big river that you couldn't see from where we sat.

Taking a cue from Walker, I made sure his grandfather had finished before speaking. "Yes, sir. We've been examining animals and fish, finding radioactive elements. We'd like to sample the water and soil on the reservation. Prove the radiation has traveled here too."

Roy added, "Sir, for much of your land, here and near the river, there is no public data. No proof of the harmful practices. We want to change that."

The old man rose, holding Roy in his gaze before his eyes moved to mine. "Do your work, but don't trust in their ability to see. They have proven blind since they first came." He turned to his grandson. "Like Tommy John. Why do they let that guy pitch?"

The reference to Cleveland's worst pitcher this season threw me off, but Walker laughed. "At least they don't let him bat very often."

The old man moved inside the house.

The incongruity of it all got the better of me. "He's a baseball fan?"

"A priest at the resident school was a baseball fan. He used to let my grandfather and some other boys listen on the radio."

In the last fifty years, over sixty-thousand Indian children had been forcibly taken from their families and forced into government-run residential schools, disallowed from using their native language, beaten if they did, and stripped of anything that represented their native culture. The incongruous image of boys gathered around a radio to listen to the great American pastime rankled.

Walker stood, a half-smile competing with the grimace still on his face. "First tribal member in baseball played for Cleveland Naps. They renamed the team when Nap Lajoie's contract was sold, an insult to all of us." A baseball broadcast flowed out an open window of the small house. "But boyhood loyalties, hard to break." Walker looked at me and Roy. "Okay, watch where you step."

●   ●   ●

After two hours of sampling streams and soil, we trudged back to the village and piled our work into the trunk of the car. The sun had shifted to the backside of afternoon, making me antsy to get on the road. "Should we say goodbye?"

"No need." Walker slid back into the rear seat.

Roy sat shotgun, scanning a folder of info he'd brought along from another lab in Portland that exchanged data with our college program. He extracted the cover document. "Did you know that they've been sampling the Willamette River basin for chemicals? They have data about the quality of drinking water since 1953."

The Willamette feeds the Columbia. "Nope, but a backup baseline could be useful," I mused, leaning into a curve and fiddling with the dial. Roy Orbison spit out the first verse of "Pretty Woman" before the radio sputtered, breaking up as I veered onto the roadway that led through the pass.

"This is interesting." Roy looked up from the file. "UW researchers have opened a lab in Tacoma. Same thing. Monitoring drinking water sources specifically for phosphorus." Roy continued, "Maybe we share our water quality data from the Rez. Get them to include it in their report to the State?"

Walker sat up in the back. "They could analyze the plankton and the sediment from the bay and validate those results as well."

"Hate to admit it, but the biologist might have something there," Roy said with a snort.

I grinned at the rivalry that existed between my two pals. Roy convinced his work on pesticides in plants was far more important than Walker's work trying to convince the Department of Transportation that the removal of too many trees on a hillside would make any highway they were building subject to rockslides.

Walker shot Roy a look. "An independent lab's blessing would give your work some credibility."

Roy snorted. "You saying I've got no credibility?"

"Yep. Give me part of that," Walker grinned at the rise he'd gotten out of Roy.

Roy split the file, tossing half over the seatback to Walker, who said, "Luke, turn off that radio. It's nothing but static."

As commanded, I concentrated on the road in silence. Pine tree forests took over one side, craggy cliffs hugged the other. Flashes of sunshine cut through the green, and squirrels startled when we came into view. The road was less traveled than the north-south routes, so, like the squirrels, I flinched when a car came from the opposite direction. It blew by, going twice as fast, most likely a local more confident in their ability to make the turns than I.

"It's like a puzzle," I said, thinking out loud. "How to piece together enough accredited sources to make whatever we write up, about the water, the whale, the deer, publishable."

Roy whistled. "Ambitious, my friend, but aren't the scientists that regularly get pages in journals like *Nature* and the *American Journal of Science*, a pretty small club?"

Walker piled on. "Not to mention, I thought a well-crafted thesis is—"

The logging truck shot around the bend, nearly half over the centerline, cutting Walker off mid-sentence. I jerked to the shoulder of the road, stomping on the brakes to avoid the cliff, throwing Roy and Walker into their passenger doors. The car rocked to a halt.

"Holy shit." Roy rubbed his shoulder before rolling down the window, gulping in air.

Walker caught my eye in the rearview. "You okay?"

My hands held the wheel in a death grip. "That guy came out of nowhere."

Walker, who made this trip more than I, said, "Those loggers are lethal." He leaned back in his seat, his eyes reflecting the almost of it before pointing to the sign perched on the cliff just beyond us. "Anyone else ready for pie?"

After looking twice in the mirror and over both shoulders, I eased back onto the road and crept the last half-mile to the café. We slid into a booth, and Roy flipped the vinyl-covered pages of the wall-mounted jukebox. An affable waitress brought coffee and water, noted our orders, and moved off to the kitchen.

Roy slid a coin in the machine, and a big band filled the booth. "Don't you just love Benny Goodman?"

My palms were still moist from panic. I wiped them down my trousers, hoping no one saw, and flipped open my menu. "My dad's favorite, he—" The Packwood Café logo at the top of the menu shrank the space between young adult-me and now-me.

A reactor does not have an on-off switch. In layman's terms, place the right elements in proximity of one another, and a reaction is triggered. Uranium naturally throws off neutrons, and once released, they hit other atoms that split another and another, the chain reaction. You can moderate the reaction with water or stop it altogether by inserting the control rods, but man doesn't start it, nature does, releasing an inordinate amount of heat and radiation.

The Packwood Café, my mother had said. I'd put it so far back in my mind that the thought of where we were, Packwood Pass, the last place Mary had been seen, hadn't registered until now. I dropped my menu and fumbled for my coffee cup, my hands shaking and my face heating.

"You okay?" Walker's face held a concern, privy to many a story of my Dad.

"Be right back." I staggered to the restroom and slammed the door behind me.

The faucet in the sink ran ice cold. I splashed my face twice, but I couldn't will away the reliving: the flood, the stars, the feel of Mary's skin on mine. My face stinging, I gripped the sink, straightened and there she was. Her face beside mine in the mirror. At first, I couldn't face her, letting a moment crawl by, not wanting to leave her side. But then I pivoted to the faded flier taped to the back of the bathroom door. Her smile froze me in place. Just like it had the very first time I'd seen it, beaming toward me over a stack of boxes the day she and Matt had moved into the other side of our A-house.

My breathing slowed. The tape that held her up had yellowed, and the printing below her chin was drained of color. A childlike scrawl asked if anyone seeing her would please call this number. My eyes locked on hers.

A knock on the door jolted me loose. Someone tried the knob. "Hey, buddy? Coming out anytime soon?"

I brushed past the guy, mumbling, "Sorry," and moved out into the light of the café. The waitress hung over the counter delivering another order to the kitchen.

"Excuse me. That poster on the restroom door." I wasn't sure what I wanted to ask.

"Oh, yeah." The woman's eyes softened. "It's old, but I can't bear to take it down. A young boy came in, all by himself, maybe four, five years ago. His mother went missing after she was here."

"Here?" My mind wouldn't work. It couldn't have been Ben. Five years ago, he would have been only eight years old. And then it hit me, the summer Lucy died. The boy had come looking for his mother when his sister disappeared, as if they might both be found together.

"According to the cops, having lunch here was the last thing anyone saw her do. Right, Bernie?"

The guy in a chef's paper hat nodded and stopped dicing carrots. "I saw her drive away. A decade ago, my third day on the job, was coming on for the late shift." He grinned as if it were a happy memory.

My hands clutched at a leather counter stool, but it spun, and I almost hit the floor.

The waitress grabbed my arm. "You okay, mister?" She pushed me onto the stool. "You knew her?"

I didn't trust myself to do anything but nod.

"We told the cops about the guy who met her here." She raised an eyebrow. "Her husband, though they didn't seem too happy to see each other."

Bernie shook his head. "Such a weird day, thunderstorms out of nowhere, off and on that afternoon, every time I tried to grab a smoke."

The waitress shoved a glass of water toward me. "Take a swig, you look green."

More unfiltered water, why the hell not? I chugged it. "They left together?"

Bernie piped up. "Nope, just like we told the cops, they had separate cars. He took off before her. Seemed in a hurry to get away. She left a few minutes later, in the same direction. I remember wondering why they hadn't taken the same car. And then, maybe forty-five minutes later, he drove back by, headed in the opposite direction."

Outside the café's front window, the road emptied into the sky. An optical illusion that made the ledge below invisible. My mother had told me the police had questioned every business and residence along the route to Chinook and halfway to Richland, but no one had remembered Mary or the car she drove. No signs of any accident either, although any summer rainstorm could have spoiled what might have been.

After a while, her husband, Matt, had told people she'd left him. He brought the twins back to Richland, but according to my mother, that didn't last long. Not the fathering type, which I could certainly attest to, having been bullied by his son for years.

My mother never believed Mary would have left her children, despite the rumors that Matt perpetuated to the contrary. Mrs. Peters had come to Richland to claim her grandchildren a few months after Mary's disappearance. Matt had been all too happy to hand them over. The company transferred him to Tennessee a short time after that.

"You said a small boy put up the flier. Who was he?"

The waitress turned to slide an order under Bernie's stack and leaned back against the wall. "The woman's son. He'd hitched a ride here."

"Hitched? Wasn't he pretty young?"

"Yeah, about eight I think, but Mel picked him up. He makes the regular run for Kellogg's. I got Joe, another regular, to take him home." She moved behind the counter, refilling the coffee pot. "That kid had a lot of guts, but luck too. No telling what could have happened if he'd taken the wrong ride." She motioned out the window. "Those woods can cover up most anything."

I pushed up from the stool, nodded my thanks to the waitress, and trudged back to the booth. "Walker, can you drive the rest of the way?" I didn't want to miss one bit of the territory, not one detail, between here and the coast.

Chapter Fourteen/Mary

September 1948

It was the end of summer, the real end. Not some lazy, hot August day, a late September one, crisp in its promise of change. The baby had ceased having its way with my stomach, but my renewed interest in food, and lots of it, seemed out of sync with normality, even for a pregnant woman.

Jimmy, in between assignments, his blonde spike of hair cowed by the merchant marine barber, had situated himself on the couch, close enough to slap Matt's thigh with each joke Milton Berle issued. Any observer would think the father and son had missed each other, but having witnessed their relationship for years, I couldn't believe that was true.

The supper dishes done and the Boone men glued to "The Texaco Star Theater" and the comedian's debut as sole host, I pushed out the screen door to have a smoke, though the Camels didn't taste as good as they used to, and I lost interest after the first inhale.

Luke and his father rounded the end of the block, returning from the first Richland High football game of the season.

"Our Bombers won." Ralph proclaimed, taking the front porch steps slower than normal. "Too bad Luke will miss the rest of the season." Ralph's smile felt tired, like an inner exhaustion thwarted his ability to grin. Luke was leaving the next day for college.

I stubbed out my cigarette, careful not to make eye contact. "Off you go, into the big wide world. Or at least, Seattle, a wider lens than here."

I shot a smile at Ralph, afraid to look in Luke's direction, knowing what I had to do.

"Orientation on Monday." Luke stared right at me. "Classes begin Tuesday."

Ralph pushed inside, but Luke stayed, as I knew he would. Conjuring up all the words I'd practiced in my head, I stalled, shifting the ashtray on the porch ledge. Despite rehearsal, my lead-off was pathetic. "All packed?" I added a bright smile which I hoped read detached.

Luke nodded and cut right through the falseness of my smile and my crossed-arms protection. "Come with me."

His whisper was so quiet, I wasn't sure he'd said it at all, when laughter burst out from the living room, Jimmy and Matt giving me cover. Pretending that I hadn't heard Luke, I forced myself to take another drag off my Camel, cocking my head in fake nonchalance. "Jimmy's last weekend for a while, too. Off to Hawaii. God knows what trouble he'll make there."

But, Luke wouldn't let me ignore him. "Come," he repeated, firm in his insistence.

"No." I let that sit for a minute, hoping he'd take the no and leave the rest. "I can't leave now. Not with the baby coming."

"Precisely why you should leave." Luke glanced behind me. "With Jimmy gone, and me gone, you'll be alone. With him."

"I'll have your Mom and Dad." Behind the walls, but I didn't say that. "And Matt's been bragging about being a father again." Which was oddly true, but I didn't add that he'd also been absent a lot lately.

Luke jerked his head, anger flushing his cheeks. "You think I don't know?"

Finally, the part I'd rehearsed. "What exactly do you think you know?"

The whisper again. "That it's mine."

That was when I released the laugh, the one I'd used in every play I'd ever been in. The laugh that responded to any ridiculous line. The laugh that pooh-poohed the unbelievable statement. The don't-be-silly laugh that torpedoed any foolish notion and any chance of his continuing to believe. A laugh that disguised the rip in my heart.

Once his face crumbled, I knew I had him. "At the risk of being indelicate, I got my period right after the flood. This baby is Matt's." In a cruel, but necessary move, I laughed again. "You didn't think..." My voice trailed off into the applause of the live audience on the television. *Please believe me.*

Luke gave it one last shot. "You and I don't lie to one another."

But I did. I lied to everyone every day. Lied every time I covered a bruise with makeup or replied fine to a How-are-you. I smiled a lie when someone said how proud I must be of Matt's work and every time I passed out of the guard gate of The Area with a folded carbon copy of a classified document tucked into my brassiere. And now, right now, I lied to protect the soon-to-be man whom I cared for more than he might ever know.

"No, we don't," I lied, and the next day he was gone.

•   •   •

With the new year rolling in, my belly swelled to the point of no return. Folks could have rested a book on it, and don't think some didn't try. The rest of me was the skinniest I'd ever been, as if the life inside me grabbed every bit of nutrition before my tummy could claim its due. My nesting mode kicked in, and my neighbor Lois loaned us a crib, saying with her girls grown she wanted it put to good use. My job with Harry had been suspended months prior, a small relief from the daily threat in The Area. Pregnant women were barred from Hanford, not that a woman-with-child could continue to work in any workplace in America.

After running Saturday errands, I came home to find Matt, a tarp splayed on the side yard, paintbrush in hand, white paint dripping down the side of the can. I paused mid-walk, not quite believing the extraordinary tableau: Matt, in the role of a honey-do husband, anticipating the arrival as if it were his first. "I thought this small chest of drawers would be perfect for the nursery. It was just gathering dust in the basement."

"No baby blue? Thought you were hoping for a boy," I teased before I thought about what it might trigger, but Matt grinned, something indiscernible in his smile.

He dipped his brush back in the can. "Your mother called. I told her she should come visit when the baby's born. Your sister's spring break coincides with your due date. Ellen could stay with your father."

That made my head spin, and not because this baby would enter the world well before March. Who was this guy, welcoming my mother into our house, all smiles about a baby? I plopped down on the patchy grass, my parcels resting in the middle of the sidewalk. "And mother could make your favorite chicken," I said, playing along, uncertain, trepid.

Matt squee-geed his brush against the rim of the can. "You know, until your mother came along, no one ever made me a special meal." He gazed at his handiwork with what looked like tenderness before continuing. "My mother spent all her time just dodging my father's blows. When she wasn't drinking, that is."

His eyes were those of a small boy full of what I could only interpret as hope. He took a step toward me and put a hand on my shoulder. I flinched before I could help it. But Matt seemed not to notice. "Anyway, this baby, it could be a new start for us." He almost choked on "us" before saying, "Mary, I..." The rest of the words didn't come, and the remorse felt sincere, but all I could think was: people don't change, and what happened to the other gal?

•   •   •

Matt—or rather his new persona—gave me permission to fill up the newly-painted chest of drawers. The Elite clothing store on The Greenway carried a decent selection of infant clothing and other necessities. The shop door chimed as I pushed through, pulling the clerk out of her chair from behind the counter. I fingered a little girl's party dress in the window, wishing I knew whether it would be a boy or a girl.

"Hello, I'm Hetta." The fresh-faced young woman sported a helpful grin. "You look like you're about to pop." Her giggle softened the accusation.

"March, another month or so to go, I'm afraid."

Her eyes swept over me, taking in my enormous bump. "I would have guessed much sooner. You wouldn't believe how many women are due in February. Seems the flood prompted lots of action." She winked, inviting me into her joke.

A tremor slid through me. What if my baby were a bruiser? How to explain that when the baby would most likely come a month earlier than my narrative?

"Guess when the lights are out there's nothing to do but entertain yourselves." She giggled again, but, any return smile on my part was stymied by a sudden fear.

What if the baby looks just like a Hinson? What if? I tossed my head back, gathering my wits, and steadying myself on a nearby display table. I managed a gush as if sharing the salesgirl's fun. "Guess I'd better pick up a couple few essentials before the February rush then?"

Hetta sifted through the bins, pulling out sleepers and booties, hats, and baby blankets, all in yellow and white. We piled my selections on the counter, and Hetta busied herself writing up a sales check.

The baby kicked. My hand flew to my tummy. Hetta grinned. "An active one?"

"More than most, my friends say."

"That's good." The girl's face sobered. "You don't want them to go quiet."

She turned away to wrap things, making me wonder how many women she'd helped, only to have their child never wear the clothing they had purchased. The city cemetery hosted a separate section with baby graves. Rectangular granite markers, most flush to the ground, commemorated the small souls whose hearts had only beat in their mother's wombs, along with those who took in a modicum of the world's oxygen for just days. The section had grown exponentially in the past few years, the miniature plots numbering in the dozens.

Clutching my packages, I pushed out of the shop door, thinking I had bigger things to worry about than just Matt.

• • •

The baby had dropped, making me a human bowling ball, and even Matt had ceased contact. Luke's absence became a constant, an ongoing, painful reminder of the choice I'd made. I could have gone with him, should have, maybe. He wouldn't risk a letter, not with the government monitoring mail, but I gathered the post each day with ridiculous hope that he might ask me again, despite knowing he wouldn't.

With no one to confide in, I took long strolls by the river a spot well beyond town, staring into the Columbia's dark blue depths, trying to discern a difference in its color and the fish beneath its surface. Silly, knowing what I knew, but I searched for that one place. That spot where I could point and say, "There it is. See what they've done."

Out of nowhere, a small group of teenagers, obviously cutting classes, barreled down the slope, coming to a halt at the water's edge. Two of the boys peeled off their shirts, their chests bared against the late February chill. I shuddered, thinking only the young could bear such cold. The boys plunged into the Columbia, turned on their backs, and waved to the others.

"Come on in. We swear it's a warm spot."

I froze in horror. A warm spot could only mean one thing, effluent, a substantive amount. I moved closer and raised my voice. "You, down there. Get back to school before I report you to the principal."

The youth on the bank shot me looks of bewilderment before scurrying back up the bank and out of sight. The two boys in the river splashed to shore, grabbed their shirts, and ran, their laughter spiraling in the breeze.

I leaned into a tree trunk, my veins pumping double time, my hands on my belly, scanning the river for surface signs, but nothing presented itself, and I couldn't get closer in my condition. Even if I could register the unlikely, warm temperature somehow, folks would turn away in denial. Harry would have to come take a sample, not me.

My shakes subsided, and I set an ambitious pace, at least for my condition, wanting to get home to call Harry, but my walk slowed as our block came into view. A brand-new Studebaker rested at the curb.

Matt bumped out our front door, bourbon in hand, jazz blaring from the radio. "What do you think of our new chariot?" He beamed in that little boy way he had when something pleased him, a glimmer of what he could have been, or might still be. The Commander Land Cruiser was a bright baby blue, a clear nod to Matt's gender preference for the baby.

"Four doors, that's good," I said, trying to sound enthusiastic about a sedan when we had discussed a station wagon. "And I hear the mileage is good."

"Cahoon gave me a great price, company discount and all." Matt ran his hand along the fender as if it were a baby's behind.

"As they should," I said. The local car dealer, Cahoon Motors, was subsidized by the government, as was every other shop in town. They kept everyone close to home by making sure any need could be fulfilled in Richland. No need to go beyond the town borders.

Matt opened the passenger door. "Let's go for a spin."

My entire body needed relief, but not in a car. My feet screamed to be propped up, my ankles swelling from my walk. The phone rang out over the jazz, saving me. "I'll get it." I waddled up the steps and into the kitchen, pulling the phone cord to the table and positioning a chair to prop up my feet.

"Boone residence."

"Mary, darling." My mother's voice said it all.

"He's gone?" The rest stuck in my throat, an unuttered whisper of a prayer.

"Yes, dear. Quietly, in the night. Ellen found him this morning. She's home for the weekend."

My father had given his life to the Stibnite mine, long hours that kept him from tucking us in most nights, so that my sister and I would want for nothing, when all we wanted was him. The baby kicked first on one side of my belly and then the other, like a cancan chorus line. My father used to scoop me up when I was kicking dirt, saying it wasn't ladylike. He'd laugh and bear hug me into submission. I always resisted, shrieking, my legs flailing in the air, but the truth was, I didn't want him to let go. His arms were the safest place in my world.

"Mama, I—" I caught myself, realizing I couldn't say that I couldn't come to the funeral. My real due date was any time now, but I was the only one who knew that. How to explain my absence to my mother? And Matt, he'd be no help, most likely jump at the chance to take his new car-baby out on the open road.

But my mother surprised me. "Mary, dear, I know the timing is terrible. You're so close to delivery. Ellen and I were talking about a private burial and then maybe a memorial when you and the baby can both come."

I wanted to creep inside my mother's arms, hole up there like I had as a child. A sob escaped me.

My mother tutted on the other end of the line. "It's all right darling, he was ready." She purred on, saying the things a mother says, but all I could hear was Maxine Sullivan crooning on the radio. I could have the moon to play with if I didn't cry. Problem was, crying was the only thing I had the energy for.

The strength to face all the bad decisions I'd made up until now, the clarity I'd found, the courage I'd summoned to change direction, all of that had been circumvented by the baby inside me. The only thing I could count on was that this change in Matt wouldn't last. The Studebaker was proof of that.

My tears had drained dry before I realized my father had, in death, given me the "stars to run away with," and that was what I would do as soon as the baby was born.

●　　●　　●

Helen was on her side of the kitchen wall when my water broke and streamed down my legs, soaking my house shoes. "Helen!" I yelled, slapping the wall, leaving my palm there to steady myself.

Helen raced in, her red waves flying. "Here, dear, let's get you into this chair." She surveyed the liquid on the floor. "Have you packed a bag for the hospital?"

I wagged my head no. Packing a bag now would have been a tip-off. "It never occurred to me it might be this early," My entire face squeezed into a contraction, pain searing through my abdomen covering the lie. "My small case is just inside the upstairs closet, my nightgown on the back side of the bathroom door. Maybe grab my hairbrush."

"And your makeup case." Helen hustled upstairs. She bumped back down with my case in record time. "All set?" She took my elbow, and I pushed off the kitchen table to a standing position.

A flock of geese soared above, rotating leaders in the wind in perfect avian choreography. We were two steps off the porch when Ralph Hinson came into view, a handkerchief at his nose. As he neared, red spots bled through his white kerchief. Helen's face detoured into a more serious concern. "Another nosebleed?"

Ralph attempted a grin behind his hand. "Not too bad this time, but the boys sent me home." His eyes targeted mine. "That time, huh?"

A smile found its way through my next contraction, thinking of how loving a grandfather Ralph would be if he knew. With Helen's hand at my back, I rolled into the Hinson's car. Helen looped around to the driver's door and called back to Ralph. "Get some ice on that. I'll get Mary settled at Kadlec and be back as soon as I can."

"Not to worry, and Mary, good luck."

Helen eased into the road, and I held my belly, panting through what felt like a swarm of babies pushing and shoving their way through me. The geese swirled above us, riding the wind toward the river and across the wide blue expanse of the Columbia.

Kadlec Hospital loomed, and a searing sensation reared its head, kicking off a crescendo of pain. This baby was well on its way.

Helen screeched into the emergency entrance and hollered at an orderly lingering outside on a smoke break. "Get a gurney. Her contractions are only three or so minutes apart."

Others took control of my body. A stiff-collared nurse directed the chorus of medical personnel. I tossed a smile at Helen through the crowd as white double doors closed me inside. Another nurse talked in my ear, but another contraction took over my entire being, and all I could do was moan. The gurney swung around a corner and into a large equipment-laden room.

The nurse's voice pierced the pain. "Mrs. Boone? Just breathe in." A nozzle lowered over my nose and mouth. The contraction peaked in my belly and then, my body was rolling over to its side and someone was holding a mask to my face. A searing pain ripped up my spine, and I cried out.

The nurse clutched me tighter. "You won't feel a thing soon."

When the next wave of pain began, it was lighter, or maybe I just felt less. A wooziness took over, and I twisted my head to the nurse by my side. "What's happening?"

"The baby is coming. Shhhh. You'll be fine." The nurse squeezed my hand.

A doctor appeared, but not the one I'd seen before. "Cutting to the chase, are we, Mrs. Boone?"

Only the top of his head showed as he sat between my feet which were now strung up in stirrups. He must be touching me, but I felt none of it in my haze. At his side, one nurse handed off an instrument and another moved in closer. The doctor had disappeared below my belly.

"Inhale," my nurse directed, and I sucked in more gas, my mind and body spinning out of the room.

Could Luke sense his baby entering into the world? Not the world I would have chosen, but the only one we had. I would have to protect him or her, and how I would do that I couldn't fathom. I couldn't trust my breast milk or anything fresh. My mind clamped onto an image of an advertisement for powdered baby formula I'd seen in a magazine a while back, puzzling over what it had said. Did I mix it with water, and what if the water was tainted too, how would I feed my baby? And then, a baby cried. My baby.

"He's here." The nurse squeezed my arm. "You have a boy."

I tried to lift my head, but it was too heavy. "Where is he?" Ben, his name was Benjamin. The name I'd told Matt was my great grandfather's, but it wasn't. Nor was Lucia my favorite aunt's name, should it be a girl.

Matt had no interest in naming the child, allowing the real reasons behind my choices to remain my secret.

"We're cleaning him up," the nurse said, but I couldn't see anything. My eyes were too heavy.

"We have some more work to do, afterbirth and all." The doctor's voice sounded like it was in a tunnel. "Hang on. I think we have another one."

A collective gasp sounded like an echo in a chamber. "Twins?"

My eyes wouldn't open. The nurse adjusted the nozzle on me again. Something pulled in my belly, but whatever pain might have been associated with the manipulation was muted by the gas. I drifted.

The nurse put a hand on my cheek. "Hold on, there's one more baby. It's crowning."

A faraway voice said, "Forceps, doctor?"

A high-pitched scream startled everyone. "No!" My voice froze them in place.

The doctor laughed out loud, a deep heartwarming chortle that reminded me of my father. "It's okay Mrs. Boone, no forceps needed. This little lady has a force of her own."

And she did, though I didn't see her, being down the rabbit hole of drugs. They told me later Lucy entered my world head first and sure-footed. If only I could be as steady in my path from here forward.

• • •

Ten days in a hospital maternity ward could drive you to drink, not that I didn't already. Someone had shaved my pubic region, God knows why, and the never-ending enemas could make a person suicidal, even if they hadn't birthed twins.

Twins. Just the thought of taking two babies home, when I was so afraid of breaking one, put me into a fast spin. But I didn't have to worry, it wasn't like anyone was letting me feed them, the nurses took care of all of that and more. They, too, were seemingly afraid I might screw them up somehow. They doled out cursory visits, but only fifteen minutes at a time, even though the twins were normal weights, Lucy at five and a half pounds and Ben at seven. I spent those minutes combing their faces for any sign, not that it would show on those angelic cheeks.

They came "specially wrapped" in baby blankets, so tight I couldn't clutch their fingers, pull on their toes, or count them. A nurse guard stayed in the room to make sure I didn't violate the rules. Little did she know that the thought of unwrapping them made me tremble.

Poor things, so innocent, so trusting, and with no knowledge of how frightened their mother was. When Lucy and Ben didn't hit some ill-determined weight goal, the nurses announced the twins would stay in the hospital another two weeks, just in case, but I'd had it with the Kadlec prison. When the doctor finally let me out of bed, I padded down the hallway to take a long look at the twins, assuring myself they were perfectly safe, and packed my bag so fast no one even noticed. I waited until Matt would be at work before fleeing.

Helen Hinson stood on her corner of the front porch, focused on the sky, when my taxi pulled up to the curb. The driver got out to hold my door. I tumbled out, my small bag throwing me off balance. Helen scurried down the walk to me. "Mary? You're home early."

"Early, like my babies." I grimaced and straightened up, determined to walk on my own two feet, even though my body felt like someone had taken an axe and cleaved me in two. Two. What was I going to do?

"Twins almost always come sooner rather than later," Helen said, parroting what I'd heard over and over in the hospital. Turns out, the perfect alibi for babies coming early is having twins. Helen took my bag and my elbow, a light, reassuring grasp that radiated safety. "At least that's the case in my family."

"Twins run in your family?"

"My older sister had twins and two of my first cousins. All boy-girl combos." Helen's smile held more, but she only said, "When can you bring the babies home?" A wistfulness permeated her question.

"Soon." Ralph's head appeared in the kitchen window. "What's Ralph doing home?" Exhaustion hit, and I dropped onto the porch steps.

"Another nosebleed." Helen's tone dulled out, flat, not herself.

"Has he seen a doctor?"

Helen snorted in disgust. "As if those doctors at Kadlec would ever tell anyone the truth." She shook her head, her blue eyes flashing her anger. "We've been arguing about it."

The Hinsons never argued, at least not that I had heard, and I'd been living on the other side of their walls for five years. "Maybe Luke can convince him?"

"He tried, but Ralph told him that just because he's a biology and botany double-major, it doesn't mean he can diagnose disease." Helen swallowed, turning her face from me.

I could tell she was holding back tears, so I went lighter. "Who knew that underneath the world's most easy-going demeanor, your husband was a stubborn old cuss?"

She side-eyed me and we both laughed. The share of it made me want to tell her even more. Say out loud how afraid I was about what ailments might befall my children and her grandchildren, but I couldn't.

I just said, "Now that I've proved I can walk twenty-foot on my own, how about accompanying a postpartum victim on a short walk? Go see that new junior high school the nurses at Kadlec were raving about." An unexpected jolt of energy propelled me onto my feet.

Helen linked arms with me, a protective move that shored me up, and we stepped off the porch into partial sunshine that held a promise of spring, despite whatever had hitched a ride on the clouds cruising southward. I focused on putting one foot in front of the other, relearning how to walk after being kept in a prone position far longer than anyone should be.

An uneven section of sidewalk loomed, and I leaned into Helen as we navigated the up and down of it. "How are the little angels?"

"The nurses tuck them into the opposite sides of their bassinets, facing each other as if they will see their mate is just over there." The thought of my mother out of reach bogged down in the mire of father's estate, and Matt way too close, made my insides quake like a 4th-grade science experiment that was about to overflow the beaker. "They're perfect," I said, forcing my trembling to stop mid-shake.

"But scary, having two of them." Helen squeezed my arm. "I'll help."

Helen spoke about organizing for the twin battle ahead as we rounded the corner. The two-block square campus of the new junior high school rolled out to greet us, the emerald green grass glistening in the spikes of sun. Fledgling pine trees lined the edge of the front sidewalk, and stone benches rested on either side of the entrance.

"Impressive, isn't it?" Helen's voice held a hint of anger.

"It should be," I answered. "According to the hospital gossip, they spent millions."

Helen frowned, shaking her head. "The schools here are among the best in the state, but heaven forbid they should spend the same amount on worker safety."

We lingered across the street from the school. The breeze had shifted and a discolored wisp of vapor sailed over the top of the building, followed by a steady stream, like someone's cigarette exhale had been magnified into a full-blown cloud current.

"That can't be?" I couldn't put words to it. It felt too horrible to say.

"Plant emissions? Yes, it is. This section of town is prone to them in the early spring." Helen sighed. "The wind picks other spots in the summer."

A bell shrilled, and the front doors burst open. Students with brown paper sacks tumbled out onto the vast lawn. Two boys started a pickup football game, the ball flying over dirndl-skirted young girls spread across the grass.

These were the sons and daughters of Hanford workers. Workers that had dedicated their lives to something they thought was bigger than themselves. But it was a mission with consequences, and the government kept such consequences classified. Adolescent giggles lifted into the sky, meeting another wave of vapor that swallowed them whole.

Helen stared straight ahead. "Luke's botany professor has him studying the effects of nuclear waste on the environment."

"They're letting them do that?" The secrecy of Eastern Washington versus the revelations likely underway on the western side of the state felt incongruous except—Luke.

Helen swallowed. "He says that it's almost as if the AEC wants to say it out loud, admit what the problems they are creating, and in doing so, get tacit permission to keep doing it."

"But he won't let that happen, will he?" Secrets pissed Luke off. All secrets.

Helen turned to me, a mother's smile wrapping her ear to ear. "No. I don't think he will." We strode to the end of the block. "So, tell me. What are you naming the little dolls?"

"Benjamin and Lucia. Ben and Lucy for short."

"Two of my favorite names." Helen's eyes never left mine.

"Mine, too." And just like that, we had a secret.

"We'd better get you home. Rest you up before tackling what's to come." Helen linked her arm in mine and pulled me along with her, my energy and the campus fading behind us. The sun shot through the clouds like a laser, disrupting the vapor thread.

As we turned the corner away from the campus, I cast a glance back over my shoulder. "The twins will never go to school there, I promise."

Chapter Fifteen/Luke

May 1964

We worked around the clock collating data and analyzing samples from the reservation and the bay, generating mixed results. I documented what served our theory, compiling the counter-research at the same time. As Miller had said, we had to prove it beyond any doubt.

We called the independent lab in Portland and compared notes. They seemed amenable but non-committal. We kept at it. Harry weighed in, pointing out holes in our data and reminding me to fix it with the boy. I called his grandmother, apologized, and suggested a new date, hoping she would help fix the mess I'd made.

More tests, more results. Walker stood up from his stool. "Nothing definitive."

My exhaustion closed around my lungs and squeezed. "Maybe we need a break."

Roy had to get back to Corvallis for finals. "Come on, Walker. I'll give you a lift."

A knock came at my cabin door two minutes after they left. "What'd you forget," I said, opening the door.

The man looked like Eliot Ness: the hat, the coat, a bump under his topcoat that I was sure was a sawed-off shotgun. He flipped his badge at me. "Luke Hinson? Mind if I come in?"

Hell, anyone who watched TV knew enough to not let that happen. I stepped out onto the porch and closed my door behind me. "What can I do for you?"

"We've been tracing leaks of classified information." He paused and cast an eye across the bramble.

My heart clutched, thinking they already had me surrounded. I shook it off, admonishing myself for an overactive imagination, but he must have thought I was denying something.

"Two folks have given us your name." He flipped open a pad. "Dr. Goodman in Richland and a Dr. Kapustka, Portland Laboratories? They both say you have been pushing for research that has not been made public."

"Huh," I said, stalling, wondering if Goodman had been threatened somehow. Kapustka was the head of the Portland lab, but we hadn't spoken to him. "Can't say that I remember asking either of those gentlemen to share any such data."

The man had an air of having the trump card in an uncertain game. "We also understand your mother, Helen Hinson of Richland, has been helping you?"

Helping is such a benign way of accusing someone of aiding and abetting a criminal. I took a step back, distancing myself from the pure evil of it: a government agency that would take anyone down in their quest to keep their secrets.

My response was that of a boy defending his mother. "You keep my mother out of this."

Card played, he said, "Afraid I can't do that unless this..." he pointed at my front window before continuing. "Unless this little project of yours comes to an end."

My laugh carried across the bramble, echoing off the hillside. "This little project is my doctoral thesis. Approved by Oregon State University and partially funded by the AEC." The minute the words came out, I realized that, unlike Eliot Ness, I was touchable.

The man wasted no time in sweeping the pot. "You might check on that with your professor."

He climbed back into the car, sparking the interior light. A man sat behind the wheel, another in the backseat, the way bullies work, three against one. They sped down the drive, spitting gravel back at me.

• • •

Miller's door was cracked, and I walked right in. He held the phone in one hand, the other on the dial. "I was just calling you." He replaced the handset in the cradle.

"You're pulling my funding?"

Dr. Miller cocked his head at my impertinence. "Not me. The AEC requested a review. A decision was made by the doctoral committee."

"Which you chair." My fury bled out in the open, clouding the air between us.

Miller folded his arms across his chest. "I gave you as much leeway as I could, but there are limits, Luke."

"You mean the rules? As set by the AEC, the biggest bullies on the planet?"

Miller held up his hands. "I'll need you to clear out your locker and any personal belongings. I'll send a letter, should you want to enroll elsewhere."

That brought me down. I sank into the chair in front of him. "You're kicking me out of the program?"

"Not me, the Board."

My lungs bottomed out. I rocked back in my chair, on tilt like I had been for months. "You're going to hide behind the Board?" I sprang to my feet. "Don't bother with the letter, I'll find my way." I slammed the door behind me, drawing the attention of everyone in the lab. I stared straight ahead, ignoring them all, and made it out into the hall.

Roy rounded the corner, an ear-to-ear grin on his face. "Perfect, you're here. Wait till I show you." His hand held a folder labeled "Rez."

Unable to target my real enemy, I glared at him. "Whatever it is, I'm no longer allowed to participate."

"Wait, what?" Roy put his hand to my shoulder, and I shook it off.

"Ejected, just like Harry. They will end anyone who gets in their way, including, it appears, my mother. Their precious mission is to keep the world safe, what a farce. They're the ones putting us all in danger." I groaned, sank against the wall, and slid to the floor, my energy spent, defeat filling my chest.

Roy squatted. "You still need to see this."

He shoved the folder into my hand. The verified results from the Tacoma lab showed radioactive elements in both soil and water from the Rez. That meant that fallout from Hanford had traveled, and recently, over seventy-five miles west. But there was more, my samples from the bayou, taken in February. The lab had charted multiple radioactive elements in the reeds, growing 270 miles from the plant. The ones I'd hacked off that day Ben came fishing.

"Shit." I scrambled to my feet. "I gotta go. Listen, hide this, don't go back into the lab with it. Understand?"

Roy stuffed the file in the backside of his pant waist and tugged his shirt over it. A pair of grad students entered the hall and shot us pitiful stares. Everyone knew.

I thrust my hand at Roy, hoping he would follow my lead. "Sorry about all this."

The grad students passed us by, casting dark glances over their shoulders. Roy faked a sad face. "Yeah, buddy, I'll miss you."

Miss. Shit, I'd forgotten about the boy again. He'd be waiting for me. I squeezed Roy's shoulder and whispered. "Suppertime, the cabin." Without waiting for an answer, I shoved off and dashed to the parking lot.

•   •   •

If I broke the speed limit, passing on uncertain, not-so-straightaways and zipped through small-town intersections, I could cut thirty minutes off my drive time to the coast. The section of road between Chinook and the cabin was almost all flatlands. I saw Ben walking ahead before he saw me. I pulled off on the side of the road and jumped out, perspiration sliding down my back, sweat that I hadn't even realized was there.

The boy reeled when he saw me and swiveled his head left to right, looking for an escape, I surmised.

Me too, I thought, but I said, sincere in my contrition. "Sorry. Unexpected summons to campus. But I'm here now. Let's go back to the cabin, okay?"

Ben shook his head. "Don't think so, mister."

"Come on, a guy can make a mistake, right?"

"Not that. It's your cabin. It's wrecked."

Of course, it was. I stared out into the blue of the day, wondering if they would ever let me be. Likely not, if I kept at it, but what else could I do? I was in it now, along with everyone else that Hanford practices had damaged or destroyed. "Get in. I need to see for myself."

Ben shrugged and dumped his load in the back seat. "It's a mess, mister." I sped up the drive to an open front door and loped up on the porch. Ben followed. "See?"

And I did. I saw it for what it was: the ransacking was a warning, a strong one. I needed to call Roy, but not from the cabin phone, sure to be bugged. "Okay then, I'll clean this up later," I said. "But, we've got work to do to get that project finished before your deadline. Right?" I put my hand on his shoulder, parroting a move of my father's.

Ben smiled. Maybe at my touch, or maybe not, but it was a smile so large that for a moment I thought it might crack his face, one as unused to smiling as mine was.

•　　•　　•

Ben's grandmother spread out a gingham cloth for the cookies and lemonade while I called Walker and told him to call Roy. The laziness of an unintentional Memorial Day porch picnic, the clink of ice in the glasses, and the crumbs on Ben's face brought a smile to mine. A new car was parked in the driveway, a white Impala. "That's a beauty. White walls and all."

"My late husband loved cars. The grill work on the side reminded me of his last one, a '47 Chevy, a Fleetline Aero Sedan." Mrs. Peters seemed pensive. "Oxblood red, waxed it every Sunday."

"A classic," I said. "You must have made the dealer happy when you traded it in for this one." Ben moved inside to search for another marker color.

Mrs. Peters' eyes followed him, waiting till the door closed behind him before sinking into the wicker bench. "Mary took the sedan when she left." Her whisper encompassed me.

"Of course," I said, wondering if she'd given up all hope and hoped not. "I'm sorry."

Ben burst back out of the screen door. "Found it."

Still mired in the past, I managed, "Okay, let's get to it." We reviewed his recent research, negated some of his excessive text, puzzled over some new photos, and reworked the set of conclusions. "Remember," I said. "Sea water has small amounts of tritium, from nuclear fallout." I charged Ben with finding the colors of various gases, emphasizing tritium. "Just fill in that bit and you're done."

Mrs. Peters mustered, "So, we'll see you at the science fair? Second Friday in June?"

"Wouldn't miss it." Hiding my growing sadness, I chomped down on a cookie, thinking they were almost as good as my mom's, and I should call her. I chugged the last of my lemonade. "Sorry, I've got some folks meeting me at the cabin."

Mrs. Peters walked me to the car. "I can't thank you enough." She cast an eye back at Ben. "You know it's been hard for him. First Mary, then Lucy. Six years ago, but summer vacations that most boys look forward to only stir up bad memories for Ben."

"How about I make it a point to take him fishing, more than once?"

She smiled, and I saw where Mary's had come from. "The sheriff called me, a decade ago now," she said. "Reporting that the storms, in the days after Mary left, likely washed away any sign of an accident." Her smile faded into her shoulders as if her cheeks couldn't support the weight of it. "Too large of an area to search with no clues, and there are none. Probably never will be."

Uncomfortable with her pain matching my own, I gave a cursory nod and hollered up to the porch. "Don't forget that last bit of research. On tritium. It's important."

Ben tossed my words back at me. "Yeah, yeah, there's always a logical answer."

•　•　•

Walker carted a huge trash sack out onto the porch as I pulled into the drive. In the settling dusk, the cabin was lit up like a Christmas tree. The cabin door swung open. Roy had a broom in hand, sweeping into a dustpan I didn't know I had. Mother. I should call her.

Someone had put candles all around. The questioning look on my face prompted Roy to point at the ceiling fixture, shattered bulbs still in the sockets. "A few lights need replacing."

"Where'd you get all the candles?

"Turns out Walker is really Abe Lincoln." He strode out to his car.

I grinned, despite the sight before me. My makeshift lab, every beaker, every test tube, and multiple instruments, were all destroyed.

Using a small brush, Walker cleared the rest of the debris from the counter. "We need something to write with."

Roy toted in a portable typewriter with the OSU stamp on it. "Figured they owed us." He extracted a half-used ream of paper from a shelf below the counter. "Good thing the FBI didn't think blank paper was a threat to the nation."

"But it is?"

Roy grinned. "You betcha." He pushed over a set of summary notes, freshly inked in his illegible cursive. "You type, we'll dictate."

Walker pulled a stack of books closer and set a candle holder on top, shedding light onto the typewriter.

"Listen, Luke, there is some bad news." Roy's smile thinned. "The AEC confiscated all of the whale samples, our data, everything left at BioHarvest."

All of the hope that had risen in me, flowed out. Without the whale samples, the only real evidence of Hanford's practices, our chances for publication were nil. I pushed away from the typewriter, defeated. How had I ever thought I would beat these government folks, decidedly not of the people?

"So, what are we doing here? Typing up my obit?"

Walker snorted. "Well, as much as I would be pleased to eulogize you at some point, we have other work." He reached inside a duffle bag and pulled out a series of paper sacks. Roy, grinning now, began emptying them onto the counter. Photos of everything we had harvested from the whale that day on the dock. In shock, I stared as Walker unboxed jarred samples, sealed with wax, lining them up along the counter with an amused look on his face.

"Did you think all the Tututni do is chant?"

• • •

The sun woke us after only a couple of hours of sleep, and we went back to it. We'd established a rhythm, one person dictating, another parsing through notes, and the third creating the list of footnotes. Then we would rotate. By midday we had a first draft of the paper, citing the whale and a clear chain of evidence. Backup data, including our bioassays on animals and plants in both the bay and Eastern Washington, created a compelling case for our conclusions, a direct connection between Hanford and the whale. Roy typed up a final copy, citing Walker as the main author and Roy and I as research assistants. I said a silent thank you for Walker's willingness to go all in. His bona fides with the state were the only among us that met the submission criteria.

"Who shall we start with? The AJS?"

I shook my head. "If this ever sees the light of day, it won't be in an American journal."

Walker agreed. Roy rubbed his chin. "The Brits?"

"I've got some pals over the pond, as they say," I said. "Might have an in," I said, thinking *Nature*, the lauded British science journal, had a worldwide audience. Glad my address book had been with me in my pack, otherwise, the FBI might have confiscated it. I paged through, searching for the Oban-drinking buddy who had a permanent position at the Marine Institute.

"Make the call. But not here." Walker motioned toward my phone. I followed his gaze, wondering what kind of bug might be planted and that Pearlie's had a phone booth.

Roy dug into his pockets, ferreting out loose change. "How much is a payphone call to the Scottish moors?"

Chapter Sixteen/Mary

March 1949

A nurse wheeled the twins out the double doors of Kadlec, following Matt to the Studebaker parked at the curb. Wishing for Luke, I scooped Lucy up first and nestled her onto the back seat, thinking she looked like her father today. When I turned back for Ben, Matt already had him, a perplexed look on his face.

"What is it?" I asked, my throat catching at the thought of Matt seeing the resemblance. But he put his fingers to Ben's forehead, making me wonder if Ben had sparked a fever. Lucy seemed to dance with fever daily, and that had been why we hadn't brought the twins home before. Their weight gain was related to a low-grade fever that had finally dissipated.

Matt's face softened. "It's just that he's so small, and yet, he seems to have a mind of his own already." Matt dropped one arm to his side, untethered like he didn't know how to use it.

Despite every blow that I'd received from that hand, I clasped it in mine. "We can figure it out as long as we stick together." Ben stretched his pudgy arm out and curled his fingers around Matt's tie. Matt and I shared a smile, one that tugged on my college girl's heart, a smile that made you remember how and why. Maybe the twins could be our beginning, again.

I plucked Ben's hand off Matt's tie, smoothed the silk, and snuggled Ben in the back seat with Lucy. "Helen says they are who they are when they come out of the box."

Matt shook his head. "I'm just not sure how good I'll ever be at this." His voice trailed off as a large garbage truck swept up the hospital drive, blocking the sun. "You don't think, I mean I...know I'm their father but..." His eyes sought mine.

A beat that shouldn't be taken, or a reflexive blink of an eye can be damning. I squeezed his hand, possibly a moment too late, and said, "Every parent has these doubts."

Was that suspicion creeping in, seeping between us? Our eyes met, questions rising in Matt's, and the possibility of change sliding away.

•   •   •

Summer served up scads of sunflowers along the edges of our A-house, the avian gardeners having done their job. Matt called, saying he had bigwigs to entertain and wouldn't be home for dinner, something that happened more and more often.

Ignoring laundry that needed doing, Helen and I were enjoying a rare moment to ourselves out on the porch when Harry pulled up. He climbed the short stoop and leaned in to kiss me on the cheek. He shot Helen a conspiratorial wink.

"Got them whipped into shape, yet?" His grin was infectious when he used it.

Helen and I laughed. "More like they have us right where they want us," I said.

"I'll put a pot of coffee on," Helen said. "To get us through the evening." She disappeared into her side of the house.

Harry took a seat on the stoop. "Long day?"

"It's been one long day since February 22nd." I rubbed my temples. "What brings you out on this one?"

"I need you back." Harry had always been a to-the-point kind of guy.

"They just started sleeping through the night," I said, waving my hand to the upstairs window. "And by night, I mean midnight to four-thirty. Brutal."

"I don't mean full-time, just a couple of days a week." His face turned serious. "Something's happening, not sure what, but I need someone I can trust."

A cry from inside drew me to my feet. "Be right back." I flew up the stairs, hoping to extract Lucy before she woke Ben, the deeper sleeper. As I leaned over her crib, her face shifted from annoyed to cherubic, her cheeks sparkling with perspiration. I scooped her into my arms, tossed another glance at Ben, snatched a fresh diaper, and crept back downstairs.

Harry held out his arms, surprising me. "Let me hold her." He cradled her like a pro.

"Who'd have thought? The crotchety old scientist, a natural."

Helen appeared with three coffee mugs and distributed them. "Already?" She put a hand to Lucy's brow. "Uh oh, another fever."

Lucy caught every bug that came along, her temperature spiking weekly. The pediatrician at Kadlec dismissed our concerns, saying some children are just more prone to catching things. Good for them to build up their immune systems, only Lucy didn't seem able to fight anything.

"This little lady needs a diaper change," Harry handed her back to me.

Laying her on the porch, I gauged her temperature for myself. "Low grade," I said with relief and secured the last pin in Lucy's clean diaper.

Helen scooped Lucy up. "I'll rock her, maybe she'll snooze a bit more." She moved inside and took a seat in the rocker my mother had brought on her last visit.

Harry waited for the door to close behind Helen. "I know you have a lot on your hands, but it's important." Two neighbor boys kicked a can down the sidewalk, giving each other noogies when a kick didn't fly. An Air Force fighter jet soared overhead. Harry pointed. "New F-80. They just ferried fourteen more over."

The can landed in the middle of our front walk with a disconcerting clunk. The boys spat out "sorry" accompanied by a carefree kick that took their game down the block. I followed their backs. "Production is gearing up along with the military?"

"Yep," Harry said, keeping something back.

Between the Russian threats and the mounting tensions in Korea, who knew what the next target might be? I didn't ask. "My next-door neighbor, Lois, is looking to earn some pin money for her daughter's confirmation dress. She might help out with the twins."

Harry nodded. "There's some talk of another test, not sure what, but most likely problematic."

"For who?"

"All of us."

•   •   •

While the Soviets tested their missiles, causing worldwide consternation at the end of August, being back in the office proved the tonic I didn't realize I needed. I'd missed adult conversations about things other than babies.

Harry and Lou progressed into final data on all the fish. By late September, they had matched the levels of radiation in our water samples to plant production. A troubling discharge of sludge had occurred at the new tank farm during construction, and Harry had managed to collect a sample. Lou spent his evenings cautioning the tribes who fished the river nearby to move upstream.

My abbreviated shift, thanks to Harry, allowed me to get home mid-afternoon and still have time to have dinner on the table, not that Matt seemed to care. Whatever his distraction, it was constant. When I rounded the corner from the bus stop, an oil company truck dwarfed the sidewalk. A trail of equipment led to the backyard.

A workman's voice carried to the curb. "Hey, Joe. What's this?"

I cut through the side yard just in time to see the worker pull out the tin canister Luke had buried. "That, gentlemen, is a time capsule. Best leave it."

"Can't do it, ma'am. We need to roll the tank. Gotta patch a leak."

"Just put it over there for now, but I'll need your help to get it back in the ground. Somewhere it won't be disturbed."

Helen stepped out onto her back porch. "Mary?" She cast a questioning gaze at the canister. The bright red paint Luke had used to label its side 'Wonders of 1948' was faded, but still legible.

"A secret project of Luke's that I'm afraid I helped facilitate." I laughed. "Do you think the universe is telling me to take my Mixmaster back? That the twins deserve cookies after all?"

"Some things shouldn't be buried, at least not permanently," Helen said with a wry smile, but her tone indicated we weren't talking about my Mixmaster anymore.

"I'm going to check on Lois. See if she'll stay long enough for me to take a shower."

After securing thirty more minutes to myself, I climbed the stairs and sank into my small dressing table chair. Out back, the oil tank had been unearthed, and a welder had set to work on the crack, torch flame flaring in the fall breeze. The men had set the canister off to the side. About ten feet away, an overly chubby squirrel sat transfixed with the action, making me wonder if the digging threatened his winter nut store.

Maybe it was the thought of that, or maybe it was just the reminder of all the things that can leak out, at the wrong time, in the wrong way. Or maybe it was that every time I looked at Ben and Lucy, I saw Luke. The perpetual half grin on Ben, the determination in Lucy's jaw, but the unadorned longing in both their eyes stopped me in my tracks most days. I pulled note paper out of the vanity drawer and wrote, *'For Luke to read: Dear Ben and Lucy...'*

Ben's high-pitched 'da-da' rang out and Lois's laughter signaled a game of peek-a-boo underway downstairs, giving me the time I needed. After folding my letter inside an envelope, I inserted the key into the drawer where I kept my diary, but couldn't get it to turn in the lock. The keyhole had been jimmied, bent inside somehow. Using a letter opener, I jostled the mechanism and then tried the key again.

The lock flipped, and I yanked my diary out, panic knifing through me. If Matt found my diary, all my plans, all my truths could be used against me. Giggles resounded below, the twins unaware of how precarious our lives were. I snatched a baby blanket off a pile of clean laundry and wrapped the diary up tight. Cupping it into the folds of my dress, the letter in my pocket, I crept down the stairs.

The men ferried their heavier tools and tarp back to their truck. After a couple of bashes with a large rock, the lid to the time capsule loosened. I stuffed the letter in the glass jar alongside the letters Luke and I had written three years prior. Wedging the diary inside the tightly packed capsule took only a few more seconds. I had the canister lid back on just as Helen came out her back door.

A worker with a shovel rounded the corner. I motioned to him. "If you could dig a hole about fifteen-foot away. Not so close to the tree that you disturb the whistle pig's stores," I said, pointing to the squirrel, before indicating a spot midway between the oil tank and the back alley.

"Hank," the lead worker hollered. "Help me get the kid's tin can back in the ground."

The two men started with pickaxes, dirt flying as I sank on the back porch.

Helen nestled in beside me to watch the action. "Did I tell you that Luke's on track to graduate from UW a year early?"

"Then what, graduate school?" Envy of that wheedled its way in. If I'd stuck to my original plan, I'd just be finishing my doctorate.

"Applying to East Coast schools. Anywhere but here, he says." Helen's face sagged a bit in the telling.

Now that I had Lucy and Ben, I couldn't imagine being without them, ever, but Luke had not been back to Richland for months. On his last holiday trip home, we'd exchanged perfunctory hellos only, passing each other on the sidewalk, feelings stuffed deeper than the capsule.

Luke and I had read our letters about life in Richland in the late 1940s out loud to one another before we buried them. His ended with a series of predictions of what might occur because of Hanford's sloppy waste practices. Even before his father's death, Luke had suspected the possible peril in Ralph's work, opinions that might be considered dissident.

"Deeper, please" I hollered at the workers. "Another foot at least." They dug until I gave them a thumbs-up, before inserting the canister into the ground and smoothing the dirt over my secrets. If they even were. How many others have to know, before it isn't a secret at all? At least my accounting of Matt and his crimes against me were buried deep in the ground, securing the list of incidents in a place he would never look. "Whoever digs that up, may or may not find it revelatory," I said, squeezing Helen's arm.

Inside, the baby talk had reached new levels. Time to get the twins fed. The workers gathered up the rest of their tools. The moon poked out on the horizon, competing with the sun in the end-of-day race. I rose to go relieve Lois, but Helen stayed seated, focused on the backyard.

•   •   •

The phone blared and then rang on top of itself, pulling Matt and me out of a sound sleep. I realized that the phone on the Hinson side of the A-house was tag-teaming our own. Other phones rang out, filling the night. Scattered conversations salted the air, snippets flying about a plant emergency. Neighboring scientists, engineers, Ralph and Matt rushed to their cars and raced toward the Area.

Unable to go back to sleep, I checked on the twins and headed out to the front porch, afraid of what might be, but the night sky held no evidence of any accident of any kind.

Helen came out and handed me a cup of tea. "Best guess?"

"Who knows," I said, hoping it wasn't a breach in a holding tank or sludge pond. The previous year muskrats had tunneled in and around a large waste storage pond, breaching the wall of earth holding back the pond. Over sixteen million gallons of radioactive effluent had flowed directly into the Columbia and contaminated every well of drinking water in the 300-Area. The company couldn't tame nature.

Helen kept her gaze on the stars. "Seems like things have settled a bit for you."

She meant Matt, being on his best behavior. Behavior that I couldn't understand and kept me on edge. I had broken the spell and inexplicably, he hadn't retaliated. Not yet. "Having an adult day or two each week helps," I said, steering away from the problem.

Helen chuckled. "Can't all be baby talk." As if summoned, a cry sounded upstairs.

I handed my teacup to Helen. "How did they know I was up?" I shot her a parting grin and moved inside. By the time I got both of the twins changed, fed, and back into their cribs, morning had dawned. I had bacon frying when Matt came through the door, haggard and hungry. He sat at the kitchen table, his face reflecting worry.

After placing a plate of bacon in front of him, I sat. "Can you tell me anything?"

"It'll be all over the news soon." Matt lowered his voice. "Something triggered the air filters on Rattlesnake Mountain. No way it was us. The scientists say it must be the jet stream carrying releases across the Pacific."

It took me a moment. "The Russians?"

Matt picked up a piece of bacon but didn't take a bite, he just nodded. Out the kitchen window, the sun covered the side yard in a blanket of gold. Things could only heat up from here.

•   •   •

The memo summoning us, me as the stenographer and Harry as the technical lab lead, promised an abbreviated meeting time. We filed into the small room, partially full of men in white lab coats from GE's Nucleonics Department. Several engineers from the reactors followed us in. A blackboard up in front held two words in all caps: CLASSIFIED MEETING. A man with an AEC identification badge escorted me to a small desk with a stenotype machine and pointed out the extra folds of paper at my feet, saying I most likely wouldn't need them. I took my seat and typed: October 7, 1949.

Harry took a chair in the front row and shot me an encouraging smile. The room quieted as an Air Force General entered. The AEC gentleman took a seat next to him up front.

Jay Harold of Hanford's Health Instrument Division, the HID, an ironic acronym, stepped to the lectern. "As you know, the HID handles radiological safety for The Area. We've determined the source of the recent spike in radioactivity on Rattlesnake Mountain."

The Air Force general stepped forward. "General Eisenhower charged us last year with the surveillance of Soviet atomic production." Murmurs rose around the room, drowning out the muted clickety-clack of my typing. The general continued. "Our intelligence sources have confirmed that the Soviets exploded their first atomic bomb."

Chatter overtook the room, but I kept to my task, recording the last words as questions peppered the air.

The general raised his hands for quiet. "While we can detect full-blown bomb tests from the other side of the globe, tracing plutonium production is much harder. We've asked you here today to help us develop a way to better monitor that."

The GE scientist stepped forward. "Our colleagues at the Oak Ridge plant in Tennessee have been conducting samplings, but the results have been disappointing."

Dr. Jackson, seated next to Harry, inserted himself. "We aren't able to measure our production gasses beyond two miles."

Harry cast a questioning look at Jackson. "But, that's by design. Our cooling periods of three months or more prevent large releases that are dangerous to the general population."

The general shook his head at Harry. "Being able to anticipate what our enemies will do next is imperative."

Only a three short years ago the Soviets had been our allies. I kept my eyes on the stenotype machine, reeling from the notion of risking public safety in order to defeat the enemy. How did that make sense?

Harold added. "Monitoring a release that's equivalent to that of the Soviets—a green run, if you will—can help determine the distance at which we might detect such emissions from the Soviet Union."

An engineer from the T-plant asked, "When?"

The general answered. "Hopefully by Turkey Day."

I eyed the engineer, wondering if he was already planning a long Thanksgiving weekend, far away from Richland, when Dr. Jackson jerked to his feet.

"But General, that's only sixty days from now, and just last year, the advisory committee agreed to control the levels of exposure. You can't just toss that aside."

The general continued. "We believe the Soviets have considerably shortened their plutonium separation cycle. To sixteen days." A hush fell over the room, everyone grappling with the implications of such a short processing time. The air in the room intensified as the General stared Jackson down. "The only way to figure this out is to duplicate their process."

Harry's hand went up again. "Do you understand the dangers of processing green fuel?"

"Do you understand the danger of not knowing what the enemy is doing?" The General shot Harry a lethal look.

A GE scientist stepped forward, glossing over Harry's question. "We'll also be testing a variety of methods to monitor contamination in animals, vegetation, and water, both on the ground and in the air, to enhance our safety protocols."

I kept typing, knowing that the irony of doing intentional harm in the name of enhancing future protections would just piss Harry off.

Sure enough, Harry jerked to his feet, shooting me a look that said, *get this all down.* "You can't expect a cloud of radioactive particles to behave a certain way. The weather, the wind, the temperature all affect how and where a plume flows." Harry looked around the room. "As humane men of science, we must insist on some meteorological requirements for this release. Minimize the danger to the public."

The general cast Harry a withering look, but Dr. Jackson jumped up, taking a conciliatory tact. "Such requirements would maximize your ability to monitor the release."

Another Hanford scientist added, "Wind speeds, rain, fog, or even low clouds could impede your aircraft's operations." The Hanford scientists and engineers all around the room nodded, showing their support. Harry and Jackson sat back down.

Harold took the lectern again. "I can assure you all that public safety is as much a priority to the Air Force as it is to the HID."

The AEC man's stern look squelched my urge to laugh out loud. He stepped over to collect the steno machine and tapes. Harold mustered a smile before adjourning the meeting. Everyone filed out of the room and dispersed in the fall afternoon.

Harry and I moved away from the crowd. "What are you going to do?" I asked, wanting to get back to my desk and write down everything I could remember.

"Initially? Help Jackson convince the Air Force to agree to certain weather conditions."

"And then?"

"Try to make sure folks are not in harm's way."

•   •   •

Harry and I rode side-by-side on the bus ride back to Richland. He offered me a ride home from the parking lot but detoured to the usual turnout. I scanned the horizon beyond the Columbia, imagining the pattern of the proposed plume, darting its tongue in and out of the clouds, depositing devastation wherever it strayed. I'd spent the bulk of the afternoon in our office, compiling a replica of the stenography notes, as close as I could remember anyway.

Harry cut into my imagination. "So, you got it all down? Names, the gist of it all."

Nodding, I rolled my eyes. "What fool thinks they can control a plume emitted during winter weather?"

Harry kept his eyes straight ahead. "Hell, they couldn't even detect the muskrats."

I wrinkled my nose. "The Red Scare is more like keeping up with the Joneses."

Harry let out a loud, heartbreaking laugh that filled the car before lowering his voice. "They want me in the control center that night. You'll have to be the one to warn people, Mary."

"How am I supposed to do that?"

"Lou and I will figure a way." Harry studied the terrain. "Think you could enlist Helen Hinson? Ralph will most likely be required to man maintenance in T-plant during the release."

Ralph was back at work. The doctors at Kadlec said his latest nosebleeds were a temporary reaction to the change in weather, that being beyond their control and all. "So, we're dreaming lucky on December 2nd?"

"If not," Harry shook his head. "I'll likely be going away."

Chapter Seventeen/Luke

End of May 1964

A telegram arrived from my Oban-drinking partner: *Nature in receipt of your paper,* STOP. *Cheers.* STOP. The telegraph formatting warned me to resist any further action until I heard more, as if worries were stoppable. My mother said I was born impatient and had a relapse, but waiting is what drives a person to distraction, and my particular distraction was Mrs. Peters's last words. Why weren't there any clues?

I called Walker. "Can you get off early? I'm thinking of an overnight hike through Packwood Pass." If the FBI was listening in, they could come help search. After slapping together some sandwiches and clearing room in my backpack for I-don't-know-what, evidence maybe, I stuffed in my camera and tossed it into the trunk next to my old two-man pup tent.

Walker was waiting at the Highway 12 junction. We drove back to the café, turned around in the drive, and retraced our route for twenty-two minutes. Half the time that had passed before Bernie had seen Matt drive back by after leaving the parking lot. Ten miles from the café, just beyond a sharp turn, what looked to be a recently installed metal guardrail held a small sign cautioning about the drop-off. I pulled to the other side of the road.

Basalt cliffs lined with pines rose in the distance, capping the valley with graduated columns formed by ancient volcanic eruptions. In the distance Goat Mountain, the now-extinct culprit, glimmered in the afternoon light. I scanned the drop-off at our feet, a series of rugged ledges that stair-stepped into a sea of green and brown before landing at the shores of the Cowlitz river.

Thick brush disrupted by large boulders and patches of fir and pine hid any possible pathway. "Seems like a good place to start."

Walker rolled his eyes. "Should've brought my machete."

"Weren't you the one who told me there's always a trail, just a question of finding it?" I pulled my pack onto my back.

Walker checked the sun. "Bring the tent."

With the tent roped on top of my pack, I swung over the guardrail and followed Walker's lead. An avid rock climber, he was better at finding footholds than I was. We sidestepped our way down the foothill, clutching the occasional shrub root to maintain balance, pausing for any cascading pebbles, lest they turn into a rock slide. Brush reached thigh-high as we neared the bottom, not that you could call it that. The real floor of the valley was a mile out, and though the slope lessened as we walked, it took us deeper into the wild, far out of sight of the road.

The sun played hide-and-seek with the clouds. The temperature rose, but there were too many bugs biting and thorny things clawing at us to risk discarding any layers. A half-hour or so into the valley interior, no trail showed itself.

Walker shimmied across a boulder and waved me over. "Look at that."

A grove of fir trees camouflaged a herd of elk, maybe a dozen or so. A bull raised his head, assessing any threat we might represent, before bowing back into a juniper bush amidst a thick bramble. "No one is scared of us." I scoffed.

"Not them, that." Walker pointed to the right of the herd.

A flash of light spiked before dying as a cloud slid over the sun. We trudged toward it, losing sight of it once, then finding it again, until we stood on top of what we thought we had seen. I kicked at the ground, stirring up nothing but dust. Walker ran a gloved hand across a bush, then raked through another. Nothing. We turned in slow circles, our eyes canvassing the foliage in our rotation. The cloud shifted, and the flash blinded me.

"There," I said, pointing and blinking away my spot-filled vision.

Walker took two steps forward and reached inside the bramble, tearing the sleeve of his flannel shirt. When he extricated his arm, he announced, "We're close."

He opened his palm, revealing a sleek rocket-like chrome ornament that had adorned the hood of every 1947 Chevrolet Fleetline Aero Sedan. It didn't prove a crash, but we were too far from the turnout for the ornament to have just rolled down. "If a car landed anywhere close, it wouldn't be seen from the highway. Any tracks washed away and then some," I said, remembering what Mrs. Peters said about the rain storms. A decade of them by now.

A sick despair filling my chest, I shrugged my pack off my shoulders and sat down on top of it. The elk trotted off, most likely not interested in my pity party.

Walker assessed the sun. "Your call, make camp here and search more tomorrow, or go now before dark takes over. Find a room."

"Shit. I think I just squashed dinner."

Walker raised an eyebrow. "You thought I was going to just eat peanut butter?" He tossed me the hood ornament. "Make camp, I'll be back."

After clearing a small circle of ground and stomping back a few threatening blackberry vines, too green for the picking, I unfurled the tent, the only remnant of my father's short tenure in the infantry before he blew out his knee in basic training. That bad knee had landed him first at an Aberdeen lumber mill in proximity to some of the best fishing in Washington.

Once we moved to Hanford, the tent saw even more service. We did overnights along the Snake River, long before the Ice Harbor Dam blocked the free flow of salmon, night fishing our favorite. We'd take turns skipping rocks across the Snake, the water shimmering in the sinking sun. My father's stamina in coaching my copious attempts, his trajectory, and the arc of his toss provided an early lesson in both fatherhood and velocity.

I pulled the ornament out of my pocket, feeling its weight in my hand. If it had popped off the hood in a crash, the force of the motion would have propelled it most likely high, then wide. After securing the ornament inside my pack, I pulled the baling twine out and measured out twelve or so yards. I tied it to the bush where we'd found the ornament.

Letting the twine loose as I walked, I headed away from camp. The length of twine stretched to a boulder. I sidestepped it, my heart in my throat, and peered to the far side. Nothing. I slogged back, defeated.

Walker showed up with a rabbit, which he skinned and skewered while I found kindling for a fire, salvaged the peanut butter sandwiches, and split one between us, saving one for breakfast. Walker set up a cross-stick rotisserie and lit the fire. The smoke traveled high into the air before the evening breeze took it.

He turned the rabbit and motioned to the loop of twine. "Which way did you walk?"

Mouth full of peanut butter, I pointed east. "About fifty feet."

Walker tracked the smoke traveling into the dusk. "I think we walk a hundred and fifty-feet tomorrow, both directions parallel to the roadway. See what we find."

Dawn was on us before I was finished sleeping, but Walker kicked me in the butt. "Let's go." Before I could stretch, he had the pup tent rolled up. I strapped it above my pack. Walker put his back to the bush where we found the rocket and walked south, establishing our line of search along the slope. The sun crept over the hills, spreading light as we trudged along, finding nothing. I dug out the last sandwich, as if eating would help.

Walker munched on his half of breakfast and licked peanut butter off his fingers, scanning the ridge that edged the roadway. "If something forced the car off the road, depending on the speed of the car, whether she hit the brakes, and assuming she was traveling west, the first bounce could have been off that ledge." He pointed. "Would propel her another thirty or forty yards." He pointed to the circle of boulders we had traversed. "Probably got another bump off those."

Halfway into swallowing, peanut butter clogged any response. My arms fell to my sides, useless. Guilt marched through me, unrelenting, unforgiving. I'd left her with that monster. My anger at her rejection, my foolish adolescent pride had wrought this. I could have kept her safe, stayed on the other side of her bedroom wall, or gutted it up and confronted Matt. But, I'd done none of that. I'd run as far away as I could from my hurt, first to Seattle, then Boston, not even considering what might happen to Mary. After that, I'd put an ocean between us, thinking distance would sever the tie, fool that I was. Still am.

When Walker said walk, he meant plow. The mire of undergrowth fought each step forward, and every time a critter scurried at my feet, I jumped, clutching the chrome ornament so tight my hand cramped. The sun inched toward a high point, and sweat ran down my back, not so much from the heat as the mounting tension of discovery.

I couldn't conceive of Mary in any state other than beautiful, her gentle smile infusing its warmth on cold afternoons on our A-house front porch. Her legs crossed, the top one pumping to the rhythm of Count Basie's orchestra. Her smoke rings would lasso me into her orbit, taking me out of my mundane teenage angst and into the world of possibilities, every one of them populated with her. She couldn't be gone.

Walker stopped and pointed. "Okay, let's try that way next."

That way spanned more of the same dense thicket, a series of small boulders rising above its fray. The secondary rise fifty or so feet beyond the hillside we had scaled the day before blocked the road from view. A hawk lit on the fire-ravaged spine of a fir tree, tracking us. Intent on any ground-level threats, I plodded behind.

Walker came to sudden stop. "Luke."

My head jerked up, and the sight, so unexpected, made me rock back. A rusted car door leaned against a boulder, shored up from behind by undergrowth. I glanced back up the rise. No one could have seen it unless they stood where we stood.

We moved closer. The door, the driver's, erect like a deserted battle shield embedded in the dirt. What remained of the shattered window pane meant it had been halfway rolled down. The weather had taken any color the door might have been, the distinctive chrome trim pocked with rust, but the aerodynamic shape of the window frame tagged with the style of a Chevrolet Fleetline of the late 40s, no question.

"Can we move it?" I whispered this, thinking a paint color might be preserved on the part of it that was buried in the dirt.

"Not yet," Walker said, a clearer thinker. Evidence, of course. "Let's go that way."

Beyond the cliff line we'd been walking, the slope steepened, and another basalt column line plunged before us, like a roller coaster track, causing us to sidestep our way across a drop-off once more. It wasn't hard to understand why no one had ever embraced Packwood's proposed path through these woods, especially back in the late 1800s. The topography would have been a nightmare for road construction.

Walker stuck his knife into the rock ledge like a piton, and we used it to pivot across. Walker reached back to extract his knife. I leaned against the ledge, surveying the territory below.

The hawk soared by. I swiped at my brow. Walker pulled a tear-shaped water bag from his pack, took a swig, and thrust it my way.

"You know," I said, grasping the larger end of the bag. "The Spanish used these for wine, not water."

"Probably why they lost the Americas."

The laughter took over, threatening our balance. We steadied ourselves, laughing again at nothing in particular, at everything: our lack of preparation for a search, our plebeian attempts at detective work, our growling stomachs. Spent, I nestled into the ledge, the stark clarity of the sky daylighting the sobering possibility that we might find her after more than a decade. Something I wasn't sure I wanted after all.

A sea of errant flora stretched before us, making it almost impossible to divine a next step, and that was when I saw it. The slit of red, but not strawberry Lucy-red, but a dark red thin line of color, threading the green and brown mass of undergrowth. Anyone could have hiked right by and never noticed.

Afraid to take my eyes off it, my hand found Walker's arm. "There."

He tracked my gaze. "Okay, after you."

We moved with new caution, the ledge precarious, the way off even more so. We slithered down the last bit of slope on our butts. After a quick scan for any other signs of life, Walker whacked off a couple of walking sticks from a fallen tree branch and handed one to me. "Watch where you're walking."

As if on cue, a skunk padded out of the brush, paused, and then turned his backside in our direction. We froze. He sniffed the air, decided not to use his powers, and ambled off.

Chest-high bramble encompassed our target. Crape myrtles, juniper berry bushes along with an assortment of prickly branches raked our arms and chests. What we couldn't bend back, we hacked away with our hunting knives, creating a passage. As we neared, my chest tightened, my hand clutched at my knife, numb, unresponsive even before I saw it.

Surrounded by thick brush, the Chevrolet lay on its side, the driver's side to the ground. Walker circumvented the wreck, ripping branches away, but a small boulder under the chassis kept us from righting her. Shattered windows all around, a plethora of dents and bashes, the screen of green could not hide the violence of the fall. The trunk lid remained intact, but the hood, crumpled and covering the windshield like an accordion squeezed in to hit a hard note, revealed a thoroughly rusted engine. "If I give you a boost, you can look inside."

My belly flipped. "Can you?"

Walker dragged over a large rock as a stepping stool. "Can't see from this angle. I'll try the door."

I nodded my agreement, and he fiddled with the passenger door handle. It broke off in his hand, but not before he had cracked it open a hair. He used his walking stick like a crowbar, tugging with all his might against the rusted hinges holding it tight. A creak echoed across the hills. His walking stick snapped in two. He pried the door the rest of the way open and stuck his head inside.

My heart froze in mid-beat, along with the rest of me. If someone had given me a slight push, I would have fallen to the forest floor with a thud. And then there was one.

Walker had let the door slam shut. He jumped off his rock and took a step toward me. "There's nothing in there. No bones, no clothing, or any sign of a human, other than this." He held up a broken gold chain, but the small cross was still on it, anchored to the clasp. "It was caught on the gear shift."

The gold chain swung off his fingers like a pendulum, taking me back to that night of warm, slow motion where every fiber in eighteen-year-old me had come alive. I had kissed this cross at the base of her throat before losing myself in her. I was lost there still.

Walker placed the chain and pendant into my outstretched palm and I squeezed it tight, thinking I'd never let it go and knowing I would have to.

"Maybe there's something in the trunk, something that would give us a clue," I said, finding my voice, praying there was no packed bag. That would mean the rumors were true, that Mary had been trying to leave, but I couldn't believe that.

The tenor of Mary and Matt's conversation that the waitress at the café had recounted meant Mary had been after something, not leaving something. She'd never willingly have left Ben and Lucy. My hands too unsteady to attempt it myself, I asked, "Any good at lock picking?"

Walker laughed out loud. "These were still in the ignition." Keys jangling, he moved to the rear of the wreck.

We worked back to back, prying away brush from the car's tail and clearing a bit of room to maneuver. A couple twists of the key and we were in, but animals had found their way through other, smaller points of entry long before. Nibbled holes strafed the carpet. Debris covered the bed of the trunk.

Walker extricated a ravaged woolen picnic blanket, snugged against the wheel bed. "Parts of this are likely feathering many a nest."

"What's that?" I pointed toward what looked like a box, or at least it once was, squeezed into the depression of the wheel bed.

Walker put gloved hands to it, and what was left of the lid, pocked with bite marks, crumbled on one end. In short, gentle tugs, he inched it out of its hiding spot.

"What do you think?" The corners of the box had been chewed away. He was asking me for permission, to remove what could be evidence of a crime, but I was too busy making sure my eyes weren't tricking me. The shoe box lid had faded writing on it, but not so faded that I couldn't read the letters. "'Riffin."

Walker put a hand on my arm to steady me. "Griffin? Harry." He eased the box out into the daylight, revealing a layer of plastic in its interior. He held it safe against his chest. "Now what?"

The forest floor was inches away, and more terrain needed searching, but I didn't have any heart left for finding what might remain. "We found the car. Let's leave the rest for the sheriff."

Walker nodded, clutching Harry's box. "Plus, we have a delivery to complete."

•   •   •

After capturing every angle of the wreck with my camera, it took us another hour to work our way back up to the car. We tied pieces of twine to branches and small trees to mark the trail as we climbed. Then spent the drive to the Lewis County sheriff's office theorizing.

"The wreck is beyond any roadway sightline. The boulders block it off completely." I stated the obvious just to get used to the words on my tongue. "So no one searched the woods."

"Weather erased any signs of the tumble." Walker gazed out his window. "The driver's door broke off. She had to have been thrown out of the car, but no telling where."

Any search party would be hard-pressed to explore it all, but the thought of her free falling, catapulted across the hillside, made me want to catch her. Be the safety net I had promised to be so long ago on the other side of the third-bedroom wall. Be the one sure thing she could count on.

"Thirteen years later, remains will be hard to find. Animals have a way of wiping things clean."

Walker's comment invoked an image that made bile rise in my throat. I tried to swallow it back down, but it stuck midway, the bitter taste fueling my guilt all over again. The shoebox nestled between us on the front seat. The plastic bag was still intact, but so thick with grime we couldn't discern the contents. I suspected the documents inside held more than just a few pieces of the puzzle, a bridge to 1951 and possibly before.

"As to clean slates, Harry needs to see this first, agree?" I motioned to the box.

Walker shrugged. "His name on it. His to tell."

Ellen, Mrs. Peters, my mother, and the hard one, Ben, they would all need telling. Say what we had found and more out loud. Something I wasn't at all sure I could do. The gold chain nestled inside my pocket, the slightest of weight against my thigh, but profound in its pressure. All the answers would not be so easily found, not by two guys out for a hike, but I was certain that Matt Boone knew more than he had ever said.

The afternoon sun rolled toward the sea as we pulled in front of the sheriff's office. The desk sergeant had the newspaper crossword puzzle in front of him, tapping his pencil.

My exhaustion kicked in, and I steadied myself against his desk. "Officer, we've found something pertinent to a missing person case."

The officer looked beyond me to Walker, casting him a suspicious look. "What?"

"An automobile in the valley, below Packwood Pass."

"And this." Walker fished the rocket hood ornament out of his pocket. "About seventy yards from the vehicle."

"The driver's door was separated from the vehicle too. The missing person is Mary Boone," I said, emphasizing missing. "Not seen since July 1950."

The desk sergeant picked up the phone, repeating the crux of our conversation, and then led us behind the gate to an office in the back. The sheriff rose to greet us, with the same not-so-favorable expression for Walker, but invited us to sit. How my friend put up with that shit, I could not imagine. We introduced ourselves.

Walker placed the hood ornament on his desk. "This is from a 1947 Chevrolet FleetLine Aero Sedan."

The sheriff regarded him. "An expert on cars, are we?"

"Among other things." Walker met the sheriff's eye.

I jumped in, proffering the gold chain. "The wreck is fairly far down the bluff. Upended on one side. We found this on the steering wheel. Her mother can attest to it being Mary Boone's." I sat back, hoping that a necklace would be all Mrs. Peters would have to identify.

The sheriff scraped back his chair, strode to the side wall, and yanked open a lower drawer of a filing cabinet. He thumbed through the folders, forward and back again, before extracting a dog-eared file. He plopped the folder in the middle of his desk.

"Let's see what we got." The sheriff removed the rubber band, and the folder sprung open.

A myriad of handwritten notes, typed ones too, spilled onto the desk, along with witness statements from the waitress, Bernie the cook's name on one, Mrs. Peters on another, and then the photo. My ability to comment ceased, but I couldn't avert my gaze.

The sheriff shoved the black-and-white photo across the desk. "Mary Boone?"

A sun ray lit the background behind Lucy and Ben digging in the sand, Mary in the foreground, smiling at the camera, her dark waves luminescent even in the monotone, eyes looking right at me. The last time I had seen those eyes, I had been so angry I had not even said goodbye. Now I wasn't sure I could. What if, I thought, what if, somehow, she survived, but couldn't come back? I shook my head at the ridiculousness of such a scenario.

The sheriff misread my head shake. "Not who you thought it was?"

"No," I struggled for air to feed my voice. "That's her. The car was her father's."

The sheriff rifled through the file. "I've got a number for the mother, Mrs. Peters."

"And Matt Boone?"

"The husband?" The sheriff nodded. "Last number is in Richland. If he's still there."

My head shake was on point this time. "Transferred to Tennessee. Same company, they can most likely give you contact info."

"Find anything else that would be of use?"

"A lot of debris and animal shit. There's a reason no one ever carved out a trail, much less a road that way." I scraped my palms across the stubble on my cheeks, realizing we had not found her purse. "No personal items other than the chain."

Walker put the spool of twine on the desk. "We marked the path down. You'll need gear to clear it. The driver's door came off. You'll find that first, along the way."

The sheriff nodded but didn't say thank you, just pulled out a map and asked us to mark the spot on the highway where the trail began. Walker put an X on the spot but said nothing. He and the sheriff exchanged a look that I would never be able to fully understand.

I broke the awkward silence, tapping the list of names. "We spoke with the folks at the Packwood Café. They said Mr. Boone drove away toward the coast, not Richland."

The sheriff pulled out a paper, stamped: FINAL REPORT. "Says here he left shortly before her, corroborated by witnesses, doesn't say in which direction."

"Mary was staying with her mother in Chinook. Matt should have gone the other way." I let that sit a moment before saying, "The café cook, Bernie, can verify that Matt came back by the café about 45 minutes later. That's how we knew where to look, about twenty minutes down the road toward the coast."

I thrust my card at him with the cabin number, hoping he'd ignore the OSU logo. "Give me a shout if you need anything else." The sheriff let us find our way out. I guess he figured we didn't need any help finding our way out, but I needed exactly that. How to navigate my way in this new world? One without the possibility of Mary ever being in it.

Chapter Eighteen/Mary

December 1949

The Air Force had overruled Jackson, saying they needed to be able to monitor in all weather conditions. A code name, "The Green Run" had been assigned to the operation. Matt left for Seattle, tossing a vague explanation about visiting bigwigs in my direction as he drove off, determined to beat the weather to the pass, spawning images of deserting rats in his wake.

Lois agreed to babysit overnight when I lied about the band's pre-holiday tour dates beginning the first day of December. She thought I was in the Dalles, singing my way back through Chenoweth. I had battened down every window, cautioning her about the wind and Lucy's condition, without telling her what the incoming storm might hold that night. After admonishing her to keep the windows closed, I'd also added that there'd been a prowler in the neighborhood, for extra measure.

Helen, far more ham radio savvy than I, commandeered the bedroom on the far, top corner of the Wang's house. Les Brown's orchestra blared from the Victrola in the Wang's parlor below us, covering the spatter of Luke's ham radio as Helen found the various channels we would need. From our second-floor perch, we could see north across the river and back south to The Area, dusk a hard gray over the barren landscape.

An iodine study a couple of years prior had revealed more than a thousand times the current permissible level in the Wang's sheep. Hanford had failed to inform Wang. His wife had dropped dead among the tomato plants a year later. Lou, through his in-laws, had built a trust with Wang and several other families in the vicinity that made up our radio operators' network tonight. The older Wang son, Joe, hung out with us until his father shooed him downstairs.

•   •   •

Helen placed a list on the table beside her. Ham operators located in almost every township within a hundred-mile radius of our frequency. Lou said we could trust them all to do the right thing. She tuned the dials on Luke's radio, adjusting and turning again, before issuing a greeting using our code call sign. "Tinseltown Tattler here, who's out tonight?"

Harry would weigh in soon from the command center, the second frequency on the list, with surreptitious updates. His seemingly innocuous comments would keep us abreast of what was transpiring with the plume.

"It's beginning," I said. A pal of Harry's had given us frequencies so we could listen in on the pilot's exchange as well as the Company's control room.

A drone of airplane engines came across the radio. Then a squawk. "Instruments not tracking—" An anxious voice of what must have been a young pilot cut out. Static filled the room. Helen touched my arm, motioning to the window. Dark clouds clogged the sky.

In my dreams, I'd imagined a purple-blue vapor. Visible only in the cavities of my mind, and it would grow larger, an ionized beauty, diving downward, subject to the whims of the wind. And I floated in the southern sky, watching it hit the ground, before spiking up again and shooting southeast, where I couldn't stop it, no matter how hard I tried. The black of the night invaded, magnifying the voices on the radio.

"Over Walla Walla now...inversion layer covering the entire town." The young pilot dropped off again. My heart stopped. We didn't have a radio operator there.

The drone of engines increased. Helen lifted the binoculars to her face, pointing as two planes came into view. She turned the radio dial to the designated frequency. A dozen operators would hear my voice, along with anyone else twisting the dial that night. I'd practiced a Bette Davis droll voice, lest I be recognized.

"A long tail of cars in Tinseltown, as Hollywood lights up the boulevard." Every operator had been given a list of code words for the various elements: Tinseltown was the entire region, cars the Air Force planes, Hollywood was the Hanford along with the scientists controlling the releases. The boulevard was the desert terrain below the flight path and of course, the lights meant the plume's possible path based on the aircraft's readings. "Spotlights are visible beyond the Hollywood Hills, as well as on the Boulevard. What a sight."

Helen twisted the dial back to The Area frequency. A frightened voice, caught halfway into a sentence, squeaked, "...6,000 curies and climbing. What the hell?"

Helen spun the dial to our designated frequency, her hand shaking.

Stifling panic, I infused my message with little girl wonder. "More lights than ever before, so unexpected, blinding all of the Boulevard and beyond."

Blinding was the mayday word, seal the house tight, shelter in place. Harry had said the plan was for a release of four thousand curies of iodine-131.

Helen tuned the dial back to The Area frequency. "Seven thousand." An audible gasp, I wasn't sure whose, followed by a telling silence in the control room. Approaching twice the planned release, the danger exceeded all our fears.

The voice of a meteorologist—the Air Force had them stationed in a variety of places to track the weather—came on, clipped, panicky. "The wind—blowing the wrong way."

They had thought they could predict the wind. I would have laughed if it wasn't so dire. Targets not chosen, terrifying in the possible random devastation to come. Helen twisted the dial back to our network.

Keeping my voice light as the Wizard-of-Oz good witch, I intoned, "The lights have animated the Boulevard, as if a road can rise up and change course, dumping the cars off as it magically cuts a new path. That's Tinseltown for you, special effects we can never predict."

The temperature dropped to a sleet level. The wind stagnated around midnight, then swirled in the icy rain, shifting directions as if targeting Walla Walla. The meteorologist in Walla Walla broke up on the frequency, clearly frantic about the low-pressure system that could draw the plume downward. "...like a blanket. Can see..." The Area control center didn't respond.

Helen dialed to the pilot's frequency. "We've lost contact, no wait. Turning 180 degrees." The pilots couldn't keep up, much less measure the emissions.

Helen covered the mic, handed me the binoculars, and pointed toward The Area. "Mary, look." The moon had peeked out just enough to light up the heavy clouds drifting toward Richland, stretching a finger over the houses of the scientists monitoring the release as well as ours. "We can't go back. Not tonight."

Thank goodness Lois had agreed to stay overnight with the twins. Helen twisted the dial and cued me.

"Imagine such a scene lighting up the main street in your town too. Tinseltown in our own backyard." I shot a look at Helen as she spun back to The Area frequency.

Static took over, drowning out what was several voices in the control room at once. "Hot spots everywhere...our equipment...lost track...Kennewick..." And then, Harry said, "Levels a thousand times greater than..." The static returned, but Harry's sentence did not need finishing. Radiation levels were always compared to background. Back when the world was supposedly normal.

The entire region had been dosed, and no one was immune. Not college students in Walla Walla, not pregnant mothers in Pasco, not the basketball crowd flowing out of the gymnasium at Spokane's high school, not the farmers and their families in the hills, not the natives on the reservation, and certainly not the families in Richland.

Radio chatter at the command center broke into my thoughts.

Harry's voice pierced the night. "They're going to do what?"

Static mixed with a low voice I didn't recognize. "Not enough results...can't measure...have to do another...tomorrow night."

Helen's hand gripped mine like a vise, as I intoned, "That's a wrap in Tinseltown for tonight folks, but stay tuned. We hear there will be an even bigger show tomorrow."

Helen clicked off the dial. Luke's radio sputtered to silent mode. A few stars twinkled against the blue-black dark to the north. Downwind, clouds laden with deadly particles clogged the sky.

Helen peered out the window as if searching for something she knew she wouldn't find. "The Clark girl, she's a junior now at Whitman. Joined an a cappella group. Her mother told me they were Christmas caroling on the campus tonight, then strolling down Main Street." Helen's face looked like it would crack in two. "I didn't say anything."

My eyes locked with Helen's, picturing the holiday lights strung across the small downtown of Walla Walla, arcs lit like a portal to heaven. "I have to get the twins out of here."

•   •   •

My suitcase sat half-full on the edge of the bed. The twins toddled around the bedroom, sliding their feet into my shoes, giggling at their inability to stand up. I caught Lucy in the crook of my arm as she toppled and kissed her forehead. It was warm, a fever in the making. Ben drew up on my leg, the three of us in a full-body huddle when Matt walked in.

"Going somewhere?"

"Going down to Mos-coh. For the holidays, remember?" I brushed past him to the bathroom and wrenched the thermometer out of the medicine cabinet. "Lucy has a temperature."

Matt gripped my forearm. "You think I don't know what you did over the weekend?"

I froze, searching his face for any sign of a bluff. We'd been so careful, but small-town gossip has a way of peeling away any façade. Hanford's tentacles stretched everywhere. Around every corner of Richland someone waited, listened, watched. Whatever Matt thought he knew, he was sure of it, so I laughed. That threw him off for the moment I needed to wrest away. I spun back to Ben, setting Lucy up on our bed and putting him beside her.

"If you're referring to the gig with the band, we played the Chenoweth Inn. Other than that," I folded my arms across my chest. "I don't know what you're talking about."

Matt took a step back, leaning into the bathroom door frame, eyeing me. "Little Miss Mary, always so contrary." He moved to block the doorway, a flash of anger in his eyes. "You think you could cheat on me and I wouldn't find out?"

He thought I was having an affair. Perfect. I exhaled my fear and sucked in air for the real fight. "Wouldn't that be the other way around, Mister?"

Matt's look wavered for a split second, giving credence to my accusation. "You can't make this about me. People have seen you at the widower Wang's." He didn't say when.

My belly seized, but I masked my panic by putting my hands on my waist and taking a firm stance, cooling my voice to an even tone. "Of course, they have." I opened a dresser drawer, feigning exasperation. "Helen and I occasionally gather eggs at the Wang farm. Happy to give you his number."

Matt's stare bored into me, but I folded my sweaters into the suitcase, holding my shaky ground, wondering who was within shouting distance. Ellen wasn't due to pick me up for another half hour. Matt's mouth twisted into a smile. "No need. The FBI is already on the trail."

"And just what trail might that be?"

"Harry's for one. You by association."

"I haven't seen Harry for almost a week. I didn't get home until late Tuesday." Mr. Wang had insisted we stay until the "dust had settled," as if it would. "Not that you were here to notice." I chanced an accusatory look of my own, steeling inside for what might come next.

Matt's eyes focused on the suitcase. "A bit early to leave for the holidays."

"Mother's clearing out the house for sale. I told her I'd help. Ellen's picking me up on her way home from Seattle."

Matt raised an eyebrow. I wondered if he had worked it out yet. Knew that I was the one responsible for losing any second chance we might have had, not that either of us wanted one. Or did he?

"Her UW medical school interviews, remember?" I picked a jack-in-the-box toy off the floor and tossed it into the suitcase. If the FBI was tailing Harry, then Lou could be exposed too, not to mention the shoebox.

Matt leaned back against the dresser, pulling out a cigarette, blocking me from packing anything else. "Your leaving now doesn't send the right signal."

There it was, the real reason. "What signal?" I wanted to make him say it. The powers that be had most likely commanded him to return from Seattle, worried about the rumors bouncing back and forth across the river between Pasco and Richland.

"That Richland isn't safe."

The fence post chatter in the hills, grocery line conversations in Kennewick, questions rising over a swath of blackened terrain here, a dead animal there, had finally culminated, at least I hoped so. Five years in and multiple atomic bombs later, did the government actually believe no one in a town of over twenty thousand was going to put it together?

"Are you accusing me of something specific?"

Matt smashed his cigarette in my ring dish. "Just reminding you that you took an oath."

My eyes met his, in the same proximity as we had been at the altar, declaring our everlasting love that had lasted just two years before the first blow. "So did you, but that hasn't stopped you from doing what you want to do." I snapped the suitcase shut.

Matt caught my arm, jerking his head in the direction of the twins. "Don't think I can't take away everything you love." His eyes, full of darkness, held the familiar threat.

But I didn't shrink away, old wounds solidifying, taking on a strength of their own. "What I think is, you're incapable of keeping any promise."

A horn honked outside. The front door creaked open, and Ellen called out. "Mary?"

Matt's grip faltered. I shrugged off his hand, gathered up the twins, and bumped down the stairs. I deposited them into Ellen's arms, knowing the danger I left behind would only fester. The shoebox was no longer safe at Lou's.

We eased away from the curb and had left the A-house in the distance before I said, "Ellen, blinker down," I said, indicating she take a left. "I need to make a quick stop in Pasco on the way out of town."

•   •   •

The holidays passed in a blur. Back in Richland, the faux-marital dance that Matt and I performed kept me spinning. Had I just imagined he'd guessed the truth of the twins? The ever-present threat of him calling me out on the lie kept me awake most nights, turning the reasons for his lack of accusation over in my head. My revised part-time schedule at the lab took me away from the twins three days a week in the new year, but at least my getaway stash was growing. Harry had taken up the slack, assisting on the coins-to-bills front. Every time I handed him a fistful of dimes, I wondered what Luke was doing and who he might be with.

Ben and Lucy didn't just crawl, they raced, their one-year-old chubby legs churning in tandem while I prepped dinner in a good wife pretense. Ben anchored himself to the kitchen door frame, peering in wonder at the steam rising from the water boiling for spaghetti. Ralph Hinson passed through my peripheral vision, home earlier than usual. Lucy swished her way past her brother and slid under a chair at the kitchen table, wrapping her pudgy hands around its legs like jail bars, grinning out at us.

I lowered the raw noodles into the pot and turned to Ben. "Well, mister—"

Helen's scream pierced the kitchen wall. "Ralph!" Another wail. "Ralph, please..."

I dashed out and burst into the Hinson's side of the A-house. Just beyond the vestibule, Helen crouched on the living room rug. Ralph lay prostrate underneath her chest, motionless, blood crusting on his nose.

"Helen? What is it?"

Helen cried, "Call an ambulance!"

I raced back to my side of the duplex. Oblivious to the drama next door, Ben and Lucy had both crawled under the kitchen table, playing tug of war with a fire engine toy. Dragging the phone cord to the stove, I flipped the burner off, dialed the Hanford emergency number, and pushed the pot of boiling water to the back of the stove. "Emergency."

"A man has collapsed. You must come right away." After giving the address, I raced back to Helen.

She had cradled Ralph's head in her lap, rocking back and forth, tears streaming her cheeks.

I knelt beside her, trying to understand what had happened to Ralph. The only thing I was sure of was who was responsible. "Is he...?"

The ambulance, siren blaring, screeched to a halt outside. Two attendants hustled up the steps, followed by Lois.

Helen shifted to Ralph's far side, and I placed my arm behind her back, afraid she might keel over. "The twins are by themselves," I said to Lois, motioning to my side of the duplex.

"I'll check on them." Lois ducked out.

"Ma'am?" One of the attendants said. "Can you tell us what happened?" His partner checked Ralph's chest with a stethoscope, then gave his head the slightest shake. He put his hand on Ralph's wrist, but after only a few seconds, the attendant let go.

Helen smoothed her hand over her husband's limp one. "He came home early, complaining of a burning sensation." She stroked Ralph's cheek, her voice halting. "Said his throat was sore too and lay down on the couch. I thought nothing of it. Too busy starting dinner." Helen flinched under my hand still on her back. "I came in to check on him. Saw his nose was bleeding. He...he gets nosebleeds sometimes." Helen looked up at the attendant, her eyes vacant. "I went back to the kitchen to get ice, a cold cloth...it only took a minute. He couldn't have..." Her voice trailed off in denial.

"About," I said, checking my wristwatch. "Ten minutes ago."

"When I came back with the ice, he was on the floor, unconscious." Helen looked lost.

"He must have tried to get up." I offered, propping Helen against the edge of the couch. Knowing she would not leave Ralph's side, I nestled in next to her. "Helen, I..." I wrapped my arm around her, unable to complete a sentence.

The attendants covered Ralph with a blanket that Helen tucked closer. We followed them out to the ambulance, a surplus State Patrol vehicle whose back cab had been retrofitted to accommodate stretchers.

"I'll drive you." I squeezed Helen's shoulder. "Where do you keep the keys?"

Helen turned to me. "Luke. I should call Luke." Her words fell between us as if she wanted me to catch them, but that was a ball I could not field.

"You can do that in a bit," I said. Ben trotted to our front door, the red tuft of baby hair catching the afternoon light. Lucy grabbed him from behind, wrapping his belly with her arms as if she'd never let go. I hoped she wouldn't.

Lois appeared behind them, wrapped in one of my aprons, holding up my purse. "You go. I'll finish dinner and stay with the twins."

Helen emerged with her car keys, and I took her elbow to navigate the porch steps. As I turned the key in the ignition, Helen said, "We have to insist on an autopsy."

The gear shift grated as I shifted into first and eased away from the curb. "I don't think you need to worry about that. The doctors at Kadlec will be more than happy to accommodate." My hands gripped the steering wheel, knowing some Hanford medical staff would most likely relish the prospect, but share the real results? Not likely.

I had typed notes for another engineer at the technical lab. He had become lethargic and gone into Kadlec several times for blood work. Five years in, they finally told him he had cancer. The hospital was staffed with doctors who may or may not tell you the truth of your situation. Timing being everything and all.

•   •   •

Ralph had been dead forty-eight hours. An unfamiliar Luke was sprawled across the front steps when I arrived home from work. College had smacked him into an angular, clear-skinned young man, but sadness framed his edges. I dropped down beside him, wanting to do more, knowing I shouldn't make the first contact. But my shoulder touched his, and he didn't pull away.

"I'm so very sorry." The apology wasn't just for his father. It was for all the hurt I'd caused.

"Those assholes at Hanford aren't." Luke shook his head into the spit of sunshine filtering through the maple trees that Ralph had planted the year they had moved. The branches drooped as if they knew he was gone. It had been dry for over two weeks, an oddity in early January.

A dandelion had sprouted or maybe just survived the winter, like me. Lucy crawled out the door to me. I scooped her up and crossed the lawn to pluck the dandelion. "Shall we blow it and make a wish?"

Lucy's cheeks puffed up to blow, and we exhaled together, the dandelion tentacles spreading into the breeze along with my wish that I could find the right way to tell Luke. The folded paper inside my bra—a carbon copy of a weekly report—scraped against my breast, reminding me I had something else to hide. Gathering my courage, I put my cheek to Lucy's, but my resolve gave way to a new concern. I drew my hand up to Lucy's forehead. Hot.

Lucy on my hip, I moved back into our side of the A-house. Lois gathered Ben up, preparing for our end-of-day handoff, but I held up a hand. "Can you watch Ben a moment longer?" Lois nodded, and I loped up the stairs to the bathroom. Extracting the thermometer from the medicine cabinet, I said, "Come on, baby, let's check your temperature."

After a minute or so in Lucy's mouth, the thermometer read 103. My mind flew to the article I'd just read on polio outbreaks, and I clipped back down the stairs with Lucy in my arms.

Helen had come out onto the porch and leaned against the stanchion, her face a mix of amusement and sadness as Luke chased Ben around the tree, tagging the toddler on the crawl. "You're it," Luke said and backed up, dragging his heels so Ben could catch him.

Ben spit out the baby talk equivalent of "you." He clutched at Luke's leg, pulling himself into a sitting position on the hard ground.

"I hate to ask," I said, huffing more from my fright than the flight down the stairs. "But, Lucy's temperature has spiked. I need to get her to the hospital. Lois needs to go. Can you watch Ben until Matt gets home? Shouldn't be long."

Helen drew a bead on me. "Don't take her to Kadlec."

I scurried to the car.

●   ●   ●

The winter sun had set while Lucy and I were at the hospital. Except for the occasional parlor light, the entire block had yielded to the dark. Smoke from Matt's Camel cigarette drifted from the porch. He hadn't brought up the band gig again, but certain he still didn't believe my story, his silence had me even more worried. I hefted a half-asleep Lucy out of the car and climbed the steps.

"Well?" Matt had a scowl on his face.

"The doctors at Lady of the Lourdes want her back tomorrow. Not polio, thank God, but they wouldn't say what. They are doing some bloodwork." I sighed, and Lucy sank into my chest.

Matt grimaced. "You couldn't have taken her to Kadlec where that sort of thing is free?"

Helen stepped out onto the porch, her timing impeccable. "How was the casserole from Lois?"

Matt found a half-smile. "Not bad in a pinch, though tuna's not my favorite."

Helen put a hand to Lucy's back. "Shall I heat you up another choice?"

"Tuna suits me fine," I said. "Where's Ben?'

Helen swiped at the perspiration on her forehead. "Inside." She pointed to her door. "He's been Luke's shadow since you left."

The fierce tug on my heart at her words had to be visible, but neither Matt nor Helen seemed to notice. "I'll put Lucy to bed and come get Ben."

"No rush. Nice having a baby in the house." A sadness swept across Helen's face, her grief ever-present.

Lucy shifted in my arms as I climbed upstairs to the nursery. Her teddy bear eyed me from the corner of the crib, and I tucked the bear in next to her. Her arm fell over the stuffed toy, covering one eye, but not the other, as if begging the question: Should I tell Luke?

•　•　•

Ralph Hinson had been dead for three weeks. No one had mentioned a funeral, and I hadn't asked. Luke had been back and forth from Seattle three times. The doctor had sent Lucy's bloodwork to a specialist, saying it would be another week and not to worry, as if that were possible. Up early, after another restless night, I perched on the front porch, migrating my position to take in the early Saturday morning sun, keeping my cardigan close.

Matt breezed past me, mumbling something about a Union-organized breakfast celebrating Washington's Birthday. He drove off. Lucy and Ben were still sleeping.

Luke stepped out onto the porch, car keys jangling, and he almost sounded friendly when he said, "You're up early."

"Couldn't sleep. Where are you off to?"

"Transporting Dad to the King County coroner."

"Why?"

"The Kadlec autopsy came back, saying Dad died of a brain aneurysm. No other causes." Luke snorted. "It's bullshit, a cover-up. My college roomie knows the coroner's family. He's arranged for him to do a second autopsy." Luke's face held the same determination that Ben's did when he had first walked, lips stretched in a straight line, forehead knotted, eyes fierce.

"Wait a second. Something you should see."

I raced up the stairs, eased past the twins' room, and stepped into my sewing room. The report I'd taken the day before was tucked under the jars of cash in my crochet basket, a hiding place that Matt had not messed with, unlike my dressing table. I extracted the document and tiptoed back downstairs.

Luke's arms were stretched across the porch railing, shoulders sagging as if his torso were too heavy to stand on its own. He straightened the moment my foot hit the threshold.

I thrust the carbon copy at him. "A copy of the monthly report for January." My finger moved down the page. "Read here."

"A Class I radiation incident occurred on January 27ᵗʰ." Luke looked at me, questions in his eyes. "The day before Dad died."

"In the same area where your father is a supervisor. The incident involved several men who worked with him."

The sun had pushed the entire block into the day, a relentless light that exposed all the imperfections of the supposed perfect family town. The siding on Lois's house had a gash from her husband tossing a shovel into it, his anger never explained. The trash cans across the street had vodka bottles forcing the lid open. The house behind them had shades drawn as they were every hour of the day. What they hid was anyone's guess. And me, standing there, next to the father of my children, unable to say the words.

Luke read out loud. "It says the men unknowingly handled barrels of radioactive waste." He shook his head.

"Read on. It says the men were 'unmonitored' and that the dose they received was not recorded."

"That can't be. Dad was so careful, so protective of his workers."

I shook my head in anger. "And no fatality is mentioned in the report, most likely because your Dad died off-site." I paused, uncertain if I should say more, but Luke deserved to know. "They don't record any death if it doesn't physically happen in The Area."

"Can I keep this?" Luke slid the report into his back pocket, not waiting for an answer.

"Something else," I said. "A burn on your father's arm, his left one. I remember because it almost looked alive. Your mother may have seen it, too."

Luke grimaced. "I've gotta go. Check in on Mom, would you?"

Baby talk wafted out from above, oblivious to the severity of the morning. I twisted my head to look up, as if Ben and Lucy might pop out the window, but the sun breaching the roofline blinded me, creating spots across my vision. When I turned back to wave, Luke was pulling away from the curb, his eyes on the road. We never said goodbye.

Chapter Nineteen/Luke

Late May 1964

We drove straight to the crab shack, catching Harry in close-out mode behind the front counter. The lingering smell of French fries from the dinner service made my stomach growl, and I said as much. Harry shot me a look and pulled some leftover clam chowder out of the fridge.

He lit a burner on the stove he had just wiped clean. "Better be worth it."

"Pretty sure it is," I said, sliding the handkerchief-wrapped, half-shoebox and its contents onto the counter.

Walker motioned to the crumbling box. "We found it in her car trunk."

The 'her' needed no definition, not for Harry. His eyes moistened, locking on the box, but he didn't touch it. This box drowned all hope, like the Columbia overflowing its banks, taking all our what-ifs in its wake. Mary was gone.

"No one knows but us." I put a hand on Harry's shoulders. "Your name. Yours to open."

Harry turned away to stir the pot, his back rising and falling in a jagged rhythm, shudders that shed a decade of maybes. He snatched a dish towel and dragged it over his face. He stretched to extract two bowls off the shelf, his hand shaking as he ladled chowder into both. Head down, he set the bowls in front of us and tossed cracker packets our way.

Walker and I dove into our bowls like men who'd been on army rations for months.

Harry used the towel to wipe away some of the grime on the plastic bag in reverent, short strokes, ginger touches relaying grief. The rubber band broke into brittle pieces at his first tug. The car trunk must have been an oven during the dry season. He pried the partially-melted plastic bag apart, so slow a slug could have crawled the length of the bar by the time he had it open.

I raised off my stool to glimpse inside. Seeing the CLASSIFIED stamp on the top document, my surprise erupted. "What the fuck, Harry?"

The night fell into a fog of do-we-don't-we as Harry lifted the papers out, remarkably well-preserved. "Luke, check the door. Be sure it's dead-bolted, the back too."

When I returned, Harry and Walker had arranged the documents on the counter, grouped by date. The earliest were dated September of '47, others bore the year 1950.

Walker, eyes wide, held one in his hands dated December 1949. "They did this?"

"With little if any remorse." Harry nodded, but he seemed removed, bogged down like putting words to it took a strength he didn't have left. "We couldn't stop them. Dr. Jackson tried, but then he caved." Harry raised his eyes to mine. "Mary made copies of a lot of our work. Summaries of others. Proof of haphazard practices around the radioactive waste. She smuggled them out. The bravest of us all."

Inside my head, a thousand past and entirely wrong assumptions crashed against one another. I hadn't believed in her. I hadn't looked past the surface, even though that was what I was trained to do.

My belly jerked, and I fled out the back door I had just bolted, past the storage locker, beyond the pile of buoys and ropes, and braced against the railing, hurling my chowder out to sea. The wind whipped around me, mocking, burning my eyes, but it couldn't compete with the brushfire of emotion devouring me.

A hand touched my back. Walker stepped to the rail beside me. "Any answers out there?"

"I should have known. Seen she was trying to protect me." I sagged, unable to explain.

"My grandfather says knowing is only the first step to understanding." Walker eyed the horizon for who knows what before turning to me. "If we ever can."

An open spillway of tears, a torrent held back in the decade since my father's death gushed out of me. Since Mary. When they subsided, Walker handed me a wet dishcloth. I mopped my face. "A dry cloth would have been better," I choked, laughing out the last of my sobs. For now.

Walker turned his back to the wind. "You know this could blow things up pretty good."

"Maybe." We stood there, letting the mist enshroud us, letting the wind lash us. Tasting the salt, I thought of all the times the government had erased the truth, blackening out the truth of my father's death on every document. "There isn't enough black marker in the world to redact a whale, right?"

•　　•　　•

My ability to acknowledge the new truth surrounding Mary's disappearance ebbed and flowed. My mother topped the list of folks to call, not just because she and Mary had been close, but because I needed her support telling Mrs. Peters and Ben about finding the car. My mother agreed to drive down early the next day. When I heard her tires on the gravel drive, my insides twisted up again after a day and a night of trying to iron them out.

My mother exited the car, a look of worry on her face when she took me in. I hadn't shaved in three days. The scruff on my chin fit with my state of mourning, as did my torn tee shirt, but I was not prepared to admit those feelings to my mother. Not yet, but just when you think you've grown past the comfort of a parent, well, you haven't. My hug almost knocked her over. We sank to the porch boards, tears in our eyes, and me wondering exactly what my mother knew.

My mother rubbed my back, hooked a finger in a hole in my tee shirt, and snorted. "Don't tell me, it's a favorite you can't let go of."

Despite my state, I laughed, remembering the tugs of war we'd played whenever she had tried to toss out my old clothes, a well-worn pair of PJs, a much-beloved pair of fishing overalls, and a too-small white shirt. The one I'd worn that night with Mary. I'd stuffed it so deep in my closet, it didn't occur to me she'd find it. But my mother always found everything.

"Tell me," I said. "Everything you remember about when she left. And after."

She shifted her focus to the bay, bright blue and glistening, filled with its own set of secrets. "She never admitted she was leaving for good. Summer vacation, she said."

"She didn't call you?"

"Long distance used to be a much bigger thing." My mother closed her eyes, swaying a bit with the breeze. "She sent a postcard. Said she was so happy here, by the sea."

"Did Harry tell you he hooked her up with a lawyer?"

My mother shook her head. "Divorce attorney?"

My turn to stare out to sea. "Yeah." The whole so-close thing bounced around my gut, along with the endless questions of how her car had ended up on the backside of that bluff. "Walker says it was probably bears."

My mother shot me a quizzical look.

"The reason we didn't find any remains," I said. "Bears return to feed over and over again until there's not much left."

"The sheriff will search, right? Clothing scraps?" Neither of us could say bones.

"She was thrown from the car, for sure," I said, finding my scientific mode center after hours of emotional upheaval. "But, most anything would be strewn high and wide by now."

The thought of Mary's favorite blouse lining a bird's nest made me oddly happy. Wisps of white silk soothing a bluebird's eggs.

My mother stood up, lifting her face to the sky. "She told me once that her father gave the best bear hugs." Her words lilted on the breeze, offering up a first line to the eulogy I was writing in my head, not that I had the strength to deliver any such thing. Mother squeezed my hand, and I squeezed back, not letting her let me go. "I'm going to make us a cup of tea," she said. "Fortification before we go see the Peters."

Her lips brushed my cheek, and she pushed off, but I stayed put, not wanting to move closer to the moment of telling. A hawk dove into the bramble on the far side of the marsh, and I thought of all the creatures that could have had a part in taking Mary, not apart, but to safety. Hiding her in every nook and cranny of the forest. Burying her spirit in the rich, undisturbed floor, a place of rebirth, a catalyst to future beauty.

The screen door screeched and slammed. My mother held up the bottle of immune tablets. "What are these?" Her accusatory look made me flinch. The BioHarvest tablets promised an immune support that could help combat cancer.

"Roy dropped them off." On the defensive, I stood, glad that I could without wobbling.

"Does this mean the cancer is back?" Mother missed nothing.

"No. Just a precaution. And I've only been taking them for a month." I didn't add that I'd had a back and forth with a man from Richland. One of the folks who endorsed the product lived downwind from Hanford. His testimonial, which had taken up a half page in the *Portland News*, credited the tablets for making him cancer-free after six months. Although he gave a lot of credit to prayers from his Mormon congregation as well. "I have another scan week after next."

"Who knew my science-based son would fall prey to charlatan medicine men?" My mother chucked the bottle at me. "Change your shirt. We need to go."

I opened my mouth to protest, wanting to justify my choices as mine to make. But my mother held up her hand, silencing me. "Luke, I can only deal with one tragedy at a time."

•   •   •

Two new large turquoise pots overflowing with poppies, zinnias, and potato vines flanked the front porch posts. Mrs. Peters set down her water pail as we pulled up. A resigned look took over her face as if she knew our visit was not one she would enjoy, but one she must endure.

My mother reached for her hand. "Is Ben here?"

Mrs. Peters nodded, casting a worried eye to the screen door, but a rustle at the side of the house produced Ben, fishing pole in one hand, his transistor in the other. Had he grown another inch in just a week? I'd grown five inches in my sophomore year of high school.

"Hey, mister," he chirped, cheerier than I'd ever seen him. "I researched that Tritium, wanna see my boards?"

"Benjamin," his grandmother interrupted. "This is Luke's mother, Helen. She was a good friend of your mother's. She and Luke, they may have some news for us."

Ben stood as still as a cornered mouse assessing his options. Most likely, he had a cadre of escape hatches, tested and true. I had several when I was fifteen too. Sometimes it was as simple as putting on the right jazz, others involved a pole like the one Ben had in his hand, but my go-to move was out my bedroom window on a starry night, flattening into the eaves of the house, where no one and nothing could touch me.

I wanted to tell him how studying the stars could help with what was to come, and how I could help too, but, instead, I said, "Before we look at your work, let's sit for a moment, okay?"

Ben's legs stiffened, but his hands dropped to his sides. The transistor clunked onto the porch. The fishing pole angled toward the ground, a string of a half-dozen flies lassoed to it, intricate in their design, colorful, sure to catch the eye of a salmon. "I'll lose the light."

I'd already lost mine. Mary had been my north star. The thing I hung my destiny on. The one true thing I'd known in my short life, no matter how much I denied it, railed against it, against her. And she was Ben's too. If I took that away, no telling what the boy would do.

My mother took a slow, sure step toward Ben. "You weren't quite two when I last saw you. Luke told me you're a scientist, too."

Ben's legs softened, kneecaps showing through his dungarees. He set the pole against the side of the house, as if he knew nothing could be a defense against what we had to say. His grandmother put an arm around him, and they shuffled to the porch steps.

My mother and Mrs. Peters flanked either side of him, their combined motherly aura almost as colorful as the flower pots. I searched the ground for a dry spot, and seeing none, I squatted, elbows on my thighs, the balls of my feet sure to give out, but the ache felt necessary, deserved.

"A couple of days ago, my pal, Walker, and I hiked into Packwood Pass. A deeper interior search than the police did a decade ago." I scanned my audience for a response, finding Mrs. Peters's eyes. Her slight nod propelled me onward. "We found what we believe to be your late husband's car, Mrs. Peters." The air in my lungs flooded out, leaving me weak. I rocked back to the ground, feeling the damp earth dig into the seat of my jeans.

My mother shot me a look of sympathy. "Luke reported it to the sheriff. They are reopening the investigation. Mary, your mother," she squeezed Ben's arm, "appears to have been in an accident."

A voice so small, it could have been the breeze instead. Just a rustle of words, unrecognizable, except they sounded just like Lucy. "But you didn't find her."

To give him our theories, theories that would only beget nightmares in a teenage boy's mind, seemed cruel. I shook my head. "We found her cross necklace."

Ben jerked to his feet and bolted past me, leaping over his fishing gear and pivoting into the forest behind the house. He had his go-to places too. None of us rose, statues in our spots.

"Ben!" His grandmother's half-hearted cry carried little weight, more plaintive than one meant to call him back. A Blue jay landed on the pot beside her, pecking at the poppy. Mary had insisted we put flower seeds into the time capsule when I'd negated her canned peaches. Promise of life, she'd said, and who knows what people may or may not grow in the future.

My mother linked her arm to Mrs. Peters's. "The sheriff will call you. They'll match the vehicle plates, but will want you to identify the necklace most likely."

"So." Mrs. Peters's face went stoic. "No sign of a body?"

My head shook itself, so used to going through the motion at this point, it was the only direction it would move. No to everything, no to signs of life, to bones, to further clues, to hope. The only no I could voice was, "No guardrails back then. Happened in a split second."

Mrs. Peters cast an eye to the sky, the sun holding strong in the west, dusk still hours away. "Her father used to say that she was prone to jumping off cliffs, the higher the better."

Had I been one of them? A jump worth taking? In uncomfortable moments like these, I tended to offer up useless observations to cover my insecurities. "She picked a good one. There's a reason they call it Goat Rocks Wilderness."

My mother rolled her eyes at me as she wrapped Mrs. Peters in a hug. "Should Luke go after Ben?"

Mrs. Peters dug for a handkerchief and swiped at her eyes. "He'll need some time to himself, but he'll be back."

"Mrs. Peters, I'm so—" But then I was stuck. Sorry didn't cover it. I was devastated, frustrated by the lack of final answers, and defiant of the facts at the same time. A limbo landscape that felt more welcoming than any resolution. Uncertainty I could wallow in. I swallowed the choke in my throat. "Tell Ben I'll call tomorrow. Set a fishing date up."

Mrs. Peters pulled away from my mother's embrace and slid her hand down my arm. "That last summer, Mary told me about you. Said you were off to do grand things."

I dragged my hands down the scruff on my cheeks. "I'm not so sure."

Mrs. Peters smiled Mary's smile. "She was."

• • •

Roy received the letter from *Nature* magazine four weeks later. We had used his parents' address in Portland, not trusting our mailboxes. Walker leaned against the railing, peering at what looked to be a summer storm brewing. Uncertain of my ability to stay standing no matter what the letter said, I sank into the rocker.

Roy held up the envelope. "On three?"

"Just open the damn thing." My annoyance with all things in my universe had only mounted since we had found the car. At my last checkup, Mary's sister Ellen had scurried around a far corner of the hallway as if trying to avoid me. My scan had shown a reduction in the cancerous cells, but my mother was at me again, taking issue with the immune supplements. Her argument—that I had no idea what I was consuming—fell flat when I assured her I'd analyzed every ingredient before swallowing the first tablet.

Roy ripped open the flap and slid out the single sheet of paper. "Dear Sirs," Roy said, and paused. "We regret to inform you..."

The rest didn't matter. They had rejected us. I sprang out of the rocker and stomped off the porch. I scooped up a handful of gravel and slung it into the bramble. Roy finished reading, but the words didn't register. Walker focused on the sky.

Roy dropped the letter on the small table next to my rocking chair. "Now what?"

"How the hell should I know?" I spit out the words, mad at the entire universe.

Walker kept his eyes to the blue. "Who signed the letter?"

Roy retrieved it from the table. "An assistant editor, some guy named Patrick."

"Not the editor-in-chief?" Walker's face held the hint of a smile.

"A rejection is a rejection by the editorial team." I kicked at the dirt in the drive. "He would have been in on the decision." I stomped back up on the porch and snatched the letter from Roy, scanning its contents for myself. The masthead listings bled down the left side of the stationary, a litany of names representing the rungs on the editorial ladder to climb, taunting me like a childhood dare. "Are you saying we should send an appeal to this Brimble, the head guy?"

"Did I ever tell you how Colonel Matthias gave us our fishing rights back, despite the entire federal government being against it? Not one person expected it, but my grandfather convinced him." Walker smiled at the memory. "Showed the colonel our ways, promising we would only fish for personal consumption, not commercial. A one-on-one conversation."

"So, I should call the guy?"

"No, go meet with him in person. And take Mary's box."

Chapter Twenty/Mary

Late February 1950

Helen doled out another week's worth of nonstop condolence casseroles, being careful not to give us tuna. I inserted some funeral potatoes into the mix, creamed with ample butter, but didn't tell Helen the title of my mother's recipe. Matt, preoccupied with other matters, came home, ate, and left again. Sleep-deprived from worry about Lucy's on-again, off-again fever, I couldn't focus. The days after Luke's departure blurred.

After rocking the twins to sleep, I brought my dinner plate of chicken and spuds out onto the porch. A spotty breeze offered inadequate relief from the tension pervading both sides of the duplex. The phone rang on the Hinson side. Helen's voice lowered after her initial hello, muffling the rest of the conversation.

A surprise gust blew the skirt of my dress above my knees, signaling a stronger wind to come. A stricken-looking Helen stepped outside. I jumped up and gripped her elbow, afraid she might collapse. We sank to the steps in silence. The wind whipped into a frenzy, blowing a child's plastic ball down the block. Ralph's street trees bent into it.

Helen swept her red mane back from her face with both hands. "The King County coroner issued his report. Luke just read it to me." Her face defiant, as if daring the wind to blow her away, she continued. "Those workers who stopped by to pay their respects on Washington's birthday, saying that Ralph got dosed. That's true and more."

Several of Ralph's crew had told Helen that Ralph had not wanted them to handle a large load of waste, but the barrels were too much for one man. One barrel had tipped and spilled over Ralph's arm, causing the burn I'd told Luke about. The workers told Helen that they had reported it to the higher-ups the same day, but those details were not included in the incident report I'd given Luke.

Helen whispered. "The coroner is certain that Ralph died from radiation poisoning, but over time, not just that accident. Says I should file an insurance claim against GE." She sniffed, her mouth breaking into a wry smile. "He doesn't understand Hanford."

"Still, this is good, right?" I said though nothing about this was good or right.

Helen turned her entire body to me, her face leaking grief, her chest heaving. "Some things, evidence Luke called it, skin on Ralph's arm and other organs, had been removed." She collapsed into my chest, the sobs taking over. "What did they do to my Ralph?"

After Helen cried every tear, after I checked on the twins twice, after I scraped the rest of dinner into the trash bin, washed the dishes, and placed them on the drying rack, I lit the first cigarette I had smoked in a week. Then I called my mother and told her I was going to spend the summer with her at the beach. What I didn't say was that I was leaving Matt for good.

•   •   •

Doctors at Lady of the Lourdes hospital did a second round of tests on Lucy, promising more answers this time. Helen sent a letter to GE asking for compensation, citing the second autopsy from the King County coroner. GE pushed back. After all, the AEC had just won an award from the U.S. government for exceptional safety at Hanford. When the King County coroner stood by his conclusions, the deputy to the head of Hanford's Health Physics Department, Dr. Foster, called in a raft of experts, all AEC acolytes.

The coroner called Helen to tell her about the so-called expert testimony delivered to him in his office in Seattle. He had listened to it all but refused to alter his report. I considered starting a fan club for him.

Ralph's body remained in limbo for weeks, Luke being unwilling to bury his father for fear that it would have to be exhumed for further study. The FBI trailed Helen around town, not even trying to look innocuous. Experts lined up against Helen's claim. Insurers refused to pay. And the government did what it did best. It shoveled dirt over the truth.

The cloudless blue sky of the soon-to-be-spring day offered no answers to the dilemma. When the twins went down for their afternoon nap, I cracked the living room window to let in some fresh air and traipsed to the side of the house to find the snow shovel. A late-March frost on the front sidewalk was a danger I could negate.

The phone rang inside, and Matt caught it on the third ring. "Yes, sir. That's the one." Matt's voice went soft in deference. Whoever was on the other end of the line must be a higher up. "Troublesome, yes." Matt paused, and I took a step back, making sure I wasn't where he could see me.

Everything was troublesome in this town. Under the eave, I flattened my back against the house, my ears on alert, trying to figure out if the bigwig had any idea of what was really going on at Hanford.

Matt's voice grew quieter. "Hinson, that's the one. The coroner called you?" My stomach twisted. Matt chuckled. "Convenient, straight from the horse's mouth." Matt snorted. "The Union president is a member of the state labor board. He could help." A beat. "Any reference to radiation could be redacted before it goes to the state board."

The seam of the house siding dug into my shoulder blades. I gripped the shovel handle, my palm numbing against the frigid metal.

"Much appreciated," Matt said. "I'll call my Union man and let the others know."

The clunk of the phone dropping back into its cradle followed by the sound of ice cubes dropping into a glass meant Matt was finished for the day. What had he done? Before I could think it through, the phone rang again. Matt called out, "Mary, it's for you."

Dodging icy patches in the yard, I dropped the shovel and loped to the front steps. The phone handle was still moist from Matt's grip. "Hello?"

"Mrs. Boone?"

"This is Mary Boone." The "Mrs." did not fit anymore, not that it ever had.

"This is Dr. Soren, at Lady of the Lourdes Hospital. We've got the other specialist's report on Lucy's blood tests."

The air seeped out of my lungs, not leaving enough to respond. Out the window, Ralph's trees swayed, a menacing gust that threatened more. I squeezed the receiver with all my might, trying to shut off the voice saying my baby was doomed, but the doctor droned on. "... a troublesome condition we are seeing in quite a few children in the region."

There it was again, that word. A word that meant there was a problem, but with no crisis response attached. Things happened at Hanford, troublesome things. Every day, more trouble. Another war: Korea. Bombs had to be built, more and more bombs, despite the consequences of that production. More trenches to dig, more waste to be dumped, and more Ralph Hinsons to give their lives to the cause. And Lucy? My heart started to rip.

I mustered, "Yes, no, I mean, what do I do?"

"Bring her back in on Monday. We'll start a regimen of treatment." He paused. "Mary, we've had some success." He left it there, no promises made.

Matt came back into the living room. "I have to make a call."

My hand froze around the receiver, staring at him. Couldn't he see me? See what was happening? See how the Hanford was killing everyone? A scream worked its way up my throat, but I couldn't find the air to force it out. And if I did, what would happen next?

Matt took a step closer. "Are you done?"

Dr. Soren, still waiting for my reply, said, "Mrs. Boone?"

"Yes. Monday then." I mumbled and hung up. Knowing I would only lose if I forced a confrontation, I brushed past Matt, but the second I was outside, my heart cleaved right down the middle. I sank to my knees on the front porch stoop, but no prayer came. Only the end-of-day glow and Matt's relentless cranking of the rotary dial.

Inside, Matt intoned, "Dr. Foster, please."

Helen's screen door creaked open. "Mary? Are you all right?"

My head shook, words impossible. A stream of melting sleet flowed toward the gutter, draining off the front slope, and revealing the first patches of spring-green grass. They'd be short-lived. Summer always browned anything that grew here.

Helen took a seat beside me, wrapping her arm around my shoulders. "Lucy?"

My head fell to her chest, my tongue testing out the new word. "Leukemia."

Matt's voice bled through from inside. "The report can be redacted before the labor board hearing." A pause. "Simple really. Just sat next to the Union president at a breakfast."

I reared my head back. "Oh, God," I said, not knowing how to tell Helen that Matt had just orchestrated a whitewash of the King County coroner's report. My husband, the man who held the strings, purse and otherwise, had just torpedoed any hope of justice for Ralph.

Helen, thinking I was still talking about Lucy, tugged me in tighter.

•   •   •

Matt's labor union pal had been more than happy to facilitate GE's request to redact the KC coroner's autopsy report. The GE lawyers filed the paperwork with the Washington State Labor Board and presto-change-o, Helen's claim was denied. Plant production droned on. Helen and Luke found a burial plot overlooking Puget Sound, and buried Ralph in a quiet family-only ceremony. Luke stayed away, determined to finish his bachelor's degree in record time.

Lucy spent one morning a week in treatment, a regimen that zapped her energy, and the winter cold persisted into April, casting an ominous chill on everything. Helen started sweeping, her grief driving every swipe of the broom, beating back the constant swirl of dust and doubt, storm after storm inundating the late spring and my senses.

At the first rays of sunshine in a week, I wrangled the stroller off my side of the porch and went back inside for the twins. A little over the one-year mark, they had grown shocks of red hair that never failed to draw comment.

The doctor had said Lucy's treatment might make her hair fall out, but there it was, sprouting against all odds. I nestled her into the stroller with the stuffed bunny the doctor had given her for Easter. Ben pulled up on the side.

"Come with us," I said to Helen. "We all need a stretch before the next storm."

Helen leaned the broom against the door frame, untied her apron, and stepped off the porch. I hoisted Ben in beside Lucy, and we took the street that led to the Greenway.

"I'll push for a while," Helen said, taking control of the stroller.

A storm brewed in the distance, and I noted the direction of the winds blowing through town. A force that might spread trouble in its wake.

I linked my arm to Helen's, matching her pace. "Has Luke decided what's next after undergrad?"

"He says he'll go east for his master's, maybe MIT. He wants to apply for a fellowship after that, some program in Scotland. I think he just wants to get as far away from all this as possible." Helen motioned to one of the trees lining the Greenway. "How can they grow here, right in the path of every windstorm?"

The silver maple's roots protruded. Roots that possibly held many things the government wouldn't want known. I lowered my voice. "Harry says the releases are being regulated again, but I can't help but feel everything is suspect."

Helen cast an eye down at the twins. Both had dozed off in the stroller. "Promise me." Her gaze lifted, locking me in. "Promise me you won't raise them here."

Her words held a possessive love, one we never spoke of. Not for the first time, I thought, even if I'm not here, Helen will always make sure they are safe. If Lucy ever could be.

Helen stroked Ben's head. "Redheads are disappearing in the bloodlines, you know." Her hand brushed Lucy's cheek, her worry as evident as mine.

I should have said it out loud, and made it official, right then, but I didn't. "Maybe they'll be the ones to reverse the trend."

Helen looked out into the distance. "Only if you get them out of here."

A familiar-looking woman approached us, slowing as she neared. "Mrs. Boone, Mrs. Hinson, how nice to see you both."

Helen reached out a hand. "Janet Clark, how are you? Your mother said you graduated from Whitman. Congratulations."

My mouth gaped open, stalling any response. This young woman who I knew to be twenty looked fifty. A comb-over concealed bald spots on her scalp, her skin splotched and yellowed, her once svelte figure pudgy. "Janet, I didn't realize you were back in town."

"Doctor's checkup." Her face twisted into a grimace, then morphed into a half-smile. "Mother told me you had twins. They're adorable."

"Tell your father I miss working with him. And the band."

Janet tucked in a corner of the baby blanket that had gone astray, her hand shaky. "They played a gig in Spokane last weekend. Dad said the new singer just doesn't have what you had." She said her goodbyes and stepped off, leaving me wondering if every artist has to experience pain to make their mark.

Helen's eyes followed Janet's departure, intoning the answer to my silent question. "Hyperthyroidism." Helen lowered her voice to a whisper. "Diagnosed a few months after The Run. Several of her classmates have sudden afflictions. Janet's mother is beside herself."

"Harry finally got the follow-up report," I said. "The snowstorm wreaked havoc that night. Downdrafts made Walla Walla a hotspot, among others." We walked on in silence, my thoughts raging, and Helen consumed by her own. The wind whipped the baby blanket loose again as we rounded the corner to home. I pulled it into the crook of my arm.

Helen saw them first. "Will they ever stop?" A dark sedan rested at the curb of our A-house. The FBI had followed Helen around for weeks after Ralph's death but had fallen away since his burial. Helen stopped walking. "Do you think they found out? About the broadcast?"

"Not sure, but Harry's been on edge." I wrapped the blanket around my forearm as if I might fend off any knives aimed at Helen, but I was the one that they wanted this time.

•   •   •

The room was on the back side of the 100-Area, where I had first begun at Hanford. Two FBI agents hovered over me as I sat in a chair facing the desk behind which neither of them sat. A scientist from the 300-Area, who I assumed the agents needed to translate technical answers I might give, sat off to the side.

Their questions, perfunctory at first, turned to probing. "Can you tell us Mrs. Boone, what Dr. Griffin required of you during December 1949?"

"As you prolly know, I'm the secretary who regularly types up and categorizes the handwritten notes of the technical lab personnel. Dr. Griffin oversees that work."

"He didn't ask you for anything out of the ordinary last December, or perhaps a month or so prior, in October 1949?"

Amazing how easy it was to shake my head, denying them the real truth. "Gentlemen, I'm sure you also know that I served as the stenographer in a meeting with an Air Force general and many others. A meeting called by the AEC that I was told was classified." I gave them just enough to make them believe me. "A job that I am sworn by oath not to discuss."

The taller of the two agents leaned against the unused desk, staring down at me. "Mrs. Boone, our questions are only about what was asked of you after that meeting."

He hadn't asked a question so I waited. The shorter one perched on the desk, his eyes aimed at mine. "Describe the content of your work in the days following that meeting."

Harry and I had planned for this. The files held all kinds of data, typed by me as a screen for the other summaries I'd created during that time. "I typed up data from the retrofitting of jackets on the slugs." I cast an eye toward the scientist who just nodded for me to continue. "We're constantly refining the process."

"Nothing else?"

"Not that I recall. It's all in the file."

"You were not asked to create a summary after that meeting in October?"

"No sir, I was not." And that was true. It was my idea, not Harry's, to type up the Air Force meeting minutes by memory, make two carbon copies, and add them to the growing mound of evidence in the shoebox. Harry had fed me additional info during our lunch breaks by the river, about the other meetings he had with Jackson after The Run. No way these guys would know any of that. Harry checked his car and house regularly for bugs.

"One last question, Mrs. Boone." The shorter one leaned back in the desk chair. "Can you tell us what you were doing the evening of December 2nd?"

My gaze cooled even as my heart clutched. "I'd have to check my calendar, but that first weekend of December..." I paused, wondering what Lois might remember, might say if asked. "I believe I was singing in The Dalles."

•   •   •

Hanford revved to a level of production not seen before, and every Manhattan Project site reactivated with renewed purpose. Talk of war with Korea, not to mention Russian bomb tests, peppered every classified memo, but that wasn't what had Harry and me jittery. The FBI followed us everywhere, checking every incoming supply, including carbon paper.

Out my single office window, about fifty yards away, a dilapidated picnic table rested in blackened grass, yet another casualty of an accidental release. Waste leaks, events unreported to the public, of course, had increased in number with the rising level of production.

Harry was late. I assumed the latest leak was the reason, but when he arrived, an FBI agent, the tall one, escorted him. I stood up. The agent motioned me to sit, but I didn't.

Harry cast a wary look my way and opened his top desk drawer. The shorter agent entered and placed an empty box on the top of Harry's desk. "Only personal items, Dr. Griffin."

"What's going on here?" Fury rising, I stepped out from behind my desk. The tall agent crossed the room and blocked my path.

"Stay where you are, Mrs. Boone."

I tried to sidestep him, but he blocked me, taking my arm. I wrestled my arm from the agent, meeting his glare.

"It's okay, Mary," Harry said, shooting me a wry smile. "I've been wanting a change." Harry sank into the chair and pulled open the bottom drawers, ferreting out an old sweater, a pocket knife, and a spare pair of rubber boots, never worn. Boots that had once had a box.

That shoebox held all our carbon copies, hopefully still hidden in Lou's garage lab, but I couldn't be sure the FBI hadn't gotten to Lou. Not if Harry had been fired.

"I'll need a refund on these." Harry stuffed the boots into the corrugated box. "Good thing I kept the box," he said, wriggling the boots in his hand.

And just like that, I knew the box was safe. Harry had made sure of it.

•   •   •

Harry moved in with a cousin on the Washington coast, and no method of communication felt safe: not the phone, not the U.S. Mail, and certainly not meeting in person. Two more months went by before the FBI let up on their surveillance of me, but the shadow of their suspicions kept me tied to Richland. That, Lucy's treatments and Matt's checkbook. June came in sticky and wet, but the onslaught paused after a few days, and miraculously, Lucy went into remission.

That Saturday, Helen suggested we pick up eggs at the Evans farm. She checked on Mr. Evans regularly. His wife had dropped dead of a heart attack, still fresh even after five years. In search of the eggs that Mr. Evans, struggling with a cancer diagnosis, could no longer bring himself to gather, we looped around to the backside of the barn.

Lou and Harry stood there grinning. I fell into Harry's bear hug and swiped Lou's cheek with a kiss that embarrassed him. Nestling on a bale of hay, I snugged my cardigan closer and asked for the answer I was most afraid of.

"Did they find out about the ham radio operation?"

"Nope," Harry said, laughing. "Turns out they just didn't like my attitude."

"Imagine that." My grin widened across my entire face before I caught myself.

"But, if they didn't find out about us, everything," Helen said. "Why fire you?"

"I spoke up about the sand filters. They don't work no matter how Jackson tries to sell it. They can't trap gasses, only the larger particulates and," Harry shook his head, "they've let the silver filter development, the only thing that will curtail the iodine releases, slide altogether."

Hanford engineers had been scrambling to develop a silver nitrate filter to contain the noxious gasses, especially the iodine, since 1947, with no luck.

Lou jumped in. "But now, Korea, the weapons build-up, has made it a more pressing matter."

Harry added. "Jackson thought the newly-formed Columbia River Advisory Group's assessment would prevail, but the AEC got its way.

They set aside Jackson's safety practices, shortened the cooling cycles again, and waste releases are flowing through inadequate filters."

Lou kicked at the dirt. "Safety was always secondary to production."

"Or war." Helen dropped to a nearby hay bale.

"But they can't blame you for the filters," I said, leaning against the barn wall, exhausted, realizing that the air the twins breathed everyday was filled with unseeable danger.

"I may have threatened to go public." Harry's face twisted into a sardonic smile. "About the inadequate filters. Spoke my mind about the new test site being built in Nevada, too."

Lou elbowed Harry. "Never did know how to keep your mouth shut."

"My contract was for only two years. I was on borrowed time, so they let me go." Harry's face turned sheepish. "But not without a final shot."

Helen rolled her eyes. "For what? They can't bring charges for insubordination."

Harry shook his head. "They revoked my pension from my government jobs before Hanford."

"Assholes."

All of us looked at Helen in shock, before dissolving into laughter.

Lou sobered first and motioned across the river toward Pasco. "I buried the shoebox, but it needs moving."

"That's what we wanted to talk to you about." Harry drew a bead on me, but no need.

I'd already decided to do it. "The twins and I are spending the rest of the summer with my mother in Chinook. I told you she moved after Daddy died, right?"

Harry eyed me. "Matt's okay with fending for himself all summer?"

"Matt appears to have other resources." Matt had been taking an inordinate number of business trips to Chicago, Seattle, and Nevada. Trips he said were related to the U.N. sending troops into Korea, but I suspected he did not embark as a solo passenger. "Dr. Soren thinks the salt air will do Lucy good."

"Chinook's mighty close to my cousin's place." Harry's cousin had given him a part-time job at a crab shack. "The school is great there, thanks to the cannery owners."

"I heard that." Only one last payment was left on my father's surgery bill, but I hadn't quite figured out how to tell Matt I wanted a divorce. Decamping to my mother's and taking leave from my job, were small steps, just like the twins were taking. I'd convinced Matt that we'd be out of his way. A way, that as of late, I was sure included another woman, not that I cared. I had bigger worries. The shoebox needed a safe home as much as I did.

·   ·   ·

Once you decide to go, stuffing a satchel and suitcase full of only the good parts of a soon-to-be past life doesn't take long. The bad parts, that red dress that always seemed to provoke him, that blue satin hair ribbon he'd used as a strangle cord, that patent leather belt he'd turned into a weapon, I left behind. They became the decoy. Proof I wasn't leaving him, just going for a visit, like I'd said.

Ben and Lucy circled my feet, toddlers raising each other. Sometimes I thought they didn't need me at all. Not as much as I needed them.

Ben wandered up my leg. "Mama."

That word, no one tells you how it will tug at your heart. "Yes, baby boy." I scooped him up and plopped us down on the bed next to the open satchel.

Ben unearthed a cardigan, put it over his head, and we all laughed as if sharing an inside joke. Matt had never been a part of this. Only the three of us got the punchlines. All Matt did was punch. I hugged Ben to me, and cast a last look around the room filled with violent memories, thinking the first thing I would do in Chinook was call that lawyer.

Helen, our ride to the bus station, greeted us on the front porch, the trunk of her Ford popped open. She scooped up Lucy and took Ben's hand. "Come on you two, time to get this adventure started."

The twins relished her instinctive moves, her gentle touch, her easy smile, all that of a grandmother, except they did not know that. Soon, I thought, someday I can tell them, but when? Luke was just at the beginning of his career. Now was not the time, but what if Lucy's remission didn't last? Then I was spiraling, second-guessing my decision to go, frozen to the porch and its proximity to critical support only Helen could give. Not that my mother wouldn't be of aid, but she didn't have Helen's quiet strength.

Helen looked back at me. "Forget something?"

The heat of summer crept up my ankles, and I swiped at the perspiration on the back of my neck. The brown paper bag stuffed with cash buried in the bottom of my satchel, each dollar well-earned, summoned my smile, but it was the jar I'd left on the counter that made my smile widen. "Just a mental review."

Helen closed the trunk on my suitcase, a diaper bag, and the twine-tied box of favorite toys and children's clothing that also held an innocent-looking shoebox. She slid into the front seat, turned the ignition, and tossed a grin over her shoulder. "I've never seen a mother travel so light."

Ben and Lucy snuggled on either side of me in the back seat, everything I needed. I snapped open my purse, checking the bus tickets to Chinook for the umpteenth time.

As Helen turned onto George Washington Way, a lightness infiltrated me, slipping in before it should, but welcome. "My mother said she couldn't bear to leave the remnants of her girls' childhood behind. A fully stocked nursery and playroom awaits the twins."

"I envy your spending the summer on Baker's Bay." Helen caught my eye in the rearview. "Luke and his college roommate are talking about taking a fishing trip this summer. Maybe I'll suggest the Bay."

Helen and I held each other's gaze. "Tell them, if they bring the fish, we'll do the frying." The lightness crept up a notch at the thought. Was there a way for Luke to know his children without knowing?

Helen pulled into the bus station parking lot. "I'll get the trunk."

Lucy and Ben tumbled out the door after me, unsteady on their pudgy legs. I hugged Helen, and a quake of guilt for taking her grandchildren away from her fissured my insides. "Saying we're going to miss you is inadequate."

"Volunteering as a nurse's aide at Kadlec will stave off my loneliness." Helen sighed. "Someone has to keep an eye on the doings there."

"Helen," I touched her shoulder, garnering her attention. "Promise me, if you leave Richland, you won't leave the time capsule behind." Then I laughed as if my request was mere whimsy, though it wasn't. "Luke doesn't know now, but he'll want it in the future."

Helen glanced down at the twins and then back up at me. "Yes, of course." We hugged, me wishing away her sadness as if I could. Helen grabbed up the twins for a last kiss before placing them side by side on a bench by the terminal drive. "Shall I have Matt over for dinner tonight?"

"No need," I said, a little too insistent, fearful Helen's invitation might derail my plan. "I left him the fixings for spaghetti on the counter. All he has to do is boil water."

"I'll check on him tomorrow then." Helen smiled her beautiful smile, the summer sunshine lighting her dimples. Lucy grabbed Helen's leg. Helen smoothed a hand across Lucy's cheek. "Happy summer, my angel."

The steam from The Area stacks floated across the sky behind her. The bus driver tossed our bags into the cargo hold and took Ben's hand as he climbed onto the bus, promising a moment behind the wheel. The driver tooted his horn, signaling time to go. I balanced Lucy on my hip and climbed the last three steps to freedom.

The twins pressed their noses to the windows, waving to Helen. The town of Richland with its perfectly laid streets, perfectly aligned rows of shops, and perfectly perfect neighborhoods faded behind us as the bus rolled out of the station.

I stared out the window not seeing any of it, conjuring instead a mental picture of the shoebox tucked into the bigger box of toys and then, my kitchen counter: a packet of spaghetti noodles, the colander, and a jar of canned tomato sauce that had a light spot on its lid. A spot where a small piece of masking tape had been. A good wife makes it easy for her husband.

•   •   •

A ticket to Baker's Bay cost $5.93. A second seat for the twins to share cost three dollars more. Freedom, it turns out, costs very little and finds you when you least expect it. The craggy bluffs of the river gave way to lush, conifer-filled forests. We rumbled out of the pass, and my lightness broke free of its box in the fourth hour of the trip.

As we neared the coast, green pastures filled with cows elicited oohs and aahs from the twins. The bus lumbered up the small rise toward the Chinook town center. A cluster of one-story white clapboard structures lined a newly-paved main street. A block over, the pristine schoolhouse towered, more evidence of cannery-owner largess.

My mother waved as we approached. The twins pulled up on the half-open window, wiggling their hellos. An unquantifiable peace entered my belly. Some things I could figure out later, resolving to take these first moments to just be a family.

We joined the crowd hovering around the baggage compartment below the bus. Elderly women embraced younger ones. Servicemen rejoined wives. Two teens stepped forward and helped the bus driver extract luggage, making quick work of the unloading. My mother scooped up the box of toddler paraphernalia, grabbed Lucy's hand, and traversed the dirt lot to the car at her grandchild's pace. Ben clung to the satchel handle as we followed.

My mother nodded in the school's direction. "That's where you'll go one day. Best school in the state."

The sunlight spun off Ben's cheeks, my early talker. "Go koo?"

"We'll see." I raised my eyebrow in a caution to my mother, not wanting loose-lipped toddlers to give away my plans to stay permanently. "For now, we're just going to enjoy the summer at the beach."

My mother keyed open the trunk of the '47 Chevrolet FleetLine Aero Sedan, oxblood red, my father's proudest purchase. The twins pawed their way into the back seat. My mother merged onto Main Street, and Baker Bay filled the horizon with its steely blue depths.

A guard gets let down before you know it. The second guess of sound, the sudden fear sparked by a human touch, the absence of panic at a door opening all faded into the green of the Western Washington hillside that slid toward the mouth of the Columbia, reed-filled marshes bridging the edges.

My mother's home, second rise over as she liked to say, rested just outside of town. Two neighbors, both supervisors at the largest cannery, maintained the dirt road entrance in exchange for a steady supply of my mother's peach cobblers.

The twins spilled outside after supper. Ben studied every inch of ground for ladybugs and caterpillars. Lucy gathered sticks for a house for her dolly. I set aside unpacking to squat on the front porch steps, loving them, loving this moment. After a lifetime of school and work, allowing myself time to just be had an odd effect. Joy. I didn't recognize it at first, confused by the unfamiliar buoyancy, but my delight in the oncoming twilight negated any fear of the day's end.

The phone rang. "Mary, it's for you." My mother called.

My watch read precisely six-thirty, too early. I frowned my way into the hall. "Yes?" The small, unrealistic hope I harbored that it was over Helen dashed in a gush.

"Mary? I don't want to worry you, but Matt's in the hospital."

My grip tightened on the receiver. Maybe he'd come home early for once, hungry, and couldn't wait to eat. Maybe. "What happened?" I didn't even try to sound concerned. Helen knew.

"He burned himself. Boiling water down his leg. Lois heard him scream and drove him to Kadlec. I was volunteering in Emergency."

Helen paused, before continuing. "It's not too severe. I just got home and checked on things on your side. And Mary, that jar of tomatoes on the counter. It might have gone bad, so I threw it away."

All I could think was—Matt can't even boil water? The tomatoes weren't the only thing gone bad.

Chapter Twenty-One/Luke

June 1964

The last of my research allowance went towards a ticket to London. Nothing like a twelve-hour flight, trapped between a ruddy-cheeked Irishman, whose snore crescendoed with any change in altitude, and a matronly, grammar school teacher who bragged non-stop on her former students.

Both had achieved notoriety in questionable scientific endeavors: one drilling for oil in distant desert plains and another heading a gold-mining company in Sudan, both destroying the earth, one unnecessary hole at a time. By the time the Pan Am jet touched the tarmac, my neck had a giant cramp, and a mean headache revved as the plane wound its way along the maze of terminals at London Airport.

A Brit from my Scottish moor days, Thomas-call-me-TJ, the sixth in his family to have those initials, met me at the gate, his straight blonde hair longer than usual. "Luke, me old mucker," he said, slapping me on the back and jumpstarting the part of my brain that sorted British Isle accents. "You look as if you could use some uncorking."

The thought of drinking at ten a.m. in the morning never would have appealed without a transatlantic leap. My logic mechanism rewound to a graduate student's way of thinking, and I assented to making a pub our first stop. The Tube deposited us in Chelsea, near TJ's flat.

Over a pint and pasties, TJ gave me the lowdown on my sole chance at L. J. F. "Jack" Brimble, *Nature*'s editor. "MacMillan is moving their publication works to Little Essex Street. Brimble's set up a veritable office at the Athenæum Club. My dad's a member."

"I'll need to borrow some clothes."

"It would be a bit naff to go as you are." TJ grinned, giving me the once-over. "We're about the same size. I'll have you looking wicked in no time."

"The meet, it's today?" My stomach did a flip at the thought of pitching my findings so soon.

TJ tossed a couple of quid on the table and pushed back his chair. "It was a bit of a dither, but we managed a private face-to-face tea time with mad Jack."

Squelching my rising panic, I guzzled my brew. Only four hours to transform into a man of science, one whom man-about-town Jack Brimble would find credible. I scurried after TJ, who'd already pushed through the pub door and flagged down a cab.

•   •   •

The venerable club on Pall Mall, founded in the early 1800s by intellectuals, claimed many members who had attained some distinction, mostly in science. We breached the Athenæum's column-laden portals with me yanking at the neck of the loaned dress shirt, chafing already. TJ steered me north, and we entered a satellite to the main library. Dozens of bookcases filled with scientific tomes towered against the four walls that surrounded a small table for four.

An older version of TJ and a white-haired, genial-faced man had already taken up residence, tea cups and bottles of whiskey splayed across the Queen Anne table. TJ's father, a chemist by profession, knew Jack Brimble well, having served as an informal advisor to *Nature* for decades. My belly let loose a growl. In the flurry of fittings of my Saville-Row-loaned suit, we hadn't eaten lunch.

"Mr. Brimble, an honor sir." TJ thrust out a hand. "May I present my colleague, Lucas Hinson? We survived the Scottish moors and the rigors of the marine science institute together."

Brimble rose to shake TJ's hand with a knowing look. "Your father and I were just discussing the merits of peer review accompanied by the right Scotch." His affable laugh ended when he turned his gaze on me, casting an eye to my too-tight shoes. The pulled laces were the one imperfect detail of my costume.

"Mr. Hinson, I understand you've made the trip over the pond just for me?"

"I appreciate your seeing me, sir." I waited for him to invite me to sit, but he kept me on my feet.

"My schedule is in shambles with the office move, but Thomas," Brimble nodded at the older of the two TJs, "said you had a pitch for me. Nothing dodgy I hope." Having issued the warning, he sat.

I plopped into the chair across from him. A waiter appeared with sandwiches. I said a silent prayer of thanks as TJ poured me a shot of Oban that I needed even more.

TJ jumped into the opening. "Did my dad mention Luke started out as a botanist too?"

Brimble shook his head. "A bit of a leap into nuclear waste research."

And with that, my heart dropped into my dress socks. He'd read my paper. Probably been an active part of the decision to reject. TJ disrupted my wallowing with a swift kick to my shins under the table. He glared me into mounting my defense.

"Actually, sir, no." Quiet at first, my voice gained momentum. "It's in the roots of every plant in and around my hometown, not to mention the water."

Brimble sat back in his chair, fingers laced. "I don't recall seeing those supporting documents."

"I brought them for your review, sir. And some documentation you might find even more intriguing." I pulled my leather case onto my lap and popped open the clasp. The snap echoed in the small chamber. "This file in particular. I made copies for you, trusting that you will hold them in the closest of confidence," I said, relaying my own warning.

The 'Classified' stamp, even in a photocopy, was prominent at the top. Brimble took it in but didn't make a move.

The older Thomas weighed in. "Odd to see that stamp again, isn't it, Jack? Wasn't it Chadwick who gave you a similar batch from Halban and Kowarski?"

The inside baseball of this comment might have blown by me had TJ not filled me in during the afternoon-long coaching session on all-things-*Nature*-magazine. Nobel prize winner Chadwick had forwarded the Halban-Kowarski research findings on nuclear chain reactions to the editors of *Nature* early in the war years, but the British government suppressed it all, fearing the Axis powers would use the info to develop nuclear weapons of their own.

"Those, I understand, could not be published, not then." My tone was one of quiet confidence, banking on Brimble's advocate side. His weekly editorials touted social awareness alongside scientific advancement. "But this discovery deserves the light of a new day, especially in a world now armed with nuclear weapons. A world that may be at war again soon."

TJ slid the sandwiches my way. I bit into one as gentlemanly as possible, savoring the cucumbers and chicken, hungry for more, but more ravenous for validation.

Brimble separated Mary's notes, laying them flush on the table as he scanned each document. The horrors of the releases, the knowledge up the chain, the Geiger counter findings on farms and valleys, and the summary of college co-ed calamities at Walla Walla painted a graphic picture of the devastation to the entire region.

"Even so, I'm loath to become involved in criminal activities." Brimble drew a bead on me. "We are not whistleblowers, Mr. Hinson. Our journal catalogs scientific discoveries."

"As did these, sir." I handed him the file of fish studies, studies never published in any journal. "Discoveries hidden from those who needed to know most."

Brimble sifted through the charts, running his fingers across the data, shaking his head. "So, your whale, is it proof that the waste has migrated?"

My tea tasted bitter and sweet all at once. "As far as the wind can blow and the river runs, taking up residence wherever there is life," I said, hoping to put a human face on it.

Brimble cast a guarded look at TJ's father, who cleared his throat and said, "We had a bit of a wind-driven to-do ourselves, didn't we, Jack?"

Brimble nodded, turning back to me. "Are you familiar with the Windscale Plutonium Plant?"

"A post-war facility in Cumberland, as I recall."

Brimble leaned in, his voice low, though we were the only ones in the room. "An accident, somewhat minimized by our government, released over 20,000 curies in 1957."

"The wind dog-legged, like the Bridge at Prestwick Golf Club," TJ's father grimaced. "Carried the fallout across most of Europe."

Brimble's face turned grave. "But no one was evacuated."

TJ sat back in his chair, rubbing his chin. "I remember that. Fleet Street reported that all the milk in Cumbria was gathered up and thrown into the Irish Sea."

"Which means your government, as well as mine, knew about the milk-iodine connection back then." I jutted out my chin. "The threat to humanity."

TJ's father shot Brimble a wry smile before adding, "Since 1919, according to your own *American Chemical Society* journal."

TJ side-eyed his father in a what-the-heck look sure to lead to a heated discussion later.

Brimble pulled my files closer. "These copies, are they for me?"

"Yes, sir. We've established the relationship of both flora and fauna to multiple releases over the last two decades, accidental as well as intentional."

Brimble raised an eyebrow at the word 'intentional,' before lowering his head back to the files that Roy had copied on the new Xerox machine at his father's office.

My gaze drifted upward to the texts that lined the walls, tomes by learned men. Men who had let this happen with little consideration for a Klickitat maiden, my father or the Evans, much less the lambs, the sockeye, the mule deer or the whale, and certainly not Lucy. Sweet Lucy, cursed from conception.

"These phenomena," I intoned. "Like all others, demand an ultimate exposition of the truth."

Brimble jerked his head up from the file. "Quoting my own words, Mr. Hinson?"

"Words that I believe got you hired at *Nature*, sir."

Brimble gave up a half-smile. "Some called it the golden age of physics, but after Hiroshima, Churchill mourned the new energy, saying it had been 'Long mercifully withheld from man.' Arthur and I wanted to be Britain's conscience. An elusive goal, I'm afraid."

"It's inside us now," I said, stroking my throat. "Someone needs to say that out loud."

•   •   •

My mother, privy to my return flight information, was rocking on my porch when I dragged in from Seattle. A showdown over the immune tablets was overdue after my ten-day absence. I winced, even in the wake of my good news.

My mother rose to embrace me. "Success?"

"Think so." I decided to get it over with. "About the supplements—"

She cut me off with a shake of her head. "That's not why I'm here. Your time capsule, it's been unearthed."

"You drove all the way from Richland to tell me about a childhood project being derailed?"

The entire past week felt unreal, and now, my mother had fallen into some 1940s fairy tale that she thought needed my permission to retell. I heaved a sigh and dropped into the other chair, relieved, but a tickle of there-must-be-something-else stirred inside my chest.

"The city was laying in new sewage pipes, the easement through our back yard. Near the alley. Anyway, they had pickaxes, and I asked them to dig it up." She pulled an envelope out of her pocket. "I opened the mason jar."

Mary and I had read our letters out loud, making sure we were giving different information before sealing them into the jar. "I already know what's in them," I said, sinking into the other chair, not looking at the envelope. "Did you think it was a secret or something?"

"I don't think I ever told you about the gas leak. When you were a junior maybe, at UW." My mother's voice softened. "Workers came to patch the tank and unearthed the capsule once before. Mary had the workers dig a deeper hole and I saw her put something inside before the workers buried it again."

All air escaped my lungs. My chest shrank into my frame in sudden inexplicable panic.

"When I dropped her at the bus station to come here, she told me to dig up the capsule if I ever moved." My mother winced, glancing at the stark cabin interior through the door I'd left open. "I decided it was time to see what she'd hidden."

Following her gaze, I took in the sparseness: no curtains on the windows, no eiderdown quilt on the twin bed with no room for anyone else. After rising from being the bullied victim in high school, transforming myself into a desired candidate for scholarship after scholarship, I was in fact, back where I'd started: lonely.

"Her diary was wrapped in a baby blanket," my mother said. "I gave it to the Lewis County sheriff this afternoon on my way here. Lots of incriminating entries. Matt Boone will have a hard time talking his way out of things." She set an age-yellowed envelope on the small table in between us. "But this is addressed to you."

My mother recited a few details of Mary's diary, but all I could focus on was the letter, sitting there, mocking me. *Fool*, it radiated, you don't know everything. In fact, you hardly know anything at all.

It took on a red glow, I swear. I checked the sun to see if it was lighting it up, but a cloud had covered it. I moved a hand toward the table, for the first time noticing the different heading: 1950, *Luke to Decide When* written in cursive.

The envelopes that held the letters we'd written to the future I had printed in all capitals: TO THE FINDERS. But my mother had found something entirely different. My mother quieted as my thumb slid under the flap. I grasped the paper, letting the envelope float to the porch.

"Dear Ben and Lucy..." My eyes raced past the greeting, but I couldn't read the rest of the words, certainly not out loud. Not with my mother there.

"If it's any consolation," my mother said, squeezing my free hand. "I've always known."

The woman never missed anything, but in my disarray, I couldn't piece it together. "How..." was all I could muster.

"Your father told me you didn't come in until five in the morning the night of the flood. And of course, I can count." She wrapped me up in a hug. "But red-haired twins named Ben and Lucy? A dead giveaway." My mother stroked my cheek. "I'm meeting Harry for dinner. Want some crab?"

My body frozen, I managed a head shake.

She tossed her fiery waves, now laced with gray, off her shoulders and strode across the drive. At the car door, she cast one last shot. "Lots of reasons in that letter, I suspect, to reconsider next steps." And then, my mother, my beautiful, accepting, fearless mother, caregiver to so many, backed down the drive and left me to read the truth that I, Lucas Benjamin Hinson, had always known in my heart.

•   •   •

After a restless night's sleep that ended in my waking at dawn and making a completely inadequate list of ways to tell Ben, I drove straight to Harry's, needing advice on my newly-found fatherhood. I pushed through the crab shack's double doors with a renewed energy that had nothing to do with the immune tablets.

Harry swung out of the kitchen door, unusually chipper, making me wonder if my mother had something to do with that. "So," he said. "The trip worth it?"

Despite my current worry, I grinned as I took a seat at the counter. "Brimble did not commit, but he'll publish it. Maybe December." I'd had plenty of time on the plane to sort through the publishing timeline, figuring about five to six months in lead time. I'd even conjured a list of possible places that might let me finish my doctorate.

"So, Merry flipping Christmas?"

"And a happy damn new year." And then I let loose a full-throated laugh that ejected all my angst, launching it into the café's high ceiling. The fan anchored to the cross beams twirled, stirring the old excitement of discovery with all my worries and wishes in my belly. A feeling I'd forgotten. Maybe I was more like my father than I realized.

"Well, congratulations." Harry checked a pot on the stove, side-eying me. "I can see how this whole thing could take your attention away from other obligations."

"What do you mean?"

"A high-school science fair, for instance."

My gut twisted from the punch, more personal than Harry yet knew. "Shit."

"Yeah, well," Harry held my gaze. "You were missed." Harry's tone meant more.

"What happened?"

"I guess some older kids made a joke of Ben's project. Started calling him spook-boy. Been dogging him pretty good the last couple of days."

"Assholes," I said, checking my watch. School should have been out by then. "I'm on it."

I hustled to my car, threw myself behind the wheel, and screeched out of the pier parking lot. Speeding past the first rise, I scanned the road, thinking Ben might have cut school, based on my own experience with bullies, but no sign of him.

I stopped halfway up the road to the cottage, afraid for the undercarriage of my car. Recent rains had pocked the dirt drive. Mud-laden, I trudged up the front porch steps, hesitant about my reception, knowing I'd screwed up royally.

Mrs. Peters opened the door before I hit the porch. "School just called." Her jaw twitched, her worry visible. "Ben's been missing since third period. That was two hours ago."

The high school was a half-hour drive down the road. Walking it, even at a clip pace, would take at least an hour or more, but he could have hitched a ride. My brain traced through our conversations, searching for what would draw Ben. The last time we'd worked on his project, I'd reminded him about tritium being visible in seawater. In some weird way, would he just want to prove me wrong?

"I have an idea about where he might be," I said, knowing for certain he had blown right past me.

"You know about today?"

"The bullies?"

Mrs. Peters shook her head as if shedding the most impossible burden. "Not that." She pushed back inside and returned with a familiar jacket. "Seven years to the day that Lucy died."

Chapter Twenty-Two/Mary

Summer 1950

Lucy's earache morphed into a fever that just wouldn't let go. Dr. Soren had referred us to a pediatrician at Ocean Beach Hospital, a kind gentleman who waited for me to sit before he did.

"Have you met Milly?" He handed Lucy a doll to distract her while he listened to her heart. After examining Lucy with a soft touch, he almost whispered. "Mrs. Boone, I'm going to order a new round of blood tests."

At first, the underlying message did not register, but then it crept in, destroying my hope cells one by one. "But the doctors at Lady of the Lourdes said she was in remission." I flattened my palms against the hard metal chair, admonishing myself for believing any treatment could stymie the demon leukemia's progress and knowing I deserved any punishment the gods doled out. But not Lucy.

"We know so little about this disease still, and in young children, with all their other systems growing and changing," the doctor shook his head, a sorrow-filled motion. "It's hard to track what might kick it off again."

I nodded, not understanding how Lucy could burrow into my shoulder like Lucy, smell like Lucy, giggle like Lucy, and yet have this thing inside her that would take all the Lucy away. I shook my head against the thought, refusing to believe that my daughter would succumb to any disease. Her heart was too big.

The doctor spoke in low tones, a new regimen of treatment, injections of some kind, he would begin them on Monday. Lucy needed as much rest as possible. "Try to keep her quiet and her fever down." He smiled at Lucy. "Would you like to take Milly home for the weekend? Bring her back to see me on Monday?"

Lucy clutched the doll to her tummy, giggled, and slid off the exam table, just like any other can't-sit-still toddler. All I could think was, if my daughter had only a short time to live, it wouldn't be in Richland. I called Matt and told him that we were staying at the shore indefinitely. That I trusted the doctor here.

•   •   •

The salt air had a healing effect on all of us, drawing us up and out early into each day. The nearby bayou offered a litany of adventures for Ben. My mother gave him his first fishing pole, and he slept with it at night. Lucy's treatments stretched through July. By week four she showed signs of improvement, and I allowed myself to hope again. The doctor's encouraging words rang in my head as I pulled up to the small row of buildings just off Cherry Street. My appointment wasn't for another ten minutes.

The driver's door handle loosened in my palm, jiggling in its socket. Mother had warned me it was finicky, missing a bolt or something. I reached out the window, freed myself with the outside handle, and swung out onto the street. The wind whipped at my skirt, the incoming weather challenging the sunny day. American flags flapped atop the masts of the boats anchored north of the marina, signaling a port-of-call patriotism I questioned.

Along a short pier, two men hauled in a morning catch. The younger man hollered, "Dad, re-tie that line." The older man replied something unintelligible and they both broke into laughter, peals of love. The easy pleasure of being father and son.

Maybe one day Ben could know too. Hopeful, I made my way back to the corner building. A sign mounted to the right of the door denoted J. Swenson, Attorney at Law. The desk where a receptionist might sit was empty, but a small bell rested on its corner. My chime triggered a rustle behind the closed door.

A tallish man, with a life-carved face, a wrinkled suit, and shaggy gray-laced brown hair stepped out. "Mary Boone?"

"I believe Harry Griffin told you about me."

"It's good to have him back." Swenson shot me a grin. "Did he tell you we were childhood ruffians, pushing every boundary?"

"No, but he said you would help, and I need someone willing to fight, Mr. Swenson."

"John, please." He motioned for me to sit. "The laws are changing, but the courts are slow to catch up."

"By courts, I assume you mean male judges?"

John Swenson shot me a crooked smile, swiveled in his chair, and snatched a folder off his credenza. "After reviewing recent rulings, I don't think there's a problem with the minors. Most courts default to the mother in terms of custody."

Harry may or may not have told him, but no need to hide anything. "We won't need to argue abuse?" I asked, wondering if I should dig up my journal.

Swenson didn't blink. "Not if we determine a mutually acceptable reason for filing."

"It's my understanding that the national organization of female attorneys is pushing for a no-fault divorce law." I'd done my research, too.

"Their efforts are picking up steam, but, I'm afraid we are caught in the soon-to-be, not the actual moment of change." He tapped the file in front of him. "Your husband was the spokesperson for The Area at its inception?"

"A master at misdirection," I said.

"Then he'll most likely be very persuasive on any witness stand, well-practiced." John pulled another document out from the rest. "How is he with the children, Lucy and Ben?"

"Absent. He has a grown son. Wasn't looking to do it all over again."

Out the side window an abandoned newspaper blew out of a trash can in the narrow alley, pages separating into flight. The front page glued itself to the window pane, announcing armistice negotiations in Kaesong, Korea, despite the ongoing strife. Neither side wanted to appear weak or lose face. Was an agreement with Matt even possible?

"The establishment of the Family Court last year, that helps," John said. "We can file a petition invoking their jurisdiction."

"I assume that's better than having the judges in the Tri-Cities hear my case?"

"A more neutral arena. One not as subject to, shall we say, corporate influences." He paused, rubbing his chin. "It's still best to go in uncontested."

"So, I have to get him to agree to let me go?"

"That or prove adultery."

While I did not doubt that Matt was capable of that and much more, he was a careful man. I needed to be equally so.

·   ·   ·

The phone rang for the fifth time before Matt picked up, sounding annoyed. "Boone residence." That's all it had been, a place to hang our hats, not a home. A heart has to be put into a home, and I had none left in me by the time we got to Richland.

"It's me." I hesitated, uncertain as to what to say next. Matt would have practiced before making a call like this. He rehearsed his presentations out loud sometimes, making sure every lie was well crafted, a practice I had not perfected. "Since you didn't make it for the 4th, I was hoping you could come down next weekend?"

His voice softened, surprising me. "Is it Lucy?"

"She's responding well to the treatments," I said, hedging, not wanting to be drawn into the real reason over the phone. "But, don't you want to see her and Ben?"

My question drew an exasperated sigh from Matt. "You're the one who wanted to spend the summer by the shore, 250 miles away."

"We need to talk." It slipped out before I thought about it. I braced myself, thinking I'd opened the door to more than I should. We'd let the uncertainty of the twins' parentage lie unspoken for well over a year, me afraid of what Matt might do if I confirmed the truth.

"Maybe we should." Matt's unreadable tone only added to my fears.

What would make him so receptive? If he had found someone new, then maybe like Helen had said, my luck had changed, and I had grounds for divorce. Before I had time to make sense of his agreeable tact, he suggested, "Maybe meet halfway? There's a café at the bus stop this side of Packwood."

"How about Saturday, around noon?" I paused, thinking this was all a little too easy. "Lucy's condition is less predictable. I'll let you know if I can't make it."

"You do that." Matt hung up.

•   •   •

My mother was on the phone with my little sister Ellen when I left, planning a trip back to Boise for Ellen's college graduation and her move to Seattle for medical school. Unobserved, I slipped an envelope into the side pocket of my handbag and secured the contents of the shoebox into a plastic bag before sealing it with two rubber bands.

On the hand-hooked rug at my mother's feet, Ben was offering different toys to Lucy, who sat with her legs outstretched, letting Ben create a pile in between them. Her legs had lost all their pudge, the baby fat stripped away by the treatments without me tracking its loss, though I rarely took my eyes off her. Ben took hold of her hand, pulling her toward him. Lucy's face broke into a giggle, and I scooted out the side door, the shoebox and the manila folder of divorce papers tucked under my arm.

The road east threaded the marshes before splitting family farms down the middle, tractors trawling the fields on either side. The Chevrolet Fleetline Aerosedan hummed down the road as if it had just rolled off the assembly line. During the two-plus hour drive, I strategized how to fit in part-time work around night school programs to finish my degree.

The route through the mountains split off from the north-south farm-to-market just before Chehalis, a township ensconced in a vast, forested prelude to the pass. The hills lifted me higher as I drove. The pavement twisted into a series of switchbacks, asphalt clinging to the mountainside. The radio lost reception, leaving the sun standing still on "Blueberry Hill."

A sign at the next bend announced the café. Another claiming the best pies in Lewis County followed. The dirt parking lot housed two semi-trucks, one loaded with pallets, the other emblazoned with the Rainier Beer logo, and a lone Ford station wagon that looked like it might rust in its spot, but not Matt's Studebaker.

I touched up my lipstick in the rearview and plucked the divorce papers out of the jockey box before exiting and tugging on the trunk to make sure it was secure. The shoebox cached below the spare had another destination if Matt wouldn't cooperate.

Just like him to keep me waiting. I'd eaten half of a slice of peach cobbler, despite my reservations about the origins of the peaches, when he arrived. He slid into the booth across from me with no physical show of affection. Prolly the most honest moment between us since we had met.

"The signs aren't wrong," I said, motioning to the pie.

Matt signaled the waitress. "Black coffee." He turned back to me. "Well?"

"The doctors at Ocean Beach finished the first round of Lucy's treatment. They say it went well." I lowered my eyes. "Thank you for getting the Company to pay for it."

Matt nodded, sipping his coffee, then. "She's my daughter too, right?"

Something in the way he said it, not a real question, an agreement to lie, as if my being gone for well over two months had given him time to think it through. Being a family man strengthened his credibility with the community, and maybe his pride wouldn't let him ask if the twins were truly his. Or, maybe even though he had someone new, he still needed me to complete his perfect family picture.

Unsure how to answer, I forked off a bite of pie, stalling. My hair fell forward, and I pushed it behind my ears, my face free of bruises for the first time in months. I wasn't going back. "Ben's sprouting. More energy than I know what to do with most days."

"Your mother?"

My mother had babied him early in our relationship. Mothering he'd needed, but too late to effect any real change. Any affection I could give had been stymied when the turning-the-other-cheek strategy had proven faulty.

"She's good, and a big help with Ben when I'm with Lucy at the hospital."

Matt set his cup down with a clunk. "I need to get back, so shall we get to it?"

I pulled the manila folder in front of me. "I think this won't be unexpected. We haven't been—shall I say happy—for a long time." If we had ever been. A flicker of worry about how he might react rose as I unwound the cord and let the papers slide out between us, glad to be in a public place.

Matt parsed the documents. "What makes you think I'll agree?"

"It's a no-fault document," I said, and then I threw my proverbial dice. "No need to bring your new girlfriend into this."

His eyes locked on mine, a look that telegraphed an odd respect, but before I could capitalize on it, he shifted his gaze to the shiny, new small jukebox mounted inside our booth. He ran his finger across the vinyl-encased list of titles, feigning interest, but a familiar threat lit his eyes. "That wouldn't be a good idea."

"You agree that our time together should end?" I straightened my back against the booth, pressing my palms into the wooden bench seat.

Out the window, clouds drifted across the tips of the foothills, shrouding the mid-afternoon light. "Not necessarily." Matt shot me a wry smile. "GE values a family man's perspective. Why would I divorce?"

And there it was. Confirmation that we were of use to him, nothing else. With Lucy's medical needs, Matt had most likely figured I would never leave. Not unless...I wouldn't let myself finish that thought. My hand forced, I extracted the document from my purse, a three-page report I'd kept out of the shoebox. "Because of this."

The paper-clipped carbon copies were records of the Green Run, minutes of the multiple meetings with the Air Force and The Area's scientists. The onion-skin paper had been difficult to copy and the purplish ink had blurred, but the internal reports also included a summary of the step-by-step outreach that Matt, as the official spokesperson, had led to stave off any public panic. The timeline listed specific assurances that the public had been given in the days that followed, all lies, assuring folks that the releases were at safe levels to keep naysayers at bay.

The final page had the actual data, charts tracking the horror inflicted on those two December nights. Classified reports cited the discharges of thousands of curies. All of Matt's statements, in every town meeting, were proven false by what he held in his hand now.

Matt's eyes narrowed as he scanned the copies, once and again, before looking up at me with a smirk on his face. "What do you think you can do with this without being arrested?"

"You've always underestimated me." I whisked the papers from his grasp. "Sign the divorce papers, and no one will ever question your concern for the people of Richland."

Matt straightened against the back of the booth, his face a brewing cloud. "You know the penalty for stealing classified documents, releasing secret government communications." He lit a cigarette and blew the smoke my way, his eyes telegraphing a warning.

But I was a step ahead this time. "I do. So, you can imagine the trouble you'd be in, upon returning to Richland today, to find the FBI searching our living room based on a tip that a hundred or so such documents are hidden in your desk."

Matt seized my wrist, but I yanked it away. "If I don't call a certain number in the next half hour, a different call will be made." I met his glare, willing my poker face to ring true. "Every document is tied to the lies you told at every town meeting, in every press conference, in almost every casual conversation you have ever had since coming to Richland."

Nothing was hidden, of course, except the shoebox in the car trunk. I couldn't risk anyone else getting involved. Matt believing that I had planted the documents was all I had. That and the childhood card games I'd played with my father, a master of the bluff. All in, I pushed the divorce documents closer to him and placed a pen on top. "And you know better than anyone how much the Company loves a scapegoat."

• • •

Matt strode to his Studebaker. I stepped into the phone booth outside of the café, turning my back to Matt backing out of the dirt drive, making a show of the supposed phone call. After faking a conversation for a minute or two, I hung up the receiver and turned around. Matt was gone. Rain dotted the Chevy's windshield. I flipped on the wipers, anchored the signed documents with my handbag on the seat beside me, and eased out of the parking lot.

A twist of the radio dial found Judy Garland and I sang along out loud, my heart so full that my chest could barely contain it. *Lucy, Ben, I'm coming home.*

Hundreds of feet down, the Cowlitz riverbed hid from my view by the thickets of evergreens and shrub brush. Unexpected sunshine spiked off the rocky side of the mountain that had been sliced away for the roadway. A sign of luck. I laughed out loud into the sunray, blinded to the logging truck barreling toward me. In the instant that the long bed swung over into my lane, I stomped on the brake and skidded across the road, perilously close to the cliff edge. The truck raced by.

Foot frozen to the brake pad, I waited for my heartbeat to slow, taking in the vast wilderness below with basalt boulders tossed here and there, roadblocks to any trail. In the rearview mirror, the right fender floated against the stark blue sky. I shifted my foot from the brake to the gas pedal and eased it down. The Fleetliner inched forward. After a mile or so, my confidence returned. The car glided across the asphalt. The pleasure it must have brought my father bubbled up in me. Rays of light streaked the forest in varying shades of green like an artist's paint strokes as I took the switchback at full speed, enrapt in the momentum.

The car rounding the bend toward me seemed only a small annoyance. An intruder in my happiness to just ignore. I pressed on the accelerator. The papers fluttered in the surge of wind through the passenger window, distracting me for the half-second it took to tuck the documents closer. The oncoming car swerved into my lane only yards ahead. I jerked the wheel, forcing the Chevy to the far side of the road. The next switchback loomed a few feet away.

The Studebaker veered closer, sideswiping the Chevy, pushing me closer to the edge. Too late to brake. I leaned into the wheel, pushing for the power to make the turn, but recovery was no longer an option. My necklace caught on the gearshift and ripped away as the thrust snapped my torso back. The Chevy sailed off the road in perfect flight, as if it might sprout wings, and I pushed with all my might on the faulty driver's door. It flew off the hinges and a flurry of divorce papers swirled passed me.

The look on Matt's face just before he exited the café, I'd willfully ignored in my misplaced euphoria. He hadn't been done.

Chapter Twenty-Three/Luke

Late June 1964

The paranormal has always fascinated me. Even a man of science can believe. Campfire smoke created a blurry aura on a starlit night. Whispers, groans, and an animal breaking a twig in the forest all added credibility to the unknown. Any prepubescent brain would be sure ghosts were real. Of the reasons folks feel they have encountered a ghost, the main one is that in the dark the brain can't receive much visual information, so it creates a questionable reality.

But Lucy had shown herself during the day. Foot heavy on the gas pedal, I raced back to the pier, negating every argument or excuse I might use to make Ben forgive me. The fact was, I had wasted my opportunities. Thrown away chances to get to know him in favor of seeking revenge that wouldn't give me what I really needed. I'd done the same thing with Mary.

That day, the last time I saw her, I had been so intent on getting my father's dead body to Seattle, getting the bad guys, I hadn't even said goodbye, punishing her for punishing me. She had come out into the sorrow-laden day, face full of care, full of something for me, but my anger would not let me receive it. And when she had turned her head to check on her twins—my twins—it felt like she was turning her back on me, again. I had slipped away in a veil of self-pity, not realizing the gift she had given me, and when she raised her hand in farewell, I pretended not to see.

Just like I had pretended not to see what Ben needed from me. I squeaked in between a delivery van and a restored Woody with surfboards on top and squeezed out of my door. At the sight of a lone figure atop the railing, I froze.

His long legs were tucked behind the second plank, his feet resting on the third, like a trapeze artist hooked to an invisible partner, a precarious chain of safety. But there was no fight left in the sag of his shoulder blades, only flight, and maybe not even.

Flight would necessitate momentum, and I got a distinct feeling that Ben had none. I knew that feeling. The overwhelming weight of nothing left to stave off defeat. I still hadn't found my way through it, but I had my mother, the safety net for my flying trapeze.

The pier planks whined as I neared. Ben cast a glance over his shoulder, his jaw set in defiance, eyes bleeding tears, wanting more.

I stopped a few feet away. "Thinking about going after her?"

Ben didn't answer, just turned his head back to the sea.

"I saw her too, you know. Here, that first day in the dinghy. And at my cabin."

Ben's shoulders shifted, signaling a deep breath, but no words came out. I calculated the drop. I could dive in after him, fish him out. It'd be cold, but we'd survive—probably—if the riptide wasn't as strong as they say. But the reason he might jump worried me more. A willingness to start down a path of self-destruction that I knew a bit about.

"I think she just couldn't go back to the hospital," I said, unsure as to what my follow-up was, calculating how many strides it would take to grab him.

"She hated it."

"Me too." I fought the urge to be relieved he was talking, knowing it could change, knowing I didn't know how to stop him, so I took the scientific approach. Ask questions. "Ever wonder why she got sick and not you?"

The boy's head cranked back my way, a look of disbelief encompassing his face. "How'd you know?"

"I had friends in high school, we all ate the same things, and drank the same water. They got sick, and I didn't. Not till now anyway."

"But we were twins." Ben's shoulders drooped, and his legs loosened. Fear surged in my chest. Ben turned his face back to the horizon.

Gulls soared past, side-eyeing me as if they knew better, rooting me to my spot. I couldn't make it in time, and spooking him would end badly. "I can't imagine how hard it was when she left, your mother too, but I lost my father." I recognized the survivor's guilt. "I know what it means to miss someone so much, to fall down this giant hole and not be able to find a foothold to climb out."

The boy twitched but kept his eyes out to sea. "Not the same, mister." His voice sounded like mine coming back at me. "Your father was old." He spat out his adolescent judgment with a fierce surety that landed right in the middle of my sense of humor.

A laugh bubbled up, unstoppable.

His head whipped around, his face reflecting my fear. "You think this is funny, mister?"

"No," I said, swallowing my smile. "I think they are gone, Lucy, your mother, my father. Taken too soon. And we'll never quite understand why we were left behind."

Ben lifted one hand off the rail, and my chest seized, but he just pushed his hair back off his forehead. "She's not Tritium," he said, turning his back to me again.

"No," I whispered, lost in that tangle of red for a split second. "She's not."

"She used to come a lot, but I haven't seen her for a while." His shoulders softened.

"She's traveling," I said. "She'll be back."

The wind shifted a downdraft that had a push to it. Ben's hand grasped the rail, and in seeing that simple, safety reflex, a rush of relief flooded my entire being.

Is this what it felt like to be a father? Not at all sure I could survive the parenthood-roller-coaster, the urge to try took over, throwing me into a protective mode with an odd result. Against all my instincts, I took a step backward, forcing my voice into a neutral tone, willing him to turn around, to see me, see that I was here for him. "Want to take the dinghy out?"

In the time that transpired, I compressed a thousand thoughts: I'd moved too far away to reach him—I could jump in after him—could he swim? I didn't know what he could do. Why hadn't I told Harry to come out as backup? Who did I think I was trying to talk a boy I hardly knew off a ledge? A boy whose mother was prone to cliffs—as was I—oh, God, he had both our genes. I thought I was dreaming with my eyes open when he twisted his torso my way.

"I didn't bring her clothes." Ben swung a leg back over the railing, and I steeled myself, batting away the urge to lunge at him, clutch him to me.

"I've got her jacket in the car." And it was just that simple to cross the common ground Lucy had tilled for us. He took a tentative step toward me. My hand stretched out. A trusting grip tightened around my palm. My son's hand in my own, a surge of love I'd never known, or maybe I had once before.

"Can we eat first?"

My son was hungry. Life restarted.

Epilogue/Luke

December 1964

We'd bundled up, Ben insisting that winter catches were only for the worthy. Me just happy to be with him. We'd left Harry inside the shack, paging through the latest issue of *Nature* magazine, one that included my words and top credits for Walker and Roy. In the end, it had been Walker's position at the Department of Transportation that gave us the credentials necessary for publication. The *Seattle Post-Intelligencer* staff had the shoebox. I hoped they were making the most of it.

My mother had called just before we left the house. Two Hanford reactors had been suddenly and summarily shut down by the government. I'd tried to imagine the halls of power that had been finally swayed and couldn't. Fishing off the pier with a storm whipping up whitecaps seemed more doable.

Ben insisted on cranking up the transistor radio, the soundtrack to *West Side Story* blasting into the wind. "Brings 'em to us, remember?"

"Yeah, but those lyrics about Sharks and Jets might not be the right lure." Our grins met in the middle. Another growth spurt had pushed him close to my height. An odd thing seeing your body mirror grow before you. I had lived life full-throttle forward, but Ben made me realize the value of reverse, backing up, revisiting, and thinking it all through better.

His hair had darkened, morphing into auburn, just as mine had as a teenager. Entering high school—which Ben was giving a try—had yanked the baby right out of him.

Ben's line strayed under the pier, catching my attention. "Got one?"

"He's feisty," Ben said, wrestling against the unknown force. "Give me a hand?"

I wrapped my hands around the reel just below his. We pulled together, and gave, pulled, and gave, hoping the fish would tire before we did.

"Hey Lucy, whose side are you on?" he shouted, sparking a peal of laughter that threatened our grip.

We talked about her openly now, clear about her presence. Ben shared stories of his sister, and I shared stories of Mary. Every story except one. I still hadn't told him, despite Mrs. Peters and my mother hounding me. Words came at night, how to say it, scribbles in my journal, all as wrong as that list I'd made early on.

I'd promised myself that once the trial for Mary's death was done, and we could put that to rest somehow, that would be the time to tell Ben he wasn't an orphan. That he had a father: me, not Matt.

Matt Boone had been arrested for manslaughter—turns out my old neighbor Lois had seen Matt using turpentine to get red paint off his fender, and the Packwood café cook's testimony, while circumstantial, was enough for the jury to convict. The judge, whose father had been a wife-beater, had been all too willing to issue the maximum sentence.

But the words to tell all didn't come. It wasn't like I wanted my son to think he was the spawn of some criminal, but Ben had been through so much already. I didn't want to be the one more thing to deal with despite the last round of tests showing the cancer still in remission.

"Hey, Dad, focus. We've got a croaker."

The Spotfin flashed on the surface, almost three feet long, its body torqued in the fight like a swordfish. In one awe-inspiring flip, it sliced the line with its razor-sharp fin and plunged back into the dark blue depths, but none of that held my attention.

"What did you call me?" A stupid response to the one thing I hadn't known how to voice.

"I asked Helen. She told me," he said, shrugging but not looking my way.

Leave it to my mother, taking the burden whenever she could. I let go of Ben's rod, but our shoulders still touched. "When?"

"Couple, three months ago. She said you'd probably want to tell me yourself." Ben kept his eyes out to sea. "But she wasn't going to lie."

This was a script that I hadn't imagined. He'd known for months. Months that included a visit to campus to meet Roy, an overnight hike with Walker, at least six fishing trips, four dinners at his grandmother's house, two that included Ellen who I'd asked out twice, once to the movies and once double-dating with Harry and my mother, who had confided they were officially a couple, but not this. When had she told Ben? Did it matter?

He knew, and I'd had plenty of opportunities to be the one to tell him. Was he wondering why I hadn't? "So, are you okay with it? Got any questions?"

Ben turned toward me, a tease on his face. "How much ya willing to tell?" He punched my arm and bent over to fish another line out of his gear to thread his rod. I waited for him to make eye contact again.

"All of it, but..." I said, weighing my next words. "First, you should know how much I loved your mother."

He twisted his head my way, a raised eyebrow that mimicked my mother's. "Me, too."

My son cast a new line out to sea, his chest stiffening against the wind, and I wrapped my arm around his shoulders, wondering what the ocean might offer up next.

Author's Note

For those who track geography in the Northwest, please note that I played fast and loose with the order of topography along Highway 84 and the location of Packwood for story purposes. Mary and Luke were born in the listening and reading of dozens of old-timers' stories in the Hanford History Project archives and other personal accounts. An early-on whistleblower, Tom Bailie, who passed in January (2024), inspired much about Luke's personality. The case of the whale and the subsequent paper in *Nature* magazine is based on a real incident: an irradiated whale was harpooned off the Oregon coast in September 1963. A scientific paper was published in early 1964 in the famed Brit journal tying the whale's condition to Hanford.

The peer-reviewed paper stated that there was "no danger to human health." Only a few days after publication, LBJ ordered two reactors at Hanford to be shut down. The testing and studies of livestock, wildlife, fish, and soil, the pink snow, the regular urine retrieval from Hanford employees, the birth of hundreds of deformed lambs, the infant mortality, and the incidence of childhood leukemia are all a matter of record (much of it referenced and indexed in *On the Home Front* (Michelle Gerber), *The Hanford Plaintiffs* (Trisha Pritikin) and *Plutopia* (Kate Brown)).

But most government files were not declassified until the late 1980s and even after four decades of secrecy, most of the experts and non-fiction authors I spoke with reiterated a reluctance on the government's part to respond to FOIA requests. The official spelling of Yakama changed in 1994, but for authenticity's sake, I have used the 'Yakima' spelling. The story itself started with a dream of a tangled mass of red hair floating on the water and two random conversations that occurred in the days after. Conversations that oddly included references to Hanford, a trifecta of coincidence that I came to believe was not a coincidence at all.

Author Acknowledgements

Let me begin by applauding the team at Black Rose Writing for believing in this tale and making my debut novel a reality. Huge thanks to Robert Dugoni and Kevin O'Brien, thriller authors extraordinaire, along with the gifted children's author Clare Hodgson Meeker and the talented author, editor, and teacher Samantha Dunn for championing my words. The generous support of established writers is fuel to the soul of a new author.

When you go down a rabbit hole as deep as Hanford's you need experts to not just vet your work but teach you the language. My heartfelt thanks to history professor and activist, Linda Marie Richards (Atomic Linda), historian and author, Michele Gerber, PhD, nuclear engineer, Dirk Dunning, nuclear physicist, Dr. Carl Willis, biochemist and tech reader, Beth Mundy, PhD, oncologist extraordinaire, Dr. Emily Marchiano, WA State Poet Laureate (also a former Hanford employee), Kathleen Flenniken, and former Los Alamos biologist, Dr. Anu Chaudhary for taking time out of their busy schedules to make sure I got it right.

Appreciative shout outs to Heart of America NW founder and state legislator, Gerry Pollett, Author of The Hanford Plaintiffs, Trisha Pritikin, Pulitzer Prize-winning author, Richard Rhodes, Author, and Professor Alex Wellerstein, Counterpunch's Joshua Frank, Spokane County Commissioner, Amber Waldorf, Columbia Riverkeepers ED, Simone Anter, nuclear scientist Dr. David Kaplan, NY Times Essayist and Writer Andy Kifer, and WA State Parks ranger, Debra Hogoboom for the conversations, the insights and copious emails that helped me navigate the "trail." A shout out to Richland journalistic guru, Wendy Culverwell, who generously gave of her time for a Richland walking tour, photos, and early enthusiasm for my story. Special thanks to Robert Franklin of the WSU Hanford History Project for his guidance.

I owe a debt of gratitude to John Claude Bemis, a fine author and instructor, for his expert coaching in shaping my tale. Kudos to my stellar Commuter Lit Writers Circle whose feedback was invaluable—Kathryn

Shailer, Sylvia Barnard, Norm Rosolen, Sue Bloch, Leedine Lah, and the gifted editor Nancy Kay Clark. I couldn't have done this without your support. I am forever grateful for the generosity of my talented beta readers (authors all) who offered copious suggestions, found the typos, and gave honest helpful reviews of my work: Sheila Myers, Brita Butler-Wall, Peter Curtis, Gary Bloxham, and Clare Hodgson Meeker. I am thankful for the insightful Jordan Merica of Salt and Sage and a singular thanks to Casey Decker, The Meticulous Type, for dropping her life to line edit multiple chapters. You're the best!

To Martin Piccoli, a fine editor and writer who at the very beginning of my new adventure in 2016, patiently reminded me of all I had forgotten about writing well. My best gal pals (in alpha order) who held me up along the way: Rosanna Bowles, Diana Carey, Mitzi Carletti, Jo Chatalas, Colleen Crowley, Rebecca Davidson, Brooke de Boutray, Robyn Grad, Nancy Iannucci, Patti Kahn, Pegi McEvoy, Kim Nunes, Sharon Peaslee, Patty Shephard Barnes, Iantha Sidell, Laura Svatek and Barry Thompson. You can all uncross your fingers now.

To the neutrons and protons in my nucleus, Case, Molly, Kyle, Erin, Bryce, and Adriane: many hugs for the constant support, and for producing my grandchildren whose zest for life propelled me through many rough-writer patches as well as allowing me to work out my writer's block in your gardens. Finally, love and gratitude to my life partner, Butch Blum, who gave me the space I needed—albeit by heading to the golf course he loves—to write this important tale.

Book Club Discussion Questions

1. In the prologue, Mary reveals the dangers both at Hanford and in her marriage. How do you think that affected her judgments both professionally and personally? How does she find the courage to combat the societal limitations at the time for women?

2. Helen seems happy in her role as a traditional wife, but how does her inner strength affect the story's path? If Helen hadn't embraced Mary, would she have found the courage to do what she did? If Helen had not been his mother, would Luke have found the courage to do what he did? Why do you think Helen stayed in Richland?

3. Matt is an abuser and a manipulator. And yet Mary still has some feelings for him. How is that possible? Do you think Matt loved Mary in his way?

4. How does Harry's role as an observer of both science and nature serve the story? Does the hint of a past broken heart give him a special insight into the other characters' relationships? Did Luke need Harry more than Harry needed Luke?

5. How does Lucy's death affect Ben's ability to build relationships or friendships? How long did it take you to figure out Lucy was a ghost? Do ghosts exist for all of us?

6. How did Luke's obsession with revenge for his father's death serve or not serve him? How did his relationship with Walker help him to find his way?

7. While winning the war was prioritized over giving the public warnings about the dangers of irradiation, why do you think the government continued to keep the dangers secret until the late 1980s? Were they justified in doing that?

8. Hanford remains our hemisphere's biggest environmental disaster. How can you help?
   https://www.hanfordchallenge.org http://www.hanfordcleanup.org

Tangles Playlist

Prologue
"Stardust" Natalie Cole - https://www.youtube.com/watch?v=-xiiCwhfcZA

Chapter One
Scene 1: "September " Earth Wind & Fire - https://www.youtube.com/watch?v=Gs069dndIYk
Scene 2: "California Dreamin'" The Mamas and Papas https://www.youtube.com/watch?v=N-aK6JnyFmk
Scene 3: "Autumn Serenade" Francesco Digilio - https://www.youtube.com/watch?v=5cbEzh-_uhg
Scene 4: "Leaves that are Green" Simon and Garfunkel https://www.youtube.com/watch?v=WwOgXWOX-iE

Chapter Two
Scene 1: "Sing, Sing, Sing" Benny Goodman and his Orchestra https://www.youtube.com/watch?v=u_E0UVNtJ9Y
"Mairzy Doats" The Merry Macs https://www.youtube.com/watch?v=Gjlh9HWBOik
Scene 2: "Moon Love" Glenn Miller and his Orchestra https://www.youtube.com/watch?v=QFPlit3K7rQ
Scene 3: "In the Mood" Glenn Miller and his Orchestra https://www.youtube.com/watch?v=aME0qvhZ37o

Chapter Three
Scene 1: "Long Time Gone" Crosby Stills and Nash https://www.youtube.com/watch?v=nS3l_TwPNRY
Scene 2: "Wake Me Up When Sept Ends" Cakes and Eclairs https://www.youtube.com/watch?v=V2joP93HHzs

Chapter Four
Scene 1: "The Doctor, Lawyer and Indian Chief" Betty Hutton https://www.youtube.com/watch?v=eViqnLXaXWY

Scene 2: "I Just Got a Letter" Glen Miller and his Orchestra
https://www.youtube.com/watch?v=2Q3CLWrz0FU
Scene 3: "Sent for You Yesterday" Jimmy Rushing
https://www.youtube.com/watch?v=mU2Mh85JNiU

Chapter Five
Scene 1: "Break It to Me Gently" Brenda Lee
https://www.youtube.com/watch?v=4rm7ODV1S_0
Scene 2 & 3: "Mother's Little Helper" Rolling Stones
https://www.youtube.com/watch?v=OusADDs_3ps
Scene 4 & 5: "Helplessly Hoping" Crosby Stills and Nash
https://www.youtube.com/watch?v=BdBs7JFn9Pk

Chapter Six
Scene 1 & 2: "You Can't Lose What You Ain't Never Had" Muddy
Waters https://www.youtube.com/watch?v=TWNgzbgrDe0
Scene 3, 4 & 5: "Concerto for Clarinet: 1 and 2" Artie Shaw and His
Orchestra https://www.youtube.com/watch?v=nkXz1zA4jGE

Chapter Seven
Scene 1: "Domino" Van Morrison
https://www.youtube.com/watch?v=QOsGA4_Y89c
Scene 2 & 3: "Into the Mystic" Van Morrison
https://www.youtube.com/watch?v=_6r2P4W9Yog

Chapter Eight
Scene 1 & 2: "Dangerous" Van Morrison
https://www.youtube.com/watch?v=ntur_ywcxeQ
Scene 3: "Days Like This" Van Morrison
https://www.youtube.com/watch?v=paauQuPhKaA

Chapter Nine
Scene 1 & 2: "Hey Mr. Tambourine Man" The Byrds
Scene 3: "The Boxer" Simon and Garfunkel
https://www.youtube.com/watch?v=l3LFML_pxlY
Scene 4: "The Watchman" Gordon Lightfoot
https://www.youtube.com/watch?v=SY34R5f97gU

Scene 5: "Follow Me" Peter Paul and Mary
https://www.youtube.com/watch?v=WMmbIdhP5NE

Chapter Ten
Scene 1 & 2: "Let it Snow" Dean Martin
https://www.youtube.com/watch?v=Rnil5LyK_B0
Scene 3: "Life is Fine" Jimmie Lunceford
https://www.youtube.com/watch?v=9ua982fTgBA
Scene 4: "You Better Go Now" Billie Holiday
https://www.youtube.com/watch?v=cZU6OTgaRiw

Chapter Eleven
Scene 1: "White Rabbit" Jefferson Airplane
https://www.youtube.com/watch?v=WANNqr-vcx0
Scene 2 & 3: "Let's Live for Today" The Grass Roots
https://www.youtube.com/watch?v=G5NtzB-voZo

Chapter Twelve
Scene 1 & 2: "All of Me" Billie Holliday
https://www.youtube.com/watch?v=5J18k5Sx3Dw
Scene 3 & 4: "All the Things You Are" Artie Shaw and His Orchestra
https://www.youtube.com/watch?v=ixdXJroP1qY
Scene 5: "Friend of the Devil" The Grateful Dead
https://www.youtube.com/watch?v=tXgReZFB1SY

Chapter Thirteen
Scene 1: "For What it's Worth" Buffalo Springfield
https://www.youtube.com/watch?v=80_39eAx3z8
Scene 2: "Season of the Witch" Donovan
https://www.youtube.com/watch?v=GU35oCHGhJ0
Scene 3: "Have You Seen Her Face" by the Byrds
https://www.youtube.com/watch?v=25YxNSkLDB8

Chapter Fourteen
Scene 1 & 2: "Ma Curly Headed Baby" Maxine Sullivan
https://www.youtube.com/watch?v=gennk6eH1u4

Scene 3 & 4: 'It's Only a Paper Moon" The Nat King Cole Trio
https://www.youtube.com/watch?v=Qc5RMYvXOhA
Scene 5: "Waiting for the Train to Come In" Peggy Lee and Duke
Ellington https://www.youtube.com/watch?v=aNQjoDaX1-k
Scene 6: "I've Heard That Song Before" Harry James
https://www.youtube.com/watch?v=cK0j8_N_dBg

Chapter Fifteen
Scene 1 & 2: "Subterranean Homesick Blues" Bob Dylan
https://www.youtube.com/watch?v=1I_oWQmddMk
Scene 3 & 4: "Astral Weeks" Van Morrison
https://www.youtube.com/watch?v=4ech6pZoBJ4
Scene 5 & 6: "Rainy Day Women" Bob Dylan
https://www.youtube.com/watch?v=fm-po_FUmvM&list=RDfm-
po_FUmvM&start_radio=1

Chapter Sixteen
Scene 1, 2 & 3: "Milestones" Miles Davis
https://www.youtube.com/watch?v=k94zDsJ-JMU
Scene 4: "Straight No Chaser" Thelonius Monk
https://www.youtube.com/watch?v=uJs2eCqhTN0
Scene 5 & 6: "Autumn Leaves" Cannonball Adderly
https://www.youtube.com/watch?v=CpB7-8SGlJ0
Scene 7: "Dream Lucky Blues" Julia Lee
https://www.youtube.com/watch?v=QVsgJ6yrRz8

Chapter Seventeen
Scene 1: "Judy Blue Eyes" Crosby Stills and Nash
https://www.youtube.com/watch?v=ZGT0P0XJRFM
Scene 2: 'Norwegian Wood" The Beatles
https://www.youtube.com/watch?v=Y_V6y1ZCg_8

Chapter Eighteen
Scene 1: "Sing Sing Sing" Benny Goodman
https://www.youtube.com/watch?v=u_E0UVNtJ9Y
Scene 2: "It's You Again" Dorothy Claire
https://www.youtube.com/watch?v=cgom2FjXRe0

Scene 3 & 4: "After Hours" Erskine Hawkins and His Orchestra
https://www.youtube.com/watch?v=p1m2Duxo9Eo
Scene 5 & 6: "Guilty" Billie Holiday
https://www.youtube.com/watch?v=nH7-wl2s9cE

Chapter Nineteen:
Scene 1: "Mood Indigo" Duke Ellington
https://www.youtube.com/watch?v=RFUSD23ZXEw
Scene 2 & 3: "Watching the River Flow" Bob Dylan
https://www.youtube.com/watch?v=_xRlojtDdEs
Scene 4: "Don't Think Twice, It's All Right" Bob Dylan
https://www.youtube.com/watch?v=Kv7K9ghgcgA

Chapter Twenty
Scene 1 & 2: "Good Morning Heartache" Billie Holiday
https://www.youtube.com/watch?v=-3jO-3BoGzM
Scene 3: "No More" Billie Holiday
https://www.youtube.com/watch?v=yhrdcF5XsSs
Scene 4 & 5: "Mack the KInife" Bobby Darin
https://www.youtube.com/watch?v=557lFG-qq5g
Scene 6 & 7: "Rockin' Robin" Bobby Day
https://www.youtube.com/watch?v=uLF3YZIjucs
Scene 8: "Fallin'" Connie Francis
https://www.youtube.com/watch?v=q7RUjXf9wR0

Chapter Twenty-One
Scene 1: "Shadoogie 1961" the Shadows
https://www.youtube.com/watch?v=tRCKYLq4eFY
Scene 2: "Masters of War" Bob Dylan
https://www.youtube.com/watch?v=JEmI_FT4YHU
Scene 3 & 4: Blowin' in the Wind" Bob Dylan
https://www.youtube.com/watch?v=MMFj8uDubsE

Chapter Twenty-Two
Scene 1 & 2: "Ain't Nobody's Business if I Do" Billie Holiday
https://www.youtube.com/watch?v=G0AIdxGPVYs
Scene 3: "Diamonds and Rust" Joan Baez
https://www.youtube.com/watch?v=IrVD0bP_ybg
Scene 4: "Blueberry Hill" Fats Domino
https://www.youtube.com/watch?v=bQQCPrwKzdo
"Frankie and Johnnie" Sam Cooke
https://www.youtube.com/watch?v=iqscpuCogRE
Scene 5: "Over the Rainbow" Judy Garland
https://www.youtube.com/watch?v=EKiiSRzukAc

Chapter Twenty-Three
Scene 1: "Girl from the North Country" Bob Dylan
https://www.youtube.com/watch?v=JncbFS5ek74

Epilogue
Beginning of Scene 1: Westside Story soundtrack compilation
https://www.youtube.com/watch?v=Z7OHCrp13Ho
End of Scene 1: "I'll Never Find Another You" The Seekers
https://www.youtube.com/watch?v=UKGWqzZryDk

Author's Notes:
"Indian Summer" Glen Miller and his Orchestra
https://www.youtube.com/watch?v=kn7jjLlyjY8
"A Change is Gonna Come" Sam Cooke
https://www.youtube.com/watch?v=wEBlaMOmKV4

About the Author

q

An Austin, Texas, transplant and lifetime environmental advocate, Kay Smith-Blum has called Seattle home since 1981. A former high-end fashion retailer who also served on the Seattle School Board, Smith-Blum spends her mornings writing stories that debunk the tropes of the mid-20th century and defy genre. Smith-Blum's short works have garnered Pushcart and Best of the Net nominations. In the afternoon, she works out her writer's block in her three sons' gardens or the nearest lap pool. For more, visit www.KaySmith-Blum.com and follow her on Instagram @discerningKSB

Note from Kay Smith-Blum

Word-of-mouth is crucial for any author to succeed. If you enjoyed *Tangles*, please leave a review online—anywhere you are able. Even if it's just a sentence or two. It would make all the difference and would be very much appreciated.

Thanks!
Kay Smith-Blum

We hope you enjoyed reading this title from:

BLACK ROSE ROSE
writing™

www.blackrosewriting.com

Subscribe to our mailing list – *The Rosevine* – and receive **FREE** books, daily deals, and stay current with news about upcoming releases and our hottest authors.
Scan the QR code below to sign up.

Already a subscriber? Please accept a sincere thank you for being a fan of Black Rose Writing authors.

View other Black Rose Writing titles at
www.blackrosewriting.com/books and use promo code
PRINT to receive a **20% discount** when purchasing.

Printed in the USA
CPSIA information can be obtained
at www.ICGtesting.com
JSHW020003250724
66787JS00001B/1

9 781685 135065